HIGHLAND DESIRE

"Brona," Heming groaned as he kissed her throat, "do ye ken what I want?"

"Aye, I ken it," she whispered. "I want it, too, although I will confess that I am nay all that sure of what *it* might be."

Even as Heming began to unlace her gown, he said, "It is me deep inside ye, love."

"Will that include a lot of kissing and touching?"

"Och, aye, loving, as much as I can bear ere I go mad with the wanting of ye."

"That sounds lovely."

"Are ye sure ye are awake, love, and aware of what ye are agreeing to?"

"Verra awake and verra aware."

Slowly tugging her gown down, Heming followed the line of her collarbone with soft kisses and light sweeps of his tongue. "I just dinnae want ye to have any regrets."

"Do ye ken? I ne'er thought a mon would work so hard to talk a lass out of what he wants."

Heming grinned against her skin and then finished tugging off her gown. As he began to unlace her shift, keeping them both dazed with kisses, he decided she did know what he wanted and what she wanted. In the way she gasped and trembled, even in the heady scent of arousal on her soft skin, he could tell that she wanted him as much as he wanted her . . .

LYNSAY SANDS

HANNAH HOWELL

Highland Thirst

ZEBRA BOOKS
KENSINGTON PUBLISHING CORP.
www.kensingtonbooks.com

ZEBRA BOOKS are published by

Kensington Publishing Corp.
119 West 40th Street
New York, NY 10018

All Kensington titles, imprints, and distributed lines are available at special quantity discounts for bulk purchases for sales promotion, premiums, fund-raising, educational, or institutional use.

Special book excerpts or customized printings can also be created to fit specific needs. For details, write or phone the office of the Kensington Sales Manager: Attn.: Sales Department. Kensington Publishing Corp., 119 West 40th Street, New York, NY 10018. Phone: 1-800-221-2647.

Zebra and the Z logo Reg. U.S. Pat. & TM Off.

First Kensington Books Trade Paperback Printing: September 2007
First Zebra Books Mass-Market Paperback Printing: September 2008
ISBN-13: 978-1-4201-5335-4
ISBN-10: 1-4201-5335-8

ISBN-13: 978-1-4201-0738-8 (eBook)
ISBN-10: 1-4201-0738-0 (eBook)

10 9 8 7 6

Printed in the United States of America

CONTENTS

BLOOD
FEUD

Hannah Howell

Prologue

Northern England—Spring 1511

The chill of foreboding swept through Heming Mac-Nachton's blood as he dismounted before the inn. He frowned at the sign hanging crookedly above the door. The fact that the inn was called The Hanging Tree only added to his growing sense of unease. Heming no longer thought the huge old tree a few yards away was an intriguing sight, despite how the moon turned the emerging leaves a soft silver color. At least no one was still dangling from its thick, sturdy limbs, he thought, and reluctantly handed his reins to the stable boy.

"I dinnae like this," he said to his cousin Tearlach MacAdie as they approached the door to the inn.

"We willnae stay long."

Heming nodded, recognizing that statement as Tearlach's agreement that something felt wrong. They could not falter in their search for information just because they felt a little uneasy about a place, however. Their people were being hunted and the hunters were getting more organized. The very survival of their people depended upon gathering as much information about their enemies as possible.

Once he was inside the inn, however, Heming's wariness grew even sharper. He and Tearlach found a table set away from the others, their backs to the wall, but that did little to calm him. A burly cold-eyed man served them ale and as Tearlach paid for it, Heming looked around. The first thing he noticed was that there were no serving wenches to be seen. That was odd but he knew there could be many reasons for that. What could not be so easily explained was the fact that no one paid them much attention. Two kilted Scotsmen in an English border inn should draw attention but aside from a few hasty, side-long glances, everyone continued talking and laughing. And there was a false note to all of that talk and good cheer, Heming thought as he drank his ale with more haste than enjoyment.

It was not until the three well-dressed people, two of whom had actually shown a natural curiosity about two Scotsmen in an English inn, got up and left that Heming knew he and Tearlach had made a serious error in judgment. "The ale—" he began as an odd feeling started to creep over him.

"Was poisoned," growled Tearlach as he slammed his empty tankard down on the scarred wood table.

"Nay, not poisoned. Something to weaken us or make us sleep." Heming saw that all those fleeting sidelong glances were becoming far more intent; the men obviously were watching and waiting for whatever potion he and Tearlach had just drunk to take effect. "Didnae taste it at first, but the taint of it is now verra clear. I just thought the ale wasnae a verra good brew."

Tearlach stood up and started for the door. Heming quickly joined him. The fact that everyone in the inn just sat and silently watched them caused Heming's insides to chill with alarm. Even before Tearlach opened the door, Heming knew they would not be escaping this trap. His thoughts were already clouding over and he felt as if he were trying to walk through thick mud. Once they were outside, the cool night air did nothing to ease that. Heming staggered and he saw Tearlach do the same. They both managed to stumble along for a few more feet although Heming wondered why they even bothered, for they would never make it to their horses.

The next thing he knew he was on his knees. Tearlach fell to his knees right beside him a heartbeat later. Heming tried to fight the pull of the potion but was not really surprised when he next found himself sprawled in the dirt, Tearlach quickly sprawling at his side. His last sight was of dozens of booted feet encircling them.

Consciousness came to him slowly and painfully. Heming felt as if his head were going to split apart. Then he recalled sprawling in the dirt, dragged into unconsciousness by some herb or potion slipped into his ale. He slowly opened his eyes and stared around him in utter disbelief. He was in a cage, thick silver chains holding his wrists and ankles to the heavy iron bars surrounding him. He was also naked and weaponless and there was no sign of Tearlach. Hearing footsteps, Heming fought down his rage and the panic he felt twisting inside of him. A moment later a tall, elegantly dressed man stood before his cage.

"Weelcome to Rosscurrach," the man drawled and coldly smiled.

The name sounded familiar but it took Heming a moment to place it. Then he recalled that he and Tearlach had stopped in an inn near the keep a few days ago. It was the home of the Kerrs. Their laird was named Sir Hervey Kerr and he was not well liked, if Heming recalled correctly. This slender man, dressed as if he were about to attend the king, did not look like the cold, brutal man they had heard whispers about, but Heming knew all too well that looks could be deceiving.

"Tearlach," he began, intending to demand to know where his cousin was.

"Your companion? I fear he is now the guest of the Carbonnels and enjoying all the comforts of a secure English dungeon. My ally, Wymon Carbonnel, intends to make your cousin tell us all about the hiding places of your people. We wish to locate your many nests so that we can clean them out."

"He will tell ye naught. Nor will I."

"Oh, I dinnae intend to ask about where all of ye hide yourselves. Nay, 'tis my intention to find out all of your strengths and weaknesses." He lightly rubbed his pale, elegant hands together. "I have many an idea on how to test them. I fear ye willnae find that as enjoyable as I will, however."

"And just why have ye made us your enemies?" Heming suspected the man knew far too much about the MacNachtons already, but wanted to hear the man admit to it.

"Ye and your ilk are the enemies of all men. Ye are an

abomination. I find it an insult that ye e'en look like a mon instead of displaying clearly the mark of the devil as ye should. No mon of conscience can allow such spawn of hell to continue to exist. 'Tis time the ones ye see as prey become the hunters."

Heming did not believe the man was truly on some righteous crusade against evil, but would not try to guess what his game really was. "I am but a mon," he said quietly.

"Nay, ye are far more than that. Dinnae play me for a fool. Ye will soon show me all of your strengths and weaknesses; reveal all of your secrets. 'Tis said that your kind can live forever and I mean to find out why."

Something in the tone of the man's voice told Heming that what the man had just said was a clue to his real intentions, but Heming's head was throbbing too much for him to be able to sort it all out right now. Once his head cleared, his first thoughts were going to be how to escape and then rescue Tearlach, not about what this swine wanted. Heming refused to think that this was how he would meet his end—as a caged beast for this courtier to torment. When the man took a few hasty steps back, Heming suspected his rage was revealing itself upon his face.

"Ye cannae escape," the man said, a faint tremor in his voice revealing his fear. "Those chains are made of silver and, just in case that is a myth, the cage is made of iron."

"What? In case I am fey as weel as a demon?" Heming was not surprised to hear the low rumble of a growl in his voice, for his anger was running hot and wild. "Ye have heeded too many tales told to scare bairns."

"Och, nay, MacNachton. I ken what ye are—a blood-sucking, soul-eating abomination. I *will* learn all of your secrets, including why ye and yours should be blessed with such long lives. Here is where the truth of your evil will be fully revealed and here is where ye will die."

Watching the man stride away, Heming murmured, "Nay, fool, the only one marching toward that fate is ye. Ye are now a walking dead mon." It was a vow, one Heming fully intended to fulfill no matter how long it took.

One

He had eyes like her pets, almost solidly black as if the center had grown so that he could see more clearly in the dark. Brona Kerr immediately decided that was not precisely true. The man's eyes were decidedly far more feral than her dog's or even her cat's. The fact that both of her pets were tense, their fur bristling slightly, told her that she was not the only one who sensed a dangerous wildness in the man. Yet she knew her pets were as confused as they were wary, as if they each sensed a friend as well as a foe.

The man was caged like some feral animal, thick silver chains holding his wrists and ankles to the fat iron bars of the cage. Water and a congealed stew sat in bowls set in one far corner of his cage and a bucket sat in the other. There was no bedding for him, not even the thinnest of old blankets. Despite the fact that he was naked, he did not appear troubled by the damp chill of the dungeon. In the flickering light of the torches she had lit, his skin appeared to be almost golden yet the wounds she could see on him should have left him as pale as a ghost. Those wounds should also have bled away the fury she could see glittering in his feral eyes. Eyes in which she could now see a hint of gold as the black circle eased back into a more human size.

He watched her like some stalking predator, his golden eyes narrowed slightly and fixed unblinkingly upon her. Thick raven hair hung almost to his trim waist. He was lean and tautly muscular just as a predator should be. Brona did not think she had ever seen a man like him before. He should terrify her and, in some ways he did, but she also felt drawn to him. That made no sense to her and she frowned.

Heming studied the woman who was studying him. She was an ethereal creature, not very tall and slender yet possessing lush breasts and nicely rounded hips. Horror and curiosity were evenly blended in her expression. The flickering shadows caused by the torches accentuated the fine lines of her face. A thick braid of pale hair was draped over her right shoulder and hung down to the top of her thighs. She smelled of woman, of clean skin and a hint of lavender. It was a welcome change from the damp foul air of his prison.

To her right sat a very large gray dog and to her left sat a large yellow cat. Heming got the strong feeling that the animals were as much her companions as her pets. It surprised him that Hervey Kerr even allowed pets at Rosscurrach. The fact that this woman had the pets indicated that she was no mere servant of the keep. Few of the poor had the time or the food to pamper an animal and these two animals looked very pampered.

"Who are ye?" she asked, struggling to keep her gaze fixed upon his face and fighting the urge to look him over, very carefully, from head to toe.

"Sir Heming MacNachton," he replied, wondering if she was in league with Hervey and sought to trick some important truth out of him.

"I have ne'er heard your name before. Are ye one of my cousin's enemies?"

"I had ne'er e'en met the fool ere he captured me and brought me here. And who are ye that ye dinnae ken that?"

Brona heard the suspicion in his voice but was not troubled by it. Chained naked in a cage as he was, the man had every right to be suspicious of everyone at Rosscurrach. She had a few suspicions of her own about him. She knew her cousin was not a good man, but she found it hard to believe that he would cage and torture a man he had never met and who had done no wrong.

"I am Mistress Brona Kerr, first cousin to the laird," she answered and could see by his hardening expression that she had only added to his mistrust. "I heard some quickly hushed whispers about a prisoner and decided I would see just what the secret was. No other prisoner has e'er warranted such mystery."

"Your cousin has a lot of prisoners, does he?"

"Nay." She sighed. "I fear he often just kills those he feels have wronged him. When he does hold a prisoner 'tis for ransom, or to torture a few secrets out of him ere he kills him. What secrets does he think ye have?"

"I ken naught that he needs to know."

"That doesnae really answer my question, does it." Brona idly scratched her dog Thor's ears. "Cousin Hervey is cold and cruel, but he is also lazy. He has obviously expended a great deal of time and effort to hold ye here and try to get ye to tell him something. I but wondered what it was."

"And why do ye need to ken such things?"

"Knowledge is power." Her cat, Havoc, rubbed its head against her leg in a bid for attention and Brona briefly leaned down to scratch the cat's back. "'Tis weel kenned round here that I dinnae hold with the torturing of a mon, but I doubt that it is the only reason there is such an effort at secrecy about ye. My cousin is little interested, and even less moved, by my disapproval of his actions. Nor are ye here for ransoming as no one has been sent out to take a demand to anyone." She shrugged. "I have considered many a reason for this but each one only raised more questions, so I decided to come here and ask ye."

"Ah, and I have told ye. He thinks I can tell him something."

"But what? What could he possibly wish to learn that is worth treating ye like this?"

Heming carefully considered his answer. The woman appeared honestly concerned, even appalled, over his mistreatment, but he dared not trust in that. Hervey could be trying to trick him into revealing something. Too many men had fallen victim to believing in a woman's softness, in her wiles and words of caring. Even a few of his kindred had stumbled into such traps. He could, however, tell her exactly why Hervey had caged him and was torturing him so assiduously. If he spoke in the right tone of voice, used the right words, he could make her see it all as utter nonsense. He might even get her to question her cousin's sanity.

"He thinks I can tell him how to live forever," he said, pleased by the scorn-filled drawl he was able to produce from his parched throat.

Brona stared at the man and forced herself not to gape. "Why would he think ye could do that?"

"My kin are long-lived. The fool thinks as far too many others do and sees such strength and health as the result of magic."

"Does he think ye have some potion? Mayhap some muttered spell words?"

When Heming nodded, she frowned, recalling that many of the men in her family died young and not all from battle wounds, either. It was sad but she had never seen anything unusual in their deaths. Each one was easily explained. If this man spoke the truth, however, it could be that Hervey feared some curse or the like. It would also be just like her cousin to want to find out if some rumor about a potion for long life was true, even if he doubted it at first.

"Then 'tis wrong of him to do this to ye," she said quietly. "Verra wrong."

A spark of hope stirred to life inside of Heming but he hastily doused it. Just because this woman believed her cousin was doing wrong did not mean that she would help him. Hervey was her kinsman and her laird. Even though her words implied that she held no affection for the man, going against him to the extent of releasing a prisoner could cost her dearly. A blood tie would not save her from punishment for such a betrayal.

"Do ye think that troubles him?" he asked.

Brona nearly winced at the bitterness underlying his words. "Nay, not at all."

"He will kill me in the end, ye ken."

"I ken it," she whispered.

"And ye will do naught to stop him?" He felt guilty for trying to push her into helping him when he knew it would endanger her, but he was fighting for his life and that of his clan.

"Nay on your word alone."

"Fair enough, but if ye havenae learned anything in the near sennight I have been trapped here, my word may be all ye have."

A pinch of shame pricked Brona's heart. She had been hesitant, had tried to ignore the whispers of the others at Rosscurrach and the cries of pain and rage she had heard in the night. While she had struggled to keep herself safe from Hervey's anger, this man had suffered horribly. While she had continued to do her best to stay out of Hervey's sight as much as possible, this man had been tortured and humiliated.

It was time to stop thinking only of protecting herself, she decided. Her cowardice appalled her. She had not realized how deeply it had entrenched itself within her heart. Brona knew her caution around her cousin was completely justified, but nothing Hervey could do to her was worth allowing this man to continue to suffer like this if he was truly innocent of any crime.

The urge to immediately release him from his chains and his cage was strong, but she resisted it. He could be lying to her, trying to stir her sympathies. Although what few whispers she had understood seemed to indicate that he was indeed imprisoned here because of some strange tales Hervey had heard about the man, it was not enough. Even if this man did not kill her the moment she released him, Hervey might. Her cousin would certainly punish her in ways she did not care to even think about.

She needed more information. This time she would actively seek out the truth instead of puzzling over the occasional whisper she overheard. Repulsed as she was by the way Hervey treated men guilty of some crime, she would not free a guilty man. Hervey was the laird of Rosscurrach and it was his right, his duty, to punish those who broke the law. The most she would do was protest his cruelty in meting out his punishments. But, if what this man said were true, then she would have to do far more than protest; she would have to free him.

A tremor of fear passed through her at the mere thought of doing such a thing. Simply protesting Hervey's actions often brought retribution that left her bruised and aching. What she was considering could easily get her killed if only from the severity of the punishment that followed. Brona knew she would not only have to decide what to do about this man, but make a plan to protect herself as well. A selfish, terrified part of her told her to just ignore it all as she had ignored so much else, but Brona silenced it. Some wrongs could not be ignored.

"I didnae try to learn anything," she confessed in a soft voice. "Knowledge may be power, but ignorance is sometimes all that keeps one safe. Howbeit, now I *will* try to learn something."

"And then do what?" Heming was surprised at how hard he had to struggle not to believe in this woman, not to let his hopes rise.

"If my cousin is treating ye so cruelly simply because he thinks ye may have some potion or spell that will make him live longer, then I will set ye free."

"But nay right now."

"I cannae act against my kinsmon, my laird, on your word alone. I will visit ye again soon."

Heming watched her walk away, pausing only to douse the torches she had lit, and he fought the urge to call her back, to try to convince her to act now. It was an odd feeling to suffer from since he knew he should neither trust her nor believe her. Holding out some hope to a condemned man was just the kind of cruelty Hervey Kerr would enjoy yet Heming found himself unable to believe that the fey Brona would have any part of that. He almost smiled when he realized his inability to believe she was hand in fist with her brutal cousin grew from the way she acted toward her pets and they acted toward her. It was a thin branch to hang his hopes on.

He suddenly tensed as he realized Brona had halted just a few feet away. Heming knew two men had been dragged down here two days ago and he felt sure she had halted near their prison. Closing his eyes, he concentrated on listening closely to what was said. His hearing was far better than any Outsider's and he hoped something would be said to help him come to some decision about Mistress Brona Kerr.

"Why have ye been thrown down here?" she asked the men.

"The laird says we have failed in our duty to him," replied a man with a deep, rough voice, bitterness dripping from every word.

"Failed, Colin? How could ye and your brother have failed in anything? Ye work from sunrise to sunset."

"Then mayhap we should have worked until moonrise, mistress."

"Who cares for your family? For your poor mother and your other siblings?"

"Ranald and Mangus are of an age to be the heads of the household."

"Has my cousin told ye what your punishment will be?"

"He gave us each ten lashes, mistress, and we thought that the end of it, but then he threw us in here."

"I think he means to feed us to the monster," said another man, his voice weak and a little unsteady.

"What monster, Fergus?"

"The one ye just went to look at."

"There is no monster there, just a mon."

"Nay, mistress, that is no a mon e'en if he appears to be one," said Colin. "Ye havenae heard him. He makes sounds like a beast, howling and snarling, e'en hissing. And the laird tortures him for hours demanding answers no mon could e'er give, asking questions about living forever and all of that. And the mon should be dead by now or near to it after all the laird has done to him, yet he isnae, is he."

"Colin, I was just there, seeing him and speaking with him. He is just a mon."

"He killed Peter. The laird dragged Peter down here last night and when the poor fool was carried back by us he wasnae alive and his neck was all torn up, like some beast had ripped it open."

Heming winced even as he felt an urge to protest. He had not torn up Peter's neck. Hervey had sliced the man's neck, drawing blood, and then had his guards force the poor man closer and closer to Heming. Weakened by loss of blood, nearly maddened by pain, Heming had been unable to fight the dark hunger stirred to life by the scent of Peter's blood. He could not be sure, but he may have roughened the wound already there when he had fed off the man. He was sure, however, that Peter had been alive when he had been dragged away, alive and well able to recover given a little care.

"What are ye saying, Colin? That the mon down there, the mon chained hand and foot to an iron cage, ripped open Peter's throat and fed on him?"

"'Tis what it looked like. Chained hand and foot, ye say?"

"Aye, naked and caged like an animal."

"If ye had seen Peter, mistress, ye wouldnae doubt us. Me and Fergus fear we will be next, that we are being kept here to feed that demon. Mayhap the laird thinks that will be the only way he can keep the monster alive and get the answers he seeks. The laird is bargaining with the devil, he is."

"What crime had Peter committed?" Brona asked, her voice little more than a whisper, but Heming could hear the shock she felt trembling in every word.

"Ach, mistress, 'tis nay something I can tell ye."

"Tell me, Colin. Ye have just told me I have been speaking to a demon who rips out men's throats and drinks their blood. I think there is little else ye could tell me that would shock me more than that."

"Peter was a bonnie lad, aye? Slim and fair with a bonnie face."

Heming could almost smell the tension in the silence that followed that statement.

"My cousin loves men?" Brona asked after a few moments.

"Aye, mistress. I am thinking he likes the lasses too.

'Tis against the church's law and all that, but I dinnae judge such men. They do nay harm, nay more than any other. S'truth, I ken one or two such men and they are good men, aye? Peter wasnae one of them, though, and he told the laird so, but the laird doesnae like to be told nay, does he. A lass can be forced, aye? 'Tisnae so easy to force a mon, especially when ye dinnae want the world and its mother to ken what ye are about."

"Then mayhap Peter isnae dead. Mayhap it was all done to force Peter to say aye."

"He must be dead. The demon took his soul. 'Tis what demons do, aye?"

"Colin, I find it verra difficult to believe the mon I just spoke with is a demon. If naught else, surely he would have the power to get away from Hervey. That my cousin may lust after men was something I had begun to suspect. Only the fact that I kenned all too weel that he beds women kept me from being sure of it. I didnae realize ye could lust after both. I had another cousin, a woman, who only loved other women, so I am nay ignorant of such things. Aye, I was a little shocked but, as ye say, I cannae condemn as the church does. God made us all, didnae he, and I cannae see how loving someone, anyone, can be such a great sin. Lusting as my cousin does, aye. Love, nay. But, to harm or kill a person because he or she doesnae share your lust is wrong. Verra wrong. I thought it was all done willingly."

"Most times it is, mistress. E'en the lasses who dinnae really want to warm the laird's bed make no real complaint when they are called there. It isnae worth it, aye?"

"There will ne'er be another nay uttered now," said Fergus. "Nay when it could mean a demon will be fed your soul."

"Ye cannae be sure that is what happened, Fergus," said Brona. "I came down here because I heard whispers about a mon down here, a mon caged like an animal and being tortured. I decided I needed to ken what my cousin was doing and why. Now I have e'en more I must learn about such as what has happened to Peter. And why the two of ye are still held here. I must go now, however, for my cousin will soon be arriving. Answer me this, Colin— do ye and yours have anywhere safe ye can flee to?"

"Aye, mistress. Why?"

"I am nay sure yet, but this is wrong. All of this is so verra, verra wrong."

Heming heard the soft rustle of skirts as Brona fled the dungeon. The rapid click of the dog's claws against the stone floor told him that Mistress Brona was running away. It was no surprise. The fear of being discovered down here might be enough to make her run, but he suspected talk of demons and murder gave her speed as well.

He sighed and tried to get into a more comfortable seated position. It appeared that Mistress Brona Kerr was just what she seemed to be—a young woman appalled by the actions of her kinsman and struggling to decide what, if anything, she could do to right things. Unfortunately, that young woman now had to wonder if he was a demon who had killed a man by ripping out his throat and drinking his blood along with his soul. Heming had to wonder if she would even bother to try to find out the truth now. It would not surprise him to discover that she no longer even thought he was innocent of all but attracting her cousin's interest in the impossible.

It was difficult not to rage against a lost chance at freedom. Heming knew that, if Peter was dead, all chance of Mistress Brona helping him to escape her cousin was gone.

She might not fully believe he was some soul-sucking demon, but she would certainly think him some dangerous madman.

An all too familiar footstep dragged Heming from his morose thoughts and his whole body tensed. Hervey was returning and with at least three men. The blood that had been forced upon him had almost healed all of his wounds and restored his strength, so Heming knew that this time the torture would last for a long time simply because he was now strong enough to endure it. He pushed aside a sudden overwhelming sense of defeat. He could not let Hervey know that he was slowly winning this uneven battle. He prayed that Mistress Brona would judge him innocent and find a way to free him from this hell for he knew he was doomed to madness if this constant torture continued for very much longer.

He also prayed that Hervey did not want to see the drinking of blood again. Colin and Fergus feared they were being held for just that reason and Heming knew that was a real possibility. He also knew that if he was driven to feed again on either of those men, he was doomed. No one at Rosscurrach would help him then.

Two

Brona quietly left the great hall, the meal she had eaten sitting heavily in her stomach. She was not sure what had troubled her more—the way Hervey had played the hospitable, ever-smiling laird, a man interested in and concerned about his clan, or the way Angus had watched her. A shiver went through her. She had seen lust in the man's eyes, a dark, predatory lust. She might be innocent in body but Hervey had not been laird of Rosscurrach for long before she had begun to learn all about lust, so she knew what she had seen in Angus's cold eyes and it terrified her. The man was as hard and cruel as Hervey.

Forcing all thought of Angus from her mind, she hurried up to the lady's solar. Relieved to find it empty, she hurried toward the narrow opening near the far wall. She lit a lantern and stepped inside, but instead of following the corridor all the way, she stopped about half the way through. Grabbing the rope handle of one of the chests that lined the hall, she pulled it away from the wall, revealing a hole in the floor. By the look of the thick drape of cobwebs, Brona suspected that no one had ever told Hervey about the secrets of Rosscurrach. He was not a man to ignore the advantages of such passages within his walls, either using them himself or sealing them off so no one else could use them.

She grabbed a broom used to sweep the floors of the solar and the bedchamber connected to it by the passage. Brushing away the curtain of cobwebs, she then tucked the broom in the crook of her arm and stepped onto the narrow stone steps leading down into the many passageways running through the walls of Rosscurrach. Once below the level of the floor, she grabbed another rope handle attached to the bottom of the chest and dragged it back over the hole.

Using the broom to brush aside the worst of the cobwebs in her way, Brona made her way down to the narrow passageway that would lead her to the one running behind the great hall. She knew that Angus and Hervey would have sought the chairs by the fireplace the moment she left. Even as she approached the chimney she feared she would not be able to eavesdrop on the men for too long. It was uncomfortably warm near the chimney. The sound of the men's voices quickly distracted her from the discomfort she was already beginning to feel, however.

"MacNachton isnae telling us anything," complained Hervey.

"He will," said Angus in that deep, cold voice that always made Brona shiver inside.

"Angus, I have been torturing the mon for nearly a week and he still shows no sign of weakening. The only thing left for me to do to him is to start taking off wee pieces of him. Although it might be interesting to see if he could recover from, let us say, the loss of a finger or a toe. Do ye think he would drain a mon dry ere he could fix that?"

"What I think is it was a mistake to make him drink Peter's blood."

Brona put a hand over her mouth to stifle a gasp of shock and horror. Colin and Fergus had spoken the truth. Sir Heming had drunk of poor Peter's blood. Even after hearing that horrifying truth, however, she still found it difficult to believe the man was a demon, hell-born, and a slave to the devil. Surely there would be something she could see or sense or even smell that would tell her she was in the presence of a demon. She had a gift for scenting the evil in a person, even what they felt at times, but she sensed no true evil in Sir Heming, only something feral. And since her gift worked best with animals, that feral part of him should have told her a lot, yet all she had felt was that air of a predator but one that was no threat to her.

"It gave me the proof I needed to verify all of the tales told about the MacNachtons. They are demons."

Angus snorted, the sound rife with scorn. "He isnae a demon. If he was some spawn of Satan, ye wouldnae be able to treat him as ye do. He would have some power, some ability to cast spells or the like, that would get him out of that cage and at your throat. Aye, and he would be trying to get ye or one of your men to give him his soul in trade for the information ye seek."

"He drank Peter's blood and his wounds immediately began to heal."

"That just makes him some strange creature, doesnae

it. Mayhap more animal than mon, for many a predator drinks the blood of its kill. It still doesnae prove he is a demon."

"Ye dinnae think he stole Peter's soul?"

"Nay. Peter shows signs of recovering and I see little difference in him from what he was ere ye cut his throat and handed him to the prisoner. And, dinnae forget that ye had to nearly force the mon to do what ye wanted him to, shoving a bleeding Peter right under his nose several times e'en though MacNachton was crazed and near blind with pain from the torture ye had inflicted upon him. Do ye truly think a demon would show such restraint? Nay, a demon would have drunk Peter dry and laughed as the poor fool died."

"If MacNachton isnae a demon then what *is* he?"

"I am nay sure. As I said, just a different breed of mon, mayhap. Who kens. But, nay, I dinnae think he is some spawn of the devil. We couldnae hold him if he was, nay e'en with silver and iron. There havenae been any signs of a witch's or demon's tricks about Rosscurrach, either. No curdled milk, no sickening animals, naught but the usual. The mon does have strengths and skills we dinnae have, but 'tis said the whole clan has such things. I cannae believe the devil would make a whole clan his minions and then allow them to stay hidden away within their own lands. No one creates such an army without intending to put them into battle."

"He has fangs, Angus."

"But nay any horns, aye? And, though he is a strong, weel-set lad, he doesnae really have much more than ye and I have. I have often heard it said that the devil's minions have massive rods and bollocks as big as apples."

Brona grimaced in disgust as both men laughed. She

was beginning to think she was wasting her time. They were not telling her any more than what she already knew and it was hardly worth standing so close to the heat of the fireplace. She was drenched in sweat and beginning to feel a little unwell. The heat was stealing all the strength from her body.

"Actually, I begin to think 'tis something to do with the blood," Hervey said just as Brona decided to leave and she quickly halted, pressing herself against the wall again.

"Ye may just have the right of it," agreed Angus. "The mon *did* heal and grow visibly stronger after drinking of Peter's blood. Mayhap we err in allowing so much of it to drip into the floor. We may have been wasting something as precious as gold."

"Aye, mayhap we should collect it and drink it. A disgusting thought, but it could hold the answer to the secret."

"Weel, he will have to recover a wee bit first. He lost too much blood this time. Nay sure we ought to let him just feast on another prisoner either, so we shall have to leave him be for a wee while. Once he gets his strength back, we will take some of his blood and see if the secret of what he is lies within it."

"A good plan. After all, if it *is* the blood that makes him what he is, it just might work for us and then we shall have to keep the MacNachtons alive, or at least some of them. I but wonder how we can ken that it works."

"If it is his blood that makes him what he is then ye will feel some change, I am certain."

"Any wounds we had would heal faster. Mayhap giving ourselves just a wee cut and watching how fast it heals itself will be enough to tell us. It might be that we need to drink of his blood several times before we can be sure whether that holds the secret or not."

"Agreed. We will take a potion made of his blood each day for a fortnight. If we see naught changing in ourselves by then, then we must decide if he is worth keeping alive."

"He will be worth it only if he begins to tell us what we need to know."

"True. Mayhap if the arrogant bastard realizes that he is now the prey and nay the predator, he will start telling us all his secrets in some vain attempt to save his worthless hide. And now let us speak of Brona."

"Ah, aye, my sweet wee cousin whom ye have been sniffing around for years. Are ye sure ye still want her?"

"Aye, I do and I want her soon. She is two and twenty now and ripe for a mon."

"She doesnae seem verra interested in ye, Angus."

"She will learn to be. She just needs to be ridden hard a few times. So? When can I marry her?"

"Soon, my friend. Verra soon. Just allow me to finish with the MacNachton first. Either the blood will hold the answer I seek or he is useless to me and I will be rid of him."

Angus cursed. "What does that business matter? How does my wedding Brona possibly affect that?"

"Because I think my cousin willnae come to the marriage willingly and we will need to be able to watch her verra closely until the deed is done. Come, dinnae look so fierce. Ye ken that I want ye to wed with her. 'Tis the perfect answer to both of our problems. Ye will get the woman ye have been lusting after for years and I will get her dowry to fill my empty purse. I dinnae think ye will need to wait too much longer. MacNachton will soon be dead or he will become our own source of the potion that will bring us superior strength and long lives."

Brona heard the clink of two tankards knocking together and knew the men were giving each other a silent toast to the success of their plans. Numb with shock, she decided she had heard all she could stomach for now and she started on her way back to the solar. It was not only MacNachton she needed to worry about now. Her own life was in danger for she had no doubt that marriage to Angus Kerr would kill her, if not in body, certainly in mind and spirit.

She reached her bedchamber without anyone seeing her, much to her relief. Brona was sure that anyone meeting her would have immediately seen that something was wrong and she doubted she could have given them a plausible excuse for her obvious upset. Washing up and changing into her night shift, she crawled into her small bed. Thor immediately curled up on the sheepskin rug by the side of the bed and Havoc sought his usual place at her feet, but she did not find the comfort she usually did in their presence. She needed to think about all she had heard and make some very hard decisions.

Sir Heming MacNachton concerned her first. He truly had drunk Peter's blood. It was hard to believe that a man would do such a thing, but she doubted Angus and Hervey were mistaken. They had obviously expected MacNachton to do just what he had done. And yet they did not think MacNachton was a demon. Despite hearing what he had done, Brona could not make herself believe it either. But what could he be if not a demon?

She thought of the man she had seen in the cage, of his wild beauty, and hoped she was not being swayed by his appearance. It was said that the devil tempted men and women with all they desired and any woman would desire a man like Sir Heming MacNachton. Brona knew she should be horrified that he had fed upon the blood of a man, and a part of her was, and yet she could not bring herself to condemn him for it. All she could keep thinking of was that he had not killed Peter, that he had not even sought out the man for his blood but had it forced upon him. If Sir Heming needed such sustenance then having a bleeding Peter shoved under his nose in the time of his greatest need must have been no more than another torment. She sincerely doubted the man had wanted others to see him do something like that.

As if sensing her agitation, Thor sat up and rested his head on the edge of the bed. A moment later she felt Havoc curl up against her back, his deep rumbling purr sounding quite loud in the silent room. Brona smiled faintly as she scratched Thor's ears and softly commanded him to lie back down. She left Havoc where he was, rather liking the warmth of the cat's big body on her back. Brona just wished they could help her make some decision about what to do.

Recalling Hervey's plan to take blood from Sir Heming, she decided that was all that should rule her decision, that and the fact that Hervey was brutally torturing a man who had never done him any harm. What the man was did not matter. What Hervey was doing was wrong and what he planned to do was even worse. On the one hand, Hervey condemned MacNachton for drinking blood and on the other, Hervey planned to do just that if he discovered that Sir Heming's blood held the secret of a long life.

Brona realized she had already made her decision about Sir Heming. She was going to try to save his life. Whatever manner of man he was, he did not deserve what

Hervey and Angus were doing to him. He certainly did not deserve being used by her cousin and his first as a source for whatever magical quality might lurk in his blood.

A shiver went through her as she recalled her cousin and Angus discussing how they would use the man, taking his blood every day in order to see if they could gain the man's strength and longevity. She had always known that her cousin and Angus were hard, cruel men, but their plan to keep Sir Heming caged so that they could feed off him was beyond cruel. Brona had to wonder if the two men were mad, or at least edging very close to madness. Even if one believed all the tales about the MacNachtons—and she had probably only heard a few of them in the last sennight—what her cousin planned was still madness.

She would take Sir Heming away from them. Brona intended to free Peter, if he still lived, as well as Colin and Fergus. The moment she opened the door to Sir Heming's cage she would not be able to stay at Rosscurrach, so she may as well help every man in the dungeons flee her mad cousin's rule. None of these men had done any harm to their laird or anyone else at Rosscurrach. She also had no doubt the men would stay free once their wounds healed. Brona just hoped she would be able to save herself as well.

Thoughts of the threat hanging over her own head started to creep into her mind, but she pushed them away. If she thought about how Hervey wanted her to marry Angus, of how that man lusted after her, she would never sleep or, if she did, she would be plagued by nightmares. She was fleeing Rosscurrach and that was all she would think about.

Closing her eyes, she tried to calm herself, knowing she needed her rest. There was a lot she had to do before she could help the men in the dungeons and herself. She would need to find a place for them to hide and gather some supplies. She would need all her wits clear to prepare for her escape and she needed sleep for that. The sooner she, Fergus, Colin, Peter—if he still lived—and Sir Heming got out of Hervey's reach the better.

Heming rocked slightly, struggling to fight the waves of pain washing over him. The laird of Rosscurrach had a true skill at torturing a man. Worse, Heming got the feeling the man actually enjoyed it. By the time the torture had stopped, Sir Hervey Kerr had been so enraged at Heming's refusal to tell him anything about the Mac-Nachtons that Heming was a little surprised he still had all his parts.

Not sure why he was fighting unconsciousness and thinking about just giving into it, Heming had his attention suddenly caught by the sound of voices. He wondered why he felt such a keen sense of disappointment when he did not hear the woman's low husky voice. The two men Mistress Brona had been talking to before leaving were talking to each other now that they were all alone. He doubted they would say anything of any importance, but Heming eagerly grasped the chance to think about anything except the pain wracking his body.

"Do ye think she will come back and set us free?" asked one and Heming recognized the voice as the one named Fergus.

"If she can, aye," said the man Colin.

"But ye dinnae think she can, do ye?"

"I cannae say. It willnae be easy to get us out of here and she is just a wee lass. Aye, and one who has lived here and been cared for all her life. Weel, until that bastard showed up and sat his arse in the laird's chair. She will want to and, if I recall right from when she was a bairn, she can be a stubborn lass. Just dinnae feel too unkindly toward her if she cannae do it."

"Och, nay, I wouldnae. As ye say, she is just a wee lass. But, if we do get free what shall we do? We cannae stay here yet what about the rest of the family?"

"We will get word to them to get away if they fear they may be in danger. S'truth, I dinnae think they will be. We really didnae commit any crime and we have been punished for the one that bastard tries to say we committed. That should be the end of it yet he keeps us here. I still think it may be to feed that beastie in the cage. Weel, the laird cannae say that, can he. I think he willnae be so verra concerned about us escaping. He will be too busy trying to get MacNachton back and mayhap Peter as weel, if the mistress can find him and he still lives."

Fergus cursed. "The old laird was such a good mon. How could he leave us with this bastard as his heir?"

"He couldnae make Mistress Brona the laird, could he? I like to think the mon didnae really ken what sort of mon Hervey Kerr is, e'en if that makes the old laird sound a bit of a fool."

Obviously Hervey Kerr was not the usual sort amongst the Kerrs of Rosscurrach, thought Heming. If he ever did reach his kinsmen he would have to make it clear that it was Hervey Kerr and his first who were their enemies. Them and a few of Hervey's men. For all that he ached to avenge this treatment at Hervey's hands, he could not allow the innocent to be caught up in that.

"Sweet Jesu, Colin, I hope she does get us out of here and soon. I dinnae want to be dragged afore that demon and have my soul eaten."

Heming inwardly cursed. A beastie and a demon that ate souls. It was obvious the two men did not share Mistress Brona's doubt concerning the claims about him and his clan. If there was a rescue, he might not be invited along, especially if the decision was left up to those two.

"Weel, thinking it all o'er I am nay certain he is a demon. Mistress Brona is right. Where is his power if he is a demon, eh? Why hasnae he sent those bastards straight to hell? If ye heed all the Godly men say then that mon down there shouldnae be just setting in that cage letting them torture him every night. He would be ripping those bars apart and killing the men who think themselves so strong they can torture one of the devil's minions. Aye, and e'en if he stayed a wee while, letting the laird and his men stain their souls nice and black by their own actions, wouldnae he be trying to woo us into sinning? Into giving him our souls?"

"I heard them say he is bound by silver chains and in an iron cage. Mayhap that is what has trapped him."

Colin's heavy sigh echoed through the dungeon. "Och, I dinnae ken, Fergus. I just dinnae ken what to think. I saw Peter. I heard the laird say the mon or whate'er he is drank poor Peter's blood and it healed his wounds. Yet a part of me thinks that, if a mon like our laird can capture and torment a demon, then why are we all told to be so afraid of them? Our laird is no a great warrior."

"Aye, true enough. Yet what mon drinks another mon's blood, Colin?"

"A verra thirsty one?"

Heming was almost able to smile as the two men

laughed. Unlike so many others Colin was at least trying to reason out what he had seen and heard. Too many heeded the dark tales about his clan and ne'er searched for the truth, simply hated and feared them. It was a shame that Colin's ability to hesitate before hating would do him little good. Heming needed a free man, a strong one who would know how to get him out of Rosscurrach. Colin was not that man.

"Get some rest, Fergus. I dinnae ken if the lass will be able to help us, but 'tis best if we stay as strong as we can. This place sucks the strength and life right out of a mon, so resting is e'en more important."

There followed only a few sighs and soft grunts as the two men obviously tried in vain to get comfortable. Heming closed his eyes, unable to fight the weakness anymore. He was cold and the pain in his body was so unrelenting he wanted to howl until his voice died.

The soft sound of something dripping caused him to open his eyes enough to look down. A small part of his mind was pleased that his ability to see in the dark still lingered, but what he saw chilled him even more than being naked in a cold, damp dungeon. He was still bleeding. It was a slow bleeding, one small drop at a time, but it was an ominous sign. His wounds should have closed enough by now to halt his bleeding.

Heming realized that he might well die in this cursed place. He had thought it before a time or two but had been able to push the thought aside. It was impossible to do that this time. Unless he got some blood soon, he would die. A bone deep chill in his body told him he had lost too much blood to simply rest and recover this time.

Closing his eyes again, he gave himself over to the encroaching blackness as despair swept over him. He did not want to die this way, but it was time to make his peace with it. His kinsmen would avenge him. That infuriated him, for he wanted to kill Hervey with his own hands, wanted to watch the bastard quiver with terror just before he ripped his throat out, but Heming could see no hope of accomplishing that now. He prayed that Tearlach fared better than he. At the moment his only hope of getting out of the trap he had fallen into, of escaping the torment, was a wee lass named Brona. Heming decided it might be time to make his peace with God.

Three

Her heart was pounding so hard, Brona was surprised she could not see the front of her gown moving from the force of it. She could hear the rapid beating inside her head as she crept from cell to cell in the dungeon. Hervey had few prisoners, which made her search much easier. She did not have to keep trying to see if the huddled pile of rags and misery in the corner of each cell was Peter or some other poor soul Hervey felt had wronged him in some way. It also meant she did not have to make any hard decisions about who should be freed and who should be left behind. It appeared that the four men she intended to set free were the only ones in the dungeon.

Finally the light from the lantern she carried fell upon the huddled form of a man. The fair hair falling in soft waves to a pair of broad shoulders told her that it was probably Peter. His face was pressed against his upraised knees so she could not be certain of that yet, however. It was no surprise that the man was curled up so tightly, either, for he was naked. Brona decided she did not wish to know or understand why her cousin had stripped the poor man of all his clothes. She had brought two shirts and two sets of breeches for Sir Heming, but would now use one set for Peter.

"Peter?" she called and was a little startled by how quickly the man responded to her tentative call, moving his head up enough to stare at her.

"Mistress Brona?" he asked in a raspy voice and even in the wavering glow of light from her lantern she could see him blush.

"Aye, Peter. I have brought ye some clothes. I didnae ken ye would have none at all and had brought two sets of clothing for the other mon, but I think they will fit ye as weel." When he did not move, she turned her head away and held the rough woolen breeches and jupon in through the bars. "Get dressed and I will let ye out of there."

She heard a sound as if he was dragging himself across the floor and it was several moments before he took the clothes from her hand. Brona resisted the urge to look at him and try to see why he was moving so slowly. She had the sinking feeling she was going to need Colin and Fergus to help with Peter as well as with Sir Heming, and hoped the brothers had not weakened from the lashes her cousin had given them.

"I wish naught more than to flee from this hell, mistress, but I dinnae think I am strong enough to do so."

"Are ye dressed now?"

"Aye, mistress."

Brona looked at him and had to hastily swallow a gasp of horror. She knew she had probably gone nearly as pale as Peter was for she could feel all the blood draining from her head. For a brief moment she had to clutch at the bars of his cell to steady herself. Peter's throat was not really torn out, but there was a gruesome wound there. She wondered how much of that injury had been caused by her cousin and how much by Sir Heming, but now was not the time to satisfy her curiosity.

As her horror and dizziness eased, her ability to think clearly returned and she frowned. Peter wore no bandage and had no stitches, yet he did not bleed. In truth, he should be dead, having bled his life away soon after the wound was made. Horrible as the wound looked, it was closed tight, not even oozing a small drop of blood now and again. There was livid bruising and a raw, ragged mark, but the skin was not open at any point along the wound. Since he had been wounded only a mere two days ago and she doubted he had any care taken of his wound, that made no sense at all. She was abruptly yanked from her thoughts over that puzzle when Peter began to sink to his knees, the simple matter of tugging on his clothing enough to weaken him badly.

"Nay," she said, putting as much authority into her voice as possible, "dinnae ye go and faint on me now, Peter. Then it *will* be verra difficult to get ye out of here."

"I am so verra weak, mistress. I willnae be able to flee here e'en if ye can open this cursed cell," he said.

"Dinnae worry o'er that. We shall have some help. Colin and Fergus are here." She took a deep breath, struggling to organize her thoughts so that she could adequately refute the argument she knew he was about to make. "I mean to free them as weel. Them and Sir Heming." Brona was surprised when Peter only blinked very slowly and then frowned.

"Are ye sure freeing Sir Heming is verra wise, mistress? I think that is one verra dangerous mon."

"That may be but he has ne'er wronged the Kerrs. Nay more than ye or Fergus or Colin have. This is wrong and I finally saw that I was little better than my cousin for I was closing my eyes to all of his cruelties. Nay more."

"Ye put yourself in grave danger by acting against the laird."

"I ken it, which is why I am also leaving Rosscurrach. Try to muster some strength, Peter." She unlocked his cell door, ignoring the twinge of guilt she felt for having stolen the keys. The theft had been a necessary sin. "We will gather ye up as we leave this place."

"Be careful, mistress," Peter said as he sat down and leaned against the frame of the door. "I cannae recall much of what happened to me after the laird cut my throat, but there is something verra dark in Sir Heming."

"Aye, I ken it, but he will be as eager to leave this place as the rest of ye are, willnae he. We can deal with the mon, come to some sort of truce that will get us all out of here."

Peter did not argue with her plan so she hurried along to the cell that held Fergus and Colin, pausing to check that the few cells between theirs and Peter's were empty. Both men were standing at the front of their cell obviously aware of her approach. Brona was relieved to see that neither man had a wound upon his neck. If Sir Heming had drunk from either of them she knew they would never agree to help her free the man. It was going to be difficult enough to get them to help her now.

"Mistress, who were ye speaking to?" asked Colin, his rough-hewn face revealing only a hint of the curiosity she could hear in his voice.

"Peter," she replied, pleased that she could tell them that their clansman was still alive.

"He still lives?"

"Aye, but he is verra weak."

"Because he has lost his soul," said Fergus, fear clear to read in his handsome face.

"Nay," said Brona, a little surprised by the sharp tone in her voice for she rarely spoke sharply to anyone. "He is weak from being left naked in this cold, damp place and from loss of blood, but 'tis still Peter I just talked to. There is *no* change in the mon he was ere he was dragged down here and surely there would be some change if he was now soulless, aye? I wouldst judge Hervey and Angus as lacking souls faster than I would Peter."

Colin frowned. "Ye are certain he is the same?"

"Verra certain and I shall need your help to get him out of here," she said.

"Then let us out, mistress, and we will carry the mon to safety."

"I will also need ye to help me get Sir Heming out of here." She sighed when they both stared at her in horror.

"But he is a demon," whispered Fergus.

"Nay he isnae," snapped Brona. "Do ye truly think my cousin has the strength to capture and hold firm to a creature from hell?" She nodded when they both frowned in doubt. "E'en Hervey and Angus dinnae think he is a demon."

"He drank blood, mistress."

"Aye, I begin to believe that he did and 'tis a frightening thing, but he didnae attack Peter to get it, did he. My cousin cut Peter's throat and kept shoving the mon at Sir Heming until he did take what was offered. I dinnae understand why any mon would drink blood, but what happened to Peter was the laird's doing, nay Sir Heming's. If Sir Heming has such a strange need, he fought it hard, didnae he. But, weak and wounded as he was, he obviously couldnae fight it for verra long. All I ken is that that mon has ne'er harmed a Kerr and yet he is being tortured unmercifully."

Colin slowly nodded. "Then we will help ye get the mon out of here."

"Thank ye, Colin." Brona quickly unlocked the door to his cell. "We had best hurry. I dinnae think anyone will be coming down here but 'tis wise to get out of here as quickly as we can."

When Brona reached Sir Heming's cage and held her lantern closer, she had to smother a cry of shock. Fergus and Colin both hissed out a series of profane curses, but she did not reprimand them for speaking so in front of her. She wished she knew some very profane curses herself, for spitting them out might ease some of the horror and anguish twisting knots in her stomach.

Sir Heming hung limply in his chains, the length of them not allowing his unconscious body to sprawl comfortably on the stone floor. It was just another form of torture to chain him in such a way. He was covered in blood, his body a mass of whip marks, cuts, and bruises. Some of those wounds still oozed blood. Brona saw the slow rise and fall of his chest and the fear that she had come too late to save him slowly left her.

"I dinnae ken what the mon is, but, if he isnae a demon, he doesnae deserve this," muttered Colin, and Fergus grunted in agreement. "As ye say, mistress, he has ne'er harmed us. Wheesht, I have ne'er e'en heard of these MacNachtons."

"There are a lot of dark whispers about the clan,"

Brona confessed as she struggled to find the right key to unlock Heming's cage. "I have listened to some, e'en gently sought out some information on the clan although few here had any, but I simply cannae believe the tales. If the MacNachtons were as dangerous and powerful as is hinted at then they wouldnae stay so quietly hidden away at some place called Cambrun, would they. Nay, their men would be giving the great Douglasses a fight o'er all that power they grab for themselves. Ah, there we are," she muttered as she finally got the door to Heming's cage open.

It took Brona another few minutes to find the key to unlock the shackles. As soon as she freed Sir Heming's ankles, she gave Colin the breeches to put on the man. Fergus stood ready to catch Sir Heming as she unshackled the man's wrists. With the two men helping her, Sir Heming was free and clothed in less time than it had taken her to find the right keys. Brona gently bathed the man's battered face, but it only roused him a little and she was not sure he would understand what was happening.

"I fear one of ye are going to have to carry him," she said to Colin and Fergus.

"I can do it," said Colin. "Fergus can help Peter. Once we are outside we can make a litter to carry them."

"Ah, weel, I fear we willnae be going outside the keep for a wee while."

"But ye said ye were freeing us." Colin hoisted Sir Heming over his shoulder, faltering a little under the weight of the man before he could steady himself again.

"I am but ye would find yourselves back here quick enough if we try to flee o'er land, at least right away. I couldnae get us any horses, so we would all be on foot," she said as she led them to Peter's cell. "I dinnae think

Hervey and his men would e'en work up a good sweat in catching us all."

"So where do we go?"

"This keep is riddled with hiding places and I have prepared one for us to hide in."

"Which the laird will be able to find, aye?"

"Nay. It seems no one ever told Hervey about all of the passageways, tunnels, and hidden chambers. I think many of them came about in my grandsire's time."

"Ah, aye, me da once mentioned that, I be thinking. When the old laird decided the easiest way to thicken the walls of Rosscurrach and add all those fireplaces was to simply build a new wall around the old ones." Colin frowned. "Are ye certain the laird doesnae ken aught about them?"

Brona nodded as they paused for Fergus to help a weak, unsteady Peter to his feet. She noticed that Peter groggily eyed Sir Heming with both fear and wariness, but he said nothing. Even beaten and unconscious there was something about Sir Heming that put a person on guard, but Brona was glad no one was going to argue any more about saving the man.

"As sure as I can be," Brona said as she started to lead the men to the place they would all hide, at least until Peter and Sir Heming could run for their lives and defend themselves. "I spent the day slipping in and out of passageways and taking supplies to the place I chose for us to hide in for a while. There was no sign of anyone else having used those secret passageways for many years. I cannae think my cousin or Angus would e'er miss the chance to use passages that would allow them to spy upon someone in near every room in the keep if they knew about all Rosscurrach's secrets."

"Nay, they would be wandering about in there all the time," agreed Colin. "Yet, he is the laird and should have kenned about them, aye? Why didnae your da tell the mon about them?"

"Hervey is the laird here only because he is the last male kinsmon in my father's line. My father didnae fully trust him and neither did my mother. I may have been little more than a child when my mother and then my father died, but I do recall that. Hervey did his best to deceive them about his true nature, but he failed. Unfortunately, my mother also failed to convince my father that he should choose another heir. Father felt verra strongly that the heir should be the closest male kinsmon."

"So will the king be choosing the next laird then?"

"Weel, I suppose if Hervey doesnae have a son, aye, something like that will happen."

Colin gave a short, harsh laugh. "Mistress, your cousin willnae be living long enough to wed and have himself a legal son. This mon's kinsmen will soon be sending the laird to his grave. I but pray they dinnae send too many of the rest of us there as weel."

"But how will they ken where he is or what has happened to him?"

"He will tell them when he returns home, aye?"

Brona looked at Sir Heming and then back at Colin. "Do ye think he will live?"

"Who can say, but e'en if he doesnae someone will come seeking revenge. I am that sure of it."

"Colin, he was kidnapped, sent to sleep with a potion in his ale. Someone took his cousin and Hervey took him. How can anyone ken where Sir Hervey is?"

"Such secrets will out, mistress. If this mon was kidnapped at an inn then there is someone there who kens it.

And what if this cousin ye mention gets free and comes ahunting for the truth? Nay, mistress, I fear Rosscurrach is due a reckoning for this."

That was frightening, especially since Brona could see the sense in all Colin said. If many of the MacNachtons were like Sir Heming, she feared her people were in for a very bloody future. She had no doubt in her mind that Sir Heming was a strong and fierce warrior, and one with the cunning to stay alive in battle and gain victory over his enemies. Her idiot of a cousin Hervey had certainly made this man an implacable enemy.

When she reached the chamber set deep beneath Rosscurrach and lit a few torches, Colin, Fergus, and even Peter looked around in amazement. She had gathered rough pallets for all of them and set them around the edges of the room. She had gathered clothing, blankets, and food as well. Thor sprawled on one pallet and Havoc on another. In one corner, she had set a number of weapons, swords, and daggers she had taken from the armory, feeling that the men would need them when they were finally able to flee the keep.

"Ye brought your pets with ye?" asked Fergus as he helped Peter lie down on one of the pallets.

"I had to. Hervey and the others wouldnae care for them and I kenned that, once Hervey realized I was the one to set ye all free, he would slaughter them out of anger at me." Brona fetched some water and rags in order to clean the wounds on Sir Heming as best as she could.

Colin settled Sir Heming on a pallet with surprising gentleness. "Aye, 'tis just what he would do. And where do ye plan to go when we can finally slip away from the keep?"

"Ah, weel, I havenae exactly decided on that yet."

She could tell by the looks the three men gave her that they thought she was being a foolish woman, but she ignored them. Brona turned her attention to trying to clean Sir Heming's wounds. It might have been wise to take enough time to plan where she would go and how she would get there, but she had felt there was little time for anything more than getting the men out of their prisons and to a safe place. There was also the fact that she really had nowhere to go that Hervey did not know about and could find her. It was going to take a lot of planning to decide what her next step would be.

"They did him hard this time," murmured Colin as he stared down at Sir Heming when Brona gently removed the man's jupon. "We heard him making some of them noises that sound like an animal again, but we ne'er thought they near killed the mon. And why would the laird think this mon would ken how to live forever? It looks like he is but a breath or two away from being dead to me."

Brona gently set a cloth soaked in cool water over Sir Heming's bruised and swollen eyelids. "Aye, I fear he looks the same to me. Hervey wasnae thinking clearly when he did this or mayhap he truly believes all those wild tales about the MacNachtons. He could have just lost the chance to get what he is so desperate to learn."

"About living forever? No one can do that."

"Weel, Sir Heming told me that his kin are long-lived, healthy, and strong. That may be what has spread that foolish tale of living forever. Hervey truly does believe it, I think. So much so that he and Angus are thinking of making a potion to drink using this mon's blood."

"Ere they dragged me away to my cell, I heard them say that the mon's wounds were already healing after he drank blood from me," said Peter. "Mayhap they arenae so mad to think such a thing."

"I heard them say that, too," murmured Brona, resisting the strong urge to stroke Sir Heming's hair. "If doing such a thing works for Sir Heming then mayhap it would work for someone else. I just find it all so verra hard to believe." She looked at Peter, who was lying on his side, wrapped tightly in a blanket, and watching the unconscious Sir Heming. "Can ye say whether he did something to your neck after he drank from ye?"

Peter grimaced. "He licked me."

"Your wounds are closed, Peter. The slice Hervey made with his dagger is red and raw but 'tis closed. The mark left tells me it was a deep cut yet here ye sit."

"Aye, ye have the right of it. I feared the bastard meant me to bleed my life out on the floor and there was a lot of it going there until that mon stuck his teeth in me. When he took those teeth out of me neck, he licked me. For a moment I feared he then wanted from me what the laird did, but, nay, he pushed me away and returned to glaring murder at the laird."

"I think he licked ye to seal the wound, though how he could do that is a wonder. Yet, 'tis the only explanation for why ye are still alive."

"Aye," agreed Colin. "Ye should have bled your life away and quickly, too, by the looks of that knife cut."

Brona joined the three men in staring down at Sir Heming. To all the other reasons she wanted the man to live, she could now add simple but deep curiosity. There was indeed something very strange about Sir Heming MacNachton.

Four

"He is dying, mistress."

Brona nearly snarled at Colin, but took a few deep, slow breaths to calm herself instead. Colin was only speaking the hard, cold truth and he did not need to be snapped at because of that. They had been hiding in the bowels of Rosscurrach for two days and Sir Heming grew no better. He was so pale he would probably blend into the linen he slept upon if not for his long black hair, and his breathing had grown shallow, weaker, and less even. Her constant tending of his many wounds had done nothing to help him. There was no sign of fever or infection and, horrendous though they were, his wounds no longer bled. Yet he only grew worse. It made no sense to her.

What also made no sense to her was how upset she was about that. She had seen death before. It was a part of life one could not ignore. She also did not know this man and, if even half of the things Hervey said about the Mac-Nachtons were true, that was probably a blessing. Yet Brona felt a cold fear growing inside of her, as if she was about to lose something precious. She inwardly shook her head, deciding the situation she found herself in plus working day and night to try to save a man's life was making her fanciful, if not completely delirious.

"I think he needs blood," a swiftly recovering Peter said.

It had to be the fact that she was watching a man die that was making her so irritable, Brona thought, biting back the urge to snap at Peter. He, too, only spoke the hard truth, just as Colin had. Soon after they had brought Sir Heming into this chamber set deep beneath Rosscurrach she had begun to suspect that her healing skills were not really what the man needed. Hervey speaking of how the man's wounds had healed after drinking Peter's blood had echoed in her mind time and time again, but she had fought to ignore it. She could no longer do that. If she did, Sir Heming would surely die.

"Weel, he isnae having any of mine," Fergus muttered.

Before Brona could respond to that the man on the bed groaned softly and then opened his eyes. "Where am I?" he asked.

Heming blinked, trying to clear his vision, but the beatings he had suffered had left his eyes too swollen for him to see clearly. His first thought was that Mistress Brona had decided to help her cousin torture him, for he could think of no other reason for her to be in his cage. A moment later he realized he was lying on something soft and a blanket covered him, a welcome comfort he knew would never have been given him if he was still Hervey Kerr's prisoner. Three men stood a few feet away looking at him and he could see no bars, could feel no chains weighing down his arms and legs. Then a soft hand touched his forehead and he turned his gaze toward the woman leaning over him. He was free, he thought, and was it not just his luck to be set free only to die.

"Ye must tell my kinsmen what happened to me," he said, his voice little more than a hoarse whisper.

"Ye may tell them yourself when ye return to them," Brona said.

"Nay, I willnae be seeing them again in this life." He felt the pain of that loss, but struggled against the urge to rage and grieve.

"Aye, ye will, Sir Heming." Brona took a deep breath, wanting to speak of something she found a little horrifying with some appearance of calm. "Do ye need blood?"

For a moment Heming could not think of how to answer her question. It was obvious the fact that he had been driven to feed from that poor man was no secret. He hoped the number of people who had learned about that was small. The very last thing his clan needed now was someone who had actually seen a MacNachton drink blood spreading the tale, adding veracity to some of the many whispers about his clan. Unfortunately, his choices at the moment were dismal. If he tried to deny what she already knew, claiming it as some aberration brought on by long hours of torture, he would not get the aid he needed to survive.

And he really needed to survive, he decided. He needed to help fight the hunters who wished to destroy his clan. He needed to find Tearlach and warn his clan. Heming ruefully admitted that, if there was even the smallest chance of survival, he wanted to grasp it and hold on tight. He could deal with any consequences of revealing a few of his clan's secrets later, when he was strong again.

"Ye saw that, did ye?" He tried not to blatantly sniff her clean, sweet scent when she slipped her arm around his back and helped him sip from a tankard of wine, easing the painful dryness of his throat.

"Nay, I didnae, but Peter has survived and he hides here with us. Also, I o'erheard my cousin speak of it with his first."

"Then, aye, blood will aid me to heal myself."

She could see how much he hated to admit that. The man was obviously not comfortable with those not of his ilk knowing that he had such a dark hunger. He looked both embarrassed and wary. The man might fear that such a confession would now end the life he was clinging to by the very tips of his fingers. Brona was still not sure how she felt about such a thing or exactly what such a hunger made Sir Heming, but she could not let him die.

"Will the blood of some animal work just as weel?" she asked.

"Nay this time. I am weak nigh onto death. There isnae—" Heming decided he would not get into a discussion about the varied qualities of blood right now. "'Tis nay strong enough."

That was a disappointment, Brona decided. Disgusting as it might be, there would have been no trouble amongst the men if she could have slipped up into the kitchens and gotten some animal blood. To save him, however, he was going to have to be allowed to drink from someone. It took only one glance at Fergus, Colin, and Peter to reveal that there would be no rush of volunteers from amongst them. Oddly enough she got the feeling that it had less to do with someone drinking their blood than with the fact

that that someone was a man. That left her and she was
not sure she had the stomach for it. It would probably
hurt, if nothing else, and she was a coward when it came
to pain.

Even with his poor sight Heming could see that none
of them wished to do what was needed. He could understand that. Not only was there the fear that somehow he
could suck out their soul along with their blood, but Outsiders had a natural distaste for being seen as prey, as
food. Some men also found it all a little too intimate to be
comfortable sharing blood with another man. Usually he
did not need blood, not as some of his kinsmen did. An
occasional drink of some blood-enriched wine was enough
to keep up his strength. Since he was born of a MacNachton and an Outsider, there were a lot of differences between him and a Pureblood MacNachton. One was that
he really only needed a hearty drink of blood if he was
wounded or ill. Since most of the time he had been at
Cambrun during such times, one of his clan had given
him what he had needed. Except for being forced to feed
from Peter, Heming had never drunk the blood of an Outsider before.

If given a choice he knew which one of the people
watching him he would choose to feed from. Heming
covertly watched the woman, sensing how hard she was
thinking over the problem. He desperately wanted to live
and, without blood, that would not happen, but he would
not beg.

"Weel, then, I guess we had better give ye some
blood," Brona said, pleased at how calm and brave she
sounded even though she was shaking inside. After
glancing at the three other men, she murmured, "And I
guess it shall be me who does so."

"Nay, mistress," said Colin, hastily stepping up to the side of the pallet. "I will do it."

Brona could not help it. She laughed and then reached out to pat Colin on one of his thick, muscular arms. "Nay, Colin, though I thank ye most kindly for choking out the offer." She grinned when he blushed and grimaced. "'Tis fine. I am the one who has pulled him free of my cousin's grip. Aye, and 'tis my kinsmon who has done this to him. I will do it." She looked at Sir Heming. "Just how does one do it? I hope there is no need to cut my throat first as was done to Peter, for I willnae be able to do that and I doubt any of these men will be able either."

"Nor would they allow me to try," said Heming. "Nay, 'twas your cousin who cut Peter's throat, as I had no intention of giving the bastards a show. Unfortunately, I was weak and maddened with pain so that when they kept pushing a bleeding mon beneath my nose, I couldnae stop myself. I also thought that I had best do so if only to close the wound that was made ere Peter bled to death. They didnae care and he was cut badly."

Brona had to lean closely to him to hear him clearly as his voice wavered from being clear if hoarse, to being little more than a ragged whisper. "Best we do this now. I dinnae think ye will be able to stay awake much longer. Do ye need to do it at the throat?"

"'Tis easiest."

Heming could not believe this woman was going to allow him to feed from her. She was afraid for all she sounded calm, but she was not resistant. He glanced at the men as she leaned closer, holding her thick hair away from her throat. They looked grimly curious.

"Should we leave?" asked Colin. "Nay sure I should watch this, or e'en want to."

"Stay," Heming said. "I am sitting on the edge of death and I need at least one of ye to stay here to be certain to stop me if ye think I am taking too much from her."

"How will we ken if ye have taken too much?"

"Ye will be able to see it. Trust me in this. I wouldst rather none of ye see this or e'en ken about it, but I dinnae really have a choice now, do I?"

"Nay if ye wish to live."

Brona looked at him as he slipped his hand around the back of her neck and tugged her closer. She could see the glint of the gold of his eyes behind his bruise-swollen eyelids. Otherwise he was a mess. It almost looked as if Hervey or one of his men had resented the man's handsome looks and had done his best to utterly destroy them. She felt uneasy as he pulled her so close she was laying on top of him. This seemed uncomfortably intimate.

"Be at ease, wee Brona," he whispered in her ear. "It willnae hurt."

"How can ye say that? Are ye nay about to sink something sharp into my neck?" she whispered back.

If he was not in so much pain and fighting to control the hunger the sight of her slim, lovely neck stirred inside of him, he would have laughed. "Aye, but just as I was able to make sure Peter didnae bleed to death, I can make it so that ye are barely aware of what I do."

Her eyes grew wide when she felt him lick her neck, causing a river of heat to suddenly flow through her body. Brona was just trying to figure out what that was when she felt a sharp pain immediately followed by more of that heady fire. She could feel him drawing the blood from her body, but all of her fear was gone, replaced by what she was beginning to think was pure, hot lust.

He stroked her back lightly with one hand and gently

rubbed the back of her neck with the other, his touch becoming stronger and more sure with each passing beat of her heart. Brona had the strongest urge to rub her body against his, to relieve a sudden ache in her breasts and her groin, but she held herself as still as she could, all too aware of the other men watching her. Just as she began to think she was going to have to rub against him or go mad, he was licking her throat again. Dazed though she was, Brona actually had to bite back a protest when Colin lifted her away from Sir Heming.

Heming closed his eyes and felt the magic of her blood flow through his body. It had been difficult to stop, even more difficult not to start to make love to her. There was a deep ache in his body at the moment that had nothing to do with his injuries. He took a deep, slow breath to try to calm the lust raging inside of him and for the first time in days, felt no pain as he did so. Brona's elixir was already working its magic and, to his utter astonishment, doing so as swiftly as the rich blood of a Pureblood of his clan, even an Elder. He had never heard of an Outsider's blood being so potent.

Brona struggled to shake off the effects of the strange feelings Sir Heming had stirred inside of her and found Colin, Fergus, and Peter all staring at her neck. "Is it bleeding?" she asked and hastily touched the place where Sir Heming had bitten her, but could feel nothing, which was very strange indeed.

"Nay," answered Colin. "'Tis fine. Looks like nay more than a wee love bite."

"What is a love bite?"

"Ah, weel, 'tis when a mon has a wee nibble on a lassie's neck—"

"Hush, Colin," snapped Peter. "Ye dinnae talk of such things with a weelborn lass and a maid."

"Actually, I was rather interested in what he had to say," said Brona.

"Sweet Jesu!" cried Fergus.

Turning to see Colin's brother staring wide-eyed at Sir Heming and crossing himself, Brona quickly looked at Sir Heming. For a moment she feared he had died despite taking her blood, or, God forbid, her blood had poisoned him, but she could see that he was still breathing. In fact, he was breathing very well, deeply and evenly and not even wincing a little as he did so. Looking at his face, she gasped along with Colin and Peter. She could actually see the bruises and swelling fading. She glanced down at his broad chest and watched the lash marks and knife slashes slowly fade away as well.

"Ye must have some verra powerful blood, mistress," muttered Colin.

"Are ye still sure he isnae a demon?" asked Fergus in a slightly unsteady whisper.

"He isnae a demon. I dinnae e'en feel faint so he did-nae take much blood from me. And I am quite certain I still have my soul." She shook her head. "'Tis miracu-lous."

"This is what the laird seeks," said Peter.

"And 'tis something I cannae give him e'en if I wanted to," said Heming as he opened his eyes, speaking to Peter but staring at Brona. "'Tis something that is unique to the MacNachtons, something that has been a part of us for-ever. The clan is ancient, as are these gifts."

Heming finally looked at the men, although it was hard to tear his gaze away from Brona's wide sea-green eyes. The three men staring at him looked more amazed than appalled or afraid, even a little stunned. None of them was rushing to find a weapon, either.

"And, Fergus, I am nay a demon," he said and decided that Fergus's guilty flush was a good sign, for if the man could feel uncomfortable about calling him a demon then it meant Fergus did not fully believe it. "I truly am just a mon, one with a few special gifts and a few, weel, curses."

"Curses like having to drink blood?"

"Aye, I suspicion ye could call that a curse, but I have ne'er worried o'er it much as I dinnae have to do it verra often." He shrugged, silently pleased over how his abused muscles now allowed him to do so easily. "It doesnae matter. Just cease to worry that I am about to suck out your soul. And I would like your word to nay speak of what has happened here. 'Tis talk about such things that has brought me into this hell."

"Fair enough," said Fergus. "Ye have it. Dinnae think anyone would believe me anyway." Peter and Colin nodded in agreement.

"How did my cousin come to ken about ye and your clan?" asked Brona. "None of us have really heard more than a whisper here and there about the MacNachtons, and some nay e'en that."

"Your cousin has joined with others who have made it their crusade to hunt down me and mine and kill us all. As your cousin so sweetly told me, the MacNachtons are an abomination that must be cleared from God's earth."

"Hervey sounded that pious?"

"He has become a hunter and they tend to talk that way. My cousin and I were trying to find out more about them as we kenned that they were starting to gather together, to become many instead of one here and there. Several of my clan have met gruesome ends recently and we are sure it was done by the hunters. We have declared them all our blood enemies."

"Oh, weel, aye. So ye must." She shook her head. "I confess I dinnae understand what ye are, how ye could drink blood, or how ye could heal as ye have. Howbeit, ye have ne'er harmed anyone at Rosscurrach and ye didnae deserve what was done to ye. Ye certainly didnae deserve what Hervey and Angus had planned for ye."

"Exactly what did they have planned for me? I assumed they would torture me until I died or, since I would ne'er tell them what they sought to ken, just get so furious with their failure that they simply killed me."

"I did as I said I would and tried to find out exactly what was going on. Weel, I am nay sure how much Hervey believes in what these hunters do, but he was appalled by what ye are. However, he wants your secret to a long life. When I heard him speak of that, I also heard what he meant to try next. When ye healed after drinking Peter's blood, Hervey decided that your blood was the secret to your long life. He and Angus intended to drink a potion made from your blood every day for a fortnight and see if they began to heal quickly from wounds. If they did, weel, I fear ye would ne'er have been set free. They would have continued to use ye to make their daily potions."

"Ye mean they would hold him down here forever and milk him like a cow just so they might live longer?" asked Fergus.

Brona winced, but had to admit there was a certain clarity in Fergus's words, although it was not an image she really wished stuck in her head. "Aye, in a manner of speaking."

"Wheesht, I think I have been looking for demons in the wrong place. 'Tis certain Angus and the laird have enough dark evil in them to be the devil's men."

Restricting her response to that of simply a nod, Brona fetched Sir Heming a tankard of wine. It pleased her to see him smoothly sit up and take it from her hand, to drink without aid. She still found the idea of drinking blood a little chilling, but could not subdue a touch of pride that her blood had done such a fine job of bringing Sir Heming back from the brink of death.

"Where are we exactly?" Heming asked.

"Deep beneath Rosscurrach," replied Brona. "This is where the women and children are to hide if the walls of Rosscurrach are breached. I realized that my father ne'er told Hervey about it and few of those who did ken about it are still alive. We ne'er had to use it, ye ken, and so Hervey ne'er had to learn of it. I begin to think my father didnae fully trust the mon he had to name as his heir."

"It would seem not. Why are we here and nay away from this place?"

"Because we must leave on foot and I didnae think we would get far ere Hervey and his men found us. Especially not with both ye and Peter so weak. I am hoping the hunt for us will soon spread to places away from Rosscurrach and allow us a chance to slip away."

Heming nodded and settled himself back down on the bed. He was feeling stronger and could feel his wounds healing but he knew the danger of believing himself fully cured. He had just looked death in the eye and had no interest in doing so again for a very long time. Certainly not when he had not even been in a battle. Nor did he wish to waste the gift Mistress Brona had given him.

"A good plan, mistress," he said. "'Tis best if we try to keep as close a watch as possible on Hervey and his men to see just when that search for us moves away from this land. When the chance comes to flee this place, 'tis wise if we do it as swiftly as possible."

Brona sighed and looked around the large stone chamber they sheltered in. "Aye, verra wise. As welcome as the safety of this place is, I dinnae wish to linger here any longer than I must." She smiled at him. "Do ye wish something to eat?"

"Aye, I believe I would though it should probably be weak fare for now."

After Brona had him settled with a bowl of surprisingly tasty broth, she took Thor for a walk through the passages. Heming finished his food, handed the wooden bowl to Colin, and settled himself back down intending to have a rest. He frowned at the opening Brona had left through as he began to wonder how she would save herself from any consequences of her mercy.

"And when we can flee this place, do any of ye ken where Mistress Brona intends to go?" he asked the three men still watching him carefully.

Colin scowled. "Nay, she hasnae said anything of her plans, but she must have some, aye? She cannae stay here. The laird beats her for the smallest sin as it is. He would kill her for this."

Hervey Kerr dearly needed killing, Heming thought but said only, "Then when the time comes for us to leave here we will be sure she has a safe place to go ere we all run off to our own chosen havens. Mistress Brona must ne'er fall into that mon's hands again."

When all three men grunted in agreement, Heming closed his eyes. He would find out where Brona thought to go and hide and then convince her that his choice of haven was far better. He had no intention of letting her go anywhere without him. Mistress Brona Kerr may not know it yet, but she had done more than save his life by giving him her blood, she had tied them together in ways she could not even begin to understand.

Five

Heming grabbed his sword at the sound of someone approaching. He calmed a little when he noticed that the dog did no more than briefly cock his head before returning to his nap and the cat did no more than twitch one ear. Even so he remained tensed for battle until Colin, Fergus, and Peter strolled into the chamber. They looked very pleased and, as Heming set his sword aside, he felt the thrill of anticipation go through him. It appeared that they were returning from their sortie outside the walls with good news. He hoped that after five days of hiding in the ground beneath Rosscurrach, they would finally be able to leave the cursed place. By the look upon Brona's face, he could tell that she felt the same.

It had been almost a fortnight since he and Tearlach had been taken from the inn and he did not know his cousin's fate. Despite knowing he had had no choice, had been a prisoner, had then needed to heal from days of torture, and had had to wait for the right moment to escape the keep, Heming could not fully dismiss a sense of guilt. He dared not think what his cousin had suffered or was still suffering. That way lay madness. He could only hope that Tearlach had also found someone with too kind a heart to allow such abuse.

"They have ridden away at last, mistress," Colin told Brona.

Brona stood up from the pallet she had been sitting on. "For but a short hunt or a long one?" she asked as she began to put away the chess pieces she and Heming had been playing with.

"Long one," replied Peter as he moved to his pallet and sat down. "A large force left, but they split apart soon after they were out of the gates. Some ride to your aunt's, mistress, to be sure she didnae lie when she said ye werenae there, or to see if ye have arrived there since last they went. Some go to a place just o'er the border into England. Although what possesses the fools to do that, I dinnae ken."

"They probably return to the place I was taken from," said Heming. "Was Hervey with that group?"

"Aye, him and that swine Angus," replied Peter.

"I suspicion they ride to the village where I and my cousin were taken prisoner. My cousin is being held near there by a mon called Carbonnel."

"Weel, ye will need help rescuing him from that Carbonnel fellow for the mon will soon have some hard fighters added to whate'er men he already had guarding his lands."

"Then I had best go to Cambrun first and tell my kinsmen what has happened."

Colin frowned. "Are they all like ye are?"

Heming sighed and dragged a hand through his hair. He had hesitated to tell his companions much about himself or his kinsmen and they had asked few questions. Yet, after spending five days with Brona Kerr, he was beginning to think she was his mate. He ached for her and the heady taste of her was still a strong, sweet memory. Everything about her held his interest, even when she argued with him. He knew that if they had not been sharing their quarters with these men, he would have been doing his utmost to make sure she was not sleeping alone. He would have been heartily feeding that hunger she stirred within him.

These three men were *her* men, loyal unto death. They had also accepted his having that taste of Brona. Since he had a growing hope of keeping his little savior by his side, it was probably time that he ceased to hold so tightly to all of his secrets.

"Aye and nay," he replied. "I am what is referred to as a Halfling. Nay a kind term as ye may be able to guess. Full-blooded MacNachtons are called Purebloods and can be a little arrogant about it. My father is nearly a Pureblood, having only a wee drop or two of Outsider blood, and my mother is an Outsider, a woman of the Callan clan. Ere I was born our laird decided that we needed to marry Outsiders for we were finding it difficult to remain hidden from the world and we had ceased to breed. My father was the first child born to them in forty years and he had but one child with an Outsider. We were slowly dying, like some mythical creatures."

"We are what ye are calling Outsiders, arenae we?" asked Brona, getting the distinct feeling that with at least some of his clan that was a grave insult.

"Aye, and up until our laird made that decision we had as little to do with ye as possible," Heming said. "My mother's clan has its own secrets. They are descended from a druid shape-shifter, a woman who could become a cat. If ye met her and her clan ye wouldnae find that so hard to believe e'en though they dinnae change anymore. Those qualities havenae all been bred out. We now think that there will always be a bit of both in a Callan and MacNachton child, and that all of what makes us Mac-Nachtons willnae e'er disappear completely."

"And do ye really live forever?"

"Nay, but we do live a verra, verra long time. We are nay sure just how long for too many of our Elders eventually grow weary of life and make an end to it. The laird's father courted death at every turning after his Outsider mate died and it finally embraced him. We can be killed, as ye have seen, for I was verra close to that fate. I had lost too much blood and 'tis near impossible for a Mac-Nachton to recover from that. Unlike Outsiders, though, we can count the ways we can be killed. The grave loss of blood, as weel as beheading, fire, and the sun."

"Ye cannae go out into the day?" Fergus asked.

Heming could see that Fergus was thinking of demons again. "A Pureblood cannae. We Halflings are nay so troubled as they are, or most of us arenae. I cannae go out in the full of the day when the sun is at its strongest, shining brightly. 'Tis as if it sucks all the life right out of me. Long enough beneath its light and a MacNachton *will* die, the more pure of blood they are, the faster it happens. We dinnae ken why God made us so, but it isnae such a bad thing. What we are *not* are creatures who take souls or devour bairns or any of that. Aye, in the olden times we werenae so verra weel behaved but it was a brutal time for all, aye? All I can do is swear that we dinnae take souls and we dinnae treat all who live about Cambrun as cattle for the slaughter." He shrugged. "We are different. That is all."

"As Mistress Brona is different," said Fergus.

Brona tensed and stared at Fergus. "What do ye mean?"

"That gift that ye have with animals. 'Tis as if ye speak to them and them to ye. As Old Annie is different, aye? She can see things the rest of us cannae, such as what will happen."

Deciding the safest thing to do was to simply not argue with that and change the subject, Brona turned to Colin and asked, "So ye think we can get out of Rosscurrach tonight?"

"Aye," replied Colin. "The laird has left the keep verra lightly guarded, the fool. And, I promise ye, now that the laird's gone, the guard upon the walls willnae be so vigilant."

"Then we go tonight. Do ye take your family away from here?"

"Nay. We have seen our mother and she says they are all safe enough. Fergus and I will go with ye, mistress. Ye shouldnae travel alone."

"I shall go with ye as weel," said Peter. "Exactly where do ye mean to go?"

"Weel, I had thought to go to my aunt's," Brona said quietly, a little alarmed that she had not yet made a clear plan for what to do once she left Rosscurrach.

It was foolish not to have a clear plan for her own escape, but Brona knew that was not completely her fault. She had lived a very secluded life. Her parents had kept her close out of fear of losing their only surviving child and Hervey simply had no interest in taking her anywhere. Brona now wondered if that was because her cousin had always planned to have her marry Angus. The result of all that seclusion meant she had very few people she could turn to for help and she also had very little idea of how to travel to them.

"Weel, ye cannae do that now as they have gone searching for ye there. So, where else can ye go?"

Brona frantically searched her mind for an answer but she could not find one. She could not even think of a clever lie that would soothe their obvious concern for her. All four men stared at her, waiting for an answer that would not come. It did not surprise her when they all slowly began to scowl at her.

"Ye dinnae have another plan, do ye, Brona," said Heming.

She sighed, seeing no hope in making him believe some lie even if she could think of one. "Nay, I fear not. If naught else, I simply dinnae ken verra many people outside of Rosscurrach. I am sure I can find some place to hide, however."

"Ye will come to Cambrun with me."

"Och, nay, I couldnae do that."

"Afraid ye will become a meal, are ye?"

"Nay, of course not. 'Tis just that ye and your clan have enough trouble to deal with. Ye dinnae need to have to worry about me as weel. And I might weel bring Hervey kicking at your door."

"Let him. 'Twill save me the trouble of hunting him down. Ye *will* come to Cambrun."

She opened her mouth to argue with him and quickly closed it again. There really was no argument to be made. She could go with him or she could wander about the countryside trying to find some place safe to hide until

Hervey was no longer murderously angry at her and Angus had left Rosscurrach or died so that he was no longer a threat. She did not think the men frowning at her right now would see the latter as a very sound plan. The tone of command in Heming's voice, however, made her feel compelled to disagree and she knew she was scowling at him.

"Mayhap we best give ye two a minute or so to discuss this," murmured Colin. "We will just take the dog for a wee walk. Come along, Thor," he said to the dog as Peter and Fergus stepped out of the room. As he started to follow them, Thor at his side, Colin looked down to see the cat walking at his other side. "Weel, I see that we will be taking Havoc for a walk as weel."

Brona had to smile as she watched her pets march off with Colin. Then Heming grasped her by the hand, sat down on his pallet, and pulled her down beside him. She felt the hint of a blush touch her cheeks and was not sure why. They had been sharing the chamber for five days so a moment or two alone should not make her feel so uncertain.

"Ye dinnae have anyone ye can go to, do ye, lass?" Heming asked quietly.

She sighed, hating to admit the sad truth. "Nay, save for my aunt, and I cannae go there now, can I? Aye, I have a few other kin, though we arenae close, but I cannae be sure how to get to their homes. I fear I have been kept verra secluded, verra sheltered. First by my parents and then by the fact that Hervey seems to prefer it if I stay out of sight most of the time."

Although Heming wanted to keep her at his side, he knew it was only fair to discuss any other choices she might have. Not doing so was the kind of subterfuge that could come back round and bite him in the end. He would give her what few choices she had and then try to talk her out of taking any except coming to Cambrun with him.

"Mayhap the easiest thing ye could do is stay right here until ye are certain your cousin is no longer so angry."

"I dinnae think there is much chance of avoiding punishment for what I have done if I stay near Hervey. He may nay remain so furious he would wish to kill me, but he willnae forgive either. He will also do something to make sure that I ne'er want to go against him again. 'Tis his way. But, I might weel try that if nay for one thing—Angus wishes to wed with me."

Heming actually saw red and felt his fangs slide into place. Angus had the same hard, cold cruelty in him that Hervey did. The man had also been very creative in his methods of torture, as if he spent many long hours finding or thinking of ways to make people scream in pain. The thought of any man touching Brona was enough to make him grit his teeth in jealous fury, which surprised him. The thought of Angus touching Brona, of laying claim to her as his wife, was enough to make Heming want to howl with rage and go after the man, hunt Angus down, and rip him apart.

"Ye are the daughter of a laird. I would have thought your cousin would seek a more fitting husband for one of your birth." Heming almost winced at his own hypocrisy, for if Angus was too lowborn for Brona then so was he.

"I *was* the daughter of a laird. I am now just a cousin of the laird. And, in truth, what I overheard implies that there was some dowry left for me. If I wed Angus then

Hervey gets to keep the dowry and he is in need of some coin. They planned on seeing to that matter as soon as they were done with you."

"Then ye must come with me to Cambrun. Ye will be safe there until I have killed Hervey and Angus." Heming realized stating his plans for her cousin so bluntly may not have been the wisest thing to do, for she grew a little pale.

Brona knew Hervey and Angus deserved whatever punishment this man wished to give them considering all they had done to the man. She had just not been prepared to hear his plans spoken so bluntly or with such a cold resolution. Yet, it was not just Heming that men like her cousin were threatening, it was the entire MacNachton clan. Knowing her cousin and Angus, they had undoubtedly made their distaste for MacNachtons brutally clear, insulting and humiliating Heming at every turn. Brona supposed it was Heming's right to feel as angry as he did. A man as proud as she sensed Heming was would have found his time as Hervey's prisoner a source of great rage.

"I apologize," Heming said. "The mon is your cousin—"

"Aye, but he has courted such a fate as ye promise him for years. I kenned what ye must feel, e'en what ye may have to do to save your clan, ere I unlocked your cage. I just winced a bit at hearing it said so clearly. 'Tis as if I unsheathed the knife that is now being held to my kinsmon and laird's throat. In truth, it would do the people of Rosscurrach only good if those two men were gone. My cousin isnae a verra good laird."

Heming gently grasped her by the chin and turned her face up to his. "Come with me to Cambrun. I can keep ye safe until ye can return here or anywhere else ye may wish to go." He felt sure that he would be doing his best every step of the way to convince her to stay with him for a great deal longer than that, but it was not the time to even hint at such a plan.

Brona stared up into his golden eyes and felt something inside of her melt. He was such a beautiful man, his face cut of pure clean lines, and his lips full enough to be incredibly tempting. If she went with him she could remain at his side for a little while longer and she knew that was just where she wanted to be. The way he stroked her cheek with the tips of his fingers had her trembling slightly and she had to face the fact that she would probably be willing to follow him anywhere.

Just one little kiss, she thought as she stared at his mouth. That did not seem too much to ask. Brona knew she was not the sort of woman a man as fine as Heming MacNachton would choose, but he could weaken enough for just a moment to give her a kiss. When she realized that his mouth was actually slowly moving toward hers, Brona had to fight hard to keep from throwing herself into his arms and hurrying things along. She had been dreaming of kissing this man for days and she did not want to do anything to stop him from giving her what she craved.

He knew it was a mistake, but Heming could not resist the temptation. Brona's full lips were so close and he felt a deep urge to try to do something to take the look of sadness from her eyes. The moment he brushed his lips over hers, however, all thought of gently comforting her fled. He felt a wildness seize him. Even as a voice in his head whispered that he should be cautious and gentle, he quickly deepened the kiss. He needed to taste her, needed to hold her close. Slipping one hand into her hair and wrapping an arm around her small waist, he pulled her close to him and nipped gently at her bottom lip. As a soft gasp escaped her Heming swiftly took advantage of it, thrusting his tongue into her mouth. The taste of her was almost as intoxicating as the rich taste of her blood.

Brona clung to his broad shoulders and tried not to do anything that might let Heming know that she was almost completely innocent of this sort of thing, even kisses. When he thrust his tongue into her mouth, she almost squeaked out a protest, but it died as he stroked the inside of her mouth. The same heat that had flooded her body as he had taken her blood rushed back so quickly she felt faint from the power of it. This time the hand stroking her back did not do so in a gentle soothing manner, but in a way that had her pressing her body close to his.

It was the sound of a dog's claws on stone that stopped Heming's fall into mindless passion and need. The men were coming back and he knew they would not like to see their mistress being mauled by a man they were still not sure they trusted. He also realized that he was already starting to push Brona down onto the pallet, desperate to feel her body beneath him. Heming was sure that Brona was a virgin and such rough play would not be right, nor would taking her virginity in haste, in a cold, damp chamber beneath Rosscurrach with three men about to interrupt them. A woman like Brona deserved wooing, not grabbing. Heming ended the kiss, and had to fight to ignore the soft sound of protest she made, one that tempted him to return to her arms.

"Brona," he said, lightly cupping her face in his hands, "the men are returning." For a moment he feared she had not understood but then she blushed and pulled out of his arms.

When she kept right on blushing, nervously patting a hand over her hair as if trying to tidy it, and refused to look at him, Heming inwardly sighed. She was embarrassed. It was his fault for throwing himself upon her like some untried boy, but Heming was not sure how to ease that embarrassment. What women he had been with in his life had not required gentle words and fine manners.

"I am sorry if I have upset ye," he said quietly, keeping one eye on the doorway.

"Och, nay, 'tis probably I who should apologize to ye for behaving so shamelessly," Brona said and took a deep breath to calm herself enough to look him in the eye.

"If I hadnae heard the men returning, I would still be acting verra shamelessly myself. Ye certainly have naught to apologize for."

Brona was about to argue that when she realized she had not heard anything and listened closely for the sound of the men and her pets returning to the chamber. She was just about to tell him he must have misheard when she heard the low murmur of voices. Brona looked at Heming in astonishment.

"How could ye have heard them?" she asked. "I have only just done so."

"I have excellent hearing, a gift from both my father and my mother. Although my father claims that my mother's hearing is enough to make him hang his head in shame." Heming smiled faintly. "He says she can hear a butterfly sneeze in London." Heming was pleased when Brona smiled fleetingly.

"One of those gifts ye mentioned, eh?"

"Aye, one of those. Will ye come with me to Cambrun, Brona Kerr?"

It was probably not the wisest thing to do, but Brona nodded. "Only until I can return to Rosscurrach without fear of being forced to marry Angus. I truly cannae abide the mon. I ken it sounds foolish but I believe marriage to that mon would slowly kill me in spirit and mind if nay in body."

"It doesnae sound foolish. He would destroy a woman with your kindness and compassion." He smiled when she blushed but before he could say anything else their companions had returned.

"'Tis verra near dark," said Colin as he entered. "Are we to leave now?"

"Aye," said Heming even as Brona moved to start packing her small bag of belongings. "Brona will go with me to Cambrun until it is safe to move back here." Since he did not have many belongings to pack, Heming moved to pack up the food and wine.

As Brona settled Havoc into a large woolen sack so that she could carry him, she became aware of a thick silence around her. She turned to look at the men and they were all staring at her or, more exactly, her cat. Brona had the feeling that she was soon going to be involved in a lengthy argument.

"I cannae leave my animals here," she said. "Hervey or Angus would kill them."

"Ye cannae take the cat, Brona," Heming said gently.

"He kens how to travel—" she began, even though it was the whole truth, for she had never traveled very far.

"Nay. If we had horses, I might consider it, but we will be walking, mayhap have to run and hide at times. I believe Thor will do just fine, but nay the cat, nay when ye have to carry him all the time. If naught else, ye could lose him along the way and that would grieve ye, aye?"

"Aye, but I cannae leave him here. If he was caught by my cousin, all of Hervey's anger would fall upon Havoc."

"We will leave him with my mother," said Colin. "The laird willnae recognize one cat from another outside of the keep. The beastie will be weel cared for, I promise ye. My sister Fiona will be that pleased to have him and care for him."

Knowing what a sweet girl Fiona was, Brona reluctantly agreed. When they slipped up behind Colin's home just outside of the village, his mother hurried out to greet them and readily agreed to care for Havoc. Feeling a little foolish for her urge to weep like a bairn, Brona ignored the men as she explained to Havoc why she had to leave him behind and advised him to stay close to Fiona until she returned for him. She then stiffened her spine and walked away with the men, silently promising herself that she *would* return even if it was only to collect her cat.

Brona turned her thoughts to what she now faced. She was about to go on an adventure at the side of a man who made her blood run hot. She would see things she had never seen and might even have to flee danger a time or two. A part of her was terrified while the greater part of her was excited. When Heming took her hand in his and smiled down at her, Brona decided that whatever she faced in the days ahead, it would all be worth it for she would be sharing it all with him.

Six

"I miss Havoc."

Heming smiled as he latched the door to their room. It was going to be very fine indeed to spend the next few hours until sunset cloistered in a locked room with Brona. Feeling that they were safely secured inside, he walked over to the small table where Brona sat staring at the food the maid had brought them. They had only been traveling for two nights and as much of each day as he could withstand without weakening. Except for a few short respites from the company of the others, this was the first time he and Brona had been left completely alone and Heming had every intention of taking full advantage of it.

Glancing at the heavy blanket Brona had hung over the window as he sat down, Heming realized that he was still surprised at how accepting of him the Kerrs were. He knew the trust of the men was still a little tenuous, but, to his delight, Brona appeared to fully accept him just as he was. With every step they took toward Cambrun the feeling that he was walking beside his mate grew stronger.

"Havoc will be fine," he said as he helped himself to some of the still warm bread. "Ye could see that Colin's wee sister liked the animal."

"Aye, and he liked her." Brona smiled faintly. "I ken that he will be weel cared for, but I am used to having him about."

"Ye will again have him leaving piles of fur all o'er your gowns verra soon."

Brona laughed and nodded, but quickly grew very serious. "Aye, once Hervey is gone. I understand that ye must end the threat to your clan, but Hervey is my cousin—" She stuttered to a halt when he placed his hand over hers.

The fact that his slightest touch could affect her so was a little embarrassing. Since leaving Rosscurrach he had kissed her again, several times, and each time she had felt far more than her body heat and melt at his touch. Her wits appeared to do the same and it was always Heming who knew someone was approaching, ending the kiss before they could be caught acting so wantonly. Each kiss left her aching for him more than she had before. Brona knew what that aching meant, what her body wanted from him, and the fact that she was not terrified by that both stunned and worried her.

Sir Heming MacNachton was not just some knight she might be able to have a future with. He was so different from her it made her head spin simply thinking about it. It was not just the fact that he drank blood, either, or had the fangs to do so. He could hear better than anyone, could see in the dark like a cat, could heal so fast she still questioned the truth she had seen with her own eyes, and he would undoubtedly still look much as he did now when she was bent and wrinkled. The fact that he would not age while she did was one reason she knew it was foolish to fall in love with him. Unfortunately her heart did not seem aware of that one particularly large problem and seemed to be setting itself right into his elegant hands.

What she feared now was heartbreak, utter devastation when they finally parted ways. Such a coward she was, she thought with disgust. Brona was sure many women had faced such a thing, had even suffered it, and survived. When he held her in his arms, she felt as though she could conquer the world. If there were even the smallest chance of holding onto that, would she not be a complete fool not to try and grab hold of it?

She inwardly shook her head over her own inability to decide what to do about Heming and her rapidly growing feelings for him. Brona suspected she had spent far too many years cowering before Hervey's rages and had lost whatever daring and courage she might have once had. Each day they drew nearer to the end of their journey and she really did not have the time to wrestle with all of her fears and doubts. Unfortunately, if she decided to be brave and daring and reach for what she so badly wanted, she was not sure she knew how to do so.

"Brona," Heming said, resisting the urge to ask her what she was thinking about so strenuously that her eyes were a little cloudy, "I will confess that there is a verra large part of me that wants to cut your cousin up and feed him to the carrion birds, but there is also a verra good reason aside from that. He threatens my whole clan. He is part of a group of men who wish to see all MacNachtons dead—mon, woman, and child. I cannae let him continue on that path and I see no chance of talking him into stepping off of it before he does more than what he did to me."

"And that was bad enough," she murmured.

"Aye, and I wake in a sweat from dreams of him or men like him getting hold of one of my family."

She nodded as she began to eat some of the thick mutton stew the maid had brought them. "I but weakened for a moment. He is a wretched mon. Cold and cruel. Yet, every now and then all I can think of is that I have so few kinsmen left. I can count them on the fingers of one hand. 'Tis sad that good ones have died yet a mon like Hervey lingers to make so many miserable."

"I also wish him dead for what he has done to ye."

"Me?"

"Aye. He has made your life a misery, given ye a fear that ye will be a long time shaking free of, and beaten ye. From what ye said about his wanting ye to marry Angus, I think he has also stolen from ye."

"My dowry," she murmured and felt the stab of anger. "I didnae e'en ken I had one. Hervey certainly has done nothing to try and see me married yet I am two and twenty. Now I think some of that is because he didnae wish to have to give away whate'er my dowry is." She sighed and helped herself to some bread to sop up the thick sauce of the stew. "I believe I shall just nay think on it anymore. Hervey has set his own fate and 'tis nay longer my concern."

"Good. Now eat and then we can rest so that we are fit and strong to travel tonight."

Brona nodded, knowing she needed to eat her fill, for the two nights of traveling they had already accomplished had shown her that she was not quite as strong as she had thought she was. So far the journey had offered her a lot to see and the good company of Heming, but no real adventure or danger. Hervey was hunting for them, however, and she needed to remain strong enough to fight or escape him if the need arose.

By the time they had finished the meal, Brona was yawning. The fact that she was about to share a bed with Heming, even fully dressed, should have made her nervous, but she was simply too tired to care. And that was very sad, she thought with a faint smile as she crawled onto the bed, closing her eyes the moment she settled her head on the pillow.

Heming grimaced as he yanked off his boots and climbed onto the bed. Brona muttered something as he pulled her into his arms but he could tell that she was already more asleep than awake. He was tempted to take advantage of that, but pushed the temptation aside. When he made Brona his he wanted her to be wide awake and fully aware of every kiss, every touch. For now it was enough just to hold her close as he slept. Before they left the room, however, Heming was determined to make her fully his, for there might not be another chance to get her alone before they reached Cambrun.

Brona smiled as lightly calloused hands stroked her. She was a little surprised that her dream had grown so explicit considering her lack of experience and knowledge. Heat flowed through her with every touch of Heming's hands and she savored it, drinking it in like the finest of wines. The touch of his warm lips upon the side of her neck made her shiver with pleasure. She reached back to thread her fingers through his soft hair even as she tilted her head back to give him greater access to her throat and murmured her delight when she felt the scrape of his teeth against her skin.

His teeth? a slowly waking part of her mind asked. Brona frowned, certain that she would not have put that in her lovely dream of sharing a passionate moment with Heming. It was true that letting him take her blood had made her feel all hot and needy. But she was still not sure she was comfortable with that need of his. Brona was fairly sure she would not have dreamt of such.

"Brona, love, 'tis time to wake up," said a familiar deep voice, soft lips moving against her ear in a way that made her stomach clench with want.

"I think I may already be awake," she murmured but did not open her eyes.

Heming laughed softly and lightly nipped her ear. "Then look at me."

"Must I?"

"Aye, for I wish to kiss ye."

There was a soft rumble to his voice that Brona realized was a sign of his desire. It fed her own desire almost as much as his touch did. Considering her utter lack of experience with men and desire, she was surprised she could recognize his so easily and feel it increasing her own.

Slowly she turned around to face him, making no move to slip free of his embrace. His golden eyes were dark and warm as he looked at her, the heat in them slipping into her blood. Brona knew what he wanted, knew she was wrong to want it too. He spoke no words of love or a future for them. Men did not need any deep emotion to feel lust. Brona felt deeply, however. Her passion came straight from her heart.

Give in, a voice whispered in her mind as he brushed

soft kisses over her face. *Just once take what ye want.*
And, oh, how she wanted, she thought as he teased her
lips with soft, nibbling kisses. It was the voice of temptation whispering in her head and she knew it. Brona also
knew she should ignore it as it was the sort of thing that
destroyed all too many women.

When he slid his tongue into her mouth, stroking the
inside in a way that had her trembling from the strength
of her desire, she wrapped her arms around his neck and
held on tight. Brona knew it was probably a big mistake,
would probably cause her a lot of pain in the future, but
she was going to give in to temptation. There had been so
little joy in her life since the death of her parents and she
was hungry for some, no matter how fleeting that joy
might prove to be. If she had to do a penance for it, she
decided it would be a small price to pay for all the sweet,
heady memories this beautiful man would give her.

"Brona," Heming groaned as he kissed her throat, "do
ye ken what I want?"

"Aye, I ken it," she whispered, not surprised to hear
the tremor in her voice. "I want it too, although I will
confess that I am nay all that sure of what *it* might be."

Even as Heming began to unlace her gown, he said, "It
is me deep inside ye, love."

She swallowed hard, amazed that such blunt talk
should make her womb clench with delight. "Will that include a lot of kissing and touching?"

"Och, aye, loving, as much as I can bear ere I go mad
with the wanting of ye."

"That sounds lovely."

"Are ye sure ye are awake, love, and aware of what ye
are agreeing to?"

"Verra awake and verra aware."

Slowly tugging her gown down, Heming followed the line of her collarbone with soft kisses and light sweeps of his tongue. "I just dinnae want ye to have any regrets."

"Do ye ken? I ne'er thought a mon would work so hard to talk a lass out of what he wants." Brona spoke with a touch of humor in her strangely husky voice, but she did want him to stop trying to make her think twice about her decision. She feared he just might succeed in making her change her mind.

Heming grinned against her skin and then finished tugging off her gown. As he began to unlace her shift, keeping them both dazed with kisses, he decided she did know what he wanted and what she wanted. If she did suffer any embarrassment or guilt after the loving ended, he felt he would be able to soothe it away. In the way she gasped and trembled, even in the heady scent of arousal on her soft skin, he could tell that she wanted him nearly as much as he wanted her. He wanted far more than her desire, however, but he would work for that prize later. Every instinct he had, from both sides of his family, was demanding that he take possession of her now.

The moment he had her stripped of her clothing, he sat up just long enough to throw off his own. Even in the short time that took him he could see that her desire cooled a little. Heming quickly returned to her arms, feeling himself tremble with the strength of his need for her as their skin touched for the first time. She fit him perfectly and her every rise and hollow called to him to touch and kiss the soft skin he could feel pressed so close to his.

Brona gasped as she felt the warmth of his skin press against her. Her hands trembled as she reached out to put her arms around him. A little tentatively she stroked his broad smooth back, savoring the feel of taut warm skin stretched over hard muscle. Feeling him tremble beneath her hands made her bolder, reassuring her that he liked her touch as much as she liked to touch him. Holding him like this felt so good she feared she might do something very foolish like swoon.

When his kisses reached her breasts, she tensed and then shuddered from the force of the desire that tore through her body. Brona arched into the caress of his tongue, whispering her pleasure. When he slowly covered one hard, aching nipple with his mouth and suckled, she arched up off the bed as fire shot through her to sct a blaze in her womb.

Heming feasted upon her full breasts using his hands, mouth, tongue, and even teeth to make her writhe beneath him. It was difficult to keep his wits about him as she turned to pure fire beneath his touch, but some small still sane part of him kept reminding him that she was a virgin, that he needed to be absolutely sure she was ready for him before he plunged into her hot depths as he ached to do. Sliding his hand down her flat belly, he slipped it between her thighs. For one brief moment she tensed and he feared he might have shocked her right out of her desire. Then as he lightly stroked her, her body softened and heated beneath his stroking fingers.

For as long as he could, Heming stroked her and kissed her, murmuring words of need and desire against her skin as he tried to prepare her for his entrance. Finally, knowing that he would spend himself upon the sheets like some untried boy if he was not inside her within the next few heartbeats, he slowly began to enter her. He was shaking from the strain of going slowly when all he wanted to do was thrust into her and keep on thrusting until they both reached paradise. When he reached the shield of her innocence, he took a deep breath and then thrust forward as hard as he could, bursting through and settling himself deep inside, and covering her mouth with his to catch her cry of pain.

Brona fought the urge to shove the man right out of her arms and off the bed. That had hurt. It took her a minute of thinking how disappointing this was before she realized that he was not moving. After kissing her so that she would not rouse everyone at the inn with her screech, he had buried his face in her neck and was very still. His breath came hot and fast against her neck and the slow caress of his hands began to restore the desire the pain of losing her innocence had caused.

After another moment of enjoying the way his mere touch could warm her blood, Brona realized she felt no more pain. It was being replaced with a very strong need for him to move. Cautiously, she moved her legs and wrapped them around his trim hips. A soft groan escaped him as that drove him even deeper inside of her. He thrust forward a little but stilled again. Brona had savored that short movement and decided that was what her body was now crying out for.

Unable to state bluntly what she wanted him to do, she tried to coax him into doing it. She caressed his back, trailing her fingers down his spine until she reached his taut buttocks. Feeling incredibly daring and wanton, Brona stroked his backside and got exactly what she wanted. Heming groaned out a curse and said something that sounded like he hoped she was not in pain anymore and then he began to move with a force and speed that had her clinging to him and crying out for more.

Brona soon felt an aching knot form in her lower belly,

one that grew tighter and more urgent with each thrust of Heming's body. Just as she started to fear that something was wrong, that knot snapped apart and sent a shimmering ecstasy throughout her body. She heard herself yell out his name and then lost herself in the pleasure sweeping through her, only faintly aware of how Heming drove himself in deep, stilled, and shuddered, her name a hoarse cry upon his lips.

Heming sprawled on top of a still trembling Brona and marveled that he was still alive and breathing. He was not as promiscuous as many in his clan, but he had had some experience in lovemaking, had even thought himself in love once. Never before had he felt anything like this, as if every part of him had been left sated yet knowing that he wanted more, just as soon as he could move. Hearing Brona call out his name as her body clenched around his had been intoxicating and he knew he would never get tired of the feeling it gave him.

When he was finally able to move, he staggered over to where the bowl of washing water had been set. After washing himself clean, he rinsed out the square of linen and returned to the bed. Ignoring Brona's deep blushes and muttered protests, he cleaned her off, washing away all signs of her lost maidenhead. Tossing the cloth in the general direction of the bowl, he crawled back into bed and pulled her into his arms, smiling faintly when she pressed her face hard against his chest.

Heming kissed the top of her head and gently stroked her hair. "I wish I had the words to describe the delight ye just gifted me with, loving. I have ne'er tasted anything so hot and sweet. If we didnae have to leave soon, I would be tasting it again and again until neither of us could move a finger."

They were not pretty words or even words of love, but Brona felt moved by them. She could sense that he spoke the truth and she found a great deal of satisfaction in knowing that her lack of experience had not dimmed the enjoyment of their lovemaking for him. Hearing him swear undying love would be even more satisfying, but she was not fool enough to think one time in her arms would win his love forever. They were obviously well matched in passion, but it would take some work to make him see that they were well matched in many other ways.

Brona admitted to herself that she did not want to lose him, did not want to lose the fire that flared between them. It was not a good time to fall in love and she deeply feared she had chosen the wrong man, but she was pretty sure that was what she had done. All she could hope for was that somehow she could make him see that she was perfect for him despite all she lacked and all of her faults. If sharing passion as they just had would help accomplish that, then she was going to learn how to be the best lover he had ever had. There was no promise that that would work but at least she could comfort herself later with the knowledge that she had done all she could to win his heart.

Heming held her close as they both dozed while waiting for the sun to get low in the sky. It felt good to hold her like this, his body still warm with satisfaction. This was how he wished to spend the rest of his nights. His only concern about mating with Brona was that she was a full Outsider. There could be a way to make sure she lived nearly as long as he did, but there was no real proof yet that it would work. Unfortunately, he was probably far beyond the point where he might have been able to let her go.

When they finally left the bed and began to dress, Brona said quietly, "I wish we could stay here longer." She suddenly blushed, fearing she had been too bold but her embarrassment and concern faded quickly when Heming grinned and kissed her.

"So do I, loving, but when one is being hunted 'tis ne'er wise to linger too long in one place," Heming said as he picked up her sack of belongings. "We can have the comfort of a bed once again when we reach Cambrun."

Brona had no chance to say anything about that, not even that she thought it a very poor idea to take a leman into his parents' home, for he grabbed her hand and started to lead her down the stairs to where the others would be waiting. Thor greeted her the moment she stepped off the last stair. Laughing at his effusive greeting, she took him outside to let him have a brief run.

Heming watched her go, savoring a rather primitive sense of possession, then turned around to find all three men scowling at him. "No need to look so fierce, my friends."

"Nay? Ye just spent most of the day locked in a room with the lass," said Colin.

"Nay. I just spent most of the day locked in a room with my mate. She just doesnae ken that fact yet." He winked at the men and they slowly began to smile at him in complete male understanding.

Seven

The sun was just setting when Heming dragged himself out of the small cave he had spent most of the day in. Since they did most of their traveling at night the others also sought their rest during the day, but they rose a lot earlier than he did. As he stretched he watched Colin and Fergus cook two rabbits someone had caught while Peter and Brona played with Thor.

Although he had held Brona in his arms for the last two days, there had not been enough privacy for them to make love and he was aching for her. Even telling himself that there was only one more night of travel before he reached Cambrun, where he could find that privacy he craved, did not dim his aching by much. Heming also cursed all the time he was losing in making her see how well matched they were. He knew a shared passion was not enough to build a good marriage on but he was sure it would help in winning her. Instead all he had been able to do was hold her and steal a few kisses.

"Ah, there ye are," said Colin. "I had me some good luck and caught a few rabbits. They are nearly ready for the eating."

"Good," said Heming as he walked up to the fire and took a deep breath of the welcome scent of meat cooking. One thing he was grateful for was that he could eat and appreciate all sorts of food, unlike his father. "I will just go and wash and then join ye for this feast."

"Wash?" Brona asked as she moved to stand next to him. "Is there a place to wash near here?"

Heming grinned and nodded. "It will be cold, for the water comes down from the mountains."

"Weel, cold water to wash in is better than no water at all."

"Come with me then, but dinnae say I didnae warn ye."

After Brona grabbed a clean shift, they walked through the thick wood to a small, rapidly flowing burn. She took off her boots and hose and tested the water with her toes, grimacing at the bite of the cold water. There would be no welcoming bath in this water but she felt sure she could endure it long enough to wash off the dust of travel.

Just as she started to unlace her gown, Heming walked by her and jumped into the water. It took her a moment to gather her thoughts back together, for the man had been completely naked. Brona suspected any woman would be stunned witless by the sight of a beautiful man like Heming walking around naked. She was surprised, however, that he had not made any loud protest as all of that bare flesh had hit the very cold water; he seemed totally unaffected by it.

"I cannae believe ye just leapt right in," she said, as

once she had stripped down to her shirt she carefully stepped into the water and crouched down to begin to wash herself. "'Tis but one step from being ice."

"Och, aye, it is cold, but I am nay so bothered by that. I willnae be staying in it for verra long, however. This type of cold will eventually bother e'en me."

"Does that come from your mother or your father?" she asked, used to how he would attribute each skill or gift he had to one or the other parent.

"Father. Remember, my mother is descended from a cat." He grinned. "I believe cats dinnae like water."

Brona laughed even as she hurried back onto the shore to strip off her wet shift and rub herself dry with the old blanket Heming had brought with him. Keeping her back to the burn and wondering why she would blush so in front of the man who had so vigorously bedded her only two nights ago Brona donned her clean, dry shift. She shook out her gown and was just tugging it on when Heming stepped up next to her and dried himself off. She tried not to look at him and failed miserably.

"Ye seem to lack modesty, Sir Heming," she murmured, finally forcing her gaze back to the matter of lacing up her gown.

He chuckled and kissed her cheek before starting to dress. "Mayhap, but I do have admirable restraint."

"Oh, aye?"

"Aye. Here we are all alone and out of sight of the others, I am naked and ye were wearing only your shift, yet I havenae thrown ye to the ground and had my wicked way with ye."

She had to bite back a laugh. Part of her sudden good humor was caused by the proof that he did still want her. Brona knew they had had little chance to make love since leaving the inn, but she had not been able to stop herself from worrying that once had been enough for Sir Heming. A man like him had to have had plenty of lovers in his life and ones who were far more experienced and skillful than she was.

There had been several times during the past two nights she had heartily wished Colin, Fergus, and Peter gone so that she could test Heming's desire for her. While she would prefer a big soft bed, the thought of Heming having his wicked way with her right there on the bank of the burn was enough to have her aching with need. She wondered exactly when she had become a wanton.

When Heming stepped up behind her to finish lacing up her gown for her, she smiled to herself. The moment he finished, he pulled her back against him and licked the side of her neck. That sent a delicious shiver down her spine, followed by a much stronger one when he scraped his very sharp teeth over the same spot. When she wondered if he was in need of more blood, Brona was surprised that the thought of letting him take hers again did not cause her even a twinge of unease. In fact it made her shiver inside with a sudden spear of wanton heat.

"Heming?" She was not really surprised to hear that deep husky tone in her voice, for the way he was nibbling on her neck was making her feel very warm and needy. "Is the taking of someone's blood supposed to make one feel, weel, needy?"

Heming pulled away from her neck a little so that she could not see him grin. Feeding could be a very sensuous experience, but he had rarely shared more than blood with the women he had fed from in the past. When there was no true feeling for the person one fed from, it was easy to turn away after one was finished. But if one cared for the person that sensual feeling swiftly flared into hot need. The fact that it had in Brona pleased him a great deal. The fact that she asked such a question with no more than simple curiosity, with no hint of unease or disgust, pleased him even more.

Not all Halflings felt the urge to give their mate a marking, that bite that left a mark all other MacNachtons could clearly read, but he had felt it the moment he had held her in his arms and known that they would soon be making love. Brona's apparent ease with the fact that he drank blood meant that he might actually get to give her one and satisfy the craving he had felt since that night at the inn. He knew she would not hesitate to let him feed from her and that was half the battle.

"It can be a very sensuous thing but it doesnae have to leave one feeling *needy*," he said. "To me it has always been a matter of necessity."

"Ye said ye dinnae have to drink blood unless ye are ill or hurt or the like."

"True, but it keeps me strong if I have some every fortnight or so."

"Oh." The idea of him drinking the blood of some other woman, of holding her close and rubbing her back, made Brona clench her teeth against a wave of jealousy.

This time Heming did not even try to hide his grin as he nibbled on her ear, enjoying the little shivers that went through her. "I too felt *needy* that time ye let me taste the essence of ye, Brona Kerr. E'en though I was near death, I felt verra *needy* indeed."

Brona could hear the hint of laughter in his voice but did not feel that he was making fun of her. She suspected she had revealed her discomfort with the thought of him doing that with some other woman and his male pride was rearing up. When he turned her around and pulled her into his arms, she pressed her cheek against his chest and fought to control the urge to blush. If she acted embarrassed or annoyed, it would probably only feed his arrogance.

Heming kissed the top of her head. "I have ne'er tasted anything as sweet, my Brona."

She thought that she must be rather pathetic since she found that a heady compliment, but then shook aside that thought and asked the question she had been planning to ask. "Do ye need some now?"

"Ah, Brona love, I would like nothing more than to taste ye whilst I am hale and strong, to feel your life's blood warming my insides and making me strong, but I fear I best nay do that right now."

She smiled faintly against his chest. "Because it will make ye feel *needy*?"

"Aye, ye wretch. Verra needy."

"And ye might toss me to the ground and have your wicked way with me?"

"In a heartbeat." He tilted her face up to his and kissed her, making no effort to hide the desire for her that was always there.

Breathless from his kiss, Brona stared at him when he finally ended it. He was looking at her in a way that made her want to toss him on the ground, but she fought to rein in the need he stirred within her. With Colin, Peter, and Fergus but a few yards away, it was not a good time to be rolling about in the heather. For all she was worried about being seen as no more than his leman once they reached Cambrun, she had the feeling she would allow him to take her right to his bed the minute they stepped inside the gates of his home.

"Rabbit's ready!" bellowed Colin.

Heming laughed softly and pulled away from her. "I think Colin needs a few lessons on how to slink away from one's enemy." He took Brona by the hand and led her back to their camp.

"Do ye think Hervey is anywhere near us?" Brona asked, unable to fully smother a stab of fear. The more she thought about how Hervey would react to what she had done, the more she was terrified of being caught by him.

"I have seen no sign of him, but I fear that doesnae necessarily mean he isnae near. We travel at night and he and his men wouldnae do that, so I feel we are safe. I will feel e'en better when we reach Cambrun on the morrow."

She took a deep breath to calm herself and push aside her fear. "He went in the opposite direction, so it isnae as if he will pass by us as he rides back to Rosscurrach."

Heming was tempted to let her think that, to comfort herself with that thought, but he had always felt that, when it came to danger, it was always best to know the full truth no matter how bad it was. "He may nay have gone all the way to Carbonnel and he may have stayed a verra short time. We are walking and he is on horseback. I dinnae think he can be close by but I willnae lessen my guard."

"Nay, that is probably wise. Nay verra comforting, but verra wise."

Reaching the camp, Brona sat down and accepted a hearty serving of rabbit. Colin was very good at cooking game and she knew she would enjoy every bite. He also tended to give her very large servings and she had the feeling he felt she needed to put some more meat on her bones. The faint hint of amusement she saw glittering in

Heming's golden eyes told her he thought the same and she gave him a brief scowl before starting to eat. She knew she needed the sustenance for the journey still ahead of them.

It was several hours and several miles later that Heming suddenly grabbed her by the arm and halted her. He hissed an order to stop at their three companions, who hastily obeyed him. Brona had noticed how quickly her men had accepted Heming as their leader and she had the sinking feeling that whatever had caused Heming to stop and silence them would show her exactly why her men felt Heming was a leader.

She tried to listen as he did, but could hear nothing. The growing blackness of his scowl told her that he could, however. When he suddenly shoved her into a thick stand of shrubbery, she yelped softly as the thorns cut through her clothing and stabbed her skin.

"Stay there, Brona," ordered Heming. "If aught happens to us try to get away and continue on to Cambrun but remember to stay hidden as much as possible."

Struggling to free her clothes of the brambles as silently as she could, Brona whispered, "Is it Hervey?"

"Aye," he whispered back as he silently drew his sword, the other men doing the same. "He must have run a few horses to death."

"He heads toward Cambrun hoping to find ye," said Peter in an equally soft voice.

"I believe so and he must be feeling verra desperate to come so close to a place he feels houses demons." Heming cursed under his breath as he thought of how close he had gotten to the safety of his home, but not close enough. He looked toward the place he had sent Brona to hide and inwardly grimaced when he saw that there were a lot of bramble bushes in the thicket. "Dinnae move from there, love, unless ye have no other choice."

"I willnae."

The very last thing Brona wished to happen to her was to be caught in Hervey's hands. Right beside her cousin would be Angus, who was anxious to get his hands on her, too. An icy shiver went down her spine and she prayed it was not an omen of some kind. Not only was she terrified of being caught but she was sick at the thought of watching Heming, Fergus, Colin, or Peter being hurt in the battle that she felt sure was looming over their heads.

Even as she sent up a prayer for Hervey and his men to ride right past them, her cousin entered the clearing where they all were and right behind him was a force of nearly twenty men. Brona was astounded that her cousin had been riding around in the dark, risking his men and especially his horse. Her men, Heming standing slightly to the fore of them, looked a pitiful force to stand fast against the men on the huge temperamental horses. Brona was very afraid that she was stuck there in order to watch them all die. Even if she were inclined to disobey Heming's forceful order, she had a clear view of how many well-armed men Hervey had and felt frozen to the ground in fear for Heming's life.

"I thought we would find ye creeping back to your nest," snapped Hervey, glaring down at Heming from atop his massive black warhorse.

"Weel, arenae ye the clever one," drawled Heming. "Now, if ye would be so kind as to move aside, I believe I will be going home."

Brona wondered if she should have told Heming that all that taunting of Hervey accomplished was death. Hervey became absolutely rabid if he felt he was being ridiculed, especially if he felt the one ridiculing him was of less power and wealth. Yet, it almost appeared as if Hervey was actually using some restraint, although whatever that restraint was, it was proving too weak to remain unmoved by Heming's obvious utter contempt.

"I wasnae done with ye, demon," said Hervey. "I still need the answers to a few questions. Seems my compatriot lost his prisoner as weel."

Heming breathed an inner sigh of relief but let no sign of that show itself in his expression. "I should hie myself home then and prepare to fight for your life as my kinsmen will soon be pounding at your gates and demanding ye pay for your crimes against us."

"Crimes against ye? Ye are a crime against nature! Against God! Ye will return to Rosscurrach with me now. Those traitors with ye will hang for betraying their laird and ye will give me the knowledge I seek. Whether ye live for verra long depends upon the value of what ye tell me."

"And after ye say all that do ye truly expect us to simply lay down our swords and surrender?"

"Then die here. I can always find me another Mac-Nachton to tell me what I seek."

Heming braced for the attack, placing himself to the fore of the three men standing at his side for he knew they were not hardened soldiers. He wanted Hervey and had every intention of taking the man down even if it caused him his own death. As he laid into Hervey's men, trying to get to Hervey himself, Heming caught a brief glimpse of Peter, Colin, and Fergus fighting and decided he had maligned them. They were very fine and fierce soldiers and none of Hervey's men would find them easy to kill.

Brona put her hand over her mouth as she watched

Heming throw himself into battle. He reached up to drag men out of their saddles and hurl them aside as if they were feather pillows. One of her cousin's hirelings went for Peter's back and found Heming at his, snapping his neck and tossing him aside. Heming moved with a startling speed and was deadly with both his hands and his sword. And his fangs, she thought as she watched him drag a man off of Fergus and sink his very sharp teeth into the man's throat. The terrified scream that came out of the man gave her the chills.

One thing Brona did see, despite the numbing shock that had overtaken her, was how her men seemed unfrightened by the fury they fought side by side with. Even when Heming used his fangs, they barely blinked an eye. It seemed that sometime in the days of travel they had spent together, Fergus, Colin, and Peter had fully accepted Heming. Brona was not sure why that should make her feel good despite the carnage going on all around her.

Astonished that the battle seemed to be going in Heming's favor despite the odds against him and her men, Brona wondered if she should just stay where she was. In the heat of the battle there were many times when she could slip away unseen, but Heming had told her to stay where she was unless she had no other choice. Just as she was about to at least make a way out of the thicket clear and easy to move through, she was grabbed by the back of her gown and roughly dragged out of her hiding place. When she was free of the brambles, she looked to see who was holding her. At the sight of Angus's hard cold face, she screamed.

Heming was beginning to weaken. Despite the toll he had taken amongst Hervey's men, he had suffered many a wound. The slow loss of blood from those wounds was beginning to steal away his strength. Just as he grabbed the front of the jupon of a man he was sure he had thrown away before, a scream pierced the air and he froze. He knew that was an error, that he could easily get himself captured or killed by reacting in such a way, but he could not move as the sound of Brona's fear rang through the wood. Hervey's men did not see that they had a chance to kill or capture him, however, for a harsh command sent them running for their horses.

Backing away from Hervey and his men and the chaos caused by their sudden retreat, Heming looked for Brona. His heart nearly stopped when he saw her struggling in the grip of Angus. She looked terrified and he could not blame her. The look upon Angus's face was not that of a man finding the woman he dearly wanted and had feared was in danger. Angus looked like a man who wanted to make a woman pay dearly for his humiliation.

Heming took a step toward them as Angus threw her over his saddle and mounted up behind her, but Heming suddenly found that he could barely walk. He staggered and was grateful for Peter's sudden aid. "Let her go!" he demanded, pleased that no hint of his increasing weakness was revealed in his voice.

"Oh, I dinnae think so, demon," snapped Hervey. "I have plans for her."

Angus looked sharply at Hervey and frowned, but Heming did not have the time or the strength to try to find out Hervey's little secrets and try to use them to turn Angus against his laird. "What plans? Ye have ignored her or beaten her since ye sat your arse in the laird's seat. Ye would have done something ere now if ye had truly had an interest in her care."

"My interest now is that she will gain me a verra pretty

purse. Some men are so desperate for a young wife who may be strong enough to bear them a son, they are more than willing to pay a hefty price."

"So ye would sell your own kinswoman, one of the few true kin ye have left?"

"In a heartbeat if the price was right and this one is," snapped Hervey. "Dinnae think this ends here, demon. I cannae take the time or waste the men to get ye now, but I will return ye to your cage verra soon."

"Heming!" Brona cried.

The sound of her panic hit him hard but what happened next nearly blinded Heming with rage. Angus punched her in the head and she went limp. It was only the grip of his three companions that stopped him from trying to climb over Hervey and his men and tearing out Angus's throat. Instead he had to stand there and watch Hervey and Angus take Brona away knowing that he was simply too weak at the moment to stop them.

For a moment after all the riders had disappeared, Heming just stood there staring in the direction they had gone. Then he slowly sank to his knees, what little strength he had abruptly leaving him. Peter, Colin, and Fergus quickly gathered around him. They were bruised and bloody but alive and obviously in far better condition than he was.

"What do ye need, m'laird?" asked Colin.

"I am nay a laird," Heming said, not really surprised to hear that the weakness he felt had invaded his voice.

"Oh, I think ye will soon be ours," Peter said. "How badly are ye hurt? I swear, ye moved so fast I couldnae see where or when ye were hurt but ye are a bloody mess and I have the feeling a lot of it is your own blood."

"Aye, 'tis." He looked in the direction Brona had been taken and whispered, "I want Brona."

"And we shall get the poor lass back, but ye need to get your strength back first. Aye, she willnae be treated weel by those bastards and it grieves me to think what she might suffer, but they willnae kill her. They want something from her, can gain from her, and that will keep her alive until we can get her out of there. So tell us what we need to do to get ye back to where ye can be tossing grown men around like they are pillows."

"I need blood." Despite the fact that he was so close to unconsciousness he could barely see straight, he felt how all three men tensed. "Nay, not yours. I have no wish to be sucking on your necks and I suspicion ye have no wish to have me do it. Nay, I can get what I need at Cambrun. Take me home."

"Where is Cambrun?"

Heming had to struggle to raise his arm enough to point in the direction of home. "See that rocky hill in the distance?"

"The one that has all that mist about it?"

"Aye. At the top is Cambrun."

"As ye wish then. We will get ye there."

"Thank ye. Oh, and try to remember to keep me out of the sun," he said and fell forward as the blackness finally conquered him.

Eight

"Brona?"

It took Heming only a moment to realize that the small, soft hand he held was not Brona's. He slowly opened his eyes and turned his head to see who sat at his bedside. Even as he saw his mother there, she leaned forward and brushed the hair from his forehead, giving him a kiss there just as she often had when he was a small boy. He must have been a lot closer to dying than he had realized.

"Thirsty?" she asked.

"Aye."

He waited patiently as she fetched him some wine. One sip told him it was his father's *enriched* wine and he began to believe he truly had been in far worse a condition than he had realized. He obviously needed more than just one hearty drink of blood to recover. Heming felt a great deal better than he had before he had fallen face down in the dirt, but he could tell that he was still weak.

His mother had just finished plumping up a mound of pillows at his back and helping him rest against them when his father walked into the room. Heming could tell by the tight look of anger on his father's face that Colin, Fergus, and Peter had already told their tale. He was glad, for it meant he only had to clarify a few things before he could start planning how to go and get Brona back.

"Have ye heard how Tearlach fares?" he asked his father.

"Aye, he fares weel," replied Jankyn as he moved to stand beside his wife, Efrica, and idly stroke her hair. "It seems he too had a guardian angel, an English one."

"I must get my angel back."

"Brona?" asked his mother, her eyes alight with curiosity.

"Aye, Brona," he replied. "How long have I slept?"

"Just for the day. 'Tis nay e'en full sunset yet. Ye were near to dying, Heming. That mon Colin said he e'en decided to give ye some of his blood but he couldnae rouse ye and he didnae ken how to do it without ye being awake."

"This mon Hervey Kerr is one of the hunters?" asked his father.

"Aye. I suppose ye ken what the mon holding Tearlach wanted." When his father nodded, Heming continued, "Hervey wanted me to tell him how to live forever." He smiled crookedly at his parents' identical looks of disgust. "Brona got me out of there just before Hervey decided that the secret may be in my blood and that he and his first would make a potion out of it and see how they fared after a fortnight of drinking it. If they showed signs of healing swiftly and the like they planned to hold me there and use me to keep making those potions."

Heming watched his mother shudder and his father quickly take her small hand in his to soothe her. "Aye, 'tis hypocrisy at its worst. He condemns me as a demon because I drink blood and then decides to use mine and drink it because it might make him live longer. Brona refused to believe me a demon and what her cousin wanted to do sickened her, so she set me free."

"So your men said. They said ye hid within the keep itself until ye felt it was safe to try and get away. They also said that ye will be their laird because ye are going to kill Hervey and marry Brona."

"Weel, I can see ye all had a verra nice talk."

"They are good men and only a wee bit nervous about being here." Jankyn grinned when Heming laughed. "They accept ye."

"Aye. Nay so much at first although they didnae kill me when Brona gave me her blood so that I could recover from her cousin's torture. I was near to dying then, too." He squeezed his mother's hand when she suddenly grasped his. "My Brona wasnae so sure she wanted to do it, but she couldnae let me die just because she was made uneasy about giving me what was needed so that I could live. And as we traveled here all of them saw many other things about me but didnae flee or back away. Nay, not e'en after I showed off all my strengths during the battle in which we lost Brona."

"And do ye plan to marry this Brona and become the laird of Rosscurrach?"

"Weel, I mean to marry Brona but I cannae say if that will make me laird of Rosscurrach or nay. It may weel do so as I think there isnae anyone else, no males leastwise."

"Then ye shall start with three loyal men who ken the truth about ye and dinnae care. A verra good start."

"But first I must get my Brona free of those bastards." Heming cautiously sat up, almost grinning at how hard his mother had to work at not moving to help him. "Weel, it may be a few more hours, I fear, but I am strong enough to make my plans."

"Hervey will be shut up tight in Rosscurrach. It will-nae be an easy battle."

Heming smiled and knew it was a cold smile of antici-pation. "Oh, it will be verra easy for I ken how to get in-side without being seen—the same way me, Brona, and those three nervous men of mine got out. Oh, and the dog." He winked at his mother. "We did manage to con-vince Brona that it would be best if she left her cat, Havoc, with Colin's mother."

"Do ye love this Brona, Heming?" asked his mother.

A little annoyed when he actually felt himself blush and his father grinned widely, Heming grimaced and de-cided to tell the truth. "She is my mate. Do ye ken, when she first came to me whilst I was in my cage, I tried to think of how she may be just another trick, sent to make me feel as if I had an ally and thus get me to tell her things I refused to tell Hervey. I couldnae do it. Oh, I did-nae tell her anything, but I simply couldnae believe she was part of it all. And after she rescued me and then of-fered me her blood so that I could heal, I knew. I just havenae told her yet."

"Then we had best get her free so that ye may do so. I am curious about one thing. Do ye feel the urge to mark her?"

"Och, aye. Verra strongly. Why?"

"Oh, no verra important reason. I am just trying to

keep a record so that we may eventually ken just how strong that particular urge is. At the moment, it appears to be a verra strong one indeed."

Jankyn nodded. "Your mother decided that it might be useful to keep a record of what disappears and what lingers when a child is born to a MacNachton and an Outsider. We ken verra little about such mixes and ignorance is ne'er a good thing. Ye are actually the strongest, er, mix yet, taking a great deal from both of us."

"Aye, of all the things both families tried to breed out," Heming said, smiling so that they knew he was not unhappy with what he was.

"Actually if ye look at the list your mother has made, most of what ye kept are the strengths, all the hunting and fighting skills. Weel, we shall talk of this another time. Ye will sense the importance of it when 'tis time for your own child to appear. Now we shall plan how to free your mate. Do ye think her life is in danger? Your men didnae."

"I am nay as certain as they are, but it could be because she is my mate."

"Aye, calm reason is verra hard to grasp when one's mate is threatened. Colin believes there is some gain for this mon Angus and the laird if Brona weds with Angus. He also seems to truly believe that, if Hervey Kerr dies and Brona marries, she will be heir for ye can stand in the place of the laird. 'Tis nay uncommon for a laird to have his daughter be his heir on condition that she marry. Have we nay had such a thing happen within our own family? It will need to be looked into. It would nay be so strange if this mon Hervey isnae telling your Brona the full truth about her father's last wishes."

"I will do that as soon as I put that bastard in the

ground." He grimaced and looked at his mother. "Pardon, *Maman*."

"No need, son," she said and smiled sweetly. "He is a bastard and I hope ye put him in the ground verra soon."

"Weel, I am nay sure how easy it will be to get too many men in through the way we got out," said Colin as he stood near the window of Heming's bedchamber and rubbed his chin as he thought the matter over. "We slipped out because no one was doing the work they should have been doing, aye? Resting whilst the laird was gone and all. They will all be ready for an attack this time, looking out for the enemy so that they can live through yet another of the laird's mistakes."

Heming yanked on his boots and then laced them up. He was finally feeling better, his weakness gone. It had taken the offer of blood from a cousin to finally help him recover his strength, but now he was eager to get back to Rosscurrach and find his Brona. Colin was right, however. They might know a secret way into the keep, but the guard on the walls would be tight and very watchful.

But would they all be eager to die for Hervey Kerr? Heming suddenly thought. "How many of the men now manning the walls of Rosscurrach are loyal to Hervey?"

"Wheesht, I doubt ye would find a full handful, why?"

"Because mayhap the simplest thing to do is lessen the number of men on those walls by letting them ken that 'tis Hervey who has committed a wrong and that Brona is the true heir as soon as she marries. All we want to do is save her from the brutal Angus and give her back what is hers by right of birth."

"Verra good," murmured Jankyn.

"It could work," said Peter. "I could—"

"Nay, ye must nay be seen by anyone who might feel inclined to tell Hervey ye are back at Rosscurrach. He will recognize ye. I suspicion there are others at the keep who will recognize ye as weel."

Peter sighed and acknowledged that truth with a nod. "'Tis humiliating but I fear there were a few who kenned exactly why the laird dragged me into his dungeon."

"Weel, few will say aught about me or Fergus," said Colin. "I am nay sure that e'en Hervey would. We are just shepherds, aye? Hervey doesnae look down that far. Probably afraid he will fall off his horse."

Jankyn laughed and shook his head. "If ye feel that sure ye willnae be in much danger if ye suddenly appear within the walls of Rosscurrach then ye must go. One mon may be enough if Fergus isnae wanting to slip inside that snake pit."

"Oh, I go where Colin goes," said Fergus. "If he gets me killed I will just follow him where'er he goes after and keep whining about how 'tis all his fault my promising young life was cut so short." He grunted when Colin rapped him on the head with his knuckles but then grinned. "Dinnae ye worry none, laird," he said to Heming. "We will make verra sure that a lot of the fellows inside the keep's walls find somewhere else to be when the fighting starts."

"Are ye sure they will be so willing to let me slip in?" asked Heming. "Dinnae they think I am a soul-sucking demon?"

"Nay, most dinnae e'en ken ye were locked up down there," said Colin. "Ye were the laird's special prisoner and he was seeking secrets for his own use, aye? Nay e'en for his people, just for him. Nay, the men I be thinking of will be willing to join ye as long as I assure them that ye are hard-working and nay a cruel bastard who beats people just to see how the blood runs off their back when he is done."

"Fair enough."

"They will also do it to have the lass ruling aside ye." Colin grinned widely when Heming gave him a mock glare.

"And that too is fair enough although I wouldnae go promising that as we dinnae ken if her father made any such command ere he died. No one seems to argue the fact that Hervey was the old laird's heir. Could be because Hervey has hidden a few truths or could be because he really is the laird."

Peter nodded. "True. He could be. But, I dinnae think anyone will complain about who is the laird so long as it isnae Hervey." He then looked at Heming and his father. "How will ye make the journey? 'Twas easy enough to find ye a place to tuck yourself away when the sun was high, but I dinnae think we can find that many hiding places if ye intend to bring such a large host of your kin."

"Dinnae worry on that, Peter," said Jankyn. "We ken how to do it. It may nay be the fastest way, but it will serve to get many of us there." Jankyn looked at his son. "So, do we leave in an hour or do ye wish to wait until the morrow?"

"In an hour," said Heming, even as he thought that was far too long to wait.

"I just had me a thought," said Colin, blushing when everyone looked at him.

"Tell me, Colin," Heming said when embarrassment apparently silenced the man. "Several times ye have seen something I have missed so I am interested in what ye have thought about."

"Weel, I was just thinking on how ye fought Hervey and his men when they took Mistress Brona. I am thinking we had best tell the men that, if they dinnae want to die for Hervey Kerr, they had best get out of Rosscurrach and stay hidden for a wee while. If your kin fight as ye do, there are some who may turn on ye and yours in their fear."

Heming stared at Colin for a moment before exchanging a look with his father. When Jankyn nodded faintly, Heming knew his father was thinking just what he was. Colin might appear to be a genial shepherd, a man with more brawn than wit, but there was obviously a sharp mind beneath that tangled hair and it would be a good idea to put such a man, such a loyal man, in a position of authority. If it turned out that Brona would become the heir if Hervey died and she married, Heming would certainly keep Colin out of the fields and set at his side.

The moment Jankyn left to finish a few preparations, Colin frowned at the door and then looked at Heming. "Is he really your father and the wee lass is really your mother?"

"Aye and aye," replied Heming. "I told ye, Colin, we dinnae age verra fast."

"Wheesht, it doesnae look like ye age at all. I thought ye said your mother and the laird's wife were Outsiders."

"Aye, they are. They are Callans. They do live long lives."

"Mayhap they do, but I doubt they dinnae look a day o'er twenty when they are old enough to have sons your age."

Heming just stared at Colin and then looked toward the door his father had just walked out of, briefly considering chasing the man down and asking a few hard questions. "I ne'er gave it much thought," he murmured, looking back at Colin, "but ye are right. It makes no sense. When she and her sister said they lived long lives, they meant ninety or a wee bit more, nay long-lived as we are. Weel, the moment this is settled, I will sit my mother down and try to find out what is going on. What made ye think on that?"

"I was thinking of the lass. She isnae a MacNachton and I suddenly worried about how she may fccl kenning she will age whcn ye dinnae. Not a thing any woman can think about with ease, I be thinking."

"How true. Weel, another problem to solve. Just remind me of it when this is all done and over. At the moment, I find it hard to recall anything except for the need to get my Brona away from Hervey and Angus."

"Then we had best get moving. We wouldnae want *your Brona* to think ye arenae going to save her, would we."

Watching the three snickering men who were fast becoming his very good friends walk out of the room, Heming had to fight to resist the strong urge to give each one a swift kick in the arse.

"These are verra clever things," said Peter as he ran his hand over the side of one of the covered carts the Mac-Nachtons used to travel in during the day.

"Aye," agreed Heming, taking a drink from his wineskin and handing it to Peter. "One learns to be clever when one can only see the sun as poison." Seeing how

Peter very carefully took a sip of wine, Heming grinned. "'Tis naught but pure wine, Peter. I wouldnae serve ye the other. I only drink it now and then as I dinnae have to have any blood for a fortnight or more after I feed. I can go longer, but it isnae always comfortable to do so."

"Hurts does it? Like hunger pangs?"

"Nay. If one goes too long without, it can feel as if ye have a belly full of broken glass."

"Ach, nasty." He took a long drink of wine and smiled politely at Jankyn when Heming's father joined them. "We made verra good time and I didnae think we would with the carts and all."

Jankyn nodded. "They arenae as fast as one would like them to be, but they mean we can travel during the day as weel as the night. 'Tis why we are within but a few miles of Rosscurrach. All one needs are men who can drive them during the day."

"'Tis hard, isnae it, nay being able to be out in the sun?" asked Peter and then he frowned and shook his head. "Pardon. That isnae any of my business."

"'Tis nay hard to guess the answer to that," said Jankyn. "Aye, it can be hard, especially when one is wed to someone who loves the sun. But, when one has kenned no other way, one doesnae think about it too often. 'Tis good, however, to see that our children begin to ease out from beneath the burden of that."

"Mayhap whate'er bairns Brona and I have will be able to endure e'en more of it than I can." Heming grimaced. "I can see the good in losing some of what makes us MacNachtons, but I do worry about losing some of the other things."

"Like being able to pick grown men up like they are

naught but thistledown and toss them about?" asked Peter with a grin. "Me, Fergus, and Colin near forgot to keep fighting just to watch that."

"Aye, things like that." Heming looked toward Rosscurrach and felt his belly knot with fear for Brona. "Berawald should be returning soon, shouldnae he?"

Jankyn patted Heming on the shoulder. "Aye, he will return soon and then we shall go and fetch your mate. Dinnae let her fate prey on your mind so. Think only of how ye will soon have her back."

" 'Tisnae easy. She is terrified of her cousin and Angus. They are both brutal men and they think she has betrayed them. Angus also lusts after her. Lust and anger make a verra dangerous brew."

"We arenae so verra far behind them, son. And dinnae forget, the lass had the wit to get ye all out of her cousin's dungeons, hide ye away, and then get ye out of the keep. They must also ken that ye will be coming with an army and they will be too busy readying for that to do much with her."

"True. I will try to remember that." He tensed as he watched a tall, slim man ride into the camp. "Berawald."

It was not easy, but Heming stood silently as Berawald joined them and had a drink of wine to clear the dust from his throat. Berawald was a slender, almost beautiful man, with long flowing black hair and deep blue eyes. He always looked distracted and one quickly learned that was because, to him, the veil between the living and the dead did not exist. His world was filled with the spirits of the dead. Heming sometimes wondered if there was something about the man that attracted those spirits.

When Berawald fixed his dreamy gaze on Heming, Heming asked, "What did ye find out?"

"Your lady is alive," Berawald said, his voice soft, deep, and almost musical.

Heming went weak at the knees at the news but struggled to quickly regain his composure. "The keep is weel fortified?"

"Aye and nay. There are many men on the walls but verra few wish to be there. Fergus and Colin have already slipped inside and I believe that verra soon the number of men on the walls will greatly lessen. 'Tis a verra haunted place, which may be something ye shouldnae tell your mate."

"I wish ye hadnae told me," Peter muttered, and smiled faintly when Jankyn grinned at him.

"I think many of them will move on when Hervey is killed. There are some with a lot of hatred toward that mon for he is responsible for their deaths. I told them that men are coming to send the mon to hell so I dinnae think there will be any trouble from them. Your way in is clear. It hasnae been discovered. Once the number of men upon the walls thins out, I think ye can slip in unseen." He frowned. "I fear Colin and Fergus werenae verra pleased with my methods of discovering if the way in was safe for them. Colin feels that spirits ought not to be troubling the living and he didnae want me to tell him who they were as he said he knew some of the ones who had died in the keep and he didnae want to ken that they were still lurking about. Said it would make him nervous. Trying to see him naked or something like that." Berawald smiled when the men laughed and then shrugged. "'Tis safe to go in the way ye came out and that is all that matters, aye?"

"Aye." Heming looked at his father. "How long do ye think we should wait ere we start to go inside?"

"Give Colin and Fergus a half an hour and then we will start toward Rosscurrach. It isnae that easy to convince men to give up their posts and mayhap e'en betray an oath made to the laird. Thank ye, Berawald. Do ye arm yourself and join us or has surveying the keep taken too much of your strength?"

"Nay, I shall go with ye." Berawald hurried off to arm himself.

Peter nodded and said, "Best I make sure I am readied for battle as weel."

The moment the men were gone, Jankyn looked at Heming. "I ken ye have said Brona Kerr is your mate, but do ye love the lass, son?"

"Are they nay one and the same?" asked Heming.

"Nay always. Sometimes the mating comes first and the love must be nurtured and grown."

"Mine is full grown."

"Good. I used to scoff at love until I met your mother. I felt the mating urge ere I admitted that it was more, much more. I but wished to be sure that ye had passed beyond the *She is mine* part of it all. When ye do speak to her of marriage I suggest ye use the love word and dinnae speak only of mates and mating. Women dinnae see that often, in a mon's eyes, 'tis the same. To them the word *mate* reeks too much of the word *breeder*."

Heming nodded. "I can see that. Weel, I believe I am all prepared to go, but I think I, too, will take a moment to be sure. And then we shall go and get my Brona back so that I can stumble my way into getting her to agree to marry me."

Nine

Brona heard someone groan and a moment later realized it was coming from her. She slowly opened her eyes and looked around. It took a little while for her vision to clear enough for her to know where she was, as her head was throbbing so hard she felt as if she would empty her belly at any moment. When she realized she was in her own bedchamber at Rosscurrach she nearly wept. This was the very last place she wanted to be.

Memories flooded her mind. Angus had yanked her out of her hiding place amongst the brambles. She had tried to fight him but there had been no breaking his grasp. As he had thrown her over the saddle of his horse, she had seen a bloodied Heming fighting to get to her. Her attempts to get free to go to him or at least run away and let him put all of his attention back onto the battle for his life had ended with a hard punch to the head. If she had become conscious at any time between then and now she could not remember it.

Was Heming still alive? She felt her heart twist painfully at the mere thought that that brief moment when she had seen him fighting to reach her would be the very last time she ever saw him. A part of her tried to tell her that it was all her fault he was dead or severely injured but she knew that was just the shock and fear talking. She had done exactly as he had asked and she had been attacked from behind. Nor was there any way she could have gotten away from a man the size of Angus.

What she needed to do now was push all thought and concern about Heming to the back of her mind. She was back in Rosscurrach and that meant she was in the hands of her cousin and Angus. Her cousin probably wanted her dead or beaten to within an inch of her life and Angus wanted to marry her and bed her. Angus was probably not very concerned about which came first. The mere thought of that man touching her made her shiver with revulsion. Brona did not even want to consider what the man would do to her when he discovered she was no longer a virgin. Thinking of such things would only make her panic and she knew she had to clear her thoughts of everything except a way to escape.

Feeling horribly thirsty, she attempted to slowly get up only to discover that she was tied very securely to her bed. She could think about escape all she wanted to but she was not going anywhere. With her wrists secured to the posts at the head of her bed and her ankles secured to the posts at the bottom, she could not even move enough to reach the knots securing her. Brona supposed she should not be surprised. She had escaped them once and they were not complete fools. She also doubted anyone would feel merciful enough to slip into her room and cut her loose. Most of the people at Rosscurrach were terrified of making Hervey or Angus angry.

Closing her eyes and fighting the urge to just lie there and weep until she lost consciousness, Brona tried to make a plan. Any plan would do. The chances of any plan she came up with working were undoubtedly very small but she needed something to cling to in order to maintain her sanity. Then again, perhaps Angus would no longer want her if he thought she had lost her mind. She inwardly shook her head over the idiocy of that thought. Angus wanted something and felt he could get it by marrying her. She could become a drooling, babbling idiot and he would still drag her before a priest. He would just lock her securely away after the wedding.

There was nothing she could do, she thought, and felt a huge wave of utter despair wash over her and try to drag her down. She did not have any way to free herself. Her only friends were either dead or wounded and unable to come after her. No one else would know where she was, not even her aunt, who might care enough to try and help her. It was no use thinking of how to escape or hoping for someone to help her escape. Brona took a deep breath to try and steady herself. What she had to do was try to think of some way to protect herself from Angus and Hervey. She had done it before, although not perfectly. Surely she could think of ways to do it again, at least until she found some way to flee them all over again.

"I am nay sure all of this preparation for war is necessary, Angus," said Hervey as he sat down at the head table and poured himself some wine.

"It may prove to be a waste of time, but I would rather have the men taking useless watches than have the Mac-Nachtons sneak up on us in the night," said Angus as he sat down on Hervey's right and helped himself to some wine. He finished off one tankard in several deep gulps and then poured himself another. "We tortured and humiliated one of their own and are a threat to their clan. I think that is enough to make them attack us unless they are all craven cowards, and I didnae get that feeling from Sir Heming when he was our guest."

Hervey cursed and thumped his fist on the table. "Damn my cousin for this. What possessed her to set the mon free? He certainly wasnae verra handsome when we were done with him, so it cannae be that she was lured into helping him because of his bonnie face."

"She probably just felt sorry for the mon. Look at that ugly dog she took in and treats like a child. Aye and that useless cat of hers. She probably saw him as just another poor animal that needed to be rescued." He shook his head. "She has too soft a heart and he used that to make her help him."

"The mon was nearly dead. I cannae believe he could e'en have talked to her. I also dinnae understand why she let Peter free or those two idiot brothers."

"Probably to help her with a mon who was nearly dead."

"Probably. There is one thing we must certainly get her to tell us and that is how she got everyone out of here."

Angus looked at Hervey and inwardly shook his head. The man pouted like a bairn when he did not get his way. Although Hervey had an admirable cruel streak and excelled at terrifying and torturing a man once that man was securely tied, chained, or imprisoned, he was almost useless at planning for a war that Angus was sure was coming their way. And this would be a war with people who were said to have some very strange and deadly powers. Angus could not understand how Hervey could doubt for one minute that the MacNachtons would be coming to get revenge for what they had done to Sir Heming MacNachton. After seeing the way the man fought, Angus wished he had ways to make the keep even more secure. Any man who could toss grown men around as if they weighed no more than a bairn made a formidable foe and was not someone who could be shrugged aside. The very last thing he wished to be was a meal for a MacNachton. His soul might be black as a moonless night but it was his and he wanted to keep it.

"Heming looked sorely wounded when we rode away," said Hervey. "I think he may be dead."

"Which gives the MacNachtons e'en more reason to attack us," said Angus, used to and bored with this type of conversation where Hervey went through every possible reason for not doing what needed to be done and expected Angus to agree with him, which Angus rarely did.

"Weel, if we dinnae see them by the end of a sennight, I would guess that they are nay coming. For all we ken, Sir Heming may have been utterly despised by all his kin and they are glad to be rid of him."

"Hervey, we tortured that mon nigh onto death and he ne'er told us a thing about his kinsmen. That isnae the sort of mon any kinsmon wants to see dead. Ye need that sort in a clan to keep the thieves and traitors in hand. Give it up, my friend. The MacNachtons will be coming here to make us pay as dearly as possible. Then they will go and gut your friend Carbonnel." He stared at Hervey and said, "Now let us talk about my wedding wee Brona."

"Now? When we may soon be in a war with men that can suck out a mon's soul?"

" 'Twould seem a verra good time to me. Who kens what may happen to one or both of us. Best to get the business of Brona, her dowry, and her inheritance all settled."

Narrowing his eyes at Angus, Hervey growled, "Oh, aye, her inheritance. If I dinnae beget a son, all she has to do is marry and she gets all of Rosscurrach. Ye seem verra eager to make ye the mon who would be standing at her side if I died without an heir."

It did not surprise Angus that Hervey had finally thought a little bit about that particular aspect of Brona's inheritance. The man was not as stupid as he acted at times. Angus knew he was going to have to tread very carefully to make Hervey let go of all those suspicions he could read on the man's face. Angus had no intention of marrying Brona and then killing Hervey. That would rouse far too many suspicions for his liking. He would just make sure that Hervey never had a chance to marry and beget that all-important heir.

"Hervey, ye ken verra weel that I have wanted the lass since I first set eyes on her. I didnae e'en ken what the old mon had said must be done after he died."

"Oh, I am nay questioning that ye lust after my cousin. I just wonder what else ye are lusting after. Could be the verra chair I am sitting in."

This was not good, mused Angus. "I just want Brona. Ye can keep the cursed laird's chair. The priest is cowering in the chapel because he is terrified that the MacNachton demons might sniff him out and suck up his soul. We can get Brona, take her to the chapel, and I can marry her. Then 'tis all done and settled ere we face the enemy. I may e'en have enough time to grab a wee taste of the wench. I have been wanting one for long enough."

"Nay."

Angus stiffened and subtly put his hand on the hilt of his sword. "Nay? Did ye just say nay?"

"I did. 'Tis my place as her laird to decide who she marries and I have decided that I dinnae want her married to a mon who stands so conveniently at my back."

"Ye bastard! Ye have promised me that wench for years."

"Weel, it seems I may have a much better deal than ye offered." Hervey pulled a wrinkled piece of parchment from his pocket. "It seems our neighbor wishes an alliance and it is to be sealed with the marriage of his son to my cousin."

"His son is barely fifteen years old. He has nae e'en grown a wee bit of down on his scrawny face."

"He will grow and he will breed her, which will keep her at that mon's keep and out of mine."

Angus slowly stood up. "Ye have gone back on your word."

"I do that all the time. No one should ken that any better than ye. If ye still want the wench after she is wed to this boy then go to her and take her. Since the lad has so little experience with women or in battle ye ought to be able to woo her into your bed simply because her husband is so bad there she is in need of a real mon. And if the lad catches ye cuckolding him, ye have enough experience to cut him down without e'en raising a sweat."

"And thus destroying the alliance? What do ye get out

of this, Hervey?" he asked in a hard cold voice as he began to decide which wound would kill the fool the fastest. He would prefer to have the man killed very slowly, but with the threat of the MacNachtons hanging over his head, he could not afford the time needed to really enjoy it.

"A lot of money and a strip of verra good land on our western border."

"And for that ye would break your word to me?"

"Give the marriage a few months, e'en a year, and then make her a widow if ye still want her so badly."

"I dinnae want her after some beardless boy has been rutting o'er her for months."

"And just what do ye think Sir Heming has been doing? Do ye really think she spent all that time with him and he didnae lift her skirts?"

"Mayhap he did, but with those three fools traveling with them, I doubt he did so more than once or twice and he would be careful nay to put a bairn in her. A lad of fifteen will be riding her every night and doing his meager best to fill her belly."

"Aha! I kenned it! Ye wanted to have her bear ye a son so that ye could try and claim Rosscurrach. Weel, ye can just forget that fine piece of treachery. Nay only is Brona going to marry the lad, but I am going to marry his sister. A sweet wee lass of fourteen. Young and tight and ready to breed."

Angus drew his sword and swung it. The look of petulant anger was still on Hervey's face as his head hit the floor. Wiping his sword off on the man's doublet, Angus slid it back into its sheath. He stared at Hervey's body for a minute and then cursed. He was still taut with fury and now he had to be rid of the fool's body.

Grabbing the cloth off the table, he tossed Hervey's body onto it and then set his head on his chest. Wrapping the body up, he hefted it over his shoulder and stealthily made his way down into the dungeons. A slow smile crossed his face as he made his way to the cage where they had kept Sir Heming. He tossed Hervey into the cage, pausing to put the man's head back on his chest and then went to throw the cloth from the table down into the pit where they emptied the prisoners' privy buckets.

Certain that the MacNachtons would soon be attacking, Angus was confident that he would be able to think of an explanation for Hervey's death. He doubted anyone would question the tale that Hervey tried to flee, was caught outside by vengeful MacNachtons, and murdered. Later, when it was dark, he would toss the body outside. Now he had to go and marry Brona before anyone learned the laird was dead.

The sound of the door to her bedchamber opening drew Brona out of her misery. She looked toward the door and felt as if all the blood in her body had just turned to ice. Angus walked over to the side of the bed and stared down at her. The man felt as if he was about to burst open from the anger inside of him and she greatly feared that anger would be visited upon her even if she did not deserve it.

"Ye have been a verra busy lass, havenae ye," he said. "Freeing prisoners, running about the country with four men. Did ye service them all?"

Even though a part of her mind told her not to respond to that insult, that it would only prod at Angus's anger, Brona said, "Of course I didnae. Just because ye and Hervey feel a need to rut with anything that breathes doesnae mean I do."

The slap he gave her made her ears ring and Brona tasted blood in her mouth. She felt tears of pain sting her eyes but blinked them away. She would not give the man the pleasure of seeing her cry. He was a brute who sought to cow her with harsh words and pain and she refused to allow him to win that game.

"If ye have bedded down with that demon ye will pay for that," he said as he began to untie her.

Brona felt a twinge of hope and then told herself not to be an idiot. Angus would never set her free. With that thought the fact that he was untying her began to frighten her. Mayhap he intended to put her down in the dungeon, she thought, and felt a cold knot of panic twist in her belly. She decided she did not really wish to know what he planned to do to her for that would probably stir her panic past her control.

"Now we are going to do what I have been planning to do for years but your damn cousin has continued to find ways to make me wait. Weel, he willnae be playing that game with me anymore."

Hervey is dead, she thought. Brona suddenly knew without a doubt that Angus had killed her cousin. Hervey had obviously pushed the man once too often and Angus had struck back.

And if he killed Hervey what would he do to her, she thought. Fear became a living thing inside of her but she fought its hold. If the only thing she could do to preserve any scrap of dignity was not cower and cry out for help then she would do it.

She bit back a cry of pain as he yanked her off the bed

and started to drag her out of the room. "Where are we going?"

"To the chapel," Angus replied, pulling her along after him as he went down the stairs.

"Why?"

"Because ye are going to marry me."

Brona tried to drag her feet and slow him down but he yanked her along so hard and unrelentingly that she had to move or she would end up being pulled along the floor and the rocky ground. "My cousin isnae here and he has to approve this."

"He approved this years ago and I mean to see that he finally keeps his promise."

By the time they entered the chapel Brona's arm was hurting her so badly from all the pulling that she was biting back tears of pain. She looked around the chapel and saw the priest, a plump man of uncertain morals, cowering near the altar. It was not likely that such a cowardly man would help her and stand against Angus but Brona felt she had to at least try to win his aid.

"Father, I havenae agreed to this!" she said and cried out when Angus hit her again.

The priest's only response to that brutality against the old laird's daughter was to cower some more and look around frantically for some route of escape. Brona knew there would be no help to be found there. He would do whatever Angus told him to. Just as so many other people at Rosscurrach, the priest was thoroughly cowed.

"We are here to be married, Father," Angus said.

"But where is the laird?" asked the priest. "Mistress Brona is his kinswoman and he should be here."

"He cannae be here right now, so get on with it."

"But there is a war—"

The priest squealed to a halt when Angus drew his sword and held it at the man's throat. Brona thought for just a moment that the priest was going to fall at their feet in a faint, but despite his trembling, and to her utter disappointment, he waved his shaking hand in a silent command to kneel before him. She tried to keep standing but Angus knelt and pulled her down beside him. Brona landed on her knees so hard that she knew they would be bruised and painful for days. It took all of her willpower not to faint from the force of that pain.

In a weak, shaking voice, the priest began the marriage service. Brona tried to catch the man's eye, tried to silently plea for him to help her, but he kept his gaze upon Angus's now sheathed sword. When she was asked to repeat her vows, she hesitated, but Angus drew his sword again and pointed it at the priest's throat once more. The threat was clear and she could not be responsible for the trembling priest's death. Brona repeated her vows even though she choked on each and every word. Her stomach was clenched and bile stung the back of her throat as she thought of how Angus was forcing her to lie before God, as she had absolutely no intention of honoring a single vow she was now taking.

Once the vows were done and a tremulous blessing was given, Angus started to take her back toward the keep. Brona ceased fighting his pull, for it hurt and she knew she might need to use that arm in the very near future. She kept a few paces behind him, however, refusing to walk by his side as if she had accepted him as her husband. Just as they reached the wide stone steps leading into the keep a man ran up to Angus, shouting his name, and Angus cursed viciously before turning to face the man.

"The MacNachtons are here," the man said, his fear ringing in his voice. "They are outside the walls."

Brona wanted to run up on the walls and see them. She even pulled against Angus's grip, but he yanked her right back. Brona wondered if Heming was there and she ached to see him, to see that he was alive.

"I told ye they would come. That was why ye were all put up on the walls," snapped Angus. "Told that fool Hervey, too."

"But what shall we do?"

"Ye shall watch them, fool. If they do anything more than just stand there or hurl insults at ye, then kill them."

"Are ye nay joining us?"

With a speed that was startling, Angus hit the man, sending him sprawling in the dirt at his feet. No wonder everyone was terrified of the man, Brona thought. She had become so good at staying out of his and Hervey's way, at staying hidden and quiet, that she had almost forgotten how the two men were so good at just striking out, often for what appeared to be no reason at all. That constant expectation of violence and pain striking at any moment had obviously been inside of her but she had smothered it, hiding it even from herself. It made one afraid, however, and she had been afraid all of the time. Just as this man was afraid.

"Watch the bastards," growled Angus, "and unless they are flying o'er the walls or coming up through the floor, dinnae trouble me with questions ye already have the answers to. I am going to be verra busy for a while consummating my marriage."

Shock was the first expression on the other man's face as he slowly stood up and looked at Brona. It was quickly followed by a look that Brona could only describe as pity. Brona felt as if her face was on fire she was blushing so hard with shame and embarrassment. She felt a lot of pity for herself, but it was humiliating to know that now everyone at Rosscurrach would be aware of what was happening to her. Her coming rape by Angus would never be some deep, dark, terrifying secret she could keep to herself. As Angus dragged her into the keep, Brona prayed that the MacNachtons did get inside Rosscurrach, for she knew only a real threat to Angus's life would stop him from accomplishing what he planned to do to her.

Ten

"Someone died down here."

Heming exchanged a grin with his father and then looked at his cousin Berawald. He liked the man but often got the feeling that his cousin lived in the world of spirits far more than he lived in the world of men. Then again, if he had lived surrounded by ghosts for as long as Berawald had perhaps he, too, would have some difficulty in holding fast to the line between the two.

"I am nay surprised," Heming drawled. "'Tis a dungeon. Sad to say too many have probably died here."

Berawald simply nodded, either ignoring Heming's slight sarcasm or unaware of it. "This mon didnae die down here and he died verra recently."

For a moment, Heming was terrified that he was too late to save Brona and he asked, "Ye are sure it is a mon?"

"Och, aye. Verra definitely a mon."

When Heming moved to the steps that led up into the keep, he realized that Berawald was marching off in another direction. A heartbeat later, he realized that his cousin was headed for the cage Hervey had kept Heming in. A chill ran over his body and Heming told himself not to be so foolish. He was still alive and, aside from getting Brona back, that was all that mattered. Cursing softly, he then hurried after Berawald. The man had to stop wandering off or he would get himself killed.

When Berawald stopped in front of the cage and held his lantern up, Heming had to force himself to walk up to him. Before he could say anything to his cousin, however, he glanced down at what Berawald was staring at and cursed again. Hervey's body was sprawled on the floor of the cage, his elegant clothing stained with his own blood, and his head sitting on his chest facing the door. The man's face was forever frozen into a petulant expression. Hervey had obviously never seen death coming.

"This mon didnae die here," said Berawald, and then he frowned. "His death was so recent that his spirit hasnae yet understood that he is dead."

"Weel, Hervey Kerr wasnae always the most clever cat in the pack."

Berawald actually smiled, but quickly grew solemn again. "If death is violent and occurs quickly, I have discovered, that the spirit of the dead one is often confused. This mon didnae see the blow coming."

"I thought the same thing."

"Ye ken who this mon is?" Berawald asked, looking at Heming.

"Aye, as I said, 'tis Hervey Kerr. 'Tis the laird of Rosscurrach, my Brona's cousin, and the mon who held me prisoner here." Out of the corner of his eye Heming saw his father's elegant hand curl tightly around one of the bars of the cage.

"This is where he held ye?" Jankyn asked. "In chains?"

"And naked," Heming said quietly, a little impressed by the vileness of the curses his father spit out. "I am nay sorry that the mon is dead but I am verra sorry that it wasnae I who struck the blow. I had dearly wished to kill him myself."

"Step back," ordered Berawald, yanking Jankyn's hand from the cage and pulling him away.

"What is it? Is something wrong?" Heming felt a bone-deep cold suddenly sweep through him and stepped even farther away from the cage.

"The spirit has gone back into its body. Watch."

Heming's eyes widened as a dark shadow swirled up from the floor and over the body. He felt something dark and dangerous in that shadow and could swear that he heard someone screaming in terror as if from a very long distance away. Just as he started to convince himself that he was letting Berawald's talk of spirits cause him to imagine things, the shadow retreated back into the floor. Heming felt someone pressed close against his back and looked behind him to find a white-faced Peter staring over his shoulder.

"Jesu," whispered Peter. "Something just took that bastard's soul down to hell, didnae it."

"Exactly," said Berawald. "Weel, let us go and save your woman, Heming."

Heming watched Berawald walk away, cast one last look at the floor, and then hurried after his cousin. "Have ye e'er seen that before?"

"Och, aye. A lot of spirits linger after death. The reasons are nay important and they are many. But, the ones who have sins blackening their souls, the ones bound for hell, arenae allowed to linger here. The devil isnae a patient mon. Where do ye think they are keeping your mate?"

Used to his cousin's abrupt changes of subject, Heming answered, "I have no idea. I have ne'er been in the place before. Nay, above here, in the keep itself. I am hoping Peter can help me."

"Ah, weel, I am certain we can find someone to help us if Peter cannae."

"Oh, sweet Mary, nay more spirits," muttered Peter.

Heming shook his head and hurried up the stairs, moving rapidly past Berawald. He needed to find Brona. Every instinct he had was crying out that she was in imminent peril. The moment he stepped out of the underbelly of Rosscurrach into what looked like a large solar, Heming felt all the cold resolve he needed to do battle wash over him, readying him for whatever he might face next. He moved to the side of the doorway leading to the dungeons, his father, Peter, and Berawald moving to stand with him. As the other men who had come through the passages came into the room, Heming listened to his father direct them.

Colin had sent some Kerrs to them and those men were used to show the MacNachton fighters around the keep. Heming suspected they were also there to try to keep the loss of Kerr life as low as possible. There was a wariness in the men but no more than that and Heming knew Colin was trying to ease his way, for the man was certain that Heming would be the next laird of Rosscurrach. All Heming cared about, however, was Brona, finding her and keeping her safe. The moment all the men who had come in through the doorway were gone, making their way through the keep to make it MacNachton territory, Heming turned to Peter, the only one still at his side.

"Where do ye think Brona will be?" Heming asked the man.

"Whene'er the laird secured the lass it was within her own bedchamber," replied Peter.

"Then take me there. Now."

All the breath in Brona's lungs was pushed out when Angus threw her onto her bed and then flung himself down on top of her. Brona was too desperate to catch her breath, to just breathe, to do anything to stop the man from roughly unlacing her gown. When she was able to finally breathe she began to struggle. Angus punched her in the face with such a cold calm, it was not only the pain of that blow that stilled her movements.

When Angus started to tug her gown off her shoulders the fear that held her in place fled and her sense returned. No matter what she did this man was going to hurt her. He was going to rape her. Brona doubted Angus would even try to make her want him, to ease the taking of her body by stirring even a little desire in her. She decided that, if she was going to be hurt, she would be hurt while fighting this man. He might not be planning to kill her but what he wanted to do to her would destroy her in ways she did not even want to think about.

Even as Brona punched Angus in the face she knew she was starting a fight that she had absolutely no chance of winning. It was also a battle that would leave her in a great deal of pain, but she no longer cared about that. He was going to put himself inside her, join their bodies, and leave his seed in her womb. The mere thought of that terrified and revolted her. Only Heming had been there and she would fight to the death to try and stop Angus from befouling what she had shared with Heming. She closed her mind to the pain as she fought with Angus.

To her complete shame it only took Angus a few short minutes to subdue her. As he tied her wrists to the bedposts she tried to take some satisfaction in the fact that he was bleeding from the mouth and nose and his eye was watering badly from the punch she had delivered to it. It had been a short, eerie battle, neither one of them making much noise. He had used his big fists and his much bigger body. She had used her fists, her feet, her teeth, and her nails, but she had still lost. Brona just hoped that later she might be able to find some comfort in the fact that she had tried to save herself.

"Why are ye doing this?" she asked, pleased at how calm, even cold, she sounded. "Why marry a woman who doesnae want ye?"

"Weel, I want ye," Angus replied as he drew his knife and began to cut her gown off her body. "I have wanted ye for years. I have also wanted to be the laird here from the first day I set foot inside these walls."

"Ye cannae be the laird here. Hervey is the laird."

"But when Hervey is dead ye become the next heir and, trust me, old Hervey is verra, verra dead."

Brona felt a brief pang of regret when she realized that this news did not cause even a flutter of grief. "I cannae be the laird because I am a woman. 'Tis why Hervey was chosen o'er me, my father's only bairn."

"*Ye* cannae be the laird but your husband can be."

So that was it, she thought, feeling a ridiculous sense

of insult as she worked strenuously to make her body as cold as ice and numb, so numb that she would not be able to even feel this man's touch. She had no doubt that Angus had lusted after her, but he had married her to become the laird of Rosscurrach. Brona suspected Hervey had kept Angus close and loyal for years with the promise of letting Angus marry her. Hervey had been smart enough to know that, once Angus was married to her, the man could never be trusted again, that Hervey's life would be in danger from the moment the vows were uttered. Something had happened to make Angus strike out and just take what he wanted. Brona suspected Angus would use the battle with the MacNachtons to hide his murder of the laird in some way.

"Tell me, has that demon been inside ye?" Angus asked as he gripped the front of her shift and held his knife ready to cut it off.

"Aye, he has been so blessed," said a deep familiar voice and Brona felt her body rush to life again, "and he is the only mon who e'er will be."

Angus sat up in shock and gaped at Heming for one brief moment before he was lifted off Brona and thrown across the room. Brona stared at Heming, lightheaded from the joy of seeing him alive and well and able to throw people around again. She met his golden gaze, saw the odd mixture of concern for her and rage at Angus, and smiled at him.

"Did he get what he wanted?" Heming asked her, aching to look her over more carefully but not daring to take his full gaze off Angus Kerr.

"Nay. We were just discussing the matter," Brona replied.

"I would like to set ye free right now, Brona love, but I have to kill a mon first."

"I can wait."

Angus was back on his feet now and he rushed at Heming. The way Heming avoided the man's heavy fists and kept knocking Angus down told her that Angus had very little chance of winning this fight. She glanced at the door to see Peter standing there. That man started toward her but she shook her head to stop him. The bedchamber was not big enough for two big men to fight without endangering everyone else in the room. She was safe enough where she was for now; but Peter could get hurt if he entered the room, or could cause a distraction that could get Heming hurt, especially now that both men had drawn their swords and were doing their best to cut each other into ribbons. She breathed a sigh of relief when Peter nodded and took up a guard's position at the door to make sure that no one could slip into the room and attack Heming's back.

Angus was soon staggering, blood flowing from several wounds. Brona suspected Heming was playing with the man, killing him slowly. Horrible as that was to watch, she could understand why Heming was doing it. Heming had been at the mercy of this man's cruel hands for almost a week. He had been tortured and humiliated. For a man with Heming's pride and strength that must have been unendurable.

Then, suddenly, Angus managed to knock Heming back against the wall. Instead of using that advantage to thrust his sword into Heming, however, Angus ran over to her. He stood next to the bed, his sword in his shaking hand, and glared at Heming as he slowly withdrew his dagger. Brona tried to get out of his reach, but it was impossible with her hands tied so tightly to the bedposts.

"I ken I can ne'er win this fight against ye, demon," said Angus, his voice hoarse with pain and fury, "but ere I get sent to hell I am taking something from ye as weel. Something I think ye want verra badly."

Brona stared at the knife in Angus's hand and knew what he intended to do, but she was helpless to stop him or to get away. All she could do was twist around on the bed as the knife plunged toward her chest. She felt the blow as the blade went into her body. Stunned, she stared down at the hilt of the knife sticking out of her chest. Then the pain hit and Brona knew she could not endure that for long, so she let the blackness rushing into her mind take her away from it.

Heming let out a bellow of rage as he watched Angus stab Brona. The man laughed even as Heming rushed at him and swung his sword. The look of triumph for causing one last person pain was still on Angus's face as his head hit the floor, the body slowly following it down. Heming immediately turned to Brona and gave a prayer of thanks to see that the knife had not entered her heart, that she was still alive.

"Another headless body?" asked Berawald as he stepped around Peter and into the room.

"Should we be taking that down to the dungeons?" asked Peter. "Ye ken, so that the devil can take the bastard's soul like it did the laird's?"

"Oh, we dinnae need to move the body for that to happen. So, best ye stay away from the body," Berawald added as he walked up to the bedside and looked down at Brona.

"Your mate is a bonnie lass, Cousin," he told Heming. "The wound is deep but it doesnae need to be a mortal wound."

"What do ye mean by that?" asked Heming.

"I am nay quite sure. 'Tis just what I feel. Take the knife out and I will help ye stop the bleeding. I think Peter should send word to your mother, who follows us. She needs to be here and, nay, I am nay sure of the why of that, either."

Peter did not question Berawald, just took off at a run. Heming did not even know or care how the battle for Rosscurrach fared. All of his attention was upon tending to Brona's wound and praying that she would recover.

"She is dying."

Efrica rubbed her hand over her son's broad back trying vainly to ease the grief she felt in him, the pain roughening his voice as he spoke the ugly truth. He had not left Brona Kerr's bedside for three long days and nights. The girl was very close to death and Efrica decided it was time to tell Heming what she had learned in the old journals she had been studying for years. Efrica was not sure she believed all she had read, despite her own situation, but it was worth a try. They had certainly tried everything else to help the girl recover.

"She needs some of your blood, Heming," she said.

Heming sat up and stared at his mother. "She isnae a MacNachton, *Maman*."

"I ken it." She sat down in the chair at his side and leaned forward, clasping his hands in hers, her heart breaking over the sorrow he felt now and the knowledge of the agony he would feel if they could not save Brona. "Ye ken that your father and I tend to the histories of the clan. Studying them and preserving them."

"Have ye found some connection between the Mac-Nachtons and the Kerrs of Rosscurrach?"

"Nay, but I have found something else far more important. Heming, look at me with the eyes of a man and nay those of a loving son who will probably always see his mother as the one who held him when he was small. How old do I look?"

Heming stared at his mother and began to frown. There were few lines on her face and her skin still had the soft clear glow of a much younger woman. He wondered how he had not noticed that that was odd. He was no good at guessing people's ages, the talent not having been of much use at Cambrun, but he tried to think of other women he knew and began to feel an odd mixture of wary and excited.

"Weel, I am nay so verra good at such things, but I would say ye look about thirty. But, have ye and Aunt nay told us many times that the Callans are a long-lived clan?"

"Long-lived being that they tend to live four score or more years. They certainly dinnae stop aging. I am o'er two score and ten years, son. Do I truly look anything like that age?"

"Nay, but how has this happened? If being wed to a MacNachton makes ye live as long as we do, then why did the laird's mother die?"

"Because she didnae guess the secret. None of us did. I had a small idea of the truth because I read so many books and journals and began to add up a few things I had read. The laird's mother lived to be nearly two hundred, Heming, e'en though she was an Outsider."

"And she drank of her husband's blood?"

"Nay, but I begin to think that, if she had, she would have lived as long as her husband. I think what added so many years to her life was that, weel, she and her husband were verra passionate. She did receive a fair bit of his, er, essence."

Heming had to grin, for his mother was blushing. "I ken what ye mean. But why do ye think blood will work e'en better? Mayhap what happened with the old laird's wife was all part of the mating." Even though he was questioning his mother's opinion, Heming began to feel the distinct tingle of hope.

"I began having a wee bit of your father's blood o'er twenty years ago, Heming, and I havenae aged but a few days or so since that time. I carry none of the usual signs of age an Outsider would. I feel certain the secret of what makes ye MacNachtons is in your blood. And, ere ye start to worry, I havenae suddenly grown fangs or desired to drink blood, or lost my ability to go outside when the sun is shining."

"Do ye ken, Hervey Kerr wondered if the secret of our long lives was in our blood. He had had plans to drink mine."

"Then I am verra glad the mon is dead and nay just for what he wanted to do to ye. If I am right, this is a secret we must keep verra close and quiet. People would kill for it, Heming. There would be no place a MacNachton could hide."

He nodded, chilled by that truth. He then thought about her opinion on what his blood might do for Brona for only a few more minutes and decided there was nothing to lose if he tried what his mother suggested. It caused him pure agony to admit it, even briefly, but Brona was dying. One could hear the approach of death in every soft rattle as she struggled to breathe.

"How do I give it to her?"

"Best if ye mix it with some wine and pour it down her throat. Ye can cut yourself and let her drink from ye later if ye wish it and if she will do it." Efrica blushed again. "It can be verra, weel, nice." She suddenly frowned at Brona. "Hurry, Heming, Death's hand is definitely reaching for your lass."

Heming made a drink of his blood and some rich wine. It was not easy getting the drink down Brona's throat but he finally managed. With his mother's hand in his, he sat and watched the woman he loved for any sign, however faint, that she would get strong again. The first sign was so subtle he would have missed it if he had not heard his mother take a swift indrawn breath. He listened closely and he heard it, heard the first sign that he was not going to lose his mate. The rattle in her chest was gone.

Eleven

Brona slowly opened her eyes and stared up at the ceiling of her bedchamber. A moment later memories flooded her mind and she almost leapt out of bed and went screaming for the door. Only the realization that her wrists were no longer tied to the bedposts calmed her. She knew instinctively that the warm body she could now feel curled at her back was not Angus and she lightly stroked the arm wrapped around her waist. A warm, soft kiss on the nape of her neck told her that Heming was awake and she turned on her back to look at him. She sighed, for with his sleep-warmed golden eyes and his tousled hair, he was intimidatingly handsome.

Then another chilling memory skipped through her mind and she gasped, hastily putting her hand on her chest where Angus's dagger had been buried. Brona frowned in confusion for there was no bandage. She eased aside the neck of her night shift and frowned even more. There was only the faintest of red lines where her wound would have been. Had she been unconscious for so long that it had healed without her even being aware of it?

"Just how long have I been asleep?" she asked Heming, idly poking at the remnants of her wound and feeling no pain there.

Heming took her hand in his and kissed her palm. He would have to tell her the truth for many reasons. If his mother was right, the occasional drinking of his blood would ensure that he did not have to stand over her grave when she died an old woman and he was still young and vigorous. There should also be no secrets between them.

"Ye were dying, Brona," he said quietly, needing her to understand that he would never have done something she might well find distasteful unless the need was dire. "Nothing we did could save ye and we tried everything. My mother finally told me about something she has discovered in the old histories and journals of our clan. Do ye recall how Hervey thought the secret to our strength and long lives was in our blood?"

Brona tensed. "Aye and he planned to drink yours to see if he was right."

"Weel, 'tis a surprise a mon like him could stumble upon a truth like that, but he was right. I gave ye some of my blood, Brona. Mixed it with wine and poured it down your throat."

"When was that?"

"Last night. Ye have slept through most of the day."

Brona knew she should be disgusted, maybe even looking for something to thoroughly rinse her mouth out with, but she only felt a passing twinge of unease. Then again she had overcome her unease with the fact that

Heming drank blood and did so straight from the source. She took another peek at the faint mark that was all that was left of what she suspected had been a mortal wound. Considering some of the putrid potions healers mixed up, a little blood with her wine seemed almost mild and it had obviously worked a miraculous cure.

Heming frowned, trying to guess what she was feeling about what he had done. She just looked a little puzzled and sometimes, when she glanced at her wound, a soft look of amazement crossed her face. Heming began to feel that there might not be any objection made about what he had done. That made him wonder if she would also accept drinking from him. The mere thought of that made him hard as a rock and he quickly pushed it from his mind.

"Hervey is dead, isnae he?" Brona asked.

"Aye, we think Angus killed him. Both men have already been buried. I didnae think ye would care but I can show ye where Hervey is buried."

"Aye, ye can do that at some time. I feel nothing and that makes me a little sad for he was a kinsmon and I have verra, verra few of those. Yet, I asked about his death because he *had* guessed the secret of your blood and 'tis a verra, verra dangerous secret, isnae it."

Pulling her into his arms, he kissed her cheek and rested his cheek on her hair. "Aye, verra dangerous. As my mother says, we wouldnae just have the hunters after us, we would have the whole world. I dinnae think it would just be for the fact that it can heal such dire wounds as yours. Nay, I think most would be after it because it makes ye live longer."

Brona lifted her head off his shoulder and stared at him in shock. "It can?"

"Once ye see my mother ye will ken the truth of that. I feel a fool for nay kenning that she is over two score and ten years yet looks thirty. I simply didnae pay any heed, thought naught unusual about it. My aunt is the same."

She suddenly hugged him very tightly. "None of ye would e'er be safe."

Heming idly combed his fingers through her long pale blond hair. "'Tis a reason for us to rejoice, though. It means that, if ye can stomach drinking a wee bit of my blood on occasion, ye would live as long as I do."

Brona tensed but did not lift her face from where she had it pressed against his broad smooth chest. "And why would ye wish to do that for me?" she asked softly, hearing her heart beat in her head, it was pounding so hard and fast.

He gently grasped her chin in his hand and turned her face up to his. "Because I want to keep ye. I dinnae want to wake one more morning without ye at my side."

"Are ye asking me to be your wife?" she whispered.

"Aye, I am. My wife, my mate, the mother of my children."

"Why?"

A large part of Brona just wanted to shout "aye" and do a little dance around the room in unbridled joy. Another part of her, however, needed more, needed him to love her. She inwardly grimaced as she admitted to herself that she would accept just a few words about caring for her. Considering what Heming was, and she was sure she did not know the whole of it yet, they would be facing some large challenges in the future and Brona felt that his feelings needed to have some depth to them if they were to survive them.

Heming smiled and brushed his lips over hers. "Because ye are the other half of me. Because ye are my love." He frowned when the plump bottom lip he had been licking began to wobble. "That isnae supposed to make ye cry."

She kissed him and then hugged him as tightly as she could. "Tears of joy. I love ye, too, Heming. I think I have since the start. Think on it—I set free a mon all called a demon, a mon who drank Peter's blood. I e'en let ye drink my blood and ye must ken how most, er, Outsiders feel about such a thing. Aye, I believe I loved ye from the first moment I looked at ye. It just took a wee while for it to settle into my heart and mind."

Feeling tears stinging his own eyes, Heming kissed her. He was just about to rid her of the night shift that prevented him from feeling all her soft skin when he heard someone clear her throat. Opening one eye, he saw his mother standing at the side of the bed. Feeling a little too much like a chastised child, he realized a blushing Brona and slid out of bed, heartily glad that he had kept his clothes on when he had gotten into bed beside her. He hurriedly introduced Brona to his mother, grinning slightly at the bemused look Brona wore as she studied the young, pretty Efrica.

Heming took Brona's hand in his and smiled at his mother. "Ye shall be pleased to hear that she has agreed to marry me."

After hugging Brona and kissing her cheek, Efrica looked at her son. "And I suspicion ye want that marriage to be soon."

"As soon as possible."

"Heming, there is something ye need to ken," Brona said. "I think that, if ye marry me, ye may be able to be the laird of Rosscurrach. Angus felt that was how it would be if Hervey was dead. 'Tis one reason he killed my cousin."

"Ah, aye," Heming said as he tugged one of the chairs closer to the bed, sat down, and took Brona's hand in his. "We heard that mentioned several times and, as ye slept, my father went through the ledger room. He found what your father had written, the instructions he had left about what was to be done about Rosscurrach and its heirs. It does say that if Hervey dies then ye are the heir, but only if ye marry, so that ye have a husband at your side." He grimaced. "From the moment I told Colin that I intended to marry ye, he has treated me as the laird of Rosscurrach and I couldnae get him to stop."

For a moment, Brona felt a touch of fear. Angus had wanted to marry her because it would have given him a chance to be the laird of Rosscurrach. Her fear that Heming might be doing the same passed quickly, however. Heming was not like that. She knew that for a fact deep inside her heart.

When she glanced at Heming's mother, the woman smiled in complete understanding and then winked at her. Having such a young, beautiful mother by law would be something she would have to get used to, Brona decided. Brona fixed her gaze on the man who would soon become her husband, a thought that had her trembling with pleasure on the inside.

"Then we can rest assured that Colin is more than ready to accept ye as laird and he isnae without some power amongst the men," she said.

Heming smiled and nodded. "I have seen that. He, Peter, and even Fergus and I have to wonder if that was one of the reasons your cousin had set them in the dungeon."

She sighed and nodded. "I suspicion that was verra much why. Hervey didnae like anyone to have any power except him."

"Weel, 'tis time for ye to have a bath," Efrica said to Brona, "and we must make plans for this wedding in, oh, three days?" She just smiled when Heming sighed. "Most of the ones who came to fight are still here as they waited to see how ye fared, Brona. They will remain for the wedding. Peter showed them where ye hid our Heming and they have settled in down there verra nicely. There are a lot of chambers and hollows down there." She turned to her son. "Ye can go and help your father sort through all those papers in the ledger room. Since ye are to be the laird here, 'tis important that ye ken all about Rosscurrach."

"Brona might wish me to wait as this is her home," said Heming after giving Brona a brief kiss and then standing up. "I may be laird in name, but 'tis only because of her."

"Weel, *her*," Brona said and smiled, "would be verra happy if ye searched through all of that and just told me what ye found. And, Heming, be sure to look for anything Hervey might have had concerning the hunters. He didnae come up with the plan to capture ye all on his own and I doubt that mon Carbonnel did either."

"Jankyn is already hard at work on that," said Efrica. "We ken that these men are becoming more and more organized and more and more of a threat. Go, now, Heming. I suspicion Brona is eager to have a bath."

Her bath was prepared so quickly that Brona knew Efrica had arrived much earlier because she had already done most of the preparations. Brona sighed with pleasure as she stepped into the hot, softly scented water.

When Efrica began to wash her hair, Brona studied her wound again and lightly touched it.

"'Tis wondrous," she murmured. "I am nay sure I will e'en have a scar. Did Heming give me more than one drink?"

"Nay, just one. But, ye may consider getting used to it. What has happened with ye, the way ye healed, has told me that I am right. The magic is in the blood. And, if ye have a wee drink once a week, ye will age as Heming will and nay be prey to so many of the fevers and poxes that steal the life from so many Outsiders."

Brona nodded. "I think I can do that. The need to stay with Heming for as long as I can will make it verra easy to do. And any children we may have as weel, I suppose."

"Aye. For all I ken, it may take nay more than one drink to pass along the magic but I havenae figured out a way to test that. Now, we must plan a bonnie gown for ye to wear and a feast. Many of the MacNachtons dinnae eat food as we do but they do like music and wine."

"That is something I am certain Rosscurrach can give them."

"Ye do love my son, dinnae ye, Brona Kerr?"

"Oh, aye," she answered softly. "Verra, verra much."

"Then all will be weel. Welcome to the family."

Brona laughed as Heming carried her into their bed-chamber, running all the way. He set her down on the bed and barred the door. She stopped laughing, however, when he started to walk back to her, for the hunger in his eyes was enough to set the bed linen on fire.

Her husband, she thought, and sighed like some love-struck girl. She felt a bit like one. Never in her wildest dreams had she thought she would be married to a man like this, to a man she could love and who loved her back. For the first time she felt part of a family again. The Mac-Nachtons could be a little strange, like Heming's cousin Berawald, but they had all welcomed her into the clan. From what she could tell by the way everyone acted at the wedding feast, the Kerrs were accepting the Mac-Nachtons far more easily than she had anticipated.

"I think it may be wise if ye remove that bonnie gown yourself, Brona love," said Heming.

Standing up, she began to unlace the soft blue gown she wore. Before she had gone down to the great hall to be joined in marriage with Heming by the same cowardly priest who had married her to Angus, Brona had had a good long look at herself and been astonished. With ribbons in her hair and the pretty gown, she had felt beautiful. Heming's look when she had entered the great hall had made her feel even more so. She did not want the gown ruined for she knew she would remember her wedding day every time she looked at it.

Keeping a close eye on Heming, she slowly undressed. With each item of clothing she removed he looked even hungrier and she felt compelled to do more, to try to drive him mad with desire. Placing one foot upon a stool, she lifted her shift up over her knee and untied the garter holding up her stocking. Brona then very carefully rolled it down her leg and set it aside. She was almost through doing the same to the other leg when a very naked Heming grabbed her in his arms and took her to their bed. She was not sure how he did it, but even as he settled her on top of the bedcovers he removed her shift and tossed it aside. When he sprawled in her arms, the feel of his flesh touching hers was enough to set her blood on fire.

"Brona love, ye shouldnae tease a mon so," he growled as he spread soft, warm kisses over her face. "I have been aching for another taste of ye since the day at the inn."

"Aye, I confess, I did think a lot about that myself," she said as she trailed her fingers up and down his spine.

"There is one thing I must tell ye ere we get too witless."

When he hesitated, she smiled and kissed his chin. "Just tell me, Heming, as I am verra eager to get witless."

"I am nay sure ye understand what I mean when I say ye are my mate. 'Tis more than a wife. 'Tis a bonding, a deep one, and it makes me want to mark ye. Not every Halfling feels the urge, but more do, and I have felt it."

"Mark me? How?"

"A bite right here," he replied and kissed the pulse point in her neck.

"But ye have already bitten me there and drank my blood. Why would ye still feel the urge?"

"The mating mark is given whilst the two mates make love. At the point where I give ye my seed I bite ye and take some of your blood. A blending, if ye will."

"Ah, weel, I dinnae see anything wrong with that if that is what ye wish to do. It didnae hurt when ye did it the last time and I fear 'tis the thought of pain I would shy away from. Am I supposed to drink your blood as weel? I dinnae see how I can as I dinnae have the teeth for it."

"Ye dinnae have to, but I think that, if ye could stomach it, I would like ye to try. My mother has done so with my father and she said it was verra nice. Blushed when she said it, too, which was verra telling. It would also be a way for ye to have a wee bit of my blood now and again so that we can be together for as long as possible." He nodded toward the little table near the bed. "All I need to do is give myself a wee cut on the wrist and ye could take a wee sip from there."

"Will it hurt ye?"

"Nay much and, remember, I but need to lick the wound and it closes."

Brona wrapped her hands around his neck and rubbed her body against his, delighting in his soft groan. "Weel, then, let us get about the business of consummating this marriage. I am most eager to get witless and bitten."

Heming laughed and kissed her. His need for her swiftly filled him and he knew he would have to fight for control. The fact that she was going to let him give her his mark and even try to drink from him herself only added to the strength of his need. He kissed every part of her sweetly curved body, reveling in her murmurs and sighs, in the taste and the heat of her. The feel of her small hands stroking his skin stole his wits. They were both trembling with the force of their passion by the time he knew they would have to be joined or he would be spilling his seed on the sheets.

Panting as if she had just run for her life over miles of countryside, Brona watched Heming reach for the small dagger on the table. She felt no doubt or hesitation about what they were about to do. Instead something strong and primitive swelled up inside of her and only added to her desire for Heming. She could feel a spot on her neck, the place where he had taken some of her blood before, grow warm and that warmth spread through her body adding to the heat passion had already stirred inside.

When Heming held his cut wrist to her mouth, she wrapped her fingers around it and pressed her mouth to the cut. His blood seeped into her mouth at first and her eyes widened. It was sweet and rich and it sent fire flying straight to her groin. She closed her eyes and sucked gently and felt a strong tremor go through Heming's body. A moment later she felt him bite her and begin to drink of her. Something inside of her burst and she screamed against his wrist and her release tore through her, followed by another and another as Heming thrust into her with a ferocity that had her sliding up the bed until her head was pressed against the bank of pillows.

Heming felt her soft lips on his wrist and his whole body clenched with the need to be inside of her. He felt his fangs fill his mouth as he reentered her. Every light pull of her mouth upon his wrist sent fire racing through him and he felt himself grow even harder. Without conscious thought he again sunk his fangs into her neck and closed his eyes in ecstasy as the heady warmth of her blood filled his mouth. A small part of his mind whispered that he could hurt her, but nothing could stop him from slamming into her heat again and again. He heard her cry out against his wrist, felt her body clench around his like a fist, and heard himself growl. Feeling his release at hand he thrust as deep inside of her as he could and nearly roared at the force of it. His last clear thought was that he hoped he remembered to close the wounds before he passed out from the pleasure that was tearing through him.

"Oh my," Brona whispered, rousing enough from her stupor to find herself flat on her back, Heming sprawled in the same boneless way at her side.

"Oh my, indeed," he said, forcing his limp body to

move enough to wrap an arm around her slim shoulders and pull her close to his side. "I cannae believe my mother said that was *verra nice,*" he muttered.

"Verra nice?" Brona shook her head. "I am verra surprised that we are still alive." She reached a hand up to touch the spot he had bitten and, although there was no blood there, she could feel that there would be a mark. "This one willnae fade, will it."

"Nay. 'Tis why it is called the mating mark. Anytime I bite ye after this, those marks will fade away as the other did. I am nay sure why this one doesnae. Just one of those mysteries." He took a slow deep breath to quell a sudden attack of nervousness. "Weel, do ye think ye can drink from me every now and then?"

"It had best be only every now and then or e'en your magical blood willnae keep us from dying, our poor wee hearts stopped by the strength of the pleasure we just survived."

Heming grinned. "Aye, 'tis best if we save it for special occasions. S'truth, I cannae help but wonder if it could be the sort of thing that makes one crave it dangerously."

Brona kissed his chest and then rubbed her cheek against the taut skin. "Aye, I could see that happening to some. And, in truth, I rather like the way we were at the inn. It wasnae so powerful but the pleasure was certainly all one needs and one can go a bit slower and savor it more, aye?"

He kissed the top of her head. "I have married a verra wise woman. Happy?" He grimaced, thinking it a foolish question for a grown man to ask a woman.

Brona propped herself up on her elbows and looked at him. "I cannae explain just how happy I am. I have ye, the mon I love more than life. I have the chance to spend years and years and years with ye. I have a new family. I have Rosscurrach back and the evil that has held it in its fist for too long is all gone. I think I am more than happy. I am blissful."

"Blissful, eh?"

"Verra blissful. I am even more so because I can give ye something ye like and nay cringe as so many others would. S'truth, I dinnae understand why I have nay trouble with ye biting me and especially with me drinking of ye, but I dinnae."

"And I shall be sure to go to the chapel and thank God for that." He kissed the tip of her nose. "Ye do ken that ye dinnae have to do it or let me do it."

"I ken it, but I find I like it. I liked it the first time, too. I wanted to rub myself all over ye. It troubled me a wee bit, but it doesnae trouble me anymore. I love ye and so I love all that is part of ye, e'en if it includes big pointy teeth and a strange thirst." She laughed along with him but then grew serious again. "And, Heming, it makes me feel verra good to ken that I have something in me that can always be used to heal ye."

"I think that is when I first began to think ye were my mate. Your blood healed me with the swiftness and strength of the blood of one of our Elders. It shouldnae have, for ye are an Outsider, but it did. Oh, it would have healed me anyway, but much more slowly. Another mystery, aye? I must be sure to remember to tell *Maman* about it as she is trying to gather all the information she can on the many strengths and gifts of the clan. Since she found out how we can hold our mates at our sides with a wee sip now and then, I can only praise her work."

"Will it be all right, Heming? Ye living here? I ken that

the MacNachton clan is verra close and ye willnae have any of them here. 'Twill also be difficult for them to visit verra often."

"It will most certainly be all right. And I willnae be the only MacNachton here. Several of my clansmen have decided to stay here too. It grows quite crowded at Cambrun now that children are being born again. It seems Rosscurrach has beneath it some verra fine places that they can make their own."

Heming rolled on top of her and smiled when she wrapped her arms around him. "Aye, my clan is large and lives closely together, but ye are my soul, Brona. This is your home and so it is mine." He brushed a kiss over each of her eyes when they glistened with tears. "Others of my clan have left Cambrun and have been most happy with their new homes and their mates. I will be most happy with mine."

"And I will be most happy to have ye stay here, my demon. Holding me. Loving me. Giving me golden-eyed bairns. Giving me happiness. Thank ye most kindly, my beautiful demon."

"Nay, love, your demon thanks ye for blessing the long life he has ahead of him with hope and laughter."

Brona was afraid she was going to start weeping and so reached down between their bodies and curled her fingers around him. "And lots and lots of pleasure."

"Aye, lots of it. Forever."

"That is my dearest hope, Heming, my love. My verra dearest one."

THE
CAPTURE

Lynsay Sands

One

Lucy glanced around the inn, uncomfortably aware of a strange buzz of excitement in the air. It had started when the two Scots had entered.

Nay, before that even, she thought with a frown. Everything had seemed relatively normal when she and her brother had first been ushered inside by Wymon Carbonnel. He'd insisted on seeing them back to the boundary of his land after their day at Carbonnel castle, and then had been equally insistent on their stopping for a meal at the inn on the border where his property met theirs.

Lucy had not been pleased with the delay. It had already been growing dark and she'd just wanted to go home and get this uncomfortable day behind them. It had been a long day for her. She'd spent the better part of it on tenterhooks dreading the proposal she'd feared coming, and dreading even more the man's reaction when she refused him. Wymon could be dreadfully unpleasant when crossed.

However, all that anxiety had apparently been for naught. The man finally had proposed before they'd left Carbonnel, but he'd taken her refusal much better than she'd expected, merely nodding with a half smile as if he'd expected it and was untroubled by the rejection.

Lucy supposed it was partially out of gratitude for his easy acceptance that she'd allowed herself to be convinced into stopping for the meal. She knew it was also the reason her brother, John, had given in gracefully and allowed the delay in their returning home. There had simply been no polite way to refuse and neither of them had wanted to be churlish when he'd taken her refusal so well, so they had agreed to the meal.

Apart from the fact that they really hadn't wished to be there—or perhaps because they'd been distracted by that—nothing had seemed abnormal at first. The inn had been surprisingly busy for that hour of the evening, the innkeeper and two serving wenches bustling to serve the men their ales and good hearty food. Although Lucy had been uncomfortably aware that, despite how busy it was, she was the only female there besides the two serving girls. Other than that, however, everything had been fine . . . But then one of Carbonnel's men had entered and nodded at Wymon and the room had suddenly gone oddly quiet for the briefest of moments, all conversation dying as the other men noted the gesture.

When the conversations had started up again an instant later, the sound had seemed a little louder, a little more hearty and—compared to what had passed before—quite unnatural.

Then the two Scots had entered. Both were tall, well-built men, both attractive in their own way. They'd taken seats away from the others and eyed the occupants of the inn with cold narrow eyes.

It was only when the innkeeper himself had gone to the table to serve the men that Lucy had realized that the two serving maids were now absent. That fact, along with the undertone of excitement in the air, was making her feel a bit nervous. There was a definite feeling that something was going to happen. Apparently, she wasn't the only one to think so, she realized when John touched her arm and she glanced his way to see the sharp look of concern in his eyes.

"If you are finished, Lucy. I think 'tis time we continued on home," he said quietly.

"Aye," she murmured, getting to her feet.

Thankfully, Carbonnel didn't protest, but stood silently to follow them from the inn.

Lucy frowned as they stepped out into the courtyard and she saw how dark the night had gotten. The sun had been making its downward journey when they'd stopped, but she hadn't realized how close it had been to nightfall. It appeared she and John would be making the rest of the journey in the dark, which meant they would have to travel at a more sedate pace to guard against their mounts injuring themselves on the uneven road. It would be quite late when they finally arrived back at Blytheswood, but that couldn't be helped now, she supposed and sighed inwardly.

"You wait here, Lucy. I shall see to your mount while your brother saddles his own," Carbonnel said with a smile, which Lucy automatically returned even as she once again experienced surprise at how well he was taking all this. Wymon wasn't a man to take disappointment well. She supposed that spoke of how little he'd really wished to marry her. She wasn't terribly surprised. Marrying her would have gained him very little. John had inherited the bulk of their parents' assets on their deaths a year ago, gaining Blytheswood castle and its environs, while she'd inherited a small demesne from her mother. She had no doubt Wymon, as a second son, would prefer to bride a woman with her own castle for him to run. It was really rather surprising that he'd offered for her hand at all.

Lucy started to glance back into the depths of the stable where her brother and Wymon were saddling the animals, but paused as the inn door suddenly opened and the first of the two Scots came out. She'd noted in the brief glance she'd cast their way when they'd entered the inn that both men were attractive, but hadn't really taken the time to examine those good looks. Now, as the two men stumbled out of the inn, she took the time to do so, allowing her eyes to slide over wide strong shoulders and sculpted features.

The first Scot was handsome enough, but for some reason her attention kept returning to the second man, getting caught on his stern, strong features in the torchlight of the inn yard. She finally forced her gaze to continue on, noting the long dark hair that fell about his shoulders, and wondering if it was as soft as it looked. Her gaze then dropped over the white tunic and dark plaid he wore, then touched briefly on the big, wicked sword strapped to his side before continuing on to his naked legs.

Englishmen wore leggings or braies on their own legs, so it was only with Scots that a girl could see the fine shape of a man's knee and calf. She found herself ogling the poor man, grateful that he was unable to see her standing in the shadows of the stables.

Her eyes were still on his legs when the man stumbled. Frowning, she shifted her concentration to take in the whole scene and noted that the other Scot seemed to be having trouble walking as well. Both were staggering a bit as if drunk, though she hadn't noticed them drinking much in the inn. Still, there was a definite wobble to their walk.

Even as she began to frown over this, first one, then the other of the two men suddenly stumbled and sank to his knees so that they knelt in the dirt of the inn yard, swaying weakly. 'Twas obvious they were fighting whatever was happening to them, but were unable to combat it and the next moment both of them collapsed side by side in the dirt. They'd barely settled on the ground when the inn door opened again and most, if not all of the men from inside, began to pour out. Even as they began to surround the two Scots on the ground more men began to appear from the sides of the building, milling out to join the others until she could no longer see the Scots.

Knowing something underhanded was happening, Lucy glanced back toward the rear of the stables to call her brother forward and see what they could do for the two men, only to freeze as she saw Wymon plunge a knife into her unsuspecting brother's neck from behind. She and John both stiffened in shock as the blade went in, then it was withdrawn and plunged in again, this time a little to the side of the first spot.

With her mouth still open on her unspoken cry, Lucy's horrified gaze met her brother's. They stared at each other with shared shock for a moment, then the life left his eyes and her brother crumbled like an empty cape.

"Why so shocked?"

Lucy blinked and slowly turned her eyes from her

fallen brother to Wymon. While she'd gaped in horror, he'd retrieved his knife and crossed to stand before her. She stared at him with incomprehension, her mind not yet capable of accepting anything that was happening.

"Surely you did not think I would take your refusal gracefully, did you?" he asked with a chiding smile, then shook his head and took her arm to turn her away and lead her out of the stables.

In her stunned state, Lucy followed docilely for perhaps two steps before regaining enough of her sense to begin to struggle. The moment she did Wymon paused and punched her in the side of the head. Light exploded behind her eyes, followed quickly by pain, and Lucy gasped as she began to fall. Then she felt herself scooped up and carried. She was barely conscious when she felt herself being passed off to someone else to hold.

The last thing she heard before darkness claimed her was someone saying, "Ye take the MacAdie, I'll take the other, and guid luck to us both."

Two

It was a constant, dull throbbing pain in her head that nagged Lucy back to consciousness. Grimacing against the relentless pounding, she squeezed her eyes more tightly closed, trying to block out the bright light beyond her eyelids that seemed to be aggravating her discomfort.

"Finally. I thought you should never wake up."

The voice rather than the words themselves drew her eyes abruptly open and Lucy ignored the pain in her head as she lifted her face to peer wide-eyed at the man standing before her. Wymon Carbonnel. He was so close he filled her vision, blocking out everything and anything else in the room with both his imposing size and the torch he held in his hand.

Made mute by the memories rushing into her head, she stared at him with both fear and loathing and finally said, "You killed my brother."

Wymon smiled faintly, though whether at her words or the raspy voice that spoke them she couldn't say. Then he shook his head.

"Me? Nay. I fear you are confused. Tearlach MacAdie killed your brother," he assured her with a smile. "And he carried you off after doing so. I have witnesses who say so."

"Liar," she snarled. "Murderer!"

Wymon merely arched his eyebrows with amusement. "Nay. Not I. That blow you took to the head has scrambled your sense somewhat, my lovely Lucy."

"The blow *you* gave me has done naught to my memory, Carbonnel. You killed my brother and then hit me and brought me here . . . Wherever here is," she added with a frown and glanced to both sides as she became aware of a gnawing pain in her wrists. The pain was explained away the moment she realized she was hanging from chains on her wrists. She was chained to the wall like a common thief.

"Welcome to Carbonnel's dungeons," he said easily as she forced herself to stand and take the weight off her arms. "I hope you shall soon come to think of this as home."

Lucy turned an amazed gaze back to him. "You are mad."

"Oh, now, is that any way to talk to your future husband?" he chided.

Her mouth dropped briefly. "I shall never marry you."

He shrugged, apparently unconcerned. "'Tis your choice, of course. However, I still hope to make you see the benefits of marrying me and going along with my version of events."

"Benefits?" she spat with disbelief.

"Aye. There are many," he assured her easily. "Living, for instance."

When Lucy stilled, his smile widened. "I shall give you a few days to consider the matter. Marriage is a grave undertaking and should be considered carefully," he assured her with sardonic solemnity. "If you decide to marry me, we shall be wed right here in this lovely room by torchlight. We shall probably consummate it here too to ensure you do not have second thoughts."

Lucy shuddered at the very thought of the hands that had taken her brother's life touching her, but he wasn't done.

"Understand. If you convince me that you truly have seriously considered the matter and seen the wisdom of our union, the story shall be that I hunted down the MacAdie who had killed your brother and taken you. That I rescued you and that you married me out of gratitude and, of course, undying love." His mouth widened in a toothy smile.

"And if I do not see the wisdom of our union?" she asked bitterly, suspecting she already knew the answer, but wanting everything on the table from the start.

"If you do not?" he echoed with amusement, then shrugged. "Well, the MacAdie shall need feeding, will he not?" he said as if it were the simplest matter in the world. And then he added, "And once you are dead your cousin Margaret will inherit Blytheswood. I suspect she may be more easily led than you anyway," he confided and then shrugged again. "One way or another, I shall have a Blytheswood bride and Blytheswood itself."

Lucy merely stared at him blankly, her mind caught on the comment that the MacAdie would need feeding. Feeding? If she refused to cooperate would Wymon cut her up, boil her, and feed her to this unknown MacAdie? It was the only sense she could make of the threat, and really it was rather gruesome as threats went, though she supposed she shouldn't much care what happened to her body once she was dead and had shed it. Still, the idea of being someone's dinner was just disgusting.

"Think on that," Carbonnel suggested and turned to move away toward the door of the dungeon. "Now, I shall go eat and relax. There is a fine new maid I should like to break in. Then I have to rest up. Tomorrow we start torturing the MacAdie for information and I do wish to be in fine form for that. I hope you two enjoy your evening as well."

She stared silently at the heavy wooden door as it clanged shut. There was no clink of it locking behind him. Why bother locking it? She was chained to the wall and helpless to leave anyway, she supposed.

Sighing, Lucy leaned back against the cold, hard stone behind her and allowed her gaze to slide over her present home, stiffening when she spotted the man chained to the wall opposite. She would have seen him earlier if Wymon hadn't stood directly before her, blocking her view of the dungeon. Now, she peered at the man noting that he was double chained across from her. Obviously, they hadn't trusted one set of chains to hold him like they had her. She thought that was a bit ridiculous. While the man was big and strong looking, one set of chains surely would have held him too.

Her gaze slid down to the chains at his ankles, noting there were two sets on each leg as well. And that he had naked knees. It was one of the Scots from the inn. The MacAdie whom Wymon had kept mentioning, she supposed. He was pale and looking a little the worse for wear, but his eyes were open and he was obviously awake and alert. She doubted he'd missed any of the conversation that had just taken place.

They stared at each other silently. Lucy was trying to think of something to say, but the only thing that came to mind was a compulsion to apologize to the man. However, she really had nothing to apologize for.

With her aching head making it impossible to think of anything intelligent to say, she closed her eyes with a little sigh in the hopes that the pain would ease some and give her back her faculties. Unfortunately, the moment she closed her eyes, thoughts of her brother filled her mind. The image of Wymon plunging the knife into John's neck seemed to be burnt onto the back of her eyelids. Lucy's breath left her on a small sob as the moment replayed through her head, followed immediately by recriminations. If only she hadn't allowed herself to be distracted by the Scots. If only she'd saddled her own horse. If only she'd been close enough, mayhap she could have saved him.

Lucy knew that wasn't really true, Wymon simply would have chosen a different method or time. No matter how it had played out, her brother would still be dead . . . and all because she'd refused to marry Wymon Carbonnel.

But . . . if she'd agreed to marry him, Lucy thought and then shook her head. Wymon probably still would have killed her brother to get Blytheswood for himself. Wymon Carbonnel was a second son. His older brother, Frederick, had inherited Carbonnel castle several years ago and left his brother to run it while he played at court. However, he'd fallen out of favor at court recently and returned home to take up the reins himself . . . leaving Wymon without any authority. The man enjoyed the power he'd had and wouldn't be eager to give it up. He would want a castle of his own to rule. She supposed Blytheswood had seemed easy pickings to him. Marry the sister, get rid of the brother, and voila! One castle and estate for him to be lord over.

Teeth grinding together, Lucy silently wished he'd just killed his own brother and continued ruling Carbonnel rather than come after her family and what they had. Of course, maybe he eventually planned to do that as well. How much better to have two castles? She wouldn't put it past him. It was part of the reason Lucy had refused to marry Wymon. She'd suspected the man was lacking in character, although that was putting it mildly. While he had never been anything but polite and even gallant in her presence until now, servants spoke and there were rumors about the man, his temper, and cruelty.

Lucy didn't trust him, didn't like him, didn't want him. And frankly, she'd rather be dead with her brother and the angels than married to the bastard.

It was looking like she'd get her wish.

Tears suddenly welled in her eyes and Lucy silently wept for her brother and for herself, and even for the man on the wall across from her. They had all been brought down by Lord Wymon Carbonnel. It was just that she and the MacAdie hadn't had the good fortune yet to die and escape the coming humiliations and abuses he planned for them.

"Dinnae give him yer tears."

Lucy blinked her eyes open and peered at the MacAdie. His expression was a strange mixture of compassion and anger.

"Diya fall into tears and defeat we're as guid as dead," he added solemnly.

"He killed my brother," she announced quietly. "Can I not mourn him?"

The Scot shook his head. "There's time fer mournin' later. Now yer needin' to stay strong. Once we're free o' here ye can collapse in tears and grief. Until then, turn yer grief tae anger and yer loss tae hate. 'Twill strengthen ye fer what's tae come."

Lucy almost asked what they could possibly need strength for. They were trapped here after all, but she bit back the question. He seemed strong and unafraid despite their position and she wouldn't weaken him when he had such an ordeal ahead. Torture, Wymon had said, and judging by his smile as he'd said it, he'd enjoy the task. This man was in for some terrible pain.

"My name is Lucy," she said after a moment.

He nodded solemnly in greeting. "And I am Tearlach MacAdie."

Lucy nodded a greeting in return, but she was thinking about Wymon's comment that the MacAdie would need feeding. She supposed she'd end up in his stew, a fine—if gruesome—way to get rid of a body, and wondered if he would eat it, or if they'd even tell him he was eating her.

Horrified by her own thoughts, Lucy distracted herself from them by asking, "Who was the man with you at the inn?"

"Ah." His eyes widened with realization. "I thought ye looked familiar. Ye were at the inn."

"Aye, we left shortly after you came in. We were in the stables fetching our mounts when you came out and seemed to pass out. That is when Wymon killed my brother."

"The mon whose death we shall be blamed fer," he murmured with a frown.

"Aye," Lucy whispered. It was obvious he'd been awake through the entire conversation she'd had with their gaoler and heard everything. "Wymon stabbed him in the neck, twice."

Tearlach's mouth tightened, but he didn't comment. It left them to fall into a thoughtful silence, one during which Lucy found her mind slipping back to that moment in the stables. The shocking sight of the knife plunging into her brother's neck . . . Her brother falling . . .

"The mon with me was me cousin," Tearlach announced suddenly. "Sir Heming MacNachton of Cambrun."

Lucy forced the image of her brother's death away and concentrated on his words. The name rang a bell, but she couldn't quite place it . . . Her eyes widened suddenly as she recognized it. There were rumors and tales circulating about the MacNachtons. Ridiculous tales of their being night demons, and soulless bloodsucking creatures who could steal your soul. It put a whole new picture on the feeding business, but she shook her head to herself, thinking Wymon was surely mad if he believed those nonsense tales. But then, she supposed he must be mad. He'd killed her brother and kidnapped her, after all. Those weren't exactly the actions of a sane man . . . Or, at least, not the actions of a sane man with a conscience.

"Why wid ye no marry him?"

Startled from her thoughts again, Lucy merely arched an eyebrow. "Did I mention he killed my brother?"

Tearlach smiled faintly despite their circumstances. "Aye. But I gather ye'd already refused him ere he did that. Why did ye refuse him to start with?"

Lucy's mouth twisted, but then she sighed and shrugged before explaining, "There has always been something not quite right about Wymon. I did not trust or like him and would not agree to marry someone who made me so uncomfortable. However . . ."

"However?" he prompted.

"However, had I realized it would cost my brother his life . . ." She swallowed, unable even to say the words that she may very well have married him had she thought it would save John's life . . . At least if it was the only way to save him. Or else, she would have made damned sure he was nowhere near her brother.

"From what I o'erheard, he wants Blytheswood more than he wants you," Tearlach pointed out not unkindly. "Whether ye'd married him or no, he wid ha'e killed yer brother. I'm suspecting the only thing yer agreeing to marry him wid ha'e changed was the time and place o' yer brother's death."

"Aye," she agreed wearily and then changed the subject again. "You and your cousin are Scottish?"

"Aye."

"Why were you down here in England?"

Tearlach was silent for a moment and she suspected he was deciding what he could or should tell her. Finally, he said, "Rumors had reached our people that some . . ." He paused and frowned, then said, "men," though she was sure it hadn't been his original choice of word, but was distracted when he continued, "Some men were gatherin' in groups and comin' after our clans. We came out in search o' information about it. We've been stoppin' at the various inns along the way, hopin' to learn what was about."

"And got yourselves caught instead," she said quietly and saw his mouth tighten. He obviously wasn't pleased with the outcome, but then there was no reason he should be. The man was chained to a wall, just as she was, helpless to do anything but suffer Carbonnel's cruelties.

Not wishing to think about the coming morning and what they were helpless to prevent happening, Lucy began to talk to distract them both, telling him tales of her childhood. She and her brother, John, had shared an oddly close relationship. Born less than a year apart, they'd been the best of friends despite the difference in their gender, and had spent every chance they could between lessons and other responsibilities playing together out in the bailey . . . or inside in the dungeons on inclement days.

It was during one of these stories that she had her first idea and first hope that all was not lost. Lucy and John had played all sorts of games in the Blytheswood unused dungeons, including playing prisoner. They'd actually chained each other up on occasion, though she'd never managed to keep her brother chained for long. John had been brilliant with locks and such and had quickly found a way to unlock them given a bit of metal and a little time. Lucy had tried for years to sort out how he'd done it, but hadn't been able to until he actually showed her. Of course, once they'd both known how to unlock the chains, that game had lost interest for them both and they'd forsaken it, but it might now save her life. Lucy thought if she could get her hands on a bit of sharp, pointy, and strong metal, she might be able to use that old skill to free herself and the man chained up with her. Getting the metal was the trick. She'd have to get free briefly and get it somehow.

Not wishing to raise false hopes in Tearlach, Lucy didn't mention this idea to him, but her mind began working on ways she might briefly gain her freedom on the morrow. The easiest way seemed to be to pretend to agree to marry Wymon.

Her heart cried out in protest at even pretending to agree, but it really was the easiest way for her to gain freedom . . . perhaps the only way. She just had to be convincing about it, she thought, and a sudden and outright agreement probably wouldn't work. A reluctant agreement would likely be more believable, she decided, and started considering different ways to seem to reluctantly agree to marry the odious man now holding her prisoner.

The hollow echo of footsteps coming down the stairs outside their cell drew Tearlach's attention away from his cellmate, Lady Lucy Blytheswood.

Despite Carbonnel's promise of tortures to come, he'd left them alone down there for more than a day. Tearlach supposed he hoped the anticipation of what was to come would be a torture in itself and weaken them . . . along with the lack of food and water.

All they'd had was the light from the torch and how often it was replaced to tell the passing time. By his guess, Tearlach was thinking they'd been down there for at least two days and nights.

They'd spent that time talking about everything and anything they could think of, each trying desperately to distract the other from the trials that lay ahead. At least, Tearlach had started out with that intention, but had soon found himself listening to her childhood tales with both awe and envy. It was so much different in some ways than his own childhood. Like Lucy and John, he'd been fortunate enough to have loving and affectionate parents. But Tearlach was an only child. His parents hadn't been gifted with a second despite dedicated efforts to produce one. It had left him alone and somewhat lonely in comparison to the close relationship Lucy had apparently shared with her brother.

He'd listened to her tales of their games in the sunshine of the bailey and woods with both interest and envy. Tearlach had never spent time in the sun. He'd inherited his father's inability to handle sunlight. The one time they'd risked taking him out into daylight he had been very young, too young to recall it, and the experiment had apparently left him with burns.

He didn't remember any of it and only knew about it from what his parents had told him. When he was younger, he'd heard the disappointment in their voices as they told the tale and had thought himself a disappointment to them because of it, but they'd quickly explained that he wasn't and never would be that, but they were disappointed for him. The fact that his mother was mortal, untainted by their strain of vampirism, had given them hope that he might inherit more of her nature and weaken the blood of his father. They'd hoped he'd be free to enjoy the sun as she did, and were only disappointed for him that he could not.

Tearlach had understood but been secretly pleased to be like his father, as any son would be. And he'd never felt the lack until finding himself chained in this dungeon listening to Lucy reminisce about her and her brother rolling and wrestling in piles of leaves under a warm fall sun.

It was only one of many emotions he'd experienced these last two days and nights. Tearlach had felt amusement, awe, joy, fear, anger, and any number of other emotions as she'd spoken. Lucy had a lovely voice and a full, joyful laugh and he'd been awed by her courage in the face of their troubles. She was a beautiful woman both inside and out and he was humbled by the strength she was showing when he himself felt gnarled with frustration and rage. It was very rare that Tearlach had felt bested, but he'd been well and truly bested this time. Drugged and captured like a novice, now chained to a wall by silver chains that somehow drew out his strength so that he could not break them.

His gaze shifted from the bars in the door and back to Lucy. He'd hoped to be able to save her. He would have liked to save them both, of course, but there was something about this woman that made him want very badly to save her.

Tearlach had watched and listened to her talk until her words had slowed and stopped and she'd nodded off, sagging in her own chains across from him, then he'd stayed awake, simply watching her sleep as he racked his brain for an escape plan. Unfortunately, nothing had come to mind as yet, but he found himself oddly distracted and hard-pressed to think clearly about anything at all when he looked at the petite, rounded blonde across from him.

Now it was morning once more, the third morning of their incarceration by his guess, and their gaolers finally approached. Tearlach knew this must be the moment of reckoning because of the number of footsteps he could hear. This was not one man coming down to change the torch, this was at least a dozen men by his guess and he knew the time for the real torture had arrived.

His gaze slid to Lucy and he considered waking her, but then decided against it. She was sleeping the sleep of the exhausted; not even the chains biting into her flesh preventing it. It was better to let her sleep. They probably wouldn't bother her yet. It was him they were coming for. Carbonnel had spoken to him before Lucy had awakened the night they'd been taken and made his intentions clear. The man wanted all the information he could garner about the MacNachton and MacAdic strongholds and intended to torture it out of him.

Nay, better to let her rest as long as she could. He would watch for a chance to escape and take her with him then. And if they were fortunate enough for that to happen, she would need all her strength for the escape.

The scrape of the door opening drew his gaze back to it. He watched with a sinking heart as Carbonnel entered, followed by man after man after man until the cell was crowded with them.

Tearlach was exceptionally strong and had been trained in all forms of battle from his birth, but even he could not defeat so many when exhausted, hungry, and unarmed . . . not to mention, still chained in silver. It appeared he had a long day ahead of him, for he had no intention of giving these men any information that may bring harm to his people. He also had no intention of giving the man the pleasure of his agonized screams as he was tortured. It would only please him and upset Lucy, so Tearlach determined he would suffer in silence.

"Ah, you are awake," Carbonnel greeted him with an eager smile and then glanced toward Lucy. "But I see our fair Lady Blytheswood sleeps the sleep of the innocent. 'Tis good to know she has not been distressed by the delay in my revisiting you both." His gaze swung back to Tearlach and his smile now had a touch of lasciviousness to it as he explained, "The new maid proved to be more entertaining than I had expected, a tasty little bundle who needed lessons in obedience."

He paused, obviously recalling these lessons he'd taught, then let out a robust breath and clapped his hands. "But now to work. I have been looking forward to this. I hope you have too. Men. Bring him."

Tearlach watched him strut out of the cell as the rest of the men moved to begin unchaining him from the wall and sighed inwardly.

Aye, he thought unhappily. It was going to be a very long day indeed.

Lucy was straining against her chains, her entire body hard with tensed muscles as her ears were assaulted by the sounds in the next room. There were no screams or shrieks of agony, no pleas for mercy, not even a curse of rage. The only sounds were of the instruments of torture, not the results. It was the constant, repetitive wet lash of a whip soaked in blood, singing through the air and then cracking across skin, punctuated by the occasional question or curse from Wymon as he demanded answers he wasn't getting, but even those had slowed to a stop in the endless hours Lucy had been listening.

It was Wymon's voice that had first woken her, stirring her from nightmares of her brother's death, only to bring her back into the present nightmare. She'd had one blissful moment of confusion when she'd first opened her eyes to this unfamiliar setting, but had quickly recalled where she was and why, and the confusion had cleared to be replaced by a heavy sense of dread as she saw that Tearlach was missing from their cell. Through the door they'd left open, she'd heard Wymon cursing him to hell and back for his obstinacy in not answering his questions, and then the singing of the whip had followed, fast and furious and, she feared, probably wielded with vicious spite.

It had seemed obvious from the fury and frustration in Wymon's voice that this sound had probably been occurring for quite a while, that sheer exhaustion from lack of sleep the last few nights had allowed her to sleep through a good deal of the torture Tearlach had been suffering. But once awake to it, Lucy hadn't been able to fall asleep again. She'd stood trembling with her tension as she listened to the awful song of the whip.

Tearlach himself made no sound at all; not even a grunt under each blow and she could imagine him stern and still and proud, unbending under the punishment. She had no doubt that very attitude would simply infuriate Wymon. It would drive him wild. She knew instinctively he would want to see and hear the man's pain, that he would not stop until Tearlach was either dead or groveling before him. Lucy suspected that the groveling would never happen. Tearlach would take whatever was meted out with stoic calm and die for his pride, she was sure.

It was something of a shock to her when this didn't happen and instead the whip suddenly went silent. That silence was ringing. Earlier the sound of men's voices and laughter had risen in each pause between blows as Wymon's men had taunted and belittled their captive, no doubt subjecting him to humiliations she had no desire to know about. But now the silence was absolute, almost uncomfortably so and she suspected Tearlach had earned the grudging respect of the men and they were now discomfited by this useless continued torment.

"I grow weary of this game. Take him back to the cell," Wymon suddenly snarled and there was exhaustion in his voice. Tearlach had defeated him by simply suffering in silence, Lucy thought and wondered at what cost.

She didn't have long to wonder. Within moments the clank and jangle of chains rang out and then the room was suddenly full of men as almost a dozen of them half led and half dragged Tearlach back into the cell by at least as many chains. They were on his throat, his wrists, his upper arms, his waist, his legs, and his ankles. They had taken no chance of his escaping, it seemed.

"So you are awake."

Lucy dragged her anxious gaze from Tearlach's bowed head to their captor as Wymon followed the men into the cell. He was obviously weary, his clothes disheveled and sweat stained from his labors and he wasn't looking at her as if he were happy to see her. If anything, he was eyeing her like a problem when he was sick to death of problems.

"Are you willing to marry me yet?" Wymon asked grimly and there was a threat in his very tone of voice.

Lucy bit her lip and glanced to Tearlach. She wanted to say "no" on principle alone as she caught a glimpse of his raw and bloodied back as he passed, but pride would not get them out of here this day and she was quite sure Tearlach could not survive a second day of such torture.

However, she found the lie of saying "aye" stuck in her throat, so she cleared it and said cautiously, "Mayhap."

It wasn't good enough for Wymon. After the stubborn resistance of Tearlach, any resistance on her part was too much and he was suddenly across the room and standing in front of her, fist raised. The fist never fell, however. It was stayed when one of his men suddenly stepped to his side and said, "He shall need to feed to have the strength to survive tomorrow if you choose to interrogate him some more then."

Wymon slowly lowered his fist, a bitter smile curving his lips. "Aye. You are right."

Lucy swallowed and took a slow breath, waiting. She had no idea what was coming next, but Wymon's smile was too unpleasant for it to be anything good.

"Unchain her," he ordered, turning away and Lucy blinked after him with surprise. She'd hoped to get free for a moment or more, but hadn't really been sure she could achieve it. Now, here he was ordering it.

Her attention shifted back to the two men who suddenly stepped forward on either side of her and—even as Tearlach was chained back to his wall—she found herself being freed. The moment her right hand was free, Lucy allowed her weight to fall forward as if she didn't have the strength to hold herself. It left her slumping against the man who had freed that side and she let her hand slide along his body as if for purchase, but it wasn't until she dipped her hand into his pocket that she found anything useful.

Tucking the item she found quickly up her sleeve, she allowed the man to help her upright as her second hand was freed and then he held her there while the other man bent to undo both of the chains at her ankles. The moment the last chain fell away, Wymon stepped forward and caught her arm, dragging her away from the soldier still trying to help her remain upright. He pulled her across the room to where the men were just finished securing Tearlach in his own chains.

"MacAdie's had a rough day," Wymon announced, his grip hard on her arm. "He needs strength for tomorrow's trials."

He shoved her so close she was pressed against the Scot's chest and Lucy glanced from one man to the other with confusion.

"You are going to assist him with the matter," Wymon announced with a cold smile. "Perhaps this will aid you in making up your mind and clear 'mayhap' from your vocabulary."

While Lucy was still trying to puzzle that out, Wymon glanced around.

"Move closer," he ordered several of the men. "I do not want her dead . . . yet . . . and if he loses control, you shall have to stop him."

Lucy didn't have a clue what Wymon was talking about, but he was succeeding in scaring her. He smiled when he saw that fear in her eyes as he glanced at her again.

"The MacNachtons and MacAdies are bloodsuckers. Vampire," he told her with amusement. "He has lost a lot of blood this day. He is weak. He needs blood and shall have yours."

While Lucy stared at him with disbelief, Wymon turned to peer at Tearlach. "I understand your kind prefer the jugular vein, MacAdie. Is that so?"

The look Tearlach turned his way was cold and empty. He was no more going to answer that question than he had any of the others.

"Feed," Wymon ordered, shoving Lucy even closer to

him. They were now as close as lovers, only their clothes pressed tight between them as a barrier.

Tearlach stared down into her face and she saw a struggle take place in the depths of his dark eyes, and then he turned his head away.

Wymon chuckled nastily at his reaction, then tugged Lucy away and back to his side. He slid his dagger from his waist and—before she realized what he was up to— jerked her wrist to him and sliced over it so that thick red blood immediately began to flow. She gasped as the pain of the slice struck her, then gasped again as Wymon held the wrist up before Tearlach's face.

"Feed," Wymon insisted and Lucy was about to curse the man for a fool in believing the ridiculous rumors about Tearlach and his people when movement caught her eye and her gaze locked on his face. As she watched in horrified fascination, the Scot's lips parted revealing wickedly sharp incisors that protruded past his other teeth. She stared at those fangs with a sort of disbelief as Tearlach inhaled the scent of her blood. What could only be described as a deep horror rose up on her face.

His head started to bend forward toward the offering Wymon was making, but a small sob of sound from her lips made him pause sharply. His eyes blinked open and found her face. Whatever he saw there made him stop cold. Mouth closing to hide his teeth, he lifted his head and turned away.

"Fool." Wymon laughed and then shrugged and tugged Lucy away from the man and began to drag her back across the cell. "Perhaps you shall change your mind come morning. You should be very hungry by then and will need the blood to survive another day of this."

Lucy remained silent, her gaze locked on Tearlach as she was rechained to the wall. Her mind was having trouble accepting what her eyes had seen and she was watching, hoping he would open his mouth and she would see that it had all been a mistake. Surely, she'd not seen what she'd thought she'd seen? The rumors weren't true, couldn't be. There was no such thing as vampires and—

"I shall bid you both good night."

Lucy turned her gaze reluctantly to Wymon as he ushered the other men out of the cell.

"Until tomorrow," he added with a grin as he followed the last man out and pulled the door closed with a hollow thud.

Lucy stared at the door as she listened to the footsteps fading away up the stairs.

"Are ye a'right?" Tearlach asked as the door to the main level of the castle clicked closed and Lucy turned an amazed gaze to the man.

"What?" she asked with disbelief.

"Are ye a'right?" He asked the question through gritted teeth, but there was real concern in his face and voice.

Lucy stared at him silently, wondering how he could ask that when he was the one who had suffered the tortures of the damned all day.

"Yer wrist," he added finally when she simply stared at him in stunned silence.

"Oh." She glanced toward the wrist, aware that it was still bleeding. Fortunately, it was her left wrist and she was right handed.

"He cut ye verra deeply." His gaze was locked on the blood slowly running down her arm and dripping onto the floor.

It was a hungry gaze, but Lucy decided to ignore it and simply said, "Nay. I am not all right. And neither are you. And we are getting out of here."

Tearlach gave a sharp laugh at her words and asked, "And how're ye proposin' we do that, lass?"

Lucy didn't answer. She was too busy trying to work her fingers over the chain on her wrist and reach the metal she'd retrieved from the guard's pocket and slid up her sleeve. It would be difficult to retrieve with the chains on, but she would do it. She had to.

Three

Tearlach closed his eyes and forced himself to ignore his various pains as well as the sharp scent of blood in the air. It was a difficult task. His back was on fire and his hunger was a burning that was filling his chest and mind. It would have been easier for him to ignore both agonies had Lucy seen fit to distract him by talking again. However, it seemed that although she'd talked to him through the last two days, now that she knew what he was, she wanted nothing more to do with him. She hadn't responded with more than a distracted grunt to any of the half a dozen comments and questions he'd asked since assuring she was all right. It almost made him sorry he'd spared her and not accepted the blood offering Wymon Carbonnel had made. After all, the blood was now simply wasted anyway, running down her arm and dripping from her elbow, drop after drop hitting the ground with a sound that was overloud to his straining senses. Each splash taunted him with what he could have had but had turned down in the face of her horror.

Tightening his mouth, Tearlach tried to block the sound and think of something else, but his mind was full of unpleasantness at the moment. Memories of the torture he'd suffered, the horror on Lucy's face when she'd spotted his teeth and realized what he was . . .

He felt his soul cringe at the memory of her expression. It had been a sharp contrast to the soft reminiscing and husky laughter she'd shared with him through the night and had made him feel, for the first time in his life, like the monster his people were whispered to be.

Tearlach had lost a lot of blood during the torture and had any of the men got close to him on the way back into this chamber, he'd have taken a chunk out of them without regret. However, Lucy had been another matter. He'd had little difficulty refusing the offer of blood when Carbonnel had merely shoved the woman up close to him, but once he'd cut her and Tearlach had seen the blood bubble to the surface of her skin, smelled the tinny scent, his hunger had been all consuming. Had Lucy not gasped and drawn his gaze to her horrified expression, he might very well have latched onto her wrist and—

"Tearlach? Are you awake?"

He almost ignored the soft question until his muddled mind realized that the sound had come much closer than from across the chamber and that he could actually feel her soft breath on his cheek. Blinking his eyes open, Tearlach stared down in amazement at the petite blonde now standing before him, concern on her face as she peered up at him. "What? How . . . ?"

Lucy grinned at his astonishment. "Do you not remember my telling you about those games my brother and I used to play in our own dungeon?"

"Aye," he said faintly as she moved to his hand and began to poke a bit of metal into the lock and twiddle it about. "Ye played prisoner, but yer brother always got free."

"Aye," she murmured, her voice distracted as she worked at the lock. "We stopped playing once I too knew how to work the locks. It was no longer any fun."

Tearlach watched her with bewilderment. Just moments ago, she hadn't seemed willing to even speak to him, yet now she was working at unlocking him. He'd barely had the thought when he recalled that while she'd been merely grunting or ignoring his earlier comments and questions, she'd also been shimmying about slightly in her chains, straining against them. At the time he'd paid it little attention, thinking it a waste of time anyway. Now, however, he realized she must have been distracted trying to free herself. She hadn't been ignoring him at all, at least not because she no longer wanted anything to do with him. She'd hardly be unlocking him now if she thought him a monster.

"Why didn't ye tell me ye were tryin' to unlock yerself?" he asked with exasperation.

"I did not wish to get your hopes up in case I could not get us free," Lucy admitted and then released a pleased little sigh as the first of his chains clicked open under her efforts.

Tearlach watched her set to work on the second chain on the same wrist, a small frown claiming his lips as he wondered if he'd have the strength to hold the wrist up once the chain was gone. He'd lost so much blood and was so weak he wasn't at all sure he would. In fact, he was rather certain that he wouldn't be able to stand without the chains to hold him up. Escape would be impossible whether he was unbound or not, he realized with dismay.

"Why did ye no' do this last night or the one before?" Tearlach asked with frustration. He'd still been strong and capable then. He could have got them out of there if she'd done this before the torture. After losing so much blood and strength, however, he wasn't at all sure he'd be anything but a burden to her now.

"I needed something to work the locks with," she said, her breath soft and warm against his arm. "I slid this bit of metal from the guard's pocket when he unchained me. You did not really think I meant it when I said mayhap to whether I was now willing to marry Wymon, did you?"

Tearlach grimaced at the question. He *had* actually believed it. After his suffering he wouldn't have been surprised if she'd said yes on the spot to avoid any similar torture herself. He didn't say as much now, however, but merely asked, "What is the bit of metal ye're using?"

"I am not sure," she admitted, pausing to pull it from the second lock and peer at it. "It looks like part of a broken pendant or some such thing. Whatever it is, we are lucky he had it on him."

Lucy returned to working on the lock and Tearlach watched her with a combination of admiration and regret. He had known she was courageous from the way she'd set aside her grief the night they were taken and set out to keep both their minds off the coming torture by telling him tales of her childhood. The tales she'd told had revealed a good deal of her character, and her ability to laugh at some of her memories despite their grim circumstance had told him more. He already knew she was strong, smart, and light-hearted by nature . . . and she apparently didn't think he was a monster after all, for surely she wouldn't be trying to free him were she afraid of, or repulsed by, him?

"Stop," Tearlach whispered and it was the hardest word he thought he'd ever had to say.

Lucy didn't seem to hear him but continued to work at the lock another moment before releasing a relieved breath as this lock too clicked open.

"Stop," Tearlach repeated as his arm dropped to sag at his side.

Lucy paused and glanced at him with confusion. "What?"

"Stop. Ye're wasting precious time," he said quietly.

"I am working as quickly as I can," she said apologetically and he realized she thought he was criticizing her efforts.

"Nay. I do not mean—" He stopped to take a breath, only to let it out on a sigh before saying, "Ye waste yer time with me, Lucy. I am too weak to make it out o' here with ye. I shall just slow ye down and get ye caught. Ye're better slipping out o' here on yer own."

She started to shake her head at once, and he quickly added, "Ye can send back help. Send a message to me people telling them where I am and they will come free me."

Lucy snorted at the very suggestion as she went to work on the chain at his neck. "Oh, aye, and by the time your people got here, you would be long dead from Carbonnel's tortures. I think not, my lord. I could do naught to save my brother from Wymon, but I will not leave you here to die at his hands too."

"Carbonnel will no' kill me. He wants information and needs me alive tae get it," Tearlach said quietly and then added, "Lucy, I do no' think I can even stand let alone walk, and ye surely have no' the strength tae carry me oot o' here."

"We will deal with that once I have freed you," she insisted firmly. "I have a plan."

"What plan?" he asked with interest and even some hope.

Lucy did not answer, but merely smiled with satisfaction as the lock at his neck snapped open. "I am getting better. I have not used these skills in so long they had grown rusty, but I am picking them back up quickly."

He smiled faintly at her pleasure, but repeated, "What plan?"

"I shall explain shortly, sir. Please be quiet now, I need to concentrate."

Tearlach opened his mouth to insist, but then let the question die on his lips as she knelt to work at the chain at his waist. The pose was very suggestive. At least to his mind as he stared down at the top of her head and watched her hands raise to his waist. He watched her test the tension of the chain. Seeming to realize it was helping him stay upright, instead of unlocking it, she left it for now and turned her attention to the chains on his feet instead.

Tearlach began to breathe again once her attention moved to that area, but left her to concentrate on her work rather than persist in questioning her. His own attention turned to watching the play of torch light on her hair. He had noted on first spotting her in the inn that she was a pretty woman, something he'd noted again on first awaking here in the dungeon, but in the time that had passed since then somehow that prettiness had turned to beauty in his eyes. The big eyes that had merely caught his attention had come to fascinate him as he watched the play of intelligence that ran through them and the emotions they spoke of. Her eyes were expressive, lightening with laughter, darkening with grief, sparkling with secret amusement, clouding with thought.

And her mouth, which might seem perfectly normal on first glance, stretched into sheer beauty with her smiles and laughter. But it was her spirit that attracted him most. She had seemed ready to cave in to grief after Wymon had left them the first night, but then had rallied. She was an exceptional woman, and he was grateful that if he had to be captured and chained to a wall, that it was she with whom he was captured and chained up.

"There." Finished freeing his feet, Lucy straightened and cast one of her glowing smiles his way as she shifted to set to work on the chains at his second wrist. "We shall be out of here in a trice."

Tearlach smiled faintly at her assurance and then inhaled deeply as the scent of blood struck his nose. She was working on his left wrist now, her own left arm closest to his face and the scent of blood still weeping slowly from her wound was strong and intoxicating. Tearlach's abused and weakened body clenched instinctively at the scent of what he needed to help heal and regain his strength.

Closing his eyes, he forced himself to remain in place when what he truly wanted to do was bend his head just those few inches necessary to run his tongue hungrily up her arm, licking away the blood now being wasted.

"Tearlach?"

Her concerned voice forced his eyes open and he found her standing before him, concern on her face as she peered at him.

"I am going to do the one at your waist now," she said quietly and he realized his second arm was now free and hung limply at his side like his first.

"Are you all right?" she asked with a frown. "You look pained."

Unwilling to explain what it was exactly that was paining him and what he wanted to do, Tearlach merely nodded.

Her expression remained uncertain and concerned, but Lucy took him at his word and once again bent to his waist.

Tearlach closed his eyes on the image of her kneeling before his groin and simply waited. He knew the moment the chain snapped free. He tried to stay upright, but it was impossible. The moment the chain no longer held his weight, Tearlach buckled and slid down the wall to his knees. Lucy tried to catch him and help him remain upright, but he was too heavy for her and they ended up facing each other on their knees.

"Are you all right?" she asked with concern, keeping him from collapsing against her by pressing her hands to his chest.

Tearlach moaned, his teeth actually aching with the need for blood. Fighting the urge to pounce on this precious woman, he growled, "What is yer plan tae get us both oot o' here?"

When Lucy was silent for a moment, Tearlach forced himself to straighten as much as he could, then leaned back against the wall so that he could see her. Lucy was worrying at her upper lip with her teeth as she watched him. For a moment, he thought she wouldn't answer, but then she held her arm up, offering him the wrist Wymon had cut. "Feed. Regain your strength and let us get out of here."

Tearlach almost pounced on the offering, but then his mind kicked in and made him pause. The amount of blood he would need to regain his strength and heal was more than she could give up without growing weak herself. Gritting his teeth, he shook his head. "Nay. Go. Escape and get word tae me clan. They shall fetch me."

"There shall be nothing to fetch," she said sharply. "Wymon shall be furious when he finds I have escaped and most likely beat you to death in his fury."

Tearlach didn't argue the point. He suspected she was right. While the man was supposed to torture information from him, Wymon did not seem the sort to enjoy being bested and would not take the escape of one of his prisoners well at all. In his temper and pique he might very well kill him. Sighing, Tearlach shook his head and then let his head drop wearily. "It doesnae matter, so long as you escape."

Rather than appreciate his sacrifice, Lucy snorted. "Oh, do not be a fool. I shall not escape alone." Catching him by the chin she lifted his head, stared him in the eye, and said firmly, "I need you."

Tearlach stared at her with sudden understanding. This of course explained all. The horror he'd seen on her face had been real. She did think him a monster, but she'd deal with the devil himself to get out of there. It wasn't trust and like that had moved her to take him with her, but need. Despite having known her only a matter of days, for some reason that was a bitter drink for Tearlach to swallow, it roused a rage in him that almost had him tearing out her throat with his need. But something in his face must have spoke of the emotions roiling in him, for fear suddenly rose in Lucy's eyes and she trembled against him. Fear on that face was enough to help him rein in his emotions and allow his mind to function again.

Of course she was afraid. No doubt all she knew of his kind were the rumors that claimed they were soul stealers and bloodsuckers. Who would not fear him? But Tearlach didn't want her to fear him, he wanted to reassure her and let her see what he was truly like, that his need for blood was just a part of him. That he didn't steal souls or attack unsuspecting travelers or any of the other things mortals claimed about his kind.

Swallowing his rage, Tearlach took a steadying breath. He had to feed to get them both out of there, but he would not do it as she wished and lap at her wrist like a hungry dog licking at a bit of meat as she looked on with silent disgust . . . and he would not hurt her.

"Tearlach?" Lucy whispered and there was uncertainty and concern on her face again as she peered at him.

He forced a smile to lips that felt stiff and dry and whispered, "Kiss me."

She blinked in surprise at the request but at least did not appear repulsed at the idea, instead she simply appeared confused. "Should you not feed? I fear you are very weak. If you lose consciousness before you can feed, we—"

"Kiss me," Tearlach repeated softly, insistently.

"But—I . . ." Lucy flushed a pretty pink and looked away as if for an escape.

Tearlach didn't repeat the request, but leaned forward slightly and caught her lips with his own. She didn't pull away or resist, but simply stayed still under his lips at first and then Tearlach managed to raise his hand to her shoulder and slide it clumsily into her hair to hold her head in place. Though it was a weak hold indeed and one she would have had no difficulty escaping had she tried, she didn't, but breathed out a little sigh as he tilted his own mouth on hers and slid his tongue out to tease her lips apart. The moment she allowed him in, Tearlach put all his waning strength into the kiss and suddenly found reserves he hadn't known he had.

They were both panting with the effort when he tore his lips away and began to press butterfly kisses to her cheek and then down her throat.

"Tearlach," she breathed, her voice trembling with myriad emotions. Not one of them fear.

"Aye," he breathed against her neck.

"You must feed," she whispered on a moan.

"Aye," he breathed and then sank his teeth into her neck. He felt her stiffen, but it was only a brief, automatic response. He was already infusing her with the pleasure and relief he was experiencing.

Moaning deep in her throat, Lucy sank against Tearlach and allowed her eyes to drift closed as her body shuddered and shivered under the pleasure suddenly coursing through her.

Part of her mind was full of wonder. She'd never expected offering her blood to him to be such a pleasurable experience. Another part of her mind was grateful that Tearlach hadn't bitten her when Wymon had tried to force him to earlier. The idea of experiencing this with Carbonnel and his men looking avidly on was horrifying. She suspected Wymon Carbonnel wouldn't have made the offer had he realized what feeding consisted of. He'd wanted to scare and torture her into agreeing to marry him, not offer her a pleasurable experience.

Tearlach suddenly pulled away from her with a gasp, and Lucy allowed her head to fall back against his supportive arm, watching him as he stared up at the ceiling, his mouth partly open and fangs visible. She stared at the teeth with fascination, finding it hard to believe that his bite had not been painful, but instead had given her pleasure.

Leaving the puzzle to be considered at another time, she shifted her eyes to his face and frowned. While he'd regained some of his color and wasn't quite the same shade as parchment anymore, he didn't really look much healthier than he had before he'd fed and it seemed obvious to her that he needed more blood.

"You need more," she said quietly.

Tearlach closed his eyes as if against temptation and shook his head. "Ye can no' give more without growin' weak yerself."

Lucy bit her lip. It seemed to her that his strength would come in handier than her own. Were it necessary, he could carry her. The same could not be said for her ability to carry him. "Perhaps if you took just a little more—"

Tearlach shook his head, but merely said, "Stand up."

"What?" she asked with confusion.

"Stand up," he insisted.

Lucy had no idea why he wished it, but rather than argue, she simply slid from his embrace and stood up next to him, reaching for the wall with surprise when the room swam briefly around her.

"I've already weakened ye. I've taken enough," he insisted quietly and when she made to protest, added, "the amount I need wid kill ye, lass."

Lucy frowned, but didn't argue further. Instead, she asked, "Can you walk?"

Tearlach was silent and unmoving for a moment, then gathered himself and forced himself to his feet. He stood, swaying slightly, but he stood under his own power and Lucy supposed it would have to be enough for now.

Moving under his arm, she took some of his weight as she steered him toward the door. Tearlach didn't protest her aid and that more than anything told her that he wasn't as strong as he claimed. From what she had learned these last few days as they talked, she knew he was a proud man who would not enjoy needing anyone's help, let alone a woman's. Obviously he was weak enough to swallow his pride. He definitely needed more blood, but she knew he would not take hers. Her best hope was that they would run across one of Wymon's men on his own and Tearlach was able to feed off him. Fully.

Lucy felt bad just for thinking the thought since it would mean the man's death, but they were being held prisoner here unjustly and against their will. And neither of them would meet a happy end if they did not escape. If it meant helping him to feed off of a lone soldier they caught unawares, she would do it.

Burdened by these grim thoughts and the little bit of his weight Tearlach was allowing her to take, Lucy led him out of the dungeon and to the stairs leading above.

"Where does that door come oot?" Tearlach asked when they paused at the foot of the stairs.

Lucy bit her lip and considered the question. She had been to Carbonnel half a dozen times in her life including this last visit with her brother, but had never really had a tour. Finally, she shook her head. "I do not think it leads into the great hall. Mayhap the kitchens."

Tearlach grimaced. "Let us hope not."

"Nay," Lucy murmured. The kitchens in a castle this size would be a constant buzz of activity. Not a spot where they could easily avoid being seen leaving. Sighing, she eased out from under his arm. "Wait here and I shall take a peek."

Before he could protest, Lucy slipped quickly up the stairs to the door at the top. She paused to take a deep breath, and then eased the door open enough to peer out. Her eyes widened incredulously as she realized she was looking into the Carbonnel Barracks where the soldiers slept when they were not about their duties. At the moment, those barracks were nearly empty with only two men remaining inside, both appearing sound asleep. It seemed their timing was fortuitous. The rest of the men were either up on the wall or at table.

Her gaze slid over the room, pausing on bits of clothing lying about; a tunic here, a pair of braies there, and one or two scraps of what appeared to be jupons with the Carbonnel colors. Thank God men were not the most tidy of creatures, she thought, and then peered back at Tearlach. She gestured for him to wait where he was, and then checked the room once more before slipping into it and moving along the beds, snatching up bits of cloth until she had two full uniforms.

Lucy made her way back to the door, slid onto the stairs, and eased it closed, not realizing she'd been holding her breath until she sucked a deep draught of the fetid dungeon air into her depleted lungs. Shaking her head, she hurried back down the stairs to Tearlach's side.

"The door leads into the barracks," she informed him quietly, sorting through the clothes she'd retrieved. "Here, we have to change into these."

Tearlach grimaced as he accepted the clothes she handed him and she couldn't blame him. They weren't exactly sweet smelling. Most of them appeared to be cast offs that had been replaced because of their poor condition, but neither of them were in a position to complain.

Turning away from her, Tearlach leaned against the wall and began to disrobe. All it took was one tug and his plaid fell away. Lucy flushed with embarrassment and quickly turned her back to the sight. Leaving him by the stairs, she slipped back into the dungeon they'd shared and quickly pulled the braies on under her gown, then removed the dress to don the tunic and the jupon with the Carbonnel colors. Lucy then ripped a strip of cloth from the hem of her gown and used it to tie back her hair. She then slipped it down her back under the tunic and jupon.

Finished, Lucy moved quickly back out to rejoin Tearlach, relieved to see that he had managed to don his own clothes without aid. She didn't think she had it in her to dress the man. She would have done it if she had to, but really, it would have been mortifying.

Tearlach smiled faintly when she returned, but then sighed and shook his head.

"What?" she asked with concern.

"Ye look far too pretty tae pass fer a boy, lass. We shall be spotted at once."

Lucy bit her lip and hesitated, then knelt and ran her hands over the stone floor, relieved when she lifted them and saw that they were covered in dirt. Managing not to grimace at the necessity, she raised her hands to her face and scrubbed the dirt onto her cheeks, nose, and forehead and then straightened and faced Tearlach in question.

His mouth twisted with weary amusement, but he nodded. "Better."

Shoulders sagging with relief, Lucy slid her arm under his again and they made their way slowly up the stairs. Lucy managed not to chivvy him to hurry, but had to bite her lip to keep from doing so. She was very aware of the time passing and the danger that they would reach the top of the stairs only to find that the men had finished their meal or whatever it was that was keeping them from the barracks and that they had a room full of guards to get through.

Pausing at the top of the stairs, she forced a smile for him, then eased the door open and peered out into the barracks, her eyes widening when she saw that luck was with them. Not only were the other men not returned, but one of the men who had been there sleeping when she'd been in the room earlier had apparently awoken and left. There was only one man left in the barracks and he was snoring soundly.

"Come," Lucy said and helped Tearlach into the room. They moved slowly along the row of beds until they reached the one where the lone soldier slept and then it was Lucy who stopped.

When Tearlach glanced at her in question, she glanced toward the door, and then back to the man before whispering, "Feed."

The Scot's eyes widened incredulously at the suggestion and he shook his head before whispering, "No time. Too risky."

Lucy frowned, but bowed to his decision and continued forward to the door leading out of the barracks. She was glad she had not insisted when she eased the door open and spotted the group of men moving across the bailey in their direction. They would have been interrupted and discovered for sure.

Her gaze swept the courtyard. The day was waning, the sun no longer visible in the sky as night settled in. She hoped that would aid them, it would make them less recognizable at least.

A shout from the direction of the keep doors made the group stop and turn to wait for one of their comrades and Tearlach immediately hissed, "Quickly."

Lucy was already moving. Fear and adrenaline either gave her added strength, or gave him temporary strength, either way, between the two of them they managed to rush out and around the building out of sight before being spotted. Pausing at the back of the barracks, they both leaned against the wall while they got their bearings.

"Where are the stables?" Tearlach gasped.

His question made her straighten to peer around and Lucy could have wept with relief when she realized exactly where they were. They stood in an alley of sorts between two buildings, the one they leaned against was the barracks, the building across from them was the stables. Before she could tell him so, the faint whicker of a horse drew his gaze to the building no more than ten feet in front of them. She nodded when he turned a questioning gaze her way.

"Wait here," she whispered and slipped away, hurrying to the opposite structure and then moving quickly around the side of it. She paused to glance over the busy courtyard, but when she didn't spot anyone paying her any undue attention, she straightened away from the wall, tried for a young man's swagger, and strode around front and into the stables.

Lucy had no plan and simply hoped that if she walked in and began to saddle a horse as if she were about some purpose, no one would question her. As it happened, it seemed the stable master was at his meal as well. The stables appeared empty.

Sending up a silent prayer of thanks, Lucy peered along the row of horses, her heart lightening when she spotted her mare. Trinket was a beautiful black, fast and smart and affectionate. She would also carry two riders with little difficulty. A good thing since she didn't think Tearlach could stay in the saddle on his own.

Grabbing a saddle, Lucy greeted the animal with soft whispers and soothing words as she prepared the mount. Once finished saddling the mare, she led her quickly to the stable doors.

Pausing in the shadows just inside the open doors, Lucy peered over the bailey, alarmed to see that it was quickly becoming crowded with people filing out of the keep. The meal was most definitely over.

Urgency creeping along her back, she tightened her hold on her mare's reins and led her quickly out of the stables and around the side at a quick march. Tearlach stumbled away from the back of the barracks as she approached and between them they managed to get him on the horse's back. Once he was seated, Lucy pretty much climbed up the man's leg to get on the mare as well. Settling before him on the horse, she caught the reins in hand and turned her toward the gates.

"Hold on," Lucy whispered to Tearlach, and then set her heels to the horse's sides to get her moving. Trinket, picking up on her urgency, burst into an immediate gallop that Lucy was hard pressed to slow. She herself wanted to charge out of there as if the devil were snapping at the horse's rear too, but feared it would draw unwanted attention. A fast walk would be less noticeable, she hoped, and forced the animal to slow to that.

The next few moments were the most tense and nerve-racking of Lucy's life. Were her hands not busy holding the reins, she would have been hard pressed not to chew her nails to the quick, which would have been a waste as it turned out, since they managed to ride to and out through the gates of Carbonnel without either being stopped or even really noted as far as she could tell. At least, if their passing was noted, it was assumed there was nothing odd about it. She supposed the fact that they were wearing soldiers' clothes and colors aided in convincing those at the gate and on the wall that they were about a duty for their lord.

Lucy wasn't the only one relieved when they were outside of Carbonnel's walls. The moment they'd ridden into the trees and were out of sight of the men on the wall, Tearlach sagged against her back with a long sigh that whistled past her ear. It seemed clear that he'd exerted a lot of strength to sit upright and suffer their passage through Carbonnel's bailey, and in fact used up a good portion of what strength he had. Now, he grew heavier by the moment until Lucy began to realize that they wouldn't be able to ride far. He needed to rest and regain his strength.

"I'll not be able to stay in the saddle long," Tearlach breathed apologetically by her ear.

Lucy refrained from stating that her thoughts had been running along the same lines, and instead began to wrack her mind, trying to think of somewhere safe for them to take shelter.

"Diya ken o' any caves around here where we can shelter? We'll need to be out o' the sun come morn."

Lucy didn't ask why they'd need to be out of the sun.

One of the rumors about his people was that they couldn't stand sunlight and she supposed it must be true. The mention of caves sparked a memory for her.

"Aye, there is," she admitted with a frown. "I know of one just on the edge of our property, but 'tis a good two hours' ride away. Can you last that long?"

"Aye," he murmured and she felt him straighten slightly behind her with determination.

Lucy let a little sigh of relief slip from her lips. His weight against her hadn't been a bother, in fact, it had helped to keep her warm. The night was cool and growing cooler by the minute. His straightening, however, told her he still had some reserves of strength and they might make it to the cave ere he collapsed completely and that was a relief. If he collapsed and tumbled off the horse ere they reached the cave, she didn't think she could get him back on the mare on her own.

As it turned out, Lucy had underestimated the distance. Or perhaps—as was more likely—they weren't traveling as quickly as she'd hoped, the weight of two people on the mare slowing the pace. Whatever the case it was closer to three hours before Lucy recognized that they'd crossed from Carbonnel land to Blytheswood. It took another few moments more for her to find the clearing near the cave she was searching for. The cave didn't open onto the clearing itself, but rested a good half mile farther on along a path that was barely discernible in daylight. Fortunately, it was a clear night and the moon offered some aid, otherwise, she never would have found the cave.

With Tearlach barely conscious and his full weight bearing down on her back, Lucy didn't stop, but urged the horse directly through the narrow opening of the cave. She grimaced as her legs scraped against either side of the entrance, just grateful that the horse had managed to fit through with them on. Tearlach was a large man and she didn't think she could have managed to drag him in on her own.

Trinket stopped and refused to walk farther once they were several feet inside the cave. Lucy didn't blame her. Without the moonlight to give it relief, the cave was pitch black after the first couple of feet. Lucy herself wasn't too happy to be in such stygian darkness, but there wasn't much choice. Aside from the fact that Tearlach needed to be out of sunlight come dawn, the dark cave would hide them from their pursuers . . . and there would definitely be pursuers. The moment their absence was noted, every last one of Carbonnel's men would be on the hunt for them, she was sure. Wymon couldn't risk her reaching anyone and telling them what had really happened at the inn, that he had murdered her brother . . . and lied when saying Tearlach had killed him and absconded with her. He would then be wanted for John's murder. It made it doubly unfortunate that Tearlach was so weak at the moment. She really would have rather ridden on to Blytheswood and spread the true tale of the happenings at the inn, but that wasn't possible now.

Lucy supposed she could leave Tearlach there and ride on by herself, but didn't want to abandon him alone and defenseless in the cave. He would be lost if Wymon's men found him, unable to defend himself. No, they would have to stay in the cave a day or so and let him regain his strength and then continue on to Blytheswood.

"Tearlach?" she whispered, releasing the reins and reaching back to touch him.

"Hmm?"

He stirred weakly against her and she let out a little breath of relief, and then said, "We are here. Can you dismount?"

His answer was to slide right off the mount and crash to the cave floor with a thud.

Four

A gasp of alarm slipping from her lips, Lucy hurried to dismount, nearly tripping over Tearlach where he lay. Kneeling at his side, she felt for his face, noting that his eyes were closed and he was breathing deeply. For a moment she feared he'd hit his head in the fall and knocked himself out, but a blind examination of his head revealed no wetness that might be blood. He was simply unconscious.

Sitting back on her heels, Lucy glanced around with a sigh. All she could see at first was the part of the cave close to the narrow entrance, but as her eyes adjusted she began to make out a little more. It was a cave—that was all—empty except for a few boulders and now herself, her mount, and Tearlach. There was nothing she could see to build a fire with or anything to add to their comfort and she was too tired at the moment to make the effort to go out and search out anything useful.

It had been a long few days for her, with first the stressful visit to Carbonnel, then her brother's murder, followed by her being kidnapped and chained to a wall for days on end. The last had been physically wearing, she'd struggled and strained against her bindings as she listened to Tearlach being tortured in the next room . . . and then there had been the stress of their escape. Added to that, she hadn't eaten in all that time except to pick at the meal that had been served her at the inn. Despite that, Lucy wasn't hungry. She was too exhausted for hunger.

Blowing out a breath, she pushed herself to her feet and quickly unsaddled Trinket. The chore seemed to take the last of her reserves of energy and she was definitely dragging by the time she dropped the saddle to the ground. Deciding there was nothing else urgent enough to keep her from resting as well, Lucy moved carefully back to Tearlach, and lay down beside him. Her head barely hit the ground before she dropped off to sleep and into the nightmares waiting there.

Lucy was awakened by the sound of voices. For a moment, she was blissfully confused, unsure where she was or of anything else, but as sleep slipped away memory reclaimed her. It had been a long night. Nightmares of her brother's murder had pounced the moment she lost consciousness and disturbed her rest twice. The first time, she'd woken up screaming his name. Her shriek was enough to wake Tearlach as well, at least enough that he'd murmured soothingly in Gaelic, thrown his arm around her, and drawn her against his side, holding her there as they both drifted back to sleep. The second time she'd woken up weeping and Tearlach had pressed her face to his chest and rubbed her back soothingly as they both drifted back to sleep again.

Thinking about it now, Lucy suspected he hadn't really been awake either time he'd offered her comfort. His words had been a sleepy slur rather than his usual strong voice, but she didn't mind. In fact, she rather hoped he hadn't been awake and wouldn't recall either incident. She didn't want him to think her weak.

A burst of laughter made her stiffen and blink her eyes back open. The sound seemed to come from right outside the cave entrance and she held her breath and stared at the spot where weak light crept into the cave, expecting men to come walking in any moment. When several moments passed without that happening, she began to breathe again and then wrinkled her nose in distaste at the scent she sniffed in. Dear God, something reeked!

Tearlach. She was sleeping curled in his arms, her head on his chest, and it was he who stunk. Or his clothes to be more exact, she thought and lifted her arm to give herself a sniff. Aye, their clothes.

Grimacing, she eased out of his embrace and sat up. There was little she could do about the clothes for now. They had nothing else to wear and it wasn't like she could find the river and wash them with Carbonnel's men riding about looking for them.

Reminded of the men outside the cave, Lucy got carefully to her feet and moved to the entrance as quietly as she could lest a skittering rock draw attention to their hiding place and their presence in it.

Reaching the cave's mouth, she eased up to peer cautiously out, relieved when there was no one about. She was just about to turn back to the interior of the cave when another laugh made her pause. After a hesitation, she eased farther out and peered to the left to see three men on horseback heading away from the cave. They'd obviously ridden right by without even noticing the entrance. She wasn't surprised, the opening was slanted, narrow, and partially obscured by foliage. If you didn't know it was there, it was easy to overlook.

"Aye, his expression when he walked into the dungeon and found it empty was funny," one of the men conceded on a sigh as the laughter died. "But his anger was less amusing when it followed."

There were subdued murmurs of agreement from the other two men and then one said, "Heads will roll if we don't find the pair and quickly."

This seemed to make them all solemn and the first speaker said, "'Tis late and a long ride back to the castle. Mayhap we'd do better to camp out here tonight and continue the search first thing in the morning."

The alacrity with which the other two men agreed suggested to Lucy that none of them were eager to return to Carbonnel and risk being one of those whose heads would roll. She watched them ride out of sight and then glanced to the sky, surprised to see that it was indeed growing late. The sun was low in the sky and would soon be gone. She and Tearlach had slept through the second half of last night and then through the day as well. She supposed she shouldn't be surprised, they'd had little enough sleep in the dungeon these last days, staying up most of the time talking as they had. And they'd been through a lot. The sleep had probably done them good. Besides, they couldn't travel in daylight, so it had saved them sitting in the cave twiddling their fingers until they could leave again.

A soft rustle drew her gaze back to Tearlach as he stirred in his sleep. She waited to see if he would wake up, but he didn't, simply shifted in his sleep, his hand moving restlessly about as if in search of her.

Lucy smiled at the thought and almost moved back to rejoin him, but decided against it. She was wide awake now and wouldn't go back to sleep. She was also tense now that she knew Wymon's men were out searching for them. They would have to be very careful when they left.

If they left, she thought with a frown as she recalled how weak Tearlach had been the night before. The whipping and whatever other tortures Wymon had used on him had taken a heavy toll. She suspected any normal man would have died in the dungeon that day, but Tearlach wasn't normal. He'd rallied a bit after taking blood from her, but it hadn't seen him far. It was obvious he needed more . . . and more than he was willing to take from her.

Her gaze shifted back out of the cave and in the direction the three Carbonnel soldiers had ridden. It seemed to her that if they were going to leave the cave, Tearlach would need more blood . . . and he was in no shape to go out hunting for it.

Could his kind survive on animal blood? She wondered and glanced back to him, considering waking him to learn the answer, but he looked so peaceful she couldn't bring herself to rouse him.

Blowing out a breath, Lucy peered out at the waning day. She would just wait until the sun set and it was a little darker and then she would risk going out to find them both something with which to break their fast.

* * *

The cave was silent and cold when Tearlach woke. Used to waking in dark cold places as he was, he shouldn't have felt so bereft, but Lucy wasn't there. She'd left him, he realized and sagged back against the cave wall, eyes closing as he pondered how odd it was that he'd gotten used to her presence so quickly. A couple nights together in chains and another asleep in a cave and he'd come to rely on her presence in his life and felt abandoned by her leaving.

He shouldn't be, Tearlach told himself unhappily. And he shouldn't be surprised either, or feel betrayed that she'd gone. He'd known from the moment that she said she couldn't escape alone that her only purpose for him was to help her escape. He should have expected that she'd have fled at the first opportunity.

Scowling as his body cramped, Tearlach forced his eyes open and peered around the dim interior. He was hungry and weak and needed to feed. He wasn't feeling much like moving, however. Unfortunately, there wasn't much choice in the matter, he acknowledged. He needed to feed to survive and he needed to survive to get back to his people, gather some men, and go after his cousin. Wherever he was.

Tearlach had managed to shake off the drug he and his cousin had been given in the inn long before Lucy had woken from her head wound in the dungeon. Until she was conscious and aware enough for him to torment, Wymon Carbonnel had passed his time by taunting Tearlach. He'd told him with great relish how he and his cousin had been recognized at one of the earlier inns they'd stopped at, as far back as Scotland. How they'd been followed, their route noted, and their capture planned. They'd been heading south on a pretty straight path, stopping at each village and inn to gather information. Apparently, several men had followed them at a very discreet distance, while others had ridden ahead to pass on the news of where they were to those who had gathered at Carbonnel to plan and arrange their capture.

The plan had worked well and Tearlach could only curse their arrogance and stupidity in following a straight path, never concerned that they would be set upon. Wymon had told him that his chore was to torture him until he learned all he could about their home, its defenses, and the paths of the underground tunnels that ran below it. His cousin had been taken elsewhere to be subjected to different tortures, ones meant to discover how strong his people were, what they could withstand, and what their weaknesses were.

Tearlach felt his backbone stiffen at the very idea of what his cousin might be undergoing even as he himself lay there weak and hurting, but safe in the cave. Right that moment, Heming might be being tortured, burned, or what have you.

Mouth tightening with determination, Tearlach forced himself to sit up. He needed to get out of the cave, feed to regain his strength, find out who had taken his cousin and to where, and then, either rescue him himself if he could, or head home to gather men and return to save him.

Tearlach wasn't sure which was the better alternative. If he went after him alone and failed, they would be worse off than before. However, if he went home to gather men and then returned, they might arrive too late to save Heming. He wasn't sure what to do and was too weak and distracted with his body's paining to sort out the matter at the moment. He needed to feed. His thoughts would be clearer then.

Tearlach repeated that thought to himself over and over as he slowly forced himself to his feet. While he'd fed a little from Lucy in that dungeon, it hadn't been nearly enough. His body had been badly injured by Wymon. Had he been a normal mortal man, Tearlach had no doubt the torture and whipping he'd suffered would have killed him. As it was, he'd survived, but with great damage. His body had spent the hours since trying to heal itself, using up blood at an astronomical rate. To feed as much as he'd need to repair the damage done and replace the blood lost, though, would kill a single person. The amount he'd taken from Lucy the night before had barely been enough for him to get them out of that dungeon.

Not that he'd really done much, he realized suddenly. If anything, Lucy was the one who had gained them their freedom. She'd given up her blood to give him the strength to mostly carry his own weight, but she'd also helped in taking some of his weight as they'd made their way out of the dungeons. She was the one who had risked slipping into the barracks and stealing clothes for them. She'd then helped him out of the barracks and around to the stables and then gone in alone to get the horse they'd fled on.

Truth be told, while Lucy had claimed she couldn't escape without him, she would have done better on her own. It was he who had needed her, not the other way around.

Tearlach had barely had that thought when he became aware of sounds coming from outside the cave. It was a shuffling and dragging punctuated by an occasional grunt that made him stiffen when he managed to get to his feet. He watched the mouth of the cave with narrowed eyes that widened incredulously when a behind backed through it, a behind he recognized as Lucy's. She was bent at the waist, dragging something heavy into the cave. That was the shuffling and dragging. The grunting was a little sound of effort that kept slipping from her lips with each tug and drag she gave at the body she was pulling with her.

Staggering away from the wall, Tearlach hurried to her side, using a hand on the wall to help him stay upright.

"What happened?" he asked in a growl as he reached her side and peered down at the unconscious man she'd dragged in.

"Oh." Forcing a smile, Lucy dropped the man's hands and straightened, wiping one forearm across her sweaty forehead as she explained, "I caught you something with which to break your fast."

"Ye caught me somethin' with which to break me fast?" Tearlach echoed, staring at her with disbelief. His gaze dropped to the man on the ground. The something she'd caught. She'd said it as if she'd snared a rabbit for his meal.

"He's one of Wymon's men," she explained and frowned at his expression before adding, "you need to re-build your strength. I thought since you didn't wish to take too much from me, you could . . ." Her voice trailed away and she frowned. "Why are you looking at me like that?"

Tearlach leaned his weight back against the cave wall with a disbelieving laugh and shook his head. Why was he staring at her like that? He'd thought she'd fled at the first opportunity, but instead she'd gone out and "caught" him someone to feed on. How was he supposed to look at her? He felt confused and befuddled and at the same time a seed of joy had burst to life in his chest and was growing and growing. Her bottom backing into the cave may as well have been the sun, because the cold, damp, and dark cave suddenly seemed like the sunniest spot on the earth and Tearlach found himself grinning like an idiot . . . an expression that apparently concerned Lucy no end.

"Are you feeling all right?" she asked, stepping to his side to press the back of a hand to his forehead. "You have not taken on a fever, have you?"

"I be fine," he assured her, his voice husky as he caught her hand and took it away from his forehead. He clasped it and smiled softly, wanting more than anything in the world to kiss this voluptuous little woman with the beautiful smile and caring eyes. Instead, he blurted, "Ye didnae need me to escape, lass."

Her eyes widened slightly at the change of subject, but then she just shrugged and said, "Aye, I did. My conscience would not have allowed me to leave you there, so I needed you to leave so I could."

Tearlach grinned. "Ye got us both out o' there yerself. Ye didnae need me. I was just a burden."

Lucy looked annoyed. "I would not have left without you."

"Ye saved me, lass."

Now she looked embarrassed as well as annoyed. When she waved away his words and turned to scowl at the unconscious man on the cave floor before them, he said, "I thought ye were horrified on learnin' what I was. That ye now thought me a monster and only wanted me to help ye escape and would flee at the first opportunity."

Lucy glanced back at him with surprise and then

frowned and said firmly, "A pair of fangs and a need for blood do not a monster make. Wymon has neither, yet I know no one more monstrous."

Tearlach felt pain rise and recede in his chest as he heard the pain in her voice. Wymon. The man had killed her brother, kidnapped her, chained her to his wall, and intended to force her to marry him.

"Besides," Lucy said suddenly, drawing his attention to the wry smile now curving her lips. "While you were not really very helpful in the escape, I was surely happy with the company," she assured him. "And I am certain you shall be more helpful in future if you will just feed and regain your strength."

The last was said with firm insistence and Tearlach smiled at the scowl she now cast his way. She had spoken nothing but the truth. He hadn't been any help and his earlier belief that she had sided with him only to gain his aid in fleeing was just ridiculous, a result of his muddled thoughts, he supposed. It was obvious he wasn't thinking clearly and it was time he fed and did start thinking clearly.

His gaze dropped to the "something" she'd brought him to break his fast. The man was now wholly inside the cave and not likely to be seen from outside, that being the case, there seemed little reason to make her drag the man farther inside. Dropping to his knees, he bent toward the soldier's neck, pausing when Lucy cleared her throat and asked uncertainly, "You will not need to kill him, will you?"

Tearlach paused and raised his head to peer at her curiously. She looked uncomfortable and worried.

"Not if ye dinnae wish it," he said quietly.

Lucy shifted on her feet and then sighed, "'Tis just

that . . . well, I know he is one of Wymon's men, but as such he really has to do what he is ordered to and I—"

"I willnae take sae much it kills him," he assured her solemnly and then, self-conscious about feeding in front of her, he tried to distract her by asking, "how exactly is it ye caught him, lass?"

"Oh, well, I woke up when they were riding past. I moved to the mouth of the cave and overheard them talking. They planned to camp in a nearby clearing. I waited until they had passed, then followed and climbed a tree near the clearing to keep an eye on them and watch for one of them to separate from the others." She paused and grinned. "I picked a very fortuitous tree. I had barely settled in my spot when this one got up, left the clearing, and came to the base of the tree I was in." She peered at the unconscious man. "Fortunately, it was the smallest of the three of them and the tree isn't far from here else I would never have been able to bring him back here on my own."

"Aye," Tearlach agreed, glancing at the man in question. Actually, lad was probably the better description. He was no more than sixteen and slender in build. Still it was obviously an effort for her to drag him to the cave. Raising his eyebrows, he glanced to her and asked, "Why did he walk to yer tree and how did he end up unconscious?"

"Oh . . . er . . . he needed to . . . er . . ." She wrinkled her nose, obviously finding it beyond her to state the man had stopped to relieve himself on the tree.

"I understand," Tearlach assured her and she smiled gratefully.

"Well, while he was . . . er . . . distracted with his business, I threw a rock down and hit him in the temple."

Tearlach raised an eyebrow. "Ye threw a rock? And where did ye find this rock in the tree?"

"Oh." Lucy waved that away. "I collected several and put them in my pocket before I left the cave." She reached into her pocket and pulled out several rather large stones.

Tearlach stared at her with admiration. "And ye knocked him oot with the first rock?"

She blushed prettily, but nodded. "My brother and I used to practice hitting targets with rocks when I was growing up. He used to say that the simplest weapons were often the most effective, that a stone had felled Goliath and could come in quite handy when necessary."

Tearlach smiled. "It's soundin' tae me as if yer brother was almost preparin' ye fer a situation sech as this."

"Aye." Her smile faded. "He worried about me constantly. He said it seemed foolish to him that women were the weaker sex and yet were not trained to defend themselves as they should. He said he never wanted me to come to harm because I knew not how to defend myself. He taught me many things while growing up that most ladies do not learn."

Tearlach felt his own smile fade as he watched the pain well up on her face at the loss of such a brother. He wished he could take that pain away, but knew he could not. He also wished he'd met and had the chance to get to know this man. He was sure he would have liked him, but that too was impossible, of course.

"Ye should sit and rest," he said gruffly. "Ye've had a busy mornin'."

"Aye." She forced the grief from her face. "I found a handful of berries on my walk. I shall just sit and eat them while you . . . er . . ."

Lucy never finished the words, but turned and moved farther into the cave, finding a good-sized boulder to sit on. She then pulled her berries from her pocket. They obviously hadn't fared well in there, and she grimaced at their squished and bruised state but set about eating them with determination.

Positioning himself so that he could bend over the man with his back to Lucy and thereby block her view of what he was doing, Tearlach didn't waste any more time, but knelt to feed. It was a quick business despite the amount of blood he took. He left the lad alive as Lucy wished, but the fellow wouldn't be up and about for a while.

Sitting up once he'd judged he'd taken what he could without killing the young man, Tearlach closed his eyes and allowed a moment for the blood to get to where it needed to go. He'd taken much more from the fellow than he had from Lucy the day before and felt better for it. His weakness was slipping from him by the second, leaving him feeling strong and capable again. Relief followed hard. Tearlach wasn't used to feeling weak and dependent on others and hadn't enjoyed it.

"How do you feel?" Lucy asked from her boulder when he suddenly stood.

"Better," he assured her and proved it by bending to catch the unconscious fellow by his collar and lifting him half off the ground. "I'm takin' him back where his friends will find him. I'll not be long."

Without waiting for her response, Tearlach dragged the man out of the cave and then paused. It was still light out, but the dusky light of new night, that grey place between day and full night that seemed to last so long in summer. He took in a deep breath of cooling air as his eyes slid over the area outside the cave where they had taken shelter and then his eyes found the path of crushed grass and weeds that Lucy had made dragging the man to him. He frowned at the obvious trail, knowing they were lucky one of the man's friends hadn't come looking for him and spotted it. It would have led right to them.

Aware that could still happen, Tearlach hefted the fellow over his shoulder, grimacing at the effort it took. He was much better than he had been, but more blood would help him regain full strength. With the man on his shoulder, he scrubbed one boot over the ground as he went, trying to repair some of the damage done and eradicate the trail. He gave it up after a bit, thinking it would be smarter to just relieve himself of his burden and get Lucy moving away from there as quick as they could. After all, the state of the man he was carrying would be a dead giveaway that they'd been in the area.

Thinking this made more sense, Tearlach simply followed the path to the tree where Lucy obviously had downed the man. He lay him down there, leaning him against the tree, then paused and glanced around. It wasn't far from the cave, which was probably a good thing. Lucy wouldn't have managed to drag him back otherwise. But the others would be nearby and he could do with a bit more blood.

Lifting his face to the sky he breathed in deeply, taking in the scents on the night air. His olfactory senses were better than most men's, almost as good as an animal's for scenting trouble on the air. Now he used it, hoping to get an idea of which direction he should go to find his breakfast's friends. He'd barely started scenting the air, however, when he heard the snapping of twigs and someone grumbling.

"God dammit, Jones. Where have you got to?"

Tearlach smiled wryly as he lowered his chin to peer into the woods in the direction of the sound. Luck was with him tonight. The man's friends were going to make it easy to find them. He stood waiting where he was, smiling when another soldier broke out of the trees and came to a startled halt right in front of him.

"What—?" the man began, and then his gaze dropped to the huddled form slumped against the tree behind Tearlach and the man cursed and whirled away, ready to make a run for it. He didn't manage more than one step before Tearlach was on him.

Lucy had finished her berries and was sadly contemplating her still mostly empty stomach when the crunch of feet on stone drew her gaze to the mouth of the cave. Tearlach had returned, she saw with relief and smiled, then her eyes widened as she spotted what he carried with him. A rabbit, skinned, skewered, and already roasted.

"Where did you get that?" she asked, getting eagerly to her feet and moving to join him.

"The lad's friends were camped nearby. They had this all prepared and ready when I found them. I think they were about to eat." He held the meat out. "Here, hold it for me while I saddle your mare."

Lucy automatically accepted the meat, but her attention was now on Tearlach. She bit her lip as she watched him work over the mare, hesitating until he had finished saddling the animal and turned back to face her before finally saying carefully, "They *were* camped nearby?"

"They still are," he assured her with a roll of the eyes. "They're all sleeping now."

"Oh." She relaxed and managed a smile, her attention turning back to the rabbit. Lucy licked her lips as she gazed at it. "It looks good."

"Aye. Smells good too." Tearlach grinned at the greedy look in her eyes, and then stopped teasing her. "Ye can eat while we ride. Come."

Her stomach rumbling at the very thought of eating the meat, Lucy followed him to her mount. When he turned his back and wasn't looking, she couldn't resist pinching off just a bit of meat and popping it quickly into her mouth. Lucy nearly moaned aloud at the succulent taste that exploded in her mouth. It seemed like forever since she'd eaten anything but those few berries.

A gasp of surprise slid from her lips as Tearlach suddenly leaned to the side and scooped her up off the cave floor.

"Would you like some?" she asked guiltily as he settled her in the saddle before him.

Tearlach's chest rumbled with quiet laughter as she held out the rabbit to him, but he shook his head. "I ha'e fed."

Lucy's eyes widened as she met his gaze. "Do you not eat food?"

"Aye," he answered, not appearing upset by the question and then explained, "there were two rabbits o'er the fire. I ate one on the way back to the cave and saved the other fer you."

"Oh." She relaxed and even smiled as she realized the entire rabbit was for her.

Tearlach left her to eat in peace as he urged the horse out of the cave and onto the path.

Every last trace of the sun was now gone, taking its light with it, but the moon was full and bright this night, offering its own light for them to see by. They'd traveled for perhaps five minutes before Lucy became aware of

Tearlach relaxing in the saddle behind her. It was only then that she realized that he'd been tense and alert before that. It wasn't long after that before he began to speak.

"I ha'e tae find and rescue me cousin, Heming," he announced.

Lucy frowned as she chewed and swallowed the bit of rabbit in her mouth. "Aye," she murmured, her eyebrows drawing together. She hadn't thought much about what may have happened to the second Scot. This man and her own situation had taken up too much of her mind to leave much room for Heming. Now she considered him and worried over his fate, wondering where he had been taken and what he was suffering.

She suspected whatever was happening to him was at least as bad as the torture and whipping Wymon had visited on Tearlach and shuddered at the thought of the unending torture he may be suffering.

"O' course I'll see ye home safe first," he added as if she may have feared he would dump her at the side of the road now that they were away. While she supposed another man might have, she hadn't even considered he would. She'd instinctively trusted him with her well-being. Before she could comment, he added, "How far is Blytheswood castle from the cave we slept in, lass?"

"Only about three hours' ride at this pace," she answered quietly and then bit her lip as she considered going home. Home to Blytheswood and the reality of her brother's being dead, murdered by their neighbor. Her people would be in an uproar if they knew. Whether they knew or not was the question. Had Wymon sent news of John's death and spread the story of her being taken by the murdering Scot who had supposedly killed him? Or had he stayed silent on the subject until he saw whether he could convince her to marry him or not? She doubted he'd remained silent. When she and John hadn't returned to Blytheswood, riders would have been sent to search the path between there and Carbonnel. They would have had to have been told something.

"We'll ha'e to be cautious in our approach until we learn what tale Carbonnel has spread," Tearlach said, his thoughts obviously following the same line as her own.

"Aye," Lucy agreed, her gaze on the remainder of the rabbit she held. Her appetite had fled with thoughts of John. They'd been close, friends as well as siblings. She would miss him terribly and would never forget the moment when their eyes had locked as Wymon had stabbed him. He'd been far too good a man to die like that.

"Rest if ye like, I'll wake ye when we get close," Tearlach suggested, but Lucy shook her head at once. She just knew if she closed her eyes her brother's death would replay itself in her mind with all its horror and sorrow. She'd avoid that as long as possible. It had been bad enough in the cave. Besides, she wasn't tired. She'd only been awake a matter of hours.

"Who do you think it is that took your cousin?" she asked to distract them both.

With her back to him as it was, she sensed rather than saw the way he jerked his head down to peer at her. "Diya no ken?"

Lucy leaned back against him and tipped her head up to see his face. He looked positively horrified, she saw with a frown, but shook her head. "Nay. Why would you think I would?"

"Well, surely ye saw who it was who took him from the inn?" Tearlach asked with a frown.

Lucy started to shake her head and then paused. She'd

seen a lot of men in the inn, and then later pouring into the courtyard. As many of them had been strangers as were men from Carbonnel. None but Carbonnel's men had worn colors, however, or clothing that would have told where they were from.

"I saw many men, but no one I recognized as another lord," she murmured thoughtfully and heard Tearlach curse under his breath before she continued, "but that in itself could be a clue."

"Explain," he ordered, sounding grim.

Lucy didn't obey at once, but tried to order her thoughts and recall all she could about the episode at the inn. Finally, she said, "None of the men there were from any of the neighboring castles, else I would have recognized them. They are from farther away, north I think," she murmured.

"North?" Tearlach caught at the suggestion.

"Aye. Scotland, I think. Just before I blacked out, I heard someone with a soft Scottish burr saying, 'Ye take the MacAdie, I'll take the other and guid luck to us both.'"

"Aye, a Scot," Tearlach murmured thoughtfully and then added, "Carbonnel told me that we were followed from Scotland. It makes sense that the other man was a Scottish laird, most like the leader o' the men who were set on our trail."

Lucy nodded. "Then we need only follow your trail backward starting at the border of Scotland."

"Aye, that's what *I'll* have to do," he said meaningfully, and then added, "ye'll be safe and sound at Blytheswood."

Lucy grimaced. "You should not take this on all by yourself, Tearlach. If you are captured—"

"Then I'd be happy kenning ye're safe at home," he growled, and then added, "but I'll no' be captured."

"And I'll no' be safe at home," Lucy muttered.

"What was that?" Tearlach asked with amazement and she suspected his shock was at her mimicking his accent.

Grimacing, she blew out a breath and said, "It occurs to me that Blytheswood may not be the safest place for me. It will surely be the first place Wymon looks, if he is not there already."

Lucy saw the frown now claiming his expression and added, "He probably *is* there already. He could not know we would stop to rest so soon in our journey. He would have expected us to head straight to Blytheswood, so would have gathered his men and marched right in and taken over if the men didn't raise the gate on seeing his approach. He would have to. He cannot allow me to tell anyone the truth of that night at the inn and that he is the one who murdered my brother."

Tearlach grunted what could have been an unhappy agreement and Lucy sighed and then said, "In truth it is probably better that we did stop to rest. If we had made it to Blytheswood, spread the truth of what happened, and raised the gate when he and his men approached, I have no doubt Wymon would have laid siege and attacked. I am sure he would kill every last mon, woman, and child at Blytheswood rather than risk the secret of his murderous behavior reaching the king."

"He may still be doin' that," Tearlach growled. "Yer men may ha'e raised the gate when they saw Carbonnel and his men approaching."

Lucy shook her head. "I suspect not. The men would have no reason to raise the gate. He is supposed to be our neighbor and friend. Nay. No doubt he has arrived to find we did not go there and has settled in to be on hand and keep me silent should we yet show up."

"Aye," Tearlach said thoughtfully and then released a weary sigh of his own as he added, "and obviously sent his men to scour the land in search o' us."

Lucy nodded solemnly. "He wishes you back to torture the information he needs from you, but now he probably just wants me dead and silenced."

Tearlach's arms tightened slightly around her at those words, but all he said was, "Whether he is inside waitin' like a spider in its web, or outside layin' siege, Blytheswood'll no' be a safe haven fer ye."

"Nay," she agreed quietly. "But I needs must know if my people are safe. If by some chance they did raise the gate and are now under siege, I would need head straight to court to speak with the king and ensure their welfare."

Lucy could feel the displeasure roll off of Tearlach at her words and knew he was upset. He—understandably—wished to head out straightaway to find and save his cousin, but he was also chivalrous enough that he felt he shouldn't leave her to travel alone to court and should accompany her. Before she could assure him that she would not expect him to travel with her, Trinket whinnied and reared as a figure suddenly leapt from the bushes and into their path.

Five

Lucy thought sure they were going to land on the path with Trinket rolling on top of them. The mare had gone upright, hooves pawing the air as she tried to avoid trampling the boy who had appeared in their path. Unprepared for the sudden rearing, Lucy simply fell helplessly back against Tearlach's chest. Fortunately, he had faster reflexes and apparently a good deal of strength. Somehow he managed to keep them both on their mount while at the same time turning the mare away from the boy.

When her front hooves came back down, Trinket landed hard, sending a jolt vibrating painfully through Lucy's bones. She was sure it was no pleasure for Tearlach either, but needed a moment to gather herself before she thought to glance back to see how he was doing.

It seemed the landing hadn't rattled him as much as her. By the time she peered around, he was dismounting and moving to the boy on the path. The lad had fallen back when he found himself confronted with a pawing Trinket. He now lay on the path, shaken but unharmed from what she saw before Tearlach reached him, and his body blocked her view of the lad.

Lucy quickly dismounted and hurried to join the pair as Tearlach caught the lad under the arms and lifted him to his feet.

"Are you all right?" she asked on reaching them.

"He's fine," Tearlach rumbled, giving her a reprimanding look that it took her a moment to understand. It wasn't until his gaze dropped meaningfully over her garb and back up that she realized she was dressed as a lad, but speaking in her normal woman's voice.

Grimacing, Lucy pitched her voice an octave or two lower and tried again, "Are you all right, boy?"

He stared from her to Tearlach and nodded mutely.

"Willy! What have you done now?"

Lucy glanced toward the bushes as a woman pushed her way through the densely growing branches and hurried to join them. She had a lit torch in hand and held it high to light up the situation. The woman's gaze moved from her son to them with a combination of concern and alarm as she settled a hand on Willy's shoulder, then she turned to the bushes and yelled, "William!"

Lucy glanced curiously toward the bushes, but the woman's next words brought her back around.

"You wait until yer father gets here, Will Jr.," she hissed. "How many times have I told you not to be runnin' off on yer own when we're away from the castle."

Lucy's eyes widened with alarm as she suddenly recognized the woman's voice. The way she held the torchlight kept her own features in shadow, but her voice was as familiar to Lucy as her brother's. The woman's name was Betty and she had served as her maid for the last six months since her previous lady's maid, Ilsa, had died of a chest complaint. Betty was a pretty little redhead with a charming personality and a natural skill and ability at healing. She'd quickly gained Lucy's liking and trust.

While Betty had only been her lady's maid these last six months, she'd actually worked in Blytheswood castle all her life, as had her husband, William. He ran Blytheswood's stables, having worked his way up from stable boy to stable master.

A nudge from Tearlach made Lucy glance his way to find him peering meaningfully at her mouth. It was only then she realized she was biting her lip. Probably not something a soldier would do, she acknowledged. Stopping the telling sign of anxiety, she forced herself to stand a little straighter and tried not to look as worried as she suddenly felt.

Trying to ease some of the panic she was feeling, Lucy reminded herself that her face was still filthy with the dirt she'd smeared on it to make their escape from the dungeon, and she was dressed like a man. It was also a dark night out with just a sliver of moonlight now falling on them. They would not recognize her, Lucy assured herself. Still, she took a nervous step to the side, placing herself half behind Tearlach and hopefully in his shadow. A little more shadow on her face couldn't hurt.

"Betty?" The gruff voice was followed by a man exploding through the bushes and onto the path. A couple of inches shorter than Tearlach and stocky, William had red hair like his wife and bright green eyes that shot over the tableau, warily taking in the situation as he placed himself a little in front of his wife and son. "What's happened?"

Tearlach stirred and Lucy knew he was about to speak, but couldn't allow it. His Scottish accent might give them away. Catching the back of his shirt to silence him, she tried to lower her voice even further and said, "No harm done. The lad just ran out in front of us. My comrade managed to control our mount, though, and no one was hurt. All's well."

Her words didn't make the man relax much. He still looked wary and as if expecting to need to defend his family. It made her wonder. Why? And why were the family out here so close to the edge of Blytheswood land rather than at the castle?

Noting the way his attention was now on her mare, Lucy drew his gaze back to them by asking, "You are from Blytheswood?"

"Aye," he answered slowly, his gaze sliding back to Trinket.

"Where are you headed?"

William didn't answer, he was examining Trinket with an interest that made Lucy nervous. It was Betty who said, "My mother has died. We're going to York to see her buried."

Briefly forgetting about William, Lucy's eyes widened on the redhead. She had known Betty's mother. She'd been a kind and loving woman right up until the day she'd died . . . three years ago . . . at Blytheswood where she'd spent her whole life. Betty was lying.

Her gaze moved over the woman with new interest. She was a pretty little thing with big eyes and a wide smile. Lucy knew William adored her, everyone at Blytheswood knew that. The pair were very happily married. *And*, she recalled, Wymon had a reputation for abusing the pretty young maids and other workers at Carbonnel. She supposed he would behave no differently at Blytheswood if he were there.

"Did Carbonnel hurt you?" she asked Betty.

"Nay," the maid said, but suddenly looked even more frightened and anxious than she had, her gaze searching out her husband with alarm.

Lucy glanced to William to see that he was now peering at her much as he had the mare. She supposed he was wondering if they had fled the castle and Wymon, only to run into two of his soldiers who would behave as badly or worse than their lord. Wanting to reassure the pair, she shifted uncomfortably under his eyes and muttered, "If I had a mother or sister working at Blytheswood, I would recommend they visit family until Carbonnel left. He is not a good man."

"Aye. One of your comrades who rode in with his lordship said as much to several of the pretty young maids," William murmured, apparently deciding that— despite the fact that they wore Carbonnel colors—they weren't like the man who was supposed to be their lord. "That along with the rumors of what goes on at Carbonnel was enough to make most of the women at Blytheswood suddenly find an urgent need to visit family, or suddenly too ill to work in the castle . . . And so it shall remain until Lady Lucy is back and he leaves, I would imagine."

Lucy nodded. Wymon was at Blytheswood as they'd suspected and had been allowed in. No doubt he was lording over her home as if it were already his. She could not go there.

"We were told the Scot killed your brother and carried you off with him," William commented.

"Nay. 'Twas Carbonnel who killed John," Lucy assured him, distracted by her thoughts. It wasn't until Tearlach turned sharply on her that she realized what the man had said and how she'd answered. Eyes widening with alarm, she glanced at William to see him smiling with satisfaction.

"Surely you didn't think you could fool me, my lady?" William asked with amusement. "I recognized Trinket right off."

He moved to the mare and ran an affectionate hand down her side. "I've saddled and unsaddled you every day since the old lord bought you for Lady Lucy six years ago, haven't I, beauty?" he said to the horse and then turned to glance over his shoulder at Lucy as he added, "and I chased around after you and John often enough when we were all children. Dressed as you are and with your hair down your back you look very like he did when he was a lad."

"My lady?" Betty echoed with surprise and shifted the torch to light up Lucy's face. Her eyes widened incredulously. "It *is* you."

Lucy let her breath out on a sigh. "You can not tell Carbonnel or his men that you saw us."

"Tell?" William snorted with derision. "I'm not planning on telling him anything. We are going to my brother's inn on the border with Oswald."

Lucy nodded slowly. While Carbonnel bordered their land on the south, Oswald was their neighbor to the north.

"We shall stay with him and help out to earn our keep until we hear Wymon is gone," William assured her, then paused and asked solemnly, "I don't suppose that will happen for a while?"

Lucy shook her head helplessly. "I do not know how long it will take, William. We have to find Tearlach's cousin." Seeing the confusion on his face at mention of a cousin, Lucy quickly explained the events that had taken place at the inn and told him about her and Tearlach being locked up at Carbonnel. He began to grin when she told him about their escape.

"Aye, you and John were always mucking about in the dungeons as children. Your mother used to fret, but your father said to let you be, that you were having fun and may learn something useful with the games the two of you played." His smile faded, leaving his expression solemn as he added, "He was right. It served you well."

"Aye," Lucy murmured sadly as she thought on her brother.

"I was the one to take Carbonnel's horse when he arrived," William announced suddenly. "When he heard that you weren't at Blytheswood, he sent one of his men to Rosscurrach to warn them of the escape. It may be where this cousin is."

"He said as much in front o' ye?" Tearlach asked with disbelief.

William shrugged. "He didn't mention who had escaped and since none of us knew he had the two of you, we didn't understand. Besides, lords tend to ignore servants for the most part and talk freely in front of us."

"Rosscurrach?" Lucy asked and then glanced to Tearlach. "That *must* be where they have your cousin. Why else send warning to them? If we hurry we can be there by tomorrow night."

Tearlach frowned. "We?"

Now Lucy was frowning as she met his gaze. "Aye. *We*. You can not free him on your own. You do not know how to unlock chains as I do. You need me."

He scowled. "What I *need* is to ken yer safe somewhere so I can concentrate on what needs doin' and not be frettin' o'er ye. And *you* need to get to court to tell the king the truth o' what happened so Carbonnel can no' abuse yer women or try to wed yer cousin Margaret and gain Blytheswood."

"'Tis mostly men and old women at Blytheswood now," Betty pointed out. "And they should be safe enough for the few days it would take to rescue your cousin. Then you could escort Lady Lucy safely to court and see Carbonnel cast out of Blytheswood."

"Aye." Lucy beamed at the maid for her aid and then added, "And Margaret is not a worry. She is not at Blytheswood to marry. In any case, he would not marry her until he found me and saw me dead."

Tearlach shifted on his feet. "I'd be feelin' better did ye stay here with William and his family, oot o' harm's way."

"William and his family are not staying here," she pointed out sharply, hurt at his effort to remove her from his side. "And rather than being safer, I shall surely just endanger them."

His shoulders dropped slightly and she knew she'd won. He would not leave her behind.

"Verra well, I cannae leave ye here, but 'tis findin' somewhere safe fer ye I'll be doin'. Yer no' goin' into Rosscurrach dungeons to get me cousin oot. *I'll* be doin' that."

"How?" she asked sharply. "You do not know how to work the locks."

"Ye shall show me," he said firmly as he turned and mounted Trinket. Once in the saddle, he glared down at her and then held out a hand. "Come."

Lucy rolled her eyes at his bossiness, but placed her hand in his and allowed him to help her back up into the saddle. This time he settled her sideways in his lap. He was acting so grumpy and impatient she expected him to set off as soon as she was settled, instead he paused and turned his attention to the family at the side of the path.

"I'll see Lucy is tae court by week's end. Dependin' on how quick yer king acts, Blytheswood should be free o' Carbonnel shortly after that. Keep yer ear to the ground fer news," he growled to William and his wife and then added, "safe travels."

"Aye." William nodded. "Safe travels to you too and good luck rescuing your cousin."

Tearlach nodded even as he urged Trinket to move. Lucy was forced back against his chest by the sudden action, then caught herself and sat up, leaning around his arm to wave to the family they were leaving behind, an action that nearly sent her sliding from the saddle.

Muttering something under his breath, Tearlach caught her with one hand and forced her back into place against his chest.

Lucy glanced up through her lashes at his expression. Seeing that it was stern and rather grumpy, she settled against him with a sigh and peered at the passing countryside, her mind working. She *did* wish to get to court and see Carbonnel ousted from her home, but it seemed to her that Tearlach's cousin's situation was more critical in importance. Her people were relatively safe for now, but Heming was being tortured and may die did they not find him and set him free.

And, Lucy was positive that Tearlach would need her help to accomplish that. It wasn't just the fact that she knew how to unlock chains. There was also the fact that Wymon had apparently sent warning on to Rosscurrach that Tearlach had escaped. Surely they would expect him to try to rescue his cousin and be watching for him? But they wouldn't be watching for a woman. Women were rarely thought capable of anything but breeding. No one at Rosscurrach would expect a woman to slip into the keep to find the dungeons and free Heming MacNachton. And that was what she'd come up with. It seemed a perfect plan to her, probably the best possible way to free the man, as well as the one carrying the least risk with it.

The more she thought on it, the more positive Lucy was that she was the better bet when it came to freeing Heming. However, knowing he would resist such a suggestion, she didn't mention it to Tearlach right away. He was a proud man and hadn't taken at all well to the fact that she'd had to help him escape Carbonnel. Lucy suspected he wouldn't take the suggestion of her saving his cousin any better. She needed to marshal a proper argument that would make him see sense.

Pride was a fine thing so long as it didn't make a fool of you and it was Lucy's considered opinion that if Tearlach didn't let her help, he would be acting the fool. And for naught. He was huge, strong, and really quite scary now that he was back to full health. He had no need to prove to her, or—she would think—anyone else, that he was strong, brave, and capable. The very fact that Carbonnel and the others had resorted to drugging him and his cousin told her that they hadn't thought they would win in a straight battle. He should have nothing to prove, but she suspected he would want to anyway.

Tearlach peered down at the woman in the saddle before him. She'd stayed awake most of the night chatting with him and telling him more tales of her youth, most of them focusing on her parents. However, she'd begun to doze off an hour ago. She was now sleeping in his arms, cradled against his chest, and he found himself scowling as his gaze slid over her. She was so small and defenseless. And he was apparently the only thing standing between her and Carbonnel at the moment. Her brother was dead, her home overrun by Carbonnel and his men, and he was now her only safe haven. Even as he'd suggested leaving her with William and his family, Tearlach had known he couldn't. The stableman couldn't have stood against Carbonnel's army should she have been found out and, despite the suggestion, he wouldn't have left her with him. Tearlach would not trust anyone with the chore of guarding her but himself . . . or perhaps one or two of his clan members. His people were faster and stronger and would fight to the death for her if necessary. As would he. The little slip of a woman had saved his life, freeing him from his chains and pretty much dragging him out of those dungeons. She was also smart, sweet, and spirited and he had no trouble with the idea of laying down his life for her.

He'd rather not, of course, but would if it became a necessity. Tearlach decided he would have to keep her with him until he could see Heming freed from Rosscurrach. Once that deed was accomplished, he would then escort her safely to court and then . . .

Tearlach frowned at the "and then" part. He supposed the "and then" *should* be that he and Heming would continue their information gathering for the clan, although they had most likely learned enough that that was no longer necessary. That being the case the "and then" should probably be that he gather with his clan members, decide what their next move should be, and help carry it out. Unfortunately, that left Lucy out and he found himself reluctant to leave her out of his future. He'd grown rather used to having her around and wasn't enjoying the prospect of the day when she would no longer be there.

Of course, he knew that day would come. Now that her brother was dead, she was the mistress of Blytheswood while he was the only child of Eva and Connall MacAdie and as such, heir to MacAdie castle with responsibilities there.

Despite these grim considerations, Tearlach found himself smiling faintly at the thought of his mother and father. A more unlikely pair you'd never imagine. His mother, Eva MacAdie, was fair and English, his father, Connall MacAdie, was dark and Scottish. She was a charming, cheerful birdlike woman, constantly bustling here and there. He was stern and solid and rarely seemed to smile except when in his wife's presence.

Rather like he and Lucy, Tearlach acknowledged to himself. Anyone meeting them would think they were opposites also and yet they worked well together.

Dangerous thoughts those, he acknowledged to himself. He and Lucy could not—

His thoughts scattered as Lucy murmured sleepily in

his arms and shifted to press her face into his chest. Tear-lach peered over her features soft in sleep, his sensible side suddenly going silent in the face of the rush of long-ing that rose up within him at the thought of waking every morning to have her cradled in his arms, her ex-pression that same sleepy contentment. The idea was not something he'd ever even thought he wanted, but it now lured him like a siren's song.

Sighing, he forced himself to look away. He lifted his gaze to the sky and his eyes narrowed. To someone who didn't live in perpetual night, it would probably look as if it were still pure night, but Tearlach lived in darkness. He knew it in all its nuances and knew that though it ap-peared to still be full night, dawn was coming. In fact, she would be streaking the sky with fingers of morning light right then if it weren't so overcast. Only the dense cloud cover kept it so dark.

His gaze dropped to their surroundings, searching for markers that would tell him how far they were from the cave and he relaxed as he spotted the shine of water ahead. They'd arrived at the riverside clearing where he'd planned for them to take shelter that evening. His eyes slid to the sky again, noting that it was just a bare shade lighter than it had been. By his guess they had just enough time to let Trinket drink water from the river and clean up a bit themselves before the sun burnt off a good portion of the cloud cover and they had to take cover in the shelter. At least *he* had to. Lucy had no need to hide from the sun; he on the other hand . . .

The steady roll of the moving horse had lulled Lucy to sleep. The end of that movement was what woke her.

Shifting sleepily, she lifted her head from Tearlach's chest and peered around with bleary eyes that suddenly cleared and widened when they fell on the river in front of which Tearlach had brought them to a halt.

"Where are we?" she asked, her eyes caught on the water's glistening surface. Dark as it was, the surface seemed to be catching what little light was available and reflecting it like a mirror.

"By a cave I ha'e used before. We can rest here fer the day and then continue on at nightfall."

Lucy nodded absently, but she hadn't really heard what he'd said, every iota of her attention was focused on the water before them. Between the filthy clothes they were wearing and all that they had endured the last several days, the idea of a bath was like the dream of a sweet to a starving person. She couldn't seem to even focus on anything else.

A soft breath on her ear and the contraction of his stomach at her back as he chuckled managed to distract her and bring her questioning glance up to his face.

"We ha'e a little time ere the sun rises fully, why do ye no' bathe in the river while I unsaddle Trinket?"

Lucy slid off the mare, a smile stretching her lips so wide it almost hurt. She could already feel the water washing away the filth coating her body.

Leaving Tearlach to tend the mare, she rushed to the river's edge and reached for the waist of her braies, and then paused to glance over her shoulder. Tearlach had dismounted and now stood with his back to her as he unsaddled Trinket. Not exactly proper, but he was offering her all the privacy he could under the circumstances.

Straightening her shoulders, Lucy turned back to the water and quickly pushed down the pants. The scrape of the material, stiff with filth from both herself and their previous owner made her grimace and pause again. Really, her tunic and braies needed cleaning as much as she did and it would be such a shame to bathe and then have to climb back into the filthy clothes. The very idea was really rather disgusting.

Lucy shifted from one foot to the other and then stepped out of the braies and snatched them up. Still wearing the tunic and jupon, she then marched into the river, gasping as the cool water closed around her feet, then her ankles, then her calves . . . She kept moving forward until she was in up to her waist, then pinched her nose closed with the finger and thumb of her free hand and submerged herself under the water.

Hoping that the full body dunking would help her adjust to the cold more quickly, Lucy stayed under until her lungs forced her back up. Eyes squinted shut and sputtering and gasping for air, she stood up abruptly in the water.

A curse made her blink her eyes open. They then widened as she found Tearlach before her in the water, still fully clothed.

"What's wrong?" she asked with concern as she noted the anger on his face.

Tearlach opened his mouth, closed it on whatever he'd been about to say, then tried again. "Ye disappeared," he pointed out shortly and when she simply stared back with confusion, added, "I heard ye splashin' and gaspin' about the water being cold and then silence. When I turned around ye were gone. I feared there may be a current here or someone or something had dragged ye under."

Lucy's eyes rounded with surprise as she realized he'd come charging into the water to save her. Her disappearance had given him a scare. She could still see the remnants of fear in his eyes, and he was panting slightly, his chest rising and falling rapidly from his rush to save her.

"You were worried about me," she whispered with amazement and saw annoyance flicker on his face.

"O' course I was worried about ye, ye daft woman," he snarled with irritation. His eyes, however, were speaking of other feelings. They had dropped away from her face, sliding down over her shoulders and chest with something like hunger.

Lucy glanced down, noting that the wet tunic she wore was now clinging to her curves, accentuating nipples that were erect from the cold. She felt a blush crest her face and instinctively raised her hands to cover them.

A low growl drew her head back up and Tearlach immediately covered her mouth with his. Lucy's lips parted on a gasp of surprise at the contact. That was all the encouragement Tearlach needed, in the next moment his arms were around her, drawing her through the water and against his damp tunic.

Startled, Lucy went stiff in his arms, but it was a very brief stiffening, then his tongue slid into her mouth and rasped against her own and she gave a surprised moan of pleasure.

Lucy had never been kissed. She had seen others kiss; servants she'd stumbled upon, her parents, and even her brother, John, with one of the maids once, but she'd never paid much attention to the actual mechanics of it, usually turning quickly away in embarrassment. She'd never realized that tongues were involved. Lucy had always thought it was just like the perfunctory pecks her mother had planted on her cheek at bedtime, only on the lips. She now saw how wrong she'd been. There was much more to this kissing business than she'd realized, at least there was with Tearlach. There was nothing quick or perfunctory about his kiss. It was slow and wet and deep and brought forth responses and sensations from her body that she'd never before experienced, sensations that left her feeling somewhat weak in the knees.

Lucy dropped the braies she'd been clutching, and caught anxiously at Tearlach's upper arms. At first it was to steady herself, but then she found that, rather than using the hold to help her stay upright in the water, she was slipping her fingers up around his neck and trying to press him closer. She wanted . . .

Lucy wasn't sure what exactly it was that she wanted. She just knew she wanted more, and she wanted him closer though they were already pressed as tightly together as they could get. Her breasts were actually being crushed against his chest, but rather than pain she was experiencing a tingling there that made her want to rub them more firmly against him.

As if reading her thoughts, Tearlach's hand suddenly slid between them and closed over one breast. Lucy groaned into his mouth and almost bit his tongue in reaction to the excitement sent spiraling through her. She then moaned as he tweaked at her erect nipple through the damp rough cloth of the tunic.

Shuddering as spasms of excitement shot all the way from her breast down to a spot between her legs, Lucy instinctively pressed herself against him there, but quickly drifted away again. Tearlach was taller than her and while he stood with his feet planted firmly on the river bed, he'd lifted her up out of the water a bit to kiss her. Her legs were ungrounded, floating freely in the water and not staying where she wanted.

Moaning her frustration, she wrapped her legs around

Tearlach's waist, then gasped in shocked pleasure as her naked core rubbed against a cloth-covered bulge in the front of his braies, increasing her excitement.

This time Tearlach also groaned. She felt his fingers convulse briefly on her breast, squeezing almost painfully, and then his other hand clasped her bottom. His fingers briefly froze on the naked flesh he found, and Lucy suddenly recalled that he'd had his back to her when she'd gone into the water. Apparently he'd assumed she'd gone in fully clothed. The fact that she hadn't seemed to be a pleasant surprise if she was correctly reading the growl that slid from his mouth into hers and the way his hand suddenly curved over the soft skin of her behind and squeezed even as he pressed her more tightly against the bulge in his braies.

When his hands left her moments later, Lucy clung to him feeling bereft, but then she felt the cloth of her tunic being tugged up her back. Breaking their kiss, Lucy released her hold on his neck and leaned away from him in the water, her arms rising to allow him to remove the garment.

Tearlach's eyes darkened as the tunic slid off over her head, baring her breasts to his view. He was suddenly so absorbed, he didn't even look away as he tossed the soaking cloth toward shore, but threw it blindly. Despite that, the tunic landed on shore with a splat, she noted.

"Where are yer bottoms, lass? I didnae see them on shore ere I came in after ye."

"I am not sure. I had them in my hand a minute ago, but I think I dropped them," Lucy admitted breathlessly, but wasn't feeling much concern over the item at the moment.

Tearlach still had enough sense to consider them an

important matter. Urging her back to his chest, he peered around, and then lunged slightly to the side to snatch the floating braies out of the water when he spotted them. They followed the tunic to shore, landing very near the tunic, but Lucy hardly made note of the fact. The moment they left his hand, Tearlach had turned his attention back to her breasts and her mind was fully taken up with her shock, awe, and pleasure as he lifted her slightly in the water to fasten his mouth on one erect nipple. His mouth was like the flame from a fire compared to the chill of the water and Lucy clutched at his shoulders with her fingers and tightened her legs around his hips as she shivered and shuddered against him.

The action brought Tearlach's hands down to her bottom again. This time he used both of them to urge her more tightly against his bulge, almost seeming to encourage her to ride it. Finding all of it together somewhat overwhelming, Lucy cried out and tugged at his hair, murmuring incoherent pleas for him to kiss her.

Tearlach obeyed at once, lifting his lips to claim hers in a kiss. She'd hoped it would help ease some of the tension clambering inside of her, however, this combination was just as overwhelming. Now she was being assaulted by the feel of his rough tunic brushing across her breasts, his hands urging her against his hips, and his mouth on hers, his tongue thrusting hungrily and deeply until Lucy sobbed into his mouth with need. She didn't try to break the contact, but couldn't have in any case since one of his hands had left her bottom to clasp the back of her head to tilt her face to a more satisfactory position.

Distracted as she was by all the sensations he was stirring in her, Lucy wasn't aware that he'd carried her out of the water until she felt the ground press against her back.

Shivering as the dew-covered grass cushioned her, she let her feet unhook and drop to the ground as he settled on top of her, then immediately began tugging at his tunic, eager to remove it as a barrier between them. Unfortunately it had been a bit snug to begin with and—now wet—was impossible for her to remove unaided.

Tearlach broke their kiss long enough to rise up on his knees and drag off the clinging cloth. He tossed it aside with little care or concern and lowered himself over her again, but did not return to kissing her. Instead, his attention moved lower and he pressed kisses along her collarbone before dipping to latch onto one breast again.

Lucy groaned and caught her hands in his hair, writhing under the caress as she felt his hand begin to slide up her inner thigh.

"Tearlach?" she whispered uncertainly. He immediately slid up her body, claiming her mouth once more in an almost soothing kiss. His hand, however, continued to slide gently up and down her thigh, raising goose bumps and stringing out her tension as it neared the top, then bringing about a confused disappointment and restlessness as it drifted away.

Much to Lucy's surprise, the action soon brought a low growl of frustration from her and she was the one to deepen the kiss and thrust her hips upward in demand as his fingers slid up her thigh once more. Despite that, she cried out in startled surprise when his fingers finally continued their upward journey until they found her core. Her body shook as a whole new, much more intense set of sensations exploded inside her.

Sobbing his name, Lucy pulled on his hair and kissed him frantically as he began to stoke a fire like none she'd ever experienced. Her body seemed to be aflame, every inch of skin suddenly burning for him. She wanted to be touched and kissed everywhere and wanted to touch and kiss him everywhere too, but couldn't seem to figure out how to do that without his stopping what he was doing. Lucy did the best she could, however, running her hands over his naked back and arms, then up into his hair again. She kissed him with all the passion he was eliciting until she almost couldn't bear it anymore, then she pulled her mouth free and began to press kisses to his face and forehead.

The moment Lucy broke their kiss she lost him. Tearlach immediately began to snake his way down her body, stopping here to nip and suckle, and there to lick and kiss. His mouth traveled over her collarbone, to each breast, down her stomach, to one hip, and then suddenly it was replacing his hand between her legs. Her eyes immediately shot open and she cried out loud enough to send birds flying from their nests as she bucked into the caress.

Tearlach merely caught her thighs to hold her in place as he ministered to her, driving her into a frenzy of need and want. Just when she was certain the overwhelming sensation and excitement would surely kill her, it suddenly exploded, wrenching a full scream from her throat as her body convulsed with spasm after spasm of a pleasure as hot and bright as the sun overhead.

That thought knifed through Lucy's pleasure like a hot blade through freshly churned butter. As hot and bright as the sun overhead? Dear God, the sun was up!

It was now high in the sky and burning its way through the last bit of cloud cover that had hidden it. Lucy could feel its warmth, see its brightness, and taste the fear for Tearlach that suddenly filled her . . . and then he was shifting above her, blocking the sky from her view. Feeling something nudge her between the legs, she lifted her head to peer the length of their bodies. Her eyes widened as she saw that he'd shed his braies and was preparing to mount her. Moments ago she would have welcomed him, but that was before she'd realized that they'd taken too long and the sun had snuck up on them. He couldn't. They couldn't. He had to take cover.

Before Lucy could speak, his mouth covered hers. She nearly sank under the pleasure reawakened in her as his tongue burst through her lips even as his hardness again brushed against her still tingling skin.

"Nay," she groaned into his mouth, but her hands started to slide up his arms. Surely a few moments would not kill him? Surely just this once . . . ?

While Tearlach had spoken of his family and home, they'd not spoken much on his being a vampire, or what his kind could and could not do. For some reason they'd avoided the topic since Wymon had made known the fact Tearlach was one. But she had never yet seen Tearlach in daylight. He always insisted they keep to caves and other shelters in the day, traveling only at night despite the urgent need to get to his cousin.

Lucy had heard many tales and rumors about his kind and the sun. They were said to abhor daylight. It was said they could not bear sunlight, and even that it could kill them.

She blinked her eyes open and peered down his naked back as her hands slid over it, and immediately moaned in horror. His flesh was turning bright red. It looked like a sunburn, but was happening much too quickly.

Just as Tearlach started to push his way into her, Lucy broke their kiss and shoved with all her might. "Nay, Tearlach! The sun."

She suspected it was more her words than her own puny efforts that made him stop. Stiffening, he suddenly pulled back and glanced skyward. Lucy saw the fear and realization slide over his face, followed by pain, and wondered if he'd really been so distracted he hadn't noticed it ere this, or if it had only just set in.

Tearlach's eyes shot back to her, sharp and piercing, and then he began to move. He levered himself off her, stood, and then caught her arm to help her to her feet, but Lucy's legs were still weak and trembling from the pleasure he'd given her. She wasn't at all sure they would carry her to the cave just then. Even if they did, she knew it wouldn't be quickly. She would simply slow him down.

"Go. I shall follow with our clothes and Trinket," she said, sitting up.

Tearlach hesitated, but really had no choice. Giving a quick nod, he turned and hurried across the clearing to disappear through a pair of bushes. Lucy watched, making note of the spot, knowing it must be the entrance to the cave, then drew her legs against her chest, resting her head briefly on her knees as she waited to recover enough to be able to follow.

Six

"Rosscurrach?"

The whispered question drew Tearlach's gaze away from the dark outline of the castle in the distance and down to the woman cradled in his arms. He'd thought she was still sleeping. Lucy had slept through most of this last night of their journey.

Much to his relief.

Unfortunately, Tearlach found her presence and nearness trying since that episode in the clearing the night before. The memories of her feel and taste and her little gasps and moans of pleasure—not to mention her outright shouts—had driven him wild all through their ride that night. It had been hardest when she was awake and shifting restlessly about in his lap, her bottom unintentionally rubbing against him as her soft voice caressed his ears. But it hadn't been much better when she was asleep, curled cozily against his chest.

Tearlach had spent most of that night fighting to keep himself from slipping his hands around her waist and up to cup her soft full breasts, or dip into the braies she wore to find her warm, damp core. While he'd managed to control his hands and make them behave, his mind had run rampant. In his imagination he'd done all of that and more at least twenty times that evening. He'd even found himself imagining stopping the horse, taking her to the ground beside it, and claiming her in all ways, even marking her with his bite and mating with her as his people did.

That's when Tearlach had realized just how much trouble he was in. He had liked the woman from the start, wanted her just as long, but had become more enthralled by her with every passing moment they'd spent together. He was already so attached he found it difficult thinking of the time when he would have to leave her behind, and though he wouldn't even think the word in his mind, he feared what he was experiencing for the woman was love.

Tearlach had spent what little time he hadn't been ravishing her in his thoughts, struggling with what to do about his feelings for her. If it had just been a matter of liking and wanting her, there wouldn't have been a problem. He would have taken her in the cave when she'd finally come in from the clearing and cuddled up next to him . . . but it *was* more than that. Caring for her as he did, Tearlach was reluctant to claim her when doing so would be so dangerous for her. How could he drag her into the battle now raging around his family? It was just small skirmishes so far, the kidnapping of himself and his cousin and various other attacks, but he feared soon it would be all-out war. Their enemies would try to wipe out his clan out of fear. Tearlach wouldn't claim Lucy simply to see her die. She would be better off without him, meeting and falling in love with a normal mortal man and living a peace-filled life.

That had been his decision on the matter. So, he had managed to keep from touching and kissing her anywhere but in his own mind. But it had been damned trying and made him irritable and short tempered. He feared he may have hurt her tender feelings a time or two with his snappishness and attempts to keep her at a distance as much as possible, and while he regretted that, it was probably for the best, too.

"Tearlach?"

He glanced down as she twisted in the saddle to peer at him, and—dark as it was—he could see her scowl at his inattention.

"Is that Rosscurrach?" she asked, gesturing toward the distant castle.

"Aye." He turned the horse to the west and set it moving again. "'Tis too late to do aught tonight. We'll take shelter until dusk. Then ye can explain how I can be unlocking his chains and I'll go find me cousin."

Much to his relief, she didn't argue the point, but simply leaned back against him. Tearlach urged the horse in the direction of the old abandoned bothy he knew was nearby.

Lucy woke abruptly, her eyes opening on the dark outline of the man curled beside her in the small space. Tearlach was sound asleep if she were to judge by his breathing. However, while she wasn't sure how long she'd slept since their arrival, she'd slept through most of their journey that night and was now wide awake. She was not going to sleep anymore.

Sighing, she turned onto her back and peered up at the splinters of light creeping in from overhead. There wasn't much, not enough to harm Tearlach, or even light up the area much more than to make his outline visible, but she was grateful for what little bit of light managed to make its way through the cracks in the wooden trapdoor above.

Lucy didn't like it here. The caves had been one thing, but this small six foot by six foot cell carved out of the dirt beneath the bothy was awful. She felt like she was in a dirt-lined coffin.

Grimacing at the thought, Lucy sat up on the hard packed dirt and moved to lean against the wall, hoping the change of position would make her feel less claustrophobic. It didn't help much and she stayed there for only a few moments before getting to her feet. Moving as silently as she could, she stepped around Tearlach to the rickety ladder that leaned against the wall by the trapdoor. While Lucy already knew Tearlach was a heavy sleeper, she had no interest in learning just *how* deep a sleeper he was by waking him.

Movements slow and cautious, she climbed up the ladder until her head bumped lightly against the wooden covering above. Lucy then reached up and pressed lightly on the closed trapdoor. It immediately started to lift under the gentle pressure and she continued upward, until she could crawl out into the small stone building atop the hole in the ground. She then eased the rickety trapdoor back into place and sat back to peer about.

Dawn had been streaking the sky by the time they'd reached the bothy, but it had still been dark enough that she hadn't been able to make out much when they'd entered the small stone hut the night before. Tearlach had left her on Trinket's back as he'd led the mare inside, then had been forced to lead her down the ladder into the hole as if she were blind. Now she reached out and ran a hand over Trinket's leg as she peered about the shelter.

With daylight creeping through the door, she could see that it was small and appeared very old. She thought it must be a hut shepherds had once slept in while watching over their sheep, but doubted it had been used for much of late. It certainly showed no signs of recent habitation.

Tearlach had told her as he'd led her down the ladder that one of his people had dug the pit where he presently slept beneath this bothy. Apparently there were no caves in the area where they might take cover and in such areas his people had made their own provisions for rest stops while traveling.

It suddenly occurred to Lucy that while his people were said to be stronger and faster and fearsome in battle, they were really more fragile than non-vampires in some ways, at least in their need to avoid sunlight. Though, when she'd asked him about the effect of sunlight on his kind during the first part of that night's ride, he'd said some of his kind *could* stand the sun. However, it hadn't sounded like many could, or for long. He had also mentioned that there were mortals among their clan to guard them during daylight.

Trinket shifted restlessly and eased a little closer to her, seeming to want attention. Lucy ran her hand affectionately over the beast again, then got to her feet and moved to the hole where at one time there would have been a door. She stood slightly to the side of the entrance to peer out at the grassy hill and be sure there was no one around, and then eased forward to stand in the sun.

Breathing deeply of the fresh air, Lucy peered over the area, but was unable to see the river she was sure they'd traveled past shortly before arriving here. That was probably for the best, she supposed. Tearlach would no doubt be furious if he woke to find she'd slipped out to bathe. The man had been testy and cranky since the incident in the clearing.

Lucy bit her lip and peered back toward the trapdoor. Tearlach's behavior since those heated moments in the clearing was causing her both confusion and hurt. While he'd been passionate and loving in the clearing, in the few short minutes it had taken her to join him, he'd seemed to have done an abrupt about-face.

Tearlach hadn't said a word on her entering other than to give a grunt to help her find him in the dark when she'd whispered his name. And while he'd reached out and pulled her down against his chest to sleep for the day, he hadn't continued with what they'd started in the clearing, or even given her a peck on the cheek to wish her good night, he'd simply pressed her head to his chest and muttered, "Sleep."

Thinking that he may be sore from the burn the sun had given him, Lucy hadn't worried too much at that point, but she had when his gruff and surly behavior had continued the next night when they'd broken camp. It would have been hard to miss the fact that he was suddenly touching her as little as possible, and went as stiff as a board in the saddle when she brushed against him. He also hadn't offered her a kiss, or even a reassuring touch since then. Worse still, the long intimate talks they'd previously shared in the dungeon and on their journey here had died out completely. He hadn't spoken at all except in response to her questions and then his answers had been mostly grunts or short, surly replies that had not encouraged conversation. Lucy had gotten the message and given up trying to talk to him.

She didn't understand what had caused this sudden change in him, but feared perhaps her wanton behavior had turned him from her. Perhaps he had decided she was not worth his trouble. For her, that idea had turned what had been a beautiful and exciting experience into a cheap, dirty encounter that made her cringe with shame.

Unfortunately, even her shame didn't stop Lucy from wanting to repeat the experience. She still yearned for his kisses, her very flesh aching for his touch and that had made the ride torment. She'd suffered his body behind her, his smell enveloping her, his breath on the back of her neck and her ear, and had craved a repeat of the experience. It had been unbearable, untenable, and had made her incredibly tense and unhappy until she felt emotionally drained and had fallen asleep before him.

Fortunately, their arrival at Rosscurrach meant she could avoid another night of such hellish tension . . . at least until they freed his cousin, Heming, and fled the area. Perhaps even then she might be able to avoid it since there were now three of them and they would need another horse. If Heming was in a bad way as Tearlach had been the night they'd escaped, he would be unable to ride alone and Tearlach would have to ride with him, leaving her free of being so close yet unable to touch him.

Shifting restlessly, Lucy glanced back toward the trapdoor again, wanting to return to the hole to cuddle up next to him and just listen to him breathe. A yearning filled her at the idea, but she forced herself impatiently back to peer out of the hut. The hillside looked the same as it had the last time she'd looked and the same way it would the next time, she was sure. She was going to drive herself mad bouncing her gaze between the trapdoor and the empty hillside. She needed to get out. To do something.

Raising her head rebelliously, Lucy moved out of the hut and started down the slope toward the woods below. She would go for a walk to help pass the time. She would search for the river, perhaps take a swim, and hopefully find some berries to eat along the way. It was better than standing there in the hut, yearning for someone who so obviously did not want her in return.

Pausing at the edge of the woods, Lucy turned in a slow circle until her gaze found the distant Rosscurrach castle. She stared silently at the imposing structure where Tearlach's cousin was being held prisoner.

Once they had rescued Heming, Tearlach intended to see her to court to have the king tend to Carbonnel. No doubt he would leave her then and she could stop twisting herself up over a man who so obviously didn't care for her. Mind you, that was only if they managed to save Heming and Tearlach didn't allow his foolish pride to get himself recaptured.

Grimacing to herself, Lucy turned and continued into the woods. Her eyes were automatically scanning the area for edible berries or something else that might ease her empty stomach, but her thoughts were on her fears for Tearlach. He seemed to think that she could describe how to unlock the chains and he would march merrily into Rosscurrach and be able to do it.

Foolish man. He probably wouldn't even make it to

the dungeons or wherever it was that they were holding Heming. While Tearlach was wearing Carbonnel colors, he spoke with a Scottish burr. She was sure he wouldn't even make it past the gate. She on the other hand . . .

Lucy bit her lip and raised her head, peering through the trees toward the castle again.

So long as she didn't speak and give away her English accent, everyone would just assume she was a maid. A big strong man might be noticed no matter the garb he wore, but a puny woman wouldn't draw more than a passing glance. As such, she could probably slip into the castle and have Heming out and back to the cave before Tearlach woke up.

Well, Lucy acknowledged, at least not long after that. Heming was probably no more capable of going about in daylight than Tearlach was and they would have to wait until night fell before attempting an escape. At any rate, she could have him back here shortly after sunset. Shortly enough that she felt sure Tearlach would still be in the hut, probably cursing her for disappearing.

Her thoughts and footsteps halted as she became aware of the distant sound of someone singing. The voice was a woman's, high and clear, and she wondered suddenly just how close the bothy was to the village. The castle had looked a good distance off, perhaps an hour's walk, but the village may have been nearer.

Tilting her head, Lucy turned slowly until she located where the song was coming from, then moved cautiously in that direction. A few moments later she was peering over a bush at a small clearing by the river she'd been looking for in the hopes of bathing. It appeared she would not be doing so today; the water was already occupied. A woman stood, naked and hip deep in the water, singing as she bathed.

Sighing with disappointment, Lucy had started to back away from the bush when her gaze suddenly landed on the gown lying on the ground near the water's edge. She stared at that dress for a very long time as she realized the one thing she'd not taken into consideration. She was not dressed as a woman, but wore the clothing of a Carbonnel soldier and that was one thing sure to draw attention her way.

While Lucy knew Rosscurrach and Carbonnel were in league together, she doubted very much if Carbonnel men were wandering freely around Rosscurrach bailey or castle. However, in a gown such as the one laying just a few feet away, she would definitely be able to slip into the castle unnoticed.

Hoping that God would take her need into consideration and forgive her for stealing the dress, Lucy began to make her way around the clearing to the spot closest to where it lay discarded.

She'd reached the point closest to the gown and was trying to decide whether to crawl out on her hands and knees to collect it or risk running out to snatch it up when the singing suddenly stopped. Lucy froze and glanced anxiously toward the water, afraid she'd been spotted, but relaxed when she saw that the other woman was now missing, only a growing, round ripple marking the surface of the river where she'd been a moment ago. The music had stopped because the woman had submerged herself in the water.

Taking the opportunity presented, Lucy rushed out of the trees, nearly tripping over her own feet in her hurry.

Reaching the dress, she bent to snatch it up and then bolted back into the woods. Lucy ducked behind the first tree large enough to hide her, heart racing as she peered back to the river. The swimmer had resurfaced and was pushing her wet hair back from her face.

When the woman burst back into song, Lucy relaxed, knowing that neither her foray, nor the fact that the dress was missing, had been noticed . . . yet. Fingers tightening around the dress, Lucy turned and slipped back through the woods to the bothy.

Trinket was sleeping where she'd left her, as was Tearlach, she saw after a quick peek down into the pit. Leaving them to it, she quickly shed the Carbonnel clothes and drew on the dress instead. It was a tad long, and a little loose on her, but would do if she caught up the skirt a bit.

Satisfied that she would pass for a servant, Lucy glanced toward the trapdoor, wishing she had some parchment and a quill to leave a note for Tearlach. Unfortunately, she didn't have anything of the sort so would have to hope that when he awoke and found her gone, he would wait here until she returned. The fact that Trinket was still here surely would tell him that she was returning.

Sighing, Lucy headed for the door, determined to carry out her plan. The only alternative was to wait for Tearlach to wake up and try to convince him to let her go into Rosscurrach after Heming. She already knew he would never agree to that and she herself wasn't willing to let him walk in there after his cousin alone. Lucy really felt she had a better chance to get the other man out than Tearlach did. Her plan was a good one, and much more sensible than his.

Mind you, that didn't mean she really wanted to walk

into enemy camp to rescue Heming. In truth, she'd rather neither of them had to go in there, but they could hardly leave his cousin at Rosscurrach to be tortured to death.

Her worries turning to what shape Heming would be in when she found him and the difficulties she might face getting him out, Lucy slipped out of the bothy and headed toward the castle. Such issues were forgotten, however, when her gaze moved absently skyward and she noted that the sun was well into its downward journey.

She'd thought it was late morning when she'd first left the shepherd's bothy. Apparently she'd been off by a bit. She'd slept much longer in the pit than she'd thought. Either that or she'd spent more time than she'd realized seated on the dirt floor of the bothy contemplating her relationship, or lack thereof, with Tearlach. It looked to be moving from afternoon toward evening. The sun would probably last only a couple more hours. Lucy frowned as she did some calculation. One hour to get her to the castle, then however much time it took her to get Heming out, and an hour back . . .

She'd have to be quick at the getting-him-free part, Lucy decided grimly. She wasn't at all sure she would be able to find the bothy again in the dark.

Lucy continued on the way she'd been going, keeping to a quick clip in an effort to make the best use of the sunlight she had, but her mind was on ways she could make her return journey easier should it end up being made in the dark. None of the ideas she was coming up with were very viable. She had nothing with which to leave a trail to follow back, no torch she could use to light the way, though she would probably have her hands full with Heming anyway if he was weak and injured.

Once again paying more attention to her thoughts than

her surroundings, Lucy nearly marched herself into the hands of the enemy. This time it was a burst of laughter that drew her attention back to her whereabouts. She immediately stiffened where she stood, freezing like a doe before the unexpected appearance of a rider or carriage.

When the laughter was not followed by the sudden appearance of riders coming from the trees ahead, she eased to the side of the path and strained her ears, listening for further sounds. At first, all she could hear was the rapid beating of her heart, but then that steadied and seemed to recede some and she caught the faint sound of male voices. It was coming from ahead and a little to the right of where she stood.

After a moment of indecision, Lucy began to move cautiously forward. Part of her was urging her to hurry on her way and avoid the men altogether. But another part was insisting it was better to know what sort of situation she was facing. She needed to know how many there were and whether they were traveling on foot or riding horseback. It would also be good to know if they had stopped to rest, or were heading in the same direction as she and likely to stumble on her further along the trail if she was not careful.

All of these worries circling in her mind, Lucy moved as quietly as she could until she glimpsed them through the trees ahead. Positioning herself behind the largest tree she could find, Lucy spied on them.

Much to her relief there appeared to be only two men. Both wore Scottish dress and were seated in the grass, taking their leisure. When several moments had passed with no one else appearing to add to their number, Lucy eased back behind the tree and concentrated on trying to hear what they were saying. Unfortunately, she had stopped far enough away that their conversation was all rather muffled, a jumbled rise and fall of sound.

Lucy was about to give up on listening when she thought she caught the name MacNachton. Letting her breath out on a small sigh, she decided she'd have to get closer. Rather than doing so upright and risking being spotted, she dropped to her hands and knees and began to crawl out from behind the tree, hoping the sparse foliage would hide her as she made her way to the next nearest tree.

The ground was littered with broken branches and leaves shaken free of the trees in a recent storm, making the journey somewhat awkward. The dress she now wore did not help. She kept getting caught up on it as she went. It was a relief when she stood up four trees later and found she was mostly able to hear and understand what was being said by the two men seated in the clearing ahead.

"I'm thinkin' this search is a waste o' time. He's most like met up with his cousin and fled home by now," one of the men said.

Lucy's eyebrows drew together at these words, wondering if they were talking about Tearlach. How could he have met up with his cousin, Heming, when they were holding him prisoner here at Rosscurrach? Were the men talking about his meeting up with another cousin? Or perhaps they were talking about his cousin, Heming, instead. Mayhap he too had managed an escape and it was he they were searching for.

"Nay," the second man's voice drew her attention back to the conversation. "The MacNachton was in a bad way. He couldnae ha'e gone far. Even did he meet up with his cousin they ha'e to be holed up near here somewhere, waitin' fer him to heal."

It *was* Heming they were talking about, Lucy realized

with a burst of excitement and then frowned, not at all sure if she should be happy or not. She was glad the man was free and—at least for the moment—safe from the clutches of Rosscurrach, but really, they had traveled all this way, risking capture and their very lives to save him, for naught. That was rather annoying.

A dry laugh drew her from her thoughts again as the first man said, "That's right, ye werenae there when they worked on him, were ye? Ye doonna ken what happened." He shook his head and then said, "He shouldnae ha'e survived what they did to him. No mortal man would . . . and the speed with which he healed . . . He and his people truly must be devil spawn." He spat on the ground and then added, "Nay. He's recovered and long gone."

Deciding she'd heard enough, Lucy was about to return to her hands and knees to crawl back the way she'd come when the snap of a branch to her right made her stiffen and glance that way. Her eyes widened in alarm as she realized she wasn't alone.

Looking just as startled and frozen as Lucy herself, a woman stared back. She was naked as the day she'd been born, with damp strands of long red hair barely covering her pendulous breasts. Her only other cover was a leafy branch she'd snapped off some bush and now held in front of her groin. Despite that, it wasn't until the woman scowled and snapped, "Hey! That's me dress!" that Lucy realized she was the bather from earlier.

Lucy shushed the woman, trying to warn her to silence, then leaned back to peer toward the men she'd been listening to. Her eyes widened in alarm as she noted that they were both now standing and peering in her direction.

"Doona be shushing me, ye thief. That's me dress yer wearin' and I'm wantin' it back."

Lucy tore her gaze away from the two men and back to the woman, her alarm increasing as the woman tossed her branch aside and charged forward, apparently determined to get the dress back using physical force if necessary.

Panic rising in her as she realized that not only had she the woman to contend with, but the men were now heading in her direction as well, Lucy cursed under her breath and made a run for it.

Seven

"Leave off, Hamish. 'Tis women's business!"

Lucy heard one of the men call out that laughing comment as she ran and for one moment hoped all would be well . . . until she heard the other man answer, "Nay! 'Tis *her!*"

The second voice sounded much closer, almost on her heels from what she could tell and didn't encourage optimism. She took a moment to wonder who the "her" was he spoke of. Had he recognized her? And if so, from where? The only thing Lucy could think was that the soldier was one of the Scots who had been at the inn on the day of the murder/kidnapping.

She let the matter drop from her consideration then, concentrating instead on avoiding branches and ruts in her path that might see her taking a spill and getting caught. Lucy didn't even dare to glance over her shoulder to see if the woman was still giving chase too or how close her pursuer or pursuers were. She put all her effort into running, and in truth, didn't think she'd ever run so fast in her life. Her feet were barely touching the ground before she lifted them for the next step. It felt almost as if she were flying.

And yet the soldier was keeping up with her, Lucy thought with dismay moments later. While the sounds behind her had halved, suggesting that one of her pursuers had given up the chase, a deep-voiced curse told her that it hadn't been the soldier who had given her up. She considered this most unfortunate. Of the two of them, she'd rather deal with the woman.

All was not lost, Lucy assured herself, trying to rally when she felt her energy flagging. She just needed to get back to the bothy and Tearlach would help her deal with the man.

Lucy kept repeating that refrain to herself until she suddenly broke out of the trees and found herself sprinting up the short hill toward the bothy. Her heart leapt with glee and for one brief, relief-filled moment she was sure she would reach the stone hut and Tearlach and be saved. But in the next second, just a few short feet from the door, something slammed into her back, knocking the wind from her lungs and sending her slamming to the ground.

Completely out of breath, Lucy lay where she was for a moment, trying to suck air back into her collapsed lungs. Fortunately, the chase had apparently winded her pursuer as well, for he lay panting heavily across her lower legs where he'd landed.

He was the first to recover. Shifting off her legs, he

dragged himself to his feet, and then bent to catch her by the arm to turn her onto her back. He then paused to take a good look at her face.

"Lady Blytheswood." The words were more satisfied confirmation than a greeting.

Lucy glared back at the man, wanting to kick him in the shins and claw his face, but her limbs were trembling from her efforts at escape and she simply didn't have the energy. Instead, she opened her mouth and shrieked long and loud.

She knew Tearlach was a very sound sleeper, and really had no hope that he'd hear her and wake, but was so exhausted and defeated there seemed little else to do. However, the action just seemed to anger the man standing over her. He winced as the sound assaulted his ears, then cursed, and dragged her to her feet.

When she immediately found some reserves of strength and began to struggle, the man slapped her hard enough across the face to send her back to her knees. "Ye've two choices, lass," he snapped. "Ye walk back under yer own power, or I carry ye back unconscious over me shoulder. Either way, ye *are* going back with me."

They were the last words he spoke. In the next moment Tearlach charged out of the bothy, sword in hand and a furious growl on his lips. Lucy immediately found herself falling to the side as she was released, and instinctively rolled further out of the way as the soldier drew his sword. The sound of metal clashing against metal made her glance back as her roll came to an end. The men were battling in earnest. Lucy got swiftly to her feet, half her attention on the battle now taking place, the other half searching the ground nearby for a boulder or something else to use against the soldier.

It wasn't that she did not think Tearlach could beat the man, but the sun was full out and she feared his strength would not last long. Lucy could see the red rising on his face already and knew the damage the sun was doing would quickly sap his strength. All she could think was the sooner they took care of the soldier and got Tearlach back out of the sun, the better.

Lucy had just spotted a good-sized rock and moved to collect it when a death cry brought her head around. She sagged with relief on seeing the soldier impaled on Tearlach's sword. All three of them stood still for a moment, and then Tearlach withdrew his sword. The other man immediately dropped, a marionette with his strings cut.

Forgetting the rock, Lucy hurried forward as Tearlach stumbled back a step and dropped to his knees. He may have won the battle, but the sun had taken its toll. She had to get him out of the sun at once, she realized, slipping silently under his arm to force him back to his feet.

"Inside," Lucy gasped urgently as she managed to wrest him upright. Tearlach didn't waste energy speaking, but merely stumbled forward with her help and back toward the bothy. The sword he still clutched dragged on the ground beside him.

Once inside, Lucy tried to steer him toward the open trapdoor, but Tearlach's strength gave out before she could get him there. Unable to hold him upright, she cried out with alarm as he dropped his sword and stumbled to his knees, then fell on his face.

Lucy could have wept, in fact, her eyes did well up with hopelessness as she peered toward the trapdoor and took in the distance to it. Then she forced herself to rally and glanced around the shed. The amount of light coming through the hole where a door should be didn't reach far into the stone hut. The back of the bothy was a hive of shadow, as was one side. The shadows along the side wall weren't as deep as the ones at the back, but they were closer.

Lucy caught Trinket's reins and moved the horse the few steps to the other side of the hut to make room, then dropped to kneel beside Tearlach and put all her effort into rolling him out of the light and against the wall. It was certainly easier than dragging him to the trapdoor and pushing him in would have been, but she was exhausted from the chase and it was still a lot of work. Only once she had him on his side and pressed up against the wall in the thin band of shadow did she pause to examine the damage he'd taken.

The soldier hadn't managed to land a single blow, but Tearlach was in a serious way. All Lucy could see was the exposed skin of his face and hands, but it was more than enough. The breath hissed out of her as she took in his raw red blistered skin.

The last time he'd been exposed to the sun it had seemed to barely bother him, but then it had been the pale light of dawn, further weakened by cloud cover. This time it was full light out with not a cloud to give relief, and the exposure had been longer. Tearlach was in a bad way.

His eyes opened suddenly.

"How can I help?" Lucy asked anxiously as she saw the agony in the black depths of his eyes.

"Blood," Tearlach growled and for a moment she thought he meant her own, but then he added, "find me someone."

Lucy didn't even think, she simply got quickly to her feet and scrambled back out into the clearing to the fallen man. Kneeling by his head, she caught him under the shoulders and grunted as she heaved backward, dragging him toward the door. The man didn't make a move or sound that suggested he was alive, but then she hadn't expected it. Having seen the wound he'd taken, she knew it was a killing blow, and had no compunction at all about letting Tearlach feed on him.

Getting him inside and to Tearlach was the problem. He wasn't as big as Tearlach and seemed almost light in comparison, but she had much further to move him. Determination was the only thing that allowed Lucy to get him to the door of the hut. She'd managed to get him halfway through the door when a sound from Tearlach made her peer his way. Seeing that his eyes were open and he was trying to say something, she released the soldier and moved quickly to his side.

"What is it?" she asked anxiously.

"Dead?" he asked breathlessly, his gaze sliding back to the man by the door.

"Aye," Lucy admitted, frowning when he immediately shook his head.

"No good . . . Blood o' the dead . . . poison to us."

Lucy sagged where she sat, her exhaustion crowding in and making her feel hopeless, then she forced herself to sit upright and held her arm out toward him. Only he wasn't aware of the gesture, his eyes had closed.

"Tearlach," she whispered, reaching to touch his face, only to change her mind at the last minute and settle it on his arm rather than risk causing him pain by touching his damaged face.

Much to her relief, his eyes opened at once and Lucy forced a smile and held her arm out so that her wrist was before his mouth. "Go ahead. Feed."

Tearlach merely closed his eyes with the slightest

shake of the head. "Leave me. Others will search fer 'im. Ye ha'e tae get away."

Lucy didn't need to ask who the "him" was he spoke of, but his words reminded her of the man's comrade in the woods. He was probably still there . . . healthy and with living blood.

"Tearlach?" she whispered, touching his shoulder again, but this time he didn't stir, let alone open his eyes. He was unconscious. Despite that, Lucy squeezed his shoulder and whispered, "I'll not leave you. I shall find someone for you to feed on. All will be well."

She waited a moment to see if he would respond, but he was fully unconscious now. Concern clouding her eyes, Lucy stood and turned away, picking up the sword he'd dropped as she went. She didn't have the energy to drag anyone anywhere, the weapon would come in handy to force her quarry to come back here with her to the bothy.

If she was still around the woman would be the easier target, Lucy thought, and suspected her nakedness would make sure she was still in the woods somewhere. She was probably out there stumbling around, trying to find the thief who had stolen her dress. Once Tearlach had fed on her, he should have the strength to go out and find the other soldier himself. Lucy was too weary to manage the man, though she'd try if necessary.

Her own thoughts made Lucy pause as she realized how far she had sunk. She'd stolen a dress, fed a youth to Tearlach the other night, and now planned to find and feed a woman to him too. Surely she was going to hell.

Nay, her mind argued at once. She had stolen the dress out of necessity. Besides she could give it back after Tearlach had fed on the woman. As for feeding him the youth and now this woman . . . well he had fed from Lucy herself and it had done her no harm that she could see. She was alive and well, her soul still intact as far as she could tell. As were all the others he'd fed on. The only person who had been killed was the man now blocking the doorway of the bothy and he'd died from a sword through the chest in a fair battle after trying to force her to go with him.

Speaking of the man in the doorway, she suddenly realized she would have to move him. She could hardly leave him there to draw the attention of anyone passing. The very idea of the effort needed for the task was enough to make Lucy sag where she stood. She was so tired.

Suddenly overwhelmed by it all, Lucy paused and rested the tip of the sword in the dirt, then lowered her head and wearily closed her eyes. Just a moment, she told herself. She would rest for just one moment and then go in search of the woman.

"You bitch."

That soft hiss brought her head up with a start. Lucy stared wide-eyed at the man now standing in the bothy doorway. The sun was behind him, casting his features in shadow and for one mad moment, she was sure the soldier had risen from the dead to smite her. But then she realized the man filling the doorway stood with his feet planted on either side of the fallen man. It was the second man from the clearing, and he was furious, she saw as he shifted and his stark glare was briefly caught by sunlight. She watched warily as he peered down at his dead comrade, noting with dread that his sword was out, clutched in a tight, white-knuckled hold.

Her eyes were still on the hand holding the sword when it started to move upward. Heart leaping, Lucy instinctively lifted Tearlach's sword as the man stepped over his friend and rushed her. She was too slow, however, or perhaps it was fairer to say that he was simply faster. She barely had the tip of the sword off the ground before he slapped it away with his own, sending Tearlach's weapon flying. Trinket whinnied and scooted out of the way of the flying missile. However, it really was tight quarters and she was forced to leap over the prone man in the doorway and out of the bothy to escape it.

Rather than move closer to Tearlach to escape the man, when he continued forward Lucy shifted into the space Trinket had been filling just moments ago. It took them both away from Tearlach and also drew her closer to the sword and a bit of wood leaning up against the wall at her back. They were the only weapons in the hut and she had no doubt she was going to need a weapon. The Scot she faced appeared to be in a cold rage over the death of his comrade. She didn't like the way he was brandishing that sword.

"It took me a bit o' time to realize who Hamish meant when he said, ''Tis her,'" the man growled, following her step by step. "But he was at the inn when ye were taken and talked endlessly about ye when he returned to Rosscurrach with the others. Goin' on about yer pretty blond hair and yer full lips, the kind that put pictures in a mon's head."

Lucy risked a glance back, trying to place the distance to the piece of wood she had her hopes on.

"Had he just said ye were Lady Blytheswood, I'd ha'e been hard on his heels, but he didnae and by the time I sorted it oot, the two o' ye were well ahead o' me. I had to track ye . . . else I'd ha'e been here in time to save him."

Lucy stumbled slightly as her foot came down on Tearlach's sword, but she kept her balance and forced her shoulders straight as she said, "Aye. I am Lady Blytheswood. The woman your laird's partner Wymon Carbonnel wishes to marry. You would do well not to harm me."

She wasn't encouraged when this brought a short, angry laugh from the man. "The last I heard, Carbonnel wants ye back dead or alive. I'm thinkin' it'll be dead." He smiled coldly and withdrew a *sgian-dubh* from his waist even as he tossed his sword aside. "But first I'll be makin' ye pay fer killing Hamish. He was a big stupid oaf but he was me friend and I'll enjoy makin' ye sorry ye killed him."

He lunged for her then, but Lucy had already reached back for the wood and now swung it around, aiming for his head. The wood connected with a crack that echoed in the small hut and the man stumbled back, a stunned look on his face as his hand rose to the wound she'd given him.

Lucy would have hit him again then, but she'd swung the wood one-handed and the impact had made it vibrate painfully in her hand. She almost dropped the weapon, but managed to get her second hand on it and hold on. Before she could deliver a second blow, however, the soldier recovered enough to launch himself at her. Lucy grunted in pain and fell back as he crashed into her. Her head hit the ground hard enough that Lucy lost her hold on the wood she'd been using as a weapon, but she hardly noticed the loss as pain radiated through her stomach as the Scot followed her down.

His full weight only rested on her a minute before he pushed his upper body up and away from her to peer down the length of them. When he turned his gaze back to her face there was an unholy satisfaction to his expression.

"Are ye sorry yet?" he panted with a vile grin.

Lucy stared back with incomprehension, and then glanced down as he had done. Her eyes widened and her breath grew shallow as she saw his knife impaled in her upper stomach. He'd stabbed her as he tackled her, that and not his weight had been the source of pain.

"Nay?" he asked, catching a handful of her hair to force her head viciously back until she returned her stunned eyes to him. Once she met his gaze, he promised, "Ye will be."

He then reached to begin dragging up the long skirts of the gown she wore. Lucy immediately began to struggle, but her efforts were feeble at best. Her strength was failing her as quickly as she was losing blood, and she knew it was pouring from her quickly. She could feel it dampening the front of her gown and smell it in the air. It smelled like death. Hers. And she slowly realized that this was it. This was how it would all end, raped and murdered in a Scottish bothy.

The soldier had managed to drag the dress up to her waist and now turned his attention to freeing himself. That's when she became aware of the low growl coming from the shadows along the side wall. For a moment, she thought a wolf had somehow got into the bothy, and then Tearlach rose behind the man, a great dark shadow in the waning light that swooped on her attacker.

Lucy grunted as the weight of both men was briefly on her. She saw the fury on Tearlach's damaged face, saw his mouth open to reveal his fangs, then squeezed her

eyes shut and turned her head quickly to the side, shutting
out the sounds of the attack. When the weight of both
men was removed a moment later, she still didn't open
her eyes. It simply seemed too much effort. Instead, she
curled onto her side with a little moan and allowed unconsciousness to claim her.

Tearlach straightened from the man he'd been feeding
on and leaned briefly against the wall of the hut as his
body repaired itself. The soldier wasn't dead, but he
would be soon if no one tended to him. Tearlach planned
to make sure no one tended to him. He'd drop him into
the pit under the bothy to breathe his last breaths. It was
little more than the man deserved for daring to touch his
Lucy.

That thought made him open his eyes and search out
her prone figure, but he didn't immediately rush to her
side. Tearlach found he was suddenly afraid to approach
her. Afraid she lay so still with her back to him because
she now found him disgusting. Monstrous.

It was the scent of blood and his need for it that had
roused Tearlach several moments ago. Rage had quickly
followed when he'd seen the struggling figures on the
other side of the bothy and realized someone was trying
to rape Lucy not more than a couple feet away.

Rage and hunger fueling him, he'd shot to his knees
and lunged on the man, growling with his fury as he'd
ripped into the man's throat. It hadn't been his usual feeding; a kind bite, using his own thoughts to cover the bene-
factor's pain. It had been the attack of an enraged animal
and he was sure he'd even snarled as he'd dragged the

man off of Lucy to feed on the blood gushing from the throat wound. She was probably horrified, repulsed by the very sight of him.

In one way, it may be for the best, Tearlach supposed. If she was now disgusted by him, there should be no difficulty keep his distance with her from now on. But that didn't lessen the pain he felt at the thought of her now viewing him with loathing and possibly thinking him an animal.

Sighing, Tearlach stood and moved the few feet to her side, then squatted next to her and gently touched her upper arm.

"Lucy? Are you all right?" he asked, and frowned when her only response was a low moan. For a moment he feared he'd been too late and had caught the man at the end of raping her. The scent of blood had to have come from somewhere, mayhap it had come from the raping. Horrified at the thought, Tearlach drew her onto her back to get a look at her expression, sure it would tell him whether he'd been too late or not.

The moment he rolled her onto her back, however, he knew where the scent of blood had come from. Lucy was covered with the warm liquid still oozing from a wound in her upper stomach.

Cursing, Tearlach ripped open the tear in the dress where she'd been stabbed attempting to get a better look at the wound. Part of his mind was puzzling over why she was in a dress rather than the Carbonnel clothes, but staunching the flow of her blood was a more urgent matter and he left it for now and glanced around until he spotted the clothes she'd previously been wearing. Snatching up the tunic, he tore it in strips and began to bind her wound. It was bad and she'd lost a lot of blood. She needed a healer, a skill Tearlach knew nothing about. His people had little use for healers.

"Betty," he muttered, suddenly recalling Lucy telling him that the woman was a skilled healer as well as her maid. He had to get her to Betty. She was the only healer he even knew of.

"Tearlach?"

He paused in his binding to glance to her face when she whispered his name. Much to his relief there was no disgust or loathing there for him, just a mild confusion as she peered from the wound he was binding then to his face.

"Rest," he whispered, continuing his work. "Ye need tae save yer strength, lass. Yer sore wounded."

"Have to tell you," she breathed and a band tightened around his heart at how weak her voice was. She was fading on him. He was going to lose her.

"Nay, save yer strength," he insisted. Nothing was as important as her surviving this in his opinion, but she was just as stubborn now as when she was well and persisted, gasping, "Heming escaped."

That brought his head up sharply.

"Escaped?" Tearlach echoed, shocked to realize that after all they'd been through to get here to save his cousin, he'd forgotten all about the man in the face of Lucy's injury.

"They are searching . . . for him. He escaped . . . like us," she got out faintly, but it seemed to take the last of her strength and her eyes closed with a little sigh.

For a moment, Tearlach feared she'd up and died on him, but when he pressed an ear to her chest he could hear her heart still beating. It didn't sound a very strong beat, but it was a beat. She wasn't dead, and wouldn't die on him if he had any say in the matter, he thought grimly, finishing binding her as tightly as he could to keep any more blood from leaving her.

Lifting her in his arms, he straightened then and turned to look for Trinket. The horse wasn't in the bothy and he felt a moment's panic, fearing the mare was gone, but then he spotted her through the open door of the hut. The animal stood serenely in the waning daylight, munching grass in front of the bothy.

Grateful he'd been too weary to unsaddle her that morning and he would not now need saddle her, Tearlach took a deep breath and then stepped over the dead man in the doorway and out into the dying day. Holding Lucy close to his chest, he bowed his head to protect his face as much as possible and hurried to the mare, hoping that if he got mounted and to the shade of the woods the sun wouldn't get the chance to weaken him terribly.

"We need speed this night, Trinket," he muttered as he struggled to get in the saddle with Lucy still in his arms. "Yer mistress needs help. We moost travel swiftly."

He didn't know if the horse understood him, but she did set off for the woods at a gallop the moment he took up the reins.

Eight

Lucy was dreaming of Tearlach. She knew it was a dream because he wasn't being cold and silent with her. Instead, his expression was concerned, his voice deep with worry. He also wasn't keeping her at a distance or being stiff and unbending. In her dream he was cradling her in his arms, whispering soft words in Scottish. She didn't understand a word he was saying, but his tone and eyes were so soft and full of caring, she decided they must be words of love before the dream faded into blackness again.

When next she opened her eyes it was to find a woman bending over her. Lucy blinked and then smiled uncertainly as she recognized her maid.

"Yer awake." Betty's smile was full of relief as she withdrew the damp cloth she'd been running over her face.

"Aye," Lucy said, or tried to. She frowned when her

voice came out as little more than a dry croak. She felt horrible, dried out and weak, her throat sore, eyes gritty, and body aching. All symptoms of the aftermath of fever, she realized with confusion. "What happened? Where am I?"

"You are at Harold's inn, my lady," Betty said, her voice soothing. But her expression became worried in the face of Lucy's blank expression and she prompted, "My husband, William? His brother, Harold? This is Harold's inn on the border of Blytheswood and Oswald."

"Oh, aye," Lucy breathed, but had no idea how she'd gotten there. "What am I doing here?"

Betty's eyebrows drew together. "Tearlach brought you. Do you not remember?"

Lucy frowned as she searched the foggy memories jumbling in her head. She remembered . . . For a moment her thoughts were blank and then she was suddenly bombarded with memory after memory, most of them featuring Tearlach MacAdie.

"I was stabbed," she whispered finally.

Betty's concern cleared from her face, chased off by relief. Straightening where she sat on the edge of the bed, she set aside the damp cloth she'd been using to wipe her down, and then turned back and admitted, "I was worried the fever had affected your mind. It got so very high a time or two I feared we would lose you. When it passed, I still worried that you might not come back to us as you were."

Lucy gave a weak nod of understanding. Fevers could be dangerous. Even did they not claim a body, they might take the mind and one never knew if that would be the case until the person recovered. She was pretty sure all her faculties were still intact, however. Her gaze slid to the flickering candle beside the bed and then to the window and the darkness beyond.

"Where is Tearlach?" she asked, grimacing over the pain it caused in her throat.

"He is downstairs helping Harold's wife in the kitchen while William helps Harold with serving the guests."

When Lucy's eyebrows rose at this news, Betty explained, "He does not show his face to the guests lest someone recognize him, but insisted he wanted to help out while here so settled on working in the kitchens." She paused and gave a soft laugh before adding, "Harold's wife, Louise, was fair surprised to have a man underfoot in the kitchens, but he's been very helpful."

Lucy smiled faintly, somehow not surprised that Tearlach would be willing to do what she was sure many lords would refuse to do. From all their talks and the time she'd been with him, she was quite sure that Tearlach would consider no chore beneath him and would simply set out to do what he could where he could.

"He is a good man," Betty said solemnly and then added, "he has been terribly worried about you. The man was a sight when he arrived with you in his arms. He was pale and trembling from his time in the sun, but would not let you go. We had to tend you in the cellar out of the sun because he insisted on holding you the whole first day while I tended your wound."

"He arrived in daylight?" Lucy asked, eyes wide with alarm, but then confusion set in. She had seen the effects of sun on Tearlach and pale and trembling wasn't it. The man burned under the sun's harsh rays.

"Aye. He had several blankets wrapped around and over both of you. We had no idea who the two of you were when he first rode into the courtyard and straight into the stables. William followed him in and came running out shouting for me."

"Blankets?" Lucy echoed faintly, suddenly having some recollection of being tight bundled and finding it hard to breathe in a warm cocoon.

"Aye, Lord Tearlach said he'd come upon a sleeping search party near dawn and stole the blankets so he could continue on to the inn with you."

He'd probably fed at the same time, Lucy supposed and then glanced worriedly at Betty, wondering if they'd realized what he was.

"He's a vampire," Betty said, answering the question she hadn't asked. She then frowned and gave her head a little shake. "I've heard stories of them, but didn't think they really existed."

"Vampire or not, he is a good man," Lucy said firmly. "Wymon is the monster."

"Aye," Betty agreed at once and then added, "and he loves you. That is clear from the way he's fretted over you."

Lucy's eyes filled with tears at these words, hardly able to hope they were true after how cold and distant he had been with her during the last night of travel that she actually recalled clearly.

Betty patted her hand gently and stood. "I shall tell him you're awake and fetch you something to drink to ease your parched throat. You just rest."

Lucy nodded and relaxed back in the bed, her eyes closing as Betty slid out of the room. She must have fallen asleep then, for when she next opened her eyes, the candle on the bedside table had burnt down to a stub and Tearlach was seated in a chair next to the bed, his head turned toward the window and the night beyond. Lucy's gaze slid back to the table and the goblet she'd noted sitting beside the candle. She unconsciously licked her dry and cracked lips as she wondered if there was liquid in it.

"Are ye thirsty?" Tearlach stood and moved to collect the goblet. Easing to sit on the bed beside her, he then slid one arm behind her back to raise her up so he could press the goblet to her lips. Lucy drank greedily, but not for long. Tearlach soon pulled the glass away, concern on his face.

"Slowly, love. Yer stomach may just toss it back up do ye no' go slowly," he cautioned and Lucy's eyes flickered at the term of endearment he didn't seem to realize he'd used. She didn't comment, however, he was raising the goblet to her lips again and her thirst took precedence at the moment. Drinking more slowly this time, she sipped from the goblet and swished the liquid around her mouth, making sure to wet every nook and cranny before allowing the soothing liquid to slide down her throat.

"Better," Tearlach murmured, offering her a smile.

Lucy automatically smiled back around the goblet and nearly slobbered all over herself. Deciding smiling was something else that would have to wait, she forced it away and continued drinking in little increments of liquid until the goblet was empty.

"Do ye want more?" Tearlach asked as he lowered her back on the bed.

"Nay, thank you," Lucy whispered. "I'd best see how this bit settles before I try more."

Tearlach nodded and set the goblet back on the table, but didn't move from the bed. Instead, he peered at her solemnly, taking in each feature of her face as if he'd feared he'd never see them again.

"Ye look better," he announced after a moment and

she laughed at the suggestion, knowing she probably looked a mess. She didn't know how long she'd been feverish, but knew it had probably left her looking less than her best.

"Ye do," Tearlach insisted with a frown. "Yer no' as pale as ye were. Ye looked near death's door these last two nights."

"I have been ill for two nights?" Lucy asked with surprise.

"Three if ye count the night we rode here," Tearlach answered making her eyebrows rise, but she didn't tell him she knew it had been more than a night that they'd traveled, that he'd swaddled them in blankets so that he could continue to ride in daylight.

"Thank you for bringing me to Betty," she whispered.

He nodded, and then commented, "She's as good a healer as ye claimed. I thought sure she widnae be able to save ye when we got here. Ye'd lost so much blood and were terrible pale."

Lucy nodded, then her eyes widened with recall and she told him, "Heming escaped Rosscurrach."

"Aye. Ye said as much ere we headed here."

"Did I?" she asked with surprise, not recalling doing so. When he nodded, she asked, "Have you heard news? Has he reached his clan?"

Tearlach frowned and shook his head. "I've heard nothing, but two search parties ha'e stopped here for meals while we've been here, one was made up of Scots, so I'm guessing they're still looking for him."

"And the other?" she queried quietly.

"Carbonnel men," he answered grimly.

Lucy merely nodded at this news. She'd known Wymon would still be hunting for them. In fact, she'd bet he was growing desperate by now. She was too dangerous to him to be allowed to run loose. The king wouldn't take kindly to news that Wymon had murdered her brother.

She noted Tearlach glancing toward the window and followed his gaze, alarmed to see the first streaks of sunlight crossing the sky.

Reaching for his hand, she touched it to get his attention.

"The sun is rising, I know you have to go," Lucy said softly, then frowned and asked, "where is it you are taking shelter here during the day?"

"The cellar," Tearlach answered.

Recalling Betty saying that she'd had to tend her in the cellar the first day because he wouldn't let her go, Lucy nodded and said, "You really should go."

"Aye," he agreed, but didn't move, simply peering at her worriedly. "Yer sure yer all right?"

"Aye. I am fine. I am on the mend and will be up and about in no time," she assured him and then bit her lip and added, "I know you must be worried about your cousin. There is no need to stay here with me if you wish to look for him and see to his well-being."

Tearlach shook his head as he got to his feet. "He's weel away by noo I'd think. I promised to see ye to court and the king and that's what I'll be doin'. After that is soon enough to meet up with me clan and discover what's been about and what we plan to do about it."

Lucy merely smiled, managing to hide her relief at his words. She would not lose him yet.

"Rest and mend, we'll talk more tonight," he promised, and then hesitated before bending to press his lips to her forehead. Lucy closed her eyes with a little sigh at the caress and promptly fell asleep. When she awoke again the room was full of sunlight and Betty was bustling about, humming a little tune under her breath.

"How long have I slept?" she asked with surprise, sitting up and scowling at how much effort it took to do so.

"You're awake!" Beaming as if she'd done something especially clever, Betty rushed across the room to the bed.

"Aye," Lucy agreed dryly. "I must have slept for hours. It was dawn when Tearlach said good night."

"You've slept one full day and night and about three hours then," Betty informed her.

"What?" Lucy gasped with horror.

"It was my potion," Betty said apologetically. "I put it in your drink. I told Tearlach not to let you drink too much, but he thought I meant because you'd been without water so long. He hadn't realized I'd put a sleeping potion in the drink and let you drink it all. It made you sleep long and hard."

Lucy started to close her eyes at this news, then forced them quickly wide open for fear she'd lose another day.

"'Tis all right," Betty said, patting her hand. "It should be out of your body by now."

Lucy released a breath of relief and the maid smiled.

"It was probably for the best. Sleep is the best healer and you are looking like the long rest has done you good. You have more color and appear much more alert this time," she informed her, and then asked, "how do you feel?"

"Hungry," Lucy said promptly and Betty laughed softly.

"That is always a good sign, my lady. You'll be up and about in no time. I shall go fetch you some broth."

Lucy scowled as the door closed behind the maid. She'd said she was hungry. Broth would hardly cure that, but she suspected the maid wouldn't let her move to solid food until she was literally up and about. Setting her teeth determinedly, Lucy slid her legs off the bed and slowly levered herself to her feet.

The thump of an empty barrel hitting the floor brought Tearlach awake with a start. Turning his head, he found William casting an apologetic wince his way from the opposite side of the cellar.

"I'm sorry, Tearlach. It slipped out of my hands."

He waved away the apology and ran a hand through his hair as he sat up on the pallet they had set up for him in the inn's cellar. "'Tis all right, the sun has nearly set anyway."

William's eyebrows rose at his words. "How is it you always know that?"

"I am no' sure," Tearlach admitted as he stood. "It has always just been that way."

"Hmm," William muttered and turned to move the empty barrel next to several others in the corner.

Knowing the man would be expected to bring up a fresh barrel to replace the empty one, Tearlach crossed the room to get it for him. He was hefting it onto his shoulder when Lucy's stable master turned around.

"'Tis all right, I can do that," William said, hurrying to his side when he saw what Tearlach was about.

"As can I," he answered mildly and then shrugged. "'Tis little enough effort in return fer all ye and Betty ha'e done for Lucy and me."

"She's our lady," William said quietly.

"But I am no'," Tearlach pointed out with a smile and turned to lead the way upstairs to the main floor of the inn. Despite the danger of being seen, he carried the barrel through the kitchen and out into the main room, walking quickly around behind the bar to set it down.

"Thank you, my lord, and good evening to you," William's brother greeted him as he straightened. Harold was rather barrel shaped himself, but otherwise was an older version of his brother.

Tearlach nodded a greeting, then turned and headed for the stairs, thinking just to check on Lucy before returning below to don his boots and sword.

"If it's Lucy you're looking for, you'll not find her up here," Betty announced with annoyance as she started down the stairs toward him.

Pausing on the first step, Tearlach raised his head to glance at William's wife, his gaze full of surprise. "I willnae?"

"No," Betty said grimly. "She is up and about despite my best advice and presently out in the stables."

"The stables?" he echoed with horror.

"Aye. She wanted to take Trinket a carrot."

"But—" Tearlach paused, briefly at a loss. Finally he snapped, "She shouldnae be oot o' the inn. What if Carbonnel's men come? She could be spotted."

"Aye," Betty agreed dryly as she reached the step above him and paused. "Mayhap if you tell her that, she will listen. She does not seem to want to listen to me."

Ignoring the mutters that followed about her lady being stubborn and bullheaded, Tearlach turned and hurried out of the inn. He crossed the courtyard at a quick clip and burst into the stables only to find it apparently empty. About to turn and march back out, Tearlach paused when the soft murmur of a woman's voice reached his ears.

Eyes narrowing, he followed the sound, not terribly surprised to find it led him to Trinket's stall. Pausing outside the stall, he peered over the door to see Lucy seated in the straw before the horse, holding up the last of a carrot for the mare to take.

"Lucy," he said shortly and she glanced up toward him with a start, then smiled brightly, and hopped to her feet.

"Oh, hello, Tearlach. Is it sunset already?" she asked, unhooking the stall door and slipping out to stand before him.

"Aye," he growled, scowling in the face of her good cheer. He opened his mouth to berate her for being out here where she might be seen by a passing search party, but found himself distracted when she slid her arm through his and turned him toward the door of the stables.

"I know I should not have risked coming out here, but I was very careful. I even made William check the lane to be sure no search parties were approaching ere hurrying across the courtyard to the stables," she informed him solemnly, and then added, "I just wanted to see Trinket and reassure her all was well. I usually visit her every day whether intending to ride or not so I knew she must feel neglected. Besides," she added with a grimace, "I needed a moment to myself without Betty hovering over me like a mother hen. She is not happy with my being out of bed and has been scowly faced all afternoon. Rather like you are right now," she added with amusement.

"I am no' scowly faced," Tearlach protested.

"Aye, ye are. Yer scowling right noo," Lucy teased, imitating his accent.

Pausing, he turned a narrow-eyed look her way. "Are ye makin' fun o' me, lass?"

"Just a little," she assured him with a soothing smile, then urged him to continue walking. "When can we leave for court?"

"Eager to be free o' me already, are ye?" Tearlach asked dryly and she turned wide horrified eyes his way.

"Nay!" she assured him. "I just thought . . . Well, I know you have responsibilities . . . You . . . I am not eager to be rid of you," she said finally. "But I know you are worried about your cousin and need to get news of your own well-being to your family and clan. It is only me who has kept you from already doing so."

Tearlach opened his mouth to speak, but paused as they heard what sounded to be a large party riding into the courtyard. Gesturing for her to wait where she was, he turned and crossed the rest of the distance to the stable doors to peer cautiously out.

Of course, Lucy didn't listen to him. Tearlach rolled his eyes with exasperation when he felt her press up against his back and lean out to peer into the courtyard. Shaking his head, he turned his attention back to the men in the courtyard. There were half a dozen of them, all wearing Carbonnel colors.

Another search party then, he thought with displeasure. It was the fifth in the few days that they'd been at the inn. Two more had stopped in during Lucy's prolonged sleep. Wymon had obviously stepped up the search in this area.

William had told him that they had seen none of Carbonnel's men ere the day Tearlach had ridden in with both he and Lucy wrapped in blankets. He supposed his attack on the men where he'd got the blankets had given them away. He'd come upon them before dawn, catching them sleeping. The fools hadn't bothered to leave one of their rank to stand guard and had been easy prey.

He'd fed well, taken the blankets, and left them unconscious but alive for Lucy's sake. She hadn't been conscious herself at the time, but he hadn't wanted to have to lie to her if the matter should come up later.

Now he wished he'd killed the men and hidden their bodies. The two men at the bothy by Rosscurrach had probably been found by now and news of them might have reached Wymon and encouraged him to concentrate his search efforts to the north. However, leaving the men in the camp alive had obviously revealed that they were in the area and Wymon had stepped up his hunt for them here. The Englishman probably had men searching all along the way between Blytheswood and court now. He'd expect Lucy to be heading that way and would be desperate to stop her.

Tearlach took a moment to curse his lack of forethought in leaving the men alive. If he hadn't been eaten alive with worry for Lucy, he surely would have considered the situation more carefully and taken care of the matter properly. The trip to court would now be more difficult than it need be. They would have to stay off the paths, avoiding villages and other travelers along the way—if they ever even got to head for court and were not discovered here in the stables, he thought with a scowl as he watched William greet the men in the courtyard.

"Can I take your horses for you, gentlemen?" William asked as he reached the party of riders.

Several men moved as if to hand over their reins, but

paused when one of them, the oldest and obviously the leader, narrowed his eyes on William and said, "You look familiar."

Tearlach held his breath as Blytheswood's stable master shrugged and said mildly, "I must have one of those faces. Many people say that."

"Hmm." The soldier continued to stare at him a moment, then gestured to his men and turned away. "We'll see to the horses ourselves."

The other men raised their eyebrows at his words, but no one protested and they all followed as he began to lead his mount across the courtyard.

Mouth tightening, Tearlach reached for his sword, only to curse when he found it missing. It was still in the cellar where he'd left it. He'd intended to go below and retrieve it after checking on Lucy, but the news that she was up and about and out in the stables had sent him hotfooting it out here to retrieve her. His foolishness had now left him unarmed and useless to defend her from their enemies, he realized grimly.

"Wait!" William cried almost desperately.

The men all paused and turned back to the stable master. A moment of silence passed during which Tearlach was positive the man was scrambling to think of some way to delay the men. Fortunately, his hesitation wasn't so long that the men appeared suspicious when he blurted, "Why do you not tell me what you'll be wanting to eat and drink and I'll go let them know inside so they can start preparing it."

Tearlach didn't wait to see if the stall tactic worked. If it didn't, waiting would be time wasted.

Swinging away from the doors, he shot his gaze briefly

around the stables until it landed on the hay loft at the back of the building.

Mouth setting, he caught Lucy by the arm and rushed her silently to the back of the long building. He had no need to explain what he wanted, the moment they reached the ladder she hitched up the skirt of the dress she wore and started to scramble up its rungs.

Tearlach was right behind her, his gaze shooting repeatedly over his shoulder to the doors to be sure they were not spotted. Fortunately, he saw no sign of the men before following her off the ladder and hurrying around behind the stack of bales.

Nine

Tearlach and Lucy settled swiftly in the loose straw behind the stacked hay. Both then sat completely still to
prevent giving away their presence in the loft. Nerves
stretched taut and ears straining, they listened tensely for
sounds of movement from below.

William's attempt to stall the men must have worked.
That, or he'd come up with another way to delay them
after Tearlach and Lucy had headed for the back of the
stables. Whatever the case, another few moments passed
in silence before they heard the creak of the stable doors
opening. The shuffle of footsteps soon followed, along
with the murmur of men's voices.

Lucy and Tearlach waited tensely as the men worked
below. It seemed to take forever for them to see to their
horses, but finally their voices and footsteps moved away,
fading into silence.

Wanting to be sure they'd not return, Tearlach raised a hand to his lips to warn Lucy to remain silent. She nodded and then they heard the door below creak again as someone entered. This time it was a single set of footsteps that reached their ears.

"My lady?"

Tearlach and Lucy glanced at each other as they recognized William's hissed call. They then both rose cautiously and eased around the bales to peer down into the stables.

"There you are," the stable master breathed with relief, and then announced, "they've gone into the inn, but I think it's best if the two of you just stay up there until they leave. I'm worried they might see you crossing the courtyard. They've only stopped for a meal. We'll serve them quick and try to get them out in a hurry. It will be safer for you to come down then."

Tearlach nodded at the suggestion. It seemed the most sensible idea.

Relaxing slightly at the easy agreement, William nodded and moved back to the doors. "I'll go help get them fed."

They watched him leave, then Lucy turned and moved back to the spot they'd found behind the bales. She eased down to sit on the straw and leaned her back against the bales with a little sigh, then glanced up at him expectantly.

Tearlach hesitated briefly, but there really wasn't anywhere else to sit that would offer cover. The bales took up almost half of this end of the loft, but the rest of it was open to view. Casting one last glance down into the stables, he followed her and settled himself on the straw.

"Thank you for bringing me here, you saved my life."

Tearlach blinked at the soft words, and then glanced at her with amusement. "Lass, ye've saved me more than a handful of times. 'Twas time I did a little savin' o' me own. 'Sides," he added wryly, "I hardly saved ye. I just brought ye to Betty. She did the savin'."

"She could not have done so had you not brought me. And you saved me from that Scot in the bothy too," she pointed out and then added, "I only saved you once. When I unlocked your chains in the dungeon."

Tearlach gave a short laugh at the claim. "Ye unlocked me chains, practically carried me oot o' the dungeons, brought me the lad to feed on in the cave, and then got me oot o' the sun that morning in the clearing when . . ." His voice slowed and he looked away from her, swamped by memories of what they'd nearly done in that clearing before the sun had forced a halt.

Feeling his shaft harden at the recollections, Tearlach forced the memories away and added, "And ye brought that Scottish soldier for me to feed on in the bothy after I was burnt fighting the first one."

"Actually, I did not bring the second Scottish soldier," she admitted quietly. "I intended to go out and find you someone, but he found us first."

"Oh, well . . ." Unable to think of anything to say to that, Tearlach fell silent, his gaze dropping away from her face. Unfortunately, it landed directly on the cleavage that seemed to be bursting out of the top of her blue gown. Knowing the dress she'd been wearing at Rosscurrach had been ruined when she was injured, he supposed she'd had to borrow this one from Betty. The redhead was obviously a good bit smaller than Lucy, at least when it came to bosoms. While the gown fit well enough in the waist, her breasts were squeezed tight and appeared to be trying to crawl right out of it.

Tearlach stared at the bountiful flesh and found himself licking suddenly dry lips. Dear Lord, they had to find her a properly fitting gown ere they left for court. He could not ride that distance with her dressed in such a way without touching her . . . And he'd be damned if those lascivious idiots at court were going to see her dressed so.

"Tearlach? What is it?"

He lifted his gaze to her face in time to see her glance down at her own bosom as if expecting to find something there. Obviously, she'd noted the direction his gaze had taken.

Apparently not finding anything amiss, she lifted confused eyes to his.

Rather than look like a complete arse who couldn't stop staring at her breasts, Tearlach lied.

"There's just this bit o' straw . . ." he said and then couldn't resist leaning forward and reaching out to pretend to pluck the nonexistent bit of straw from the soft, upper swell of one breast. Purely to support the lie, he assured himself.

Lucy glanced down, then back up, and turned toward him to speak as he leaned forward, but then froze as their lips met.

Tearlach froze too, his fingers pausing mid-pluck, his lips soft against hers. He knew he should back up and end the unintentional caress, but couldn't seem to bring himself to do so. Both of them just stayed frozen, both seeming to hold their breath for a minute, then Lucy released a little sigh that brushed over his lips and Tearlach was lost.

*　*　*

Lucy heard the groan come from deep in Tearlach's throat in response to her sigh, but it didn't prepare her for what followed. The sigh had been a result of her certainty that he was about to pull away from her rather than kiss her as she would like. But rather than pull away, that groan was like the opening of flood gates. Tearlach suddenly pressed his lips more firmly over hers, his tongue slipping out to request entrance.

Hardly able to believe he was finally kissing her again, Lucy opened to him at once, her arms creeping tentatively up around his neck as his tongue filled her. The action brought a riot of sensation to life in her, and she groaned into his mouth, her upper body arching invitingly as she scraped her nails over his scalp.

Murmuring something into her mouth, Tearlach deepened the kiss, his fingers rising to run over the soft flesh revealed by her décolletage before giving one side of the material the barest tug. It was all that was needed to free the breast on that side from the tight gown encasing it and Lucy gasped as she felt his warm, callused hand immediately close over it. Shuddering with pleasure, she arched her back further, pressing into the touch.

Her response to his kiss became somewhat frantic as Tearlach kneaded the sensitive flesh, and she almost bit his tongue when he caught her erect nipple between thumb and finger and tweaked it.

Breaking the kiss then, Tearlach ducked his head to catch the nipple in his mouth. Groaning, Lucy twisted her head and let it fall back, then cried out and tangled her fingers in his hair as his tongue rasped over the sensitive nipple.

"We shouldnae be doin' this," he groaned suddenly,

lifting his head. "Yer a lady. Ye deserve more than a tumble in the hay."

Lucy's eyes blinked open with dismay as his words made their way through her passion-soaked mind.

"I like hay," she insisted as he began to withdraw his hands. Then, afraid he would stop and trying to make sure he didn't, Lucy released her own hold on him and reached between them to press her fingers against his erection. She wasn't at all sure what she was doing was right, but the way Tearlach growled and bucked violently against her touch suggested she might be, so she closed her hand and squeezed slightly.

His reaction was most gratifying. The next thing she knew, Tearlach was pushing her onto her back in the straw and kneeling above her, tugging his tunic off over his head.

"Oh," Lucy breathed, reaching for his chest as it was revealed. He was so wide, so strong, so beautiful. Her hands ran across the marble-like skin with pleasure, sweeping across his upper chest, then down across his stomach until he caught them. Her eyes shot anxiously to his face, but he wasn't stopping. Tearlach merely kissed the back of first one hand and then the other before holding them out of the way in one hand so that he could reach down and free her second breast from the gown with a quick tug. Once it was revealed, he released her hands and bent to feast on her flesh.

Lucy clutched at his upper shoulders as Tearlach laved first one breast and then the other, his tongue and teeth scraping gently over her erect nipples. She was arching into the attention, her legs shifting and writhing restlessly when she felt his fingers slide beneath her skirt and begin

to run up her leg. She froze then, stomach muscles clenching and breath coming in short, excited gasps as her attention was torn between what he was doing to her breasts
and the slow, almost tickling caress of his fingers creeping up her thigh.

Lucy instinctively tried to close her legs when his hand
reached the top of her thigh, then immediately forced
them open again to give him access.

"Oh, Tearlach," she gasped, pressing her heels into the
straw and thrusting upward as his fingers brushed lightly
over the warm, slick skin that awaited him.

"Aye," he growled, releasing her breast and shifting up
her body to kiss her as his clever fingers worked their
magic.

Lucy put everything she had into her response, all her
need, all her love, and all the desire he was bringing to
life. She alternately sucked at his tongue and allowed her
own to wrestle with it, but then tore her mouth away with
a cry as he slid one finger into her.

"Please," she gasped breathlessly, her hips thrusting of
their own accord, seeking the release she'd experienced in
the clearing. Tearlach's mouth immediately covered hers
again, silencing Lucy as he continued to fan her need.

Lucy knew she should be quiet, that she risked making
their presence known should the men return, but she
couldn't help herself. She felt sure Tearlach was going to
drive her mad with his caresses . . . and then he suddenly
withdrew his touch. Her eyes immediately blinked open,
filled with the fear that he would stop, but he merely
urged her thighs further apart, and quickly freed himself
from his braies as he settled in the cradle of her thighs.

Lucy instinctively pressed her feet flat to the floor and
drew her knees up as he nudged against her and then he

was pushing his way inside. She went stiff, biting hard on her lip to keep from crying out as pain replaced the pleasure she'd been experiencing just moments ago.

Tearlach froze at once, allowing her body to adjust, and then kissed her as he eased one hand between them to begin caressing her again. Much to her amazement the pain was soon a memory and the pleasure slowly began to grow once more. Lucy was soon responding to his kiss, a moan rising up her throat.

The moment her hips shifted of their own accord, Tearlach removed his hand and used it to lever some of his weight off of her as he started to withdraw. She cried out in protest, but realized he wasn't stopping when he eased back in.

Clutching at his shoulders, she arched into Tearlach's movement, gasping as he rubbed against the sensitive nub between her legs as he entered. Desperate for the release she knew waited, Lucy gave up her hold on his shoulders and reached down to close her hands over his behind, squeezing and urging him on as her earlier tension returned and grew.

Tearlach answered her demand, his movements becoming faster, thrusting deeper until he brought them both the release she craved.

Lucy was still shuddering and gasping when Tearlach suddenly rolled to the side, taking her with him. Completely exhausted, she allowed her eyes to close, and lay limp and satisfied, barely able to appreciate the gesture as he arranged her to rest on top of him, her head nestled on his chest rather than the prickly straw.

* * *

"Hello?"

Tearlach blinked his eyes open at that call, his gaze shooting briefly around with confusion before he recalled where he was and why. Glancing down at Lucy's sleepy face as she blinked her own eyes open, he lifted a finger to his mouth, signaling for her to remain silent. He then eased them both upright and reached for his tunic.

"Tearlach? My lady?"

"William?" Tearlach called, recognizing the man's voice.

"Aye."

In the silence that followed that word, Tearlach quickly tugged his tunic on and then William said, "Are you not coming down? The men are gone."

"Aye. I'll be right there," Tearlach answered.

Grabbing up Lucy's borrowed dress, he handed it to her, then—spotting the panic on her face—couldn't resist catching her by the back of the head and drawing her to him for a quick, reassuring kiss that turned into a longer one than he'd intended. Breaking the kiss on a sigh, he hugged her briefly, whispering, "All is well. Take yer time. I'll see what he wants."

When she nodded, he stood and drew on the braies he'd been forced to wear since escaping Carbonnel. As he hopped around trying to get them up his legs, he couldn't help thinking it would be nice to return to wearing a plaid.

"Tearlach?" William called again, sounding as if he were at the bottom of the ladder now.

"I'm coming," he snapped, finally getting the braies on, and then paused to send Lucy a reassuring smile before moving around the bales.

A glance down showed the stable master at the foot of

the ladder, peering up. Tearlach grimaced, and then quickly descended to the stable floor.

"Did you not hear them leave?" William asked, backing out of the way as Tearlach stepped off the ladder.

"We dozed off waitin'," he muttered.

"Hmm." William looked rather amused, and then said, "You've straw sticking out of your shirt."

Scowling, Tearlach glanced down and plucked out the offending item.

"And in your hair," William said once he was done.

Tearlach gave his hair an impatient comb through with his fingers to get out any bits of straw there, and then took William's arm to urge him toward the door of the stables. "As Lucy is oop and aboot now, I'm thinkin' we should set out soon. Mayhap at sunset on the morrow."

"I was afraid you'd say that," William muttered on a sigh, then paused to face him and announced, "I overheard Carbonnel's men talking."

Tearlach smiled faintly, knowing the man hadn't overheard at all, but had deliberately listened in to their conversation. William was a good man. As were the rest of his family. All of them had quickly realized that he was a vampire and seemed to accept it without issue.

"From what I overheard," William continued, reclaiming his attention, "it seems they have search parties scouring the area between Blytheswood and court."

Tearlach grimaced at having his earlier worries verified. "We'll ha'e tae travel off the main trails then. Stick to the woods and keep an eye out."

"'Tis risky," William pointed out.

"Aye. But Lucy has tae get tae court and ha'e Carbonnel removed froom Blytheswood. Who kens what he's doin' tae the people there. With no young women to rape and torment, he may turn his attention tae beatin' the older women or even the men. He seems tae like tae hurt people."

"Aye," William agreed on a sigh, and then said, "I have been thinking . . . We are not far from the sea here. Mayhap rather than head straight south toward court, you would do better to head southeast, toward Skegness. They won't be watching in that direction and once there you could hire a boat to sail you down to London. They wouldn't be expecting or watching for that."

Tearlach blinked in surprise at the suggestion. It was a good one. William was a clever man. "I presume there's a reason yer suggestin' Skegness and no' one o' the closer coastal villages further north?"

"I have a cousin in Skegness who has a small boat," William admitted, and then offered, "I could take you to him and get him to take you."

Tearlach considered the matter. It was a good idea. His only concern was whether they could travel at night by boat without difficulty, and if they couldn't and had to do so during the day was there somewhere for him to shelter from the sun? Just how big was this small boat? And what of their horses?

"Tearlach?"

He turned to see Lucy stepping off the ladder and hurrying toward them. She'd done a much better job of making herself look presentable than he had. Her hair was tucked up in a tidy bun, and her clothes were a tad wrinkled, but otherwise fine. There wasn't a stray bit of straw anywhere that he could see and he gave her a most thorough examination as she approached. His eyes roved over every inch of her, his mind recalling what they'd done in the loft. The memory was enough to tempt him to turn her around and chase her back up into the loft to do it again.

Controlling that urge, he scowled instead and said, "We leave fer court tomorrow night."

"We do?" she asked with surprise.

"Aye, so ye'd best go inside and ha'e Harold's wife feed ye. Ye need tae build up yer strength fer the journey."

"Oh." She hesitated and then asked, "Will you not come with me?"

"Nay. William and I ha'e planning tae do fer the journey." Seeing the disappointment on her face, he allowed his voice to soften and added, "I shall join ye in a bit. Now go on. Eat."

Managing a smile, Lucy nodded and turned away to continue out of the stables. Tearlach moved to the door to watch. He stayed there until she was safely inside the inn, only then turning back to William. "Tell me about this boat yer cousin has."

Ten

Lucy smiled faintly as she leaned out her bedchamber window and watched Agatha berate one of the men in the bailey below. At more than eighty summers, Agatha was the oldest person Lucy knew, and the most crotchety as well. The soldier below would surely attest to that. He'd been suffering her scolding for several minutes now.

Shaking her head slightly, Lucy let her gaze run over the unfortunate soldier, sighing as she noted that he was similar in looks to Tearlach. At least, he would be if his hair was longer, and he was a little taller, and his nose was not so crooked, and . . .

Lucy grimaced with disgust at she admitted that the man really looked nothing like Tearlach. It was just that everyone and everything made her think of him. She missed the Scot.

It had been two months since the night they'd set out

for court. William had accompanied them on the journey to his cousin's in Skegness. They'd arrived well into the second night of their journey.

Dragged from his bed in the wee hours, Arthur had been reluctant at first to help them, but between William's persuasion and the coins Lucy had offered to pay him for his time once she was back at home at Blytheswood, he'd relented.

The next problem had been the horses. Arthur's boat was small, used to fish for his living. There had been no room for the horses. Finally it was decided that William would wait in Skegness for Tearlach to return and collect the mount Harold had loaned him. While the Scot rode home, William would take Trinket back to the inn. Once Lucy was back at Blytheswood, he, Betty, and Will Jr. would return, bringing the mare with them.

With that all settled, they'd set out. The boat journey had been rather long and boring. Most of it had been made during night, but when the sun rose, Tearlach had taken cover under an old sail Arthur and William had arranged for just that use.

Lucy had spent some time under the sail with him, but it had been hot and Tearlach had mostly been sleeping, so she had left him and gone to chat with Arthur for the rest of the trip. It was full daylight when they'd arrived at the docks in London. Lucy had been prepared to head out on her own so the men could start their return journey, but Tearlach had refused to let her. Afraid Wymon may have some men in town watching the palace for her approach, he'd insisted they wait until night fell and he could see her safely to the gates and into the care of the palace guards.

Arthur hadn't seemed to mind the idea of waiting,

claiming there were some shops he'd like to visit while he was there anyway. Left with little choice, Lucy had paced the boat as she waited for late afternoon to turn into night. It had been a relief when the sun had set and Tearlach had come out from under his shelter to escort her ashore.

Without horses, they'd traveled on foot. Worried as he was about a possible last minute attack, Tearlach had set a swift pace that made it impossible to talk. He hadn't slowed until they were at the palace and were greeted by the guards at the gate. Then there simply hadn't been a chance to talk in private. Tearlach had ensured the guards would see her safely inside and to the king's waiting room, and then had taken her hand, only to pause and glance toward the guards and back. Finally, he'd merely said, "I need to get back to me clan and make sure all is well with Heming, but . . ." His gaze had slid to the guards once more before he'd finished, "We'll meet again."

Lucy had nodded, relieved that he wasn't just dumping her there and happy to be rid of her, then he'd nodded, glanced toward the watching guards again, and turned away to head back to the docks and Arthur's waiting boat.

Everything after that had been a bit of a rush. Lucy had been hurried inside the palace, where she'd expected to have a long wait for an audience with the king. Fortunately, she'd run into Lord Oswald on the way. Their neighbor to the north had been a friend of her father's while he still lived and the man had stopped her, full of concern and worry.

As promised, Carbonnel had spread the tale of her brother's murder with the claim that Tearlach had done

the deed and then kidnapped her. Lucy had quickly explained the truth, leaving out the fact that Tearlach was a
vampire and simply saying Carbonnel had planned to
blame the murder on him as well as her own should she
refuse to marry him.

Oswald was a powerful ally of the king's. The moment
he understood what was happening, he'd made sure she
was taken directly to their king, accompanying her there
to insist something be done about Wymon. The very next
morning, Lucy was riding for Blytheswood with Oswald
at her side and a good-sized army carrying the king's
standard at her back. That had been enough. There had
been no battle, no need really for the army. Carbonnel
had taken to his heels the moment he heard they were on
the way.

They'd arrived at Blytheswood to find he'd fled and
was on the run. Oswald had stayed the night before traveling on home, taking his men with him. The king's men
had split into two groups, the majority of them turning to
head back to court while a much smaller group headed
out to chase after Carbonnel, following him to the coast
where he'd barely managed to escape on a boat headed
for France.

Lucy had spent the nearly two months since then learning all she needed to take over her brother's position in
running Blytheswood, but it was difficult with her mind
distracted by thoughts of Tearlach. He'd said they'd meet
again, and she knew he was probably being kept busy
with clan matters, but it had been so long and . . .

She frowned, her eyes dropping to her stomach as she
raised a hand to cover it.

"Oh, there you are."

Lucy turned away from the window to force a smile for Betty, but the maid merely pursed her lips with exasperation.

"You are mooning again."

"Nay. I am not," Lucy denied at once.

"Aye, you are," the woman insisted, then sighed and walked to her side. Once there she slid an arm around her waist to urge her away from the window. "Do not deny it, I know you miss him."

Now it was Lucy's turn to sigh. Nodding an admission, she said quietly, "I do, but he said we'd meet again."

"Well, it better be soon," Betty muttered.

"What?" Lucy asked.

Rather than repeat what she'd said, Betty blew a breath out and settled on the bed next to her and then said, "I am not sure if you are aware of it, but you are with child."

Lucy bit her lip. She hadn't had a woman's time since that evening in the loft. "Aye. I know."

"Well?" the woman prompted.

"Well what?" Lucy asked helplessly, tears pooling in her eyes.

"Well, what are you going to do about it?"

"Son?"

Tearlach glanced up idly from the ale he'd been contemplating and managed a smile of greeting for his mother as she settled on the bench next to him.

When that was his only greeting before turning his attention back to his untouched ale, she frowned with concern. "You have been distracted since you and Heming were taken at the inn on the border."

Tearlach shrugged unhappily, not bothering to deny it.

His mind hadn't been on matters they should be since leaving Lucy in London. He'd left her alive and well, and from the news he'd received since then, continued to be . . . But Tearlach wouldn't have been surprised had he been told that Lucy had dropped dead the moment he'd left her side. The woman was haunting him.

"Your father says that is why he insisted you return here to MacAdie, that you were distracted and he feared your coming to harm."

Tearlach grimaced. On arriving back in Skegness, he'd collected his borrowed mount and ridden straight home to MacAdie to assure his parents that he was well. He'd then arranged to have Harold's horse returned, sending a bag of coins along with it to thank him for his help. After that, he'd traveled with his father to gather with the clans to decide what their next move would be. It was there he'd learned of the king's men marching on Blytheswood and sending Carbonnel running. The man was now of great interest to his people as was Rosscurrach, and they had people watching the situation closely and keeping them updated.

Unfortunately, while Tearlach had soaked up every bit of news they had on Lucy, he hadn't seemed to be able to concentrate on anything else very well, and his father had finally suggested he return home to rest a bit after his recent trials. That was his diplomatic way of telling him that he was useless to them as he was. Tearlach had returned home, feeling weary and beaten.

While his last words to Lucy had been that they would meet again, Tearlach had forced himself to stay away. It was for her own good, but was doing little for his well-being. His dreams were consumed with the woman; her sweet voice whispering his name, her lips soft beneath his, her passionate moans ringing in his ears. He always woke up hard and hot, yearning to return to the dreams, but forced himself from his bed to face the night.

Tearlach found little respite in being awake, however. Lucy's smiling face kept popping into his head. Her tinkling laughter constantly rang in his ears as if carried on the wind, and he found himself smiling as he recalled the tales she'd shared about her youth . . .

Aye, she haunted him, and Tearlach was hard pressed not to give up his good intentions, mount his horse, ride straight to Blytheswood, and claim her as his own. Only the peril his people faced kept him from doing so. He would not drag her into that.

"You haven't spoken of what they did to you, son," Eva MacAdie murmured. "I know they tortured Heming. Were you tortured too?"

"They whipped me one day," he said, waving the matter away as unimportant and it truly was in his mind. With everything else that had happened since then, he hardly recalled that day of blood and pain as more than an unpleasant memory. There was no room in his mind for the experience to trouble him much, with Lucy filling his thoughts as she was.

"Your father told me that Lady Blytheswood helped you escape ere they could harm you much," Eva said tentatively.

"Aye." Tearlach smiled faintly. "Lucy got us both unchained and oot o' the dungeon."

Eva considered him silently, her eyes narrowing as she took in his smile.

Made uncomfortable by her examination, he turned his face forward and peered down into his untouched ale again, stiffening when she breathed, "You care for her."

A denial rose to his lips at once, but then he decided not to bother, his mother would see through the lie and he didn't have the heart to deny his feelings anyway. Sagging wearily, Tearlach nodded and offered her a wry smile.

"'Tis odd. When I first woke in that dungeon across from her, I thought her pleasant enough to look on. No great beauty, but passably pretty."

"And now?" Eva asked, urging him on.

He shook his head with bewilderment. "Now, no woman can compare to the beauty I found in her."

"You love her," Eva breathed with happy realization.

Tearlach glanced toward her, scowling. "Do no' say it as if 'tis such a wondrous thing, Mother. 'Tis a curse."

Eva's eyebrows drew together in concern at his words. "Did she not love you too, son? Surely she did. How could she help herself?"

An affectionate smile curved his lips at her staunch words. Of course, she could not imagine a woman not returning her son's love.

"As it happens, I think she does love me too," Tearlach admitted miserably and his mother almost bounced on the bench seat beside him in her happy excitement.

"But this is wonderful," she exclaimed, clasping her hands around his upper arm and squeezing affectionately.

Tearlach had no doubt she was envisioning the grandbabies he and Lucy could produce for her. His mother had longed to have more than one child, but it had not been meant to be. She would definitely spoil rotten any child he produced for her. The idea of the offspring he and Lucy might have produced made *him* less happy. It caused an ache in his chest, because he knew it could never be.

"Why are you still here?" she suddenly asked with a frown and he glanced at her with confusion.

"What do ye mean?"

"I mean, why are you not on your way to England to collect your love?" she said impatiently, and then smiled and said, "we can have the wedding here. A proper wedding, with a feast and all our people in attendance. We can—"

"Mother," he interrupted before she got too carried away. "There'll be no wedding."

She deflated as if he'd slapped her. "Why not?"

Tearlach looked away and sighed. "Weel, first off, now that her brother is dead, she is the Lady o' Blytheswood."

"But that is perfect," she assured him. "Blytheswood is not so far away, we could visit often. Besides, 'tis not like your father will give up the reins to MacAdie anytime soon. This would give you a home of your own to run."

"Aye," Tearlach acknowledged slowly, not having considered that himself, then shook the thought away and pointed out, "but her king'll have plans fer her. He'd no' be pleased to let her marry a Scot."

Eva snorted slightly at that and said, "Trust me, my boy. I am English born and raised and from what I know of the King of England, with enough coin he'll forgive anything."

Tearlach felt a moment's hope at this news, then recalled his main worry and shook his head. "I'll no' drag her into our battles."

Eva blinked in apparent surprise at his words and then shook her head slightly and asked, "And she would have no battles at Blytheswood? It seems to me she already has. Did Carbonnel not kill her brother and kidnap her to try to gain Blytheswood?"

When Tearlach frowned, she added, "At least we know who our enemies are. With us, she would know she has enemies, and friends, and she would be prepared for what was coming rather than taken by surprise as she was by Wymon."

She gave Tearlach a moment to consider that and then added, "Tearlach, life is full of battles; some large, some small. Every life. We just must do the best we can to get through them. And," she continued firmly when he opened his mouth to speak, "we are all stronger together than apart."

"But what if I claim her and something happens to harm her?"

"What if you do not and something happens to her at Blytheswood and you were not there to help her?" Eva countered with a shrug. "We can not foresee the future, son. We can only see the present and what I am seeing is that you are pining after the woman and useless without her."

Tearlach stiffened with affront. "I am no' pining."

"Aye," she countered. "You are."

"Our son doesnae pine," Connall MacAdie said grimly, drawing their attention to the fact that he now stood in the open keep doors. Once he had their attention, he announced, "We ha'e a guest. Several o' them actually."

"Who?" Tearlach and Eva asked together.

Connall MacAdie smiled faintly, but shook his head. "Come see."

Eleven

Tearlach and his mother exchanged a glance, then both stood and moved to join Connall MacAdie in the open door. He moved aside at once, leaving Tearlach a clear view.

He peered out at the large traveling party standing in a circle of torch light in the dark bailey and felt something like shock. Tearlach had been told on rising and coming below that a party had been spotted approaching the castle just as the sun set. He'd also been told his father had preceded him below and was already riding out to see to the matter, so he'd sat himself at the trestle table where his mother had found him.

Tearlach had assumed the party would be from Mac-Nachton, but these people were English without a plaid among them, he noted with amazement.

"Who?" he began, but then several of the soldiers at

the front of the group shifted their horses aside and his eyes fell on the woman they'd revealed.

"Lucy," he whispered, his eyes consuming her where she sat on Trinket's back. Her gown was a periwinkle blue, and her blond hair was unbound and waving around her face in the evening breeze. She was even more beautiful to him than the visions of her that had haunted his nights and disturbed his sleep.

"Lucy?" Eva MacAdie echoed with a slow smile.

"Ye'd best go talk to her, son," his father murmured and then glanced at his wife to add, "I have . . . and I like her."

Eva beamed at her husband as if he had done something quite clever, and then gave her son a gentle push. "Go. Tell her you love her. Fix this now. The girl has ridden all the way here to see you, do not keep her waiting."

Nodding, Tearlach started down the stairs with steps that started out slow, but sped up until he was nearly running when he reached the bottom. He was brought to an abrupt halt when a horse suddenly stepped in his path.

Scowling, Tearlach glared up at the rider who had dared to come between him and the woman he wanted, but then blinked in surprise as he recognized the rider.

"William," he said, a smile of greeting replacing his scowl. "'Tis guid tae see ye."

The man grinned back. "I am happy to say the same."

"And me," Betty announced, leaning to the side to peer around her husband's shoulder from where she sat behind him. "We insisted on accompanying her ladyship when she set out on this journey to collect you."

"Collect me?" he echoed with a grin.

"Aye, well, someone had to. You didn't appear to be tending the task yourself," Betty said with a reprimanding look and then added with some asperity, "and we would know why."

Tearlach's eyebrows rose at the demand, but before he could speak, William cleared his throat and said, "'Twas obvious to us at the inn that you love our lady, and yet you did not stay to claim her. Why?"

"I—She—My people—" Tearlach struggled, his thoughts in an uproar. He liked this couple and was trying desperately not to be offended at their behavior, but hadn't expected the question. Hell, he hadn't expected to find them all on his doorstep either. Finally, he simply said, "The MacAdies have enemies."

William relaxed at these words and nodded slowly. "I suspected that might be the case."

"Aye," Betty nodded. "He said as much to Lady Lucy. William told her he feared you may be trying to keep her safe from your enemies. 'Tis why she decided to come."

"That and she is with—Ouch! Wife!" William glared back at the pretty redhead who had silenced him with a pinch in the side.

"William, do you think I might talk to him now?" Lucy's dry voice reached Tearlach and he shifted, trying to see around the horse between them.

"She's a little annoyed at our insisting on talking to you first," William admitted, not sounding terribly concerned by her annoyance.

"But we had to," Betty said reasonably. "Other than her cousin Margaret, we are the closest thing she has to family now, and as such could hardly let her charge up here on her own and throw herself at you. She's a lady. She has to have some pride, I say."

"And you are absolutely right," Eva agreed, drawing

his notice to the fact that his mother and father had now descended the stairs to join them. "I hope it will ease your mind to know that Tearlach has been pining for her."

"Tearlach doesnae pine," Connall said with exasperation.

Eva ignored him and continued, "And I think had you not shown up here, he would have headed to England, if not today then on the morrow."

Betty beamed at this news and twisted on the horse to peer over her shoulder. "Did you hear, my lady? He was pining. Your pride is intact."

An exasperated little sigh reached his ears, then his father claimed his attention with a touch on the arm and muttered, "Mayhap ye should show the lass a bit o' MacAdie and have a talk with her, son, else yer mother and her people'll do it all fer ye."

Tearlach grinned at the suggestion and slid past the horse William and Betty rode.

Lucy shifted unhappily in the saddle. She'd known this was a bad idea from the first. Her original intention had been to slip away on her own, perhaps dressed as a lad and ride to MacAdie to hopefully see Tearlach and find out once and for all whether he cared for her or not.

It was something she wouldn't have dared do if not for the fact that she was carrying his child. If not for that, her pride surely would have kept her "pining" at Blytheswood until she was old and grey, but she could not force the title "bastard" on her babe. She either had to inform Tearlach and see if he would marry her and claim the child, or she would have to find a husband who would, and quickly. The second option wouldn't have been difficult. Blytheswood was a rich estate. Many would be happy to claim her child to get their hands on her home. But the child was Tearlach's, and she loved him and had to give him the choice first.

Unfortunately, Betty had quickly got wind of her intention to make her way into Scotland and insisted she wasn't to travel alone. She would need a guard, and maid, and . . .

The next thing Lucy knew, she had a small army traveling with her and William and Betty were insisting that as her brother was no longer there to speak for her, they should do it. She'd resisted the idea, but the closer they'd got to MacAdie, the more cowardly she'd turned, and when they'd spotted MacAdie castle ahead in the day's dying light, had even suggested they stop for the night rather than try to finish the journey in the encroaching dusk.

Her suggestion had been ignored. Shortly after she'd voiced it, a small party had ridden out to meet them. At first, Lucy had thought the man at the head of the party was Tearlach, but when he'd paused before them, lifting a torch to look them over, she'd realized it wasn't, but was just someone very similar in looks. She'd been shocked to learn the man was Tearlach's father, he'd looked far too young for that, but he'd been kind and even welcoming and had escorted them the rest of the way to the keep.

Lucy had spent that last short distance to MacAdie vacillating between excitement at the idea of seeing Tearlach, and fear that he'd reject her. By the time they'd ridden into the bailey, she'd wished she'd never set out on this fool's journey, and decided it would be best if William and Betty spoke for her.

Now, however, she found herself thoroughly embarrassed, impatient, and wishing she'd not let them interfere.

Lucy was startled from her thoughts when Tearlach suddenly pushed his way past the horse William and Betty rode and approached her own. Before she could decide how to greet him, he was reaching up to grasp the pommel in front of her and then using his hold on that to swing himself up on the mare with her. Eyes wide, she sat stiff before him as he took the reins from her suddenly weak hands and turned them to travel back through her men. Several started to turn their own mounts to follow, but a word from William made them pause.

"Ye've elevated William in rank," Tearlach commented, apparently noting the incident.

"Aye," Lucy said and then nodded lest he couldn't hear her over the galloping horse. On taking over the reins of Blytheswood, she'd needed people around her whom she trusted and William and Betty were definitely that. She'd made William her right hand, giving him a great deal of responsibility and—when necessary—making him her voice among the soldiers. The man was a natural leader and had taken to the new position like a duck to water.

"A smart move," Tearlach praised, as they rode back through the gates she'd just entered and into the dark night. "He's intelligent and a natural leader."

Lucy's only response was a nod, but she also relaxed a little in the saddle despite the fact that he'd ridden them into the woods where the darkness seemed complete. She could see little but darker shapes amid the night surrounding them, but knew from their previous time together that Tearlach could see more and would steer them safely to wherever he was taking them.

Neither of them spoke again until they broke out of the trees. After the dark woods, the moonlit clearing was almost like daylight to Lucy. She could actually see enough to make out separate trees, bushes, and plants. Her gaze slid over the moonlight shining off the water of the loch at the center of the clearing and she smiled faintly.

"Ye came to collect me," Tearlach said as he eased her mount to a walk as they crossed the clearing, heading for the water's edge. "Ye love me."

Lucy blinked at his words and then scowled. There had been a good deal of arrogant male satisfaction in his voice. Before she could get too riled up, he added, "'Tis good. I love you too."

Already annoyed, Lucy couldn't keep from turning a raised eyebrow his way at this claim. "Then why did you not come to claim me?"

He inspected her doubting expression in silence for a moment, then brought Trinket to a halt and quickly dismounted. When he turned and raised his arms, inviting her to join him on the ground, she hesitated, her unhappy thoughts keeping her in the saddle.

Tearlach made up her mind for her, catching her by the waist and lifting her off the horse. Once he'd set her on her feet, he caught her face in his hands and solemnly met her gaze. "I do love ye, Lucy. And that's the verra reason I didnae come to claim ye."

She tsked impatiently and tugged her face free to whirl away. "That makes no sense at all."

"Aye. It does." He caught her arm and drew her back around, pulling her forward until she raised her hands to his chest to keep some space between them. "My people ha'e enemies. Ye've seen that. And ye've seen what they're willin' to do to me, to me clansmen. I didnae wish to drag ye into that and put ye in danger. I loved ye enough I wanted to keep ye safe from that."

Lucy considered his words briefly, and then tilted her head. "And now? Will you send me away to keep me safe?"

"I should," he admitted grimly. "I should set ye back on yer mare and turn ye to England and tell ye to forget all about me."

Lucy sucked in a breath at this threat, afraid he might do just that, but instead he hugged her close. Tearlach pressed a kiss to her forehead, then sighed unhappily and admitted, "But I find I'm a much more selfish man than I kenned. I ha'e been miserable lonely without ye, lass. I miss yer sweet smile and constant silly chatter and—"

"Constant silly chatter?" she protested, pulling back as much as he would allow.

Tearlach grinned at her affront, but didn't apologize. Instead he caught his hands in the hair at the back of her head and tipped her face up for his kiss. Lucy was annoyed enough that she managed to resist his kiss and stay stiff and still in his arms for all of a heartbeat, then she gave it up with a sigh and opened her mouth to him as her hands crept around his neck.

They both moaned as the familiar heat burst to life between them.

"God, I've missed ye," he groaned, breaking the kiss and pressing kisses along her cheek to her throat as his hands began to move over her body, brushing here, caressing there. "Kissing ye, touching ye, holding ye close, and fillin' ye with me seed. I've dreamt o' nothin' else."

"Ohhh." Lucy groaned as his hand closed over one breast. When he shifted his thigh between hers, she pressed into the caress, her back arching and fingers clenching in his hair as she admitted breathlessly, "I have missed you too and dreamt of the same thing."

The minute the words left her mouth, he was tugging free of her and turning toward Trinket. "Come."

"But—" She dug in her heels, confusion clear on her face when he turned to glance at her in question. "Are we not going to . . ." She blushed, unable to give voice to the lovemaking she'd thought they were heading for. The man had got her all worked up and with so little effort. Surely he didn't intend to leave her hanging like this? she thought. But much to her dismay, while he grinned, Tearlach shook his head.

"We're getting married, lass. I can wait until then. 'Tis no sense anticipating our vows again and risking getting with child so others can claim we married fer a bairn."

Lucy's eyes widened in alarm at his words, but in the next moment he was hurrying her toward the horse.

"Come, we ha'e to return and assure them all is well. Mother will be fair pleased at the news. Ye'll like me mother," he added.

Lucy merely grunted as he caught her up, and lifted her into the saddle and then he'd mounted behind her and was heading Trinket back into the dark woods at a gallop. The speed with which they were traveling made it difficult to speak, but even if it hadn't, Lucy hadn't a clue what to say. Obviously she had to tell him she was with child, but it wasn't something she could just blurt out. She needed to work the conversation around to the topic somehow and then gently announce it.

She considered the matter seriously as they rode, but

hadn't come up with a way to work the subject into a conversation by the time they'd arrived back at the keep. She was nibbling a bit frantically at her lip as Tearlach lifted her down from the horse, then rushed her up the steps and dragged her into the keep.

"We're gettin' wed!" he bellowed as the keep door slid closed behind them.

This wasn't how Lucy had imagined him making the announcement. Not that she'd really had a chance to think about it, of course, but if she had, she'd have expected it to be at the sup, and he would have stood and made the announcement then raised a drink to cheer the occasion. Not walking in and bellowing it at the top of his lungs.

"Oh! Lovely!"

Lucy glanced toward Tearlach's mother as the woman rushed toward them.

"Welcome to the family, dear." Eva MacAdie hugged her tightly, then turned to her son and hugged him too, burbling on excitedly, "We can have a summer wedding. That would be lovely. We can have all the family there and Lucy's family too, of course, and—"

Lucy's eyes were widening in horror at the thought of her standing before the priest with a distended belly when Tearlach interrupted his mother.

"Summer is a long way off, Mother. A little sooner would suit me better."

Lucy was just sighing her relief at his words when an older woman she thought must be his grandmother crossed the hall to join them followed by Connall MacAdie and a man of an age with the unknown woman.

"I understand yer eagerness, Tearlach," the woman said gently. "But we have to give everyone time to make arrangements and travel here and we'll need to prepare a feast and so on."

"Lucy, this is me Aunt Aileen and me Uncle Ewan," Tearlach said, introducing the newcomers.

Lucy managed not to look shocked to learn that the older couple were an aunt and uncle rather than grandparents and smiled pleasantly as she offered a greeting.

"Early spring," Lady MacAdie said thoughtfully, drawing all eyes her way. "We may be able to manage early spring."

"Aye," Aileen agreed. "I will help. We can manage it all by spring."

"Verra well," Tearlach said on a sigh. "Spring then."

"Nay!"

That word was screaming through Lucy's head so it took her a moment to realize that it wasn't she who'd protested in such a panicked shriek, but Betty. Her gaze slid to the little redhead as she hurried to her side.

"Did you not tell him?" she asked, her eyes wide with amazement.

"Tell me what?" Tearlach asked with a frown.

"Spring is much too far away, my lord," Betty told him firmly. "Earlier is better. Tomorrow even would be best."

"Tomorrow?" Connall MacAdie asked with amazement, but Lucy couldn't help but notice that Lady MacAdie had gone stone still and was now appraising her with thoughtful eyes.

"Tomorrow would be all right," Tearlach said agreeably. "I really wasnae expecting tae ha'e to wait until spring or summer. A week mayhap, but—"

"Tearlach, we cannae manage a proper wedding by

the morrow, or even in a week," Aunt Aileen said with an amused shake of the head. "And there's no need to marry with undue haste."

"Undue haste is good," Betty countered.

Lucy closed her eyes briefly as Betty and the aunt began to argue the point, but blinked them open when Lady Eva said softly, "You are with child."

The woman was peering at her with soft, tear-filled eyes.

"Are you not?" she asked hopefully.

Lucy bit her lip, terribly aware that the great hall had suddenly gone silent and all eyes were now focused on her.

"Lass?" Tearlach took her arm and used his hold to turn her toward him. "Are we with child?"

A small laugh slipped from her lips at the question. Are *we* with child? She hadn't noticed him kneeling beside her getting sick of a morning.

A nudge in her side from Betty recalled her to the situation at hand and Lucy sighed and nodded her head.

"Oh, Lucy!" Eva cried, pulling her away from Tearlach and into a fierce hug. "This is wonderful. Connall, did you hear? We're to be grandparents."

"Aye," the man said with amusement. "I'm guessin' spring is oot then and I'd best be fetchin' the priest?"

"Oh, aye!" Eva released her suddenly and whirled to her husband. "Go quickly, find him." She shooed the man out the door and then turned to her sister-in-law. "Aileen?"

It was all she had to say. The other woman straightened and announced, "I'll go talk to Cook. I am sure she can whip up something special if we gi'e her until the morrow."

"Aye, the morrow," Eva agreed. "We still need to send news to the MacNachtons. Some of them can attend at least."

"I'll take the news to MacNachton," Uncle Ewan announced and seemed happy to make his escape from the pandemonium that was about to settle on MacAdie.

"Thank you, Ewan," Eva called after him, and then turned in a circle, muttering, "where is my maid? I need to make a list. So much to do, so much to do."

Lucy watched wide-eyed as the women rushed off, then glanced to Tearlach in question when he suddenly began to draw her toward the door.

"What—?" she began as he led her outside and then gasped as he suddenly swept her off her feet and jogged lightly down the steps to her mare.

"Where are we going?" Lucy asked with a laugh once they were both settled on Trinket and he was directing the mare back out of the bailey they'd only recently returned to.

"Back to the loch," Tearlach answered in a growl. "I've a mind to anticipate those wedding vows after all."

Lucy turned her blushing face up to him with surprise.

"You do?" she asked, her body beginning to tingle at the very suggestion.

"Aye. Well, 'tis no' like we need fear getting ye with child," he pointed out, his hand slipping around her waist to cover the babe they'd created. "And I ha'e missed ye, love. We've a lot o' time apart to make up fer."

"It has only been two months, Tearlach," she protested on a laugh.

"Aye," he agreed and then added solemnly, "a lifetime."

Lucy's smile softened and she leaned into him with a sigh. They rode the rest of the way in silence. Once at the loch, Tearlach brought Trinket to a halt, then slid off the mare, and reached up to lift Lucy down. He didn't embrace her right away as she expected, but instead peered down at her solemnly and said, "The news we received up here was that Wymon is on the run. Does it bother ye that he's free? If so, I'll hunt him down meself and—"

"Nay," Lucy interrupted, raising a hand to press it against his chest as she shook her head. "He will be found in time, or meet the end he deserves in some way. I will not lose any more precious time with you by having you take the time to hunt him down." She then smiled and added, "Besides, if not for the fact that he killed my brother, I might wish to thank Wymon for capturing me and locking me in his dungeon with you. Else we might never have met."

"Aye," Tearlach said with a smile, and then added more solemnly, "but while he may ha'e captured me body, *you* captured me heart, Lucy Blytheswood. And with one of my kind, that's a forever kind o' love."

"So is mine, Tearlach," she promised just before his mouth covered hers. Lucy knew what she said was true. She would love this man all of her life and beyond.

Epilogue

"My Lord!"

Tearlach lowered his sword and stepped back from the man he'd been training. Turning, he saw William rushing across the dark practice field toward him, a wide smile splitting his lips. Tearlach found himself smiling in response and thought, not for the first time that Lucy had made a smart move in promoting the stable master to first here at Blytheswood. William was a clever and likeable fellow. He'd been a great aid in helping Tearlach step into the roll of Lord of Blytheswood. The man had helped to smooth the way with Lucy's people, who easily might have resented finding themselves serving a Scot and one of the dreaded MacAdies.

The fact that Tearlach only came out at night and remained indoors during the day had caused some speculation and uncertainty at first, but William had somehow managed to soothe concerns and ease worries so that now, a month after he had married Lucy and traveled to Blytheswood, things were running smoothly.

"Riders are approaching," William announced as he entered the circle of torchlight to join him.

Tearlach was just stiffening at this news when the man added, "A small party. Scots; three men and a woman with a dog running beside them. I think it might be your cousin."

"Aye. 'Twill be Heming and Brona with that dog o' hers," Tearlach said, his smile returning. "Lucy will be pleased."

"As will my Betty," William admitted with a wry grin. "The three women get on like a stables afire."

Tearlach grunted in agreement as the two men started across the bailey toward the keep doors. It was the truth. Their party had stopped in at Rosscurrach on their journey home after the wedding at MacAdie. His cousins' new home had been on the way and Tearlach had wanted to see for himself how Heming fared. He'd also wanted to meet his cousin's new bride as well as introduce Lucy to the man she'd heard so much about, but never met.

Lucy, Betty, and Heming's new bride, Brona, had taken to each other at once. The three women had talked and laughed up a storm during the few days they'd stayed at Rosscurrach. Tearlach had originally intended to stop there to rest only for the night, but had lengthened the duration of the stay when he saw how well the women had got along. It had pleased him to see Lucy so happy. Heming had seemed pleased as well and had assured him he would soon bring Brona to visit at Blytheswood.

It seemed soon had come, Tearlach thought as he reached the foot of the steps leading to the keep. He paused there and glanced up when one of the double doors suddenly swung open, a smile curving his lips when he saw Lucy rushing out, Betty on her heels.

Spying him at the foot of the stairs, Lucy grabbed up her skirts and hurtled down the steps toward him. "Tearlach! Betty and I were in the solar and we saw riders approaching. I think it's Brona and Heming!"

Rather than answer, Tearlach braced himself and opened his arms as Lucy hurled herself at his chest. Catching her with a grunt, he closed his arms around her with a smile, pleased with the exuberance and affection she so freely displayed. It too had helped her people accept his presence at her side.

"Why did you not tell me Brona and Heming were coming?" Lucy asked, slipping her own arms around his neck as he held her close.

"Because I didnae ken," he admitted and then gave in to the temptation to kiss her. He'd meant it to be a quick peck, but when his sweet wife opened her mouth beneath his, Tearlach couldn't resist deepening the kiss. The familiar desire immediately stirred to life between them, urging his hands to slide over her body as she moaned and arched into his embrace.

"There was no message sent ahead. You do not suppose there is something wrong?"

Lucy blinked her eyes open as Betty's words penetrated her passion-dazed mind. Pulling away from Tearlach, she turned to the other woman, noting the worried frown she wore as she awaited William's answer.

The fact that the man didn't at first answer, but instead exchanged a glance with Tearlach, was not reassuring. Turning back to her husband, Lucy frowned. "Tearlach?"

"We willnae ken until they get here, will we?" he said patiently. It wasn't a very satisfactory answer to her mind, but she knew it was also true. They wouldn't know until the party arrived. Fortunately, for her peace of mind, they didn't have long to wait; even then a shout came from the wall and the bailey was filled with the clang and squeal of the drawbridge lowering.

Lucy was eager enough that she would have crossed the bailey to meet the riders, but Tearlach settled his arm around her shoulders and held her at his side. She scowled at him for it and when he merely smiled with amusement in reaction, she tsked and rolled her eyes and turned back to watch the small party cross the bailey. They approached at a sedate cantor that didn't suggest trouble may be behind this visit, she noted with relief, her eyes sliding over the foursome. Heming and Brona were accompanied by Peter and Fergus, she noted and then smiled widely as the large grey dog who had entered beside his mistress's mare spotted them and suddenly lunged forward, rushing across the bailey in front of the others to greet them.

"Hello, Thor." Lucy beamed at the well-behaved beast when he sat down directly in front of her and whined what to her sounded like a plea for petting. Kneeling, she caught his great furry head in her hands and ruffled the fur by his ears as she murmured a greeting and told him how good he was for not jumping up on her dress.

"They do not look as if they bring bad news," William commented.

Lucy glanced toward the riders again as her husband grunted his agreement. Her gaze slid over the faces, seeing no sign of trouble there.

"They look a little travel weary, though," Betty said,

and then tsked. "No doubt they'll be parched after their journey. I should go warn Cook. And a room must be prepared. I'll take care of it, my lady."

"Thank you, Betty," Lucy called after the woman now rushing back into the keep. Giving Thor one last pet, Lucy straightened as the riders drew to a halt before them and began to dismount. She beamed at Brona and stepped forward at once to hug the other woman.

"Lucy." Brona hugged her tightly and then began apologizing at once. "'Tis sorry I am we didnae warn ye o' our coming, but this visit was a sudden one. We had to bring ye the news."

"Do not be silly," Lucy assured her as they separated and then asked, "what news?"

Brona hesitated and glanced to her husband. When he merely smiled and gave a slight nod, she turned back and said solemnly, "Wymon is dead."

Lucy sucked in a breath at this news, unsure how to react to it. In truth, she was pleased at the news. The man had killed her brother, and kidnapped both her and Tearlach and tortured him horribly. He'd also planned to force her to marry him, or kill her if she wouldn't. Lucy was glad he was dead, and felt it was the end the villain deserved. Still, she felt almost guilty for the relief and satisfaction she was experiencing.

"Well," she said finally, "thank you for coming all this way to tell us. Now, you must be thirsty after your travels. Come. We shall find you something to eat and drink while a room is prepared. You are staying?" she asked as they started up the stairs.

"Aye." Brona grinned. "We will pass a night or twae ere returning, if ye'll have us?"

"We certainly will," Lucy assured her firmly.

* * *

"She didnae e'en ask how he died," Heming commented as they watched the two women disappear into the keep with Thor on their heels.

"Nay, she didnae," Tearlach murmured and then turned back to his cousin. "How did he die?"

"Verra quickly, from what I hear," Heming said with a grin, and then explained, "it seems French food didnae settle well with 'im. He landed on the coast last week. He was apparently trying to make his way back to Carbonnel, hoping his brother would help him appeal to the king for mercy. Howbeit, he had the misfortune to land in a village where one of our scout parties was nosing around, and he was daft enough to give his real name to the serving wench in the inn where they all stopped to eat."

"Wymon always did let his arrogance outrun his common sense," William muttered with disgust, reminding them of his presence.

"Aye, well, his arrogance got him killed this time," Heming said, sounding amused. "One o' the men took him on in a fair fight when he left the inn."

"Fair?" William asked with disbelief.

"As fair as a fight can be between an Outsider and one o' our own," Heming said with a shrug and then pointed out, "at least they gave him a chance and didnae jest kill him outright."

"Aye. I suppose it was more than he deserved," William said with a shrug and then turned his attention to the horses. Taking the reins of Brona and Heming's mount in hand, he left Peter and Fergus to lead their own horses and led them to the stables, the three men laughing and chattering as they went.

"This only happened last week?" Tearlach asked, turning now to lead the way up the keep steps. "I'm surprised the news reached ye so quickly."

"Oh, weel, they sent a mon back to MacAdie with the news, but he stopped to rest a night at Rosscurrach on the way. Ere he left to continue his journey, I told him to tell yer father I'd bring the news to ye meself so he needn't send a messenger."

"And I thank ye," Tearlach assured him as he pulled the keep door open for the other two to precede him inside.

"Doonae thank me, I was happy to do it. Brona has been pestering me about coming to visit yer wee wife almost since the day ye left Rosscurrach," Heming informed him as he stepped past him into the keep. "She took a shine to Lucy."

"'Tis a shine that's returned," Tearlach assured him as he followed.

A burst of laughter made both men pause just inside the door and peer toward the chairs by the fireplace where Lucy and Brona sat, heads close together, hands on chests as they laughed over something.

"We are lucky men, Tearlach," Heming murmured solemnly as his eyes slid over his wife.

"Aye," Tearlach agreed and then gave a half laugh and a shake of the head. "Ye'd ha'e been hard pressed to convince me when I woke in Carbonnel's dungeons, and e'en harder pressed to do so when Wymon was torturin' me, but I see now that the day we were taken at the inn was the luckiest day o' me life."

"And o' mine," Heming assured him and then commented, "it makes ye wonder if there's no' a grand plan to things, does it no'?"

"That it does, Cousin. That it does," Tearlach said as the two men moved to join the women who had saved their lives, and become their futures.

Please turn the page for an exciting sneak peek of
Hannah Howell's historical romance
HIGHLAND SINNER,
available now!

Scotland, early summer 1478

What was that smell?

Tormand Murray struggled to wake up at least enough to move away from the odor assaulting his nose. He groaned as he started to turn on his side and the ache in his head became a piercing agony. Flopping onto his side, he cautiously ran his hand over his head and found the source of that pain. There was a very tender swelling at the back of his head. The damp matted hair around the swelling told him that it had bled but he could feel no continued blood flow. That indicated that he had been unconscious for more than a few minutes, possibly for even more than a few hours.

As he lay there trying to will away the pain in his head, Tormand tried to open his eyes. A sharp pinch halted his attempt and he cursed. He had definitely been unconscious for quite a while and something beside a knock on the head had been done to him for his eyes were crusted shut. He had a fleeting, hazy memory of something being thrown into his eyes before all went black, but it was not enough to give him any firm idea of what had happened to him. Although he ruefully admitted to himself that it was as much vanity as a reluctance to cause himself pain that caused him to fear he would tear out his eyelashes if he just forced his eyes open, Tormand proceeded very carefully. He gently brushed aside the crust on his eyes until he could open them, even if only enough to see if there was any water close at hand to wash his eyes with.

And, he hoped, enough water to wash himself if he proved to be the source of the stench. To his shame there had been a few times he had woken to find himself stinking, drunk, and a few stumbles into some foul muck upon the street being the cause. He had never been this foul before, he mused, as the smell began to turn his stomach.

Then his whole body tensed as he suddenly recognized the odor. It was death. Beneath the rank odor of an unclean garderobe was the scent of blood—a lot of blood. Far too much to have come from his own head wound.

The very next thing Tormand became aware of was that he was naked. For one brief moment panic seized him. Had he been thrown into some open grave with other bodies? He quickly shook aside that fear. It was not dirt or cold flesh he felt beneath him but the cool linen of a soft bed. Rousing from unconsciousness to that odor had obviously disordered his mind, he thought, disgusted with himself.

Easing his eyes open at last, he grunted in pain as the light stung his eyes and made his head throb even more. Everything was a little blurry, but he could make out enough to see that he was in a rather opulent bedchamber, one that looked vaguely familiar. His blood ran cold and he was suddenly even more reluctant to seek out the source of that smell. It certainly could not be from some battle if only because the part of the bedchamber he was looking at showed no signs of one.

If there is a dead body in this room, laddie, best ye learn about it quick. Ye might be needing to run, said a voice in his head that sounded remarkably like his squire, Walter, and Tormand had to agree with it. He forced down all the reluctance he felt and, since he could see no sign of the dead in the part of the room he studied, turned over to look in the other direction. The sight that greeted his watering eyes had him making a sound that all too closely resembled the one his niece Anna made whenever she saw a spider. Death shared his bed.

He scrambled away from the corpse so quickly he nearly fell out of the bed. Struggling for calm, he eased his way off the bed and then sought out some water to cleanse his eyes so that he could see more clearly. It took several awkward bathings of his eyes before the sting in them eased and the blurring faded. One of the first things he saw after he dried his face was his clothing folded neatly on a chair, as if he had come to this bedchamber as a guest, willingly. Tormand wasted no time in putting on his clothes and searching the room for any other signs of his presence, collecting up his weapons and his cloak.

Knowing he could not avoid looking at the body in the bed any longer, he stiffened his spine and walked back to the bed. Tormand felt the sting of bile in the back of his throat as he looked upon what had once been a beautiful woman. So mutilated was the body that it took him several moments to realize that he was looking at what was left of Lady Clara Sinclair. The ragged clumps of golden blond hair left upon her head and the wide, staring blue eyes told him that, as did the heart-shaped birthmark above the open wound where her left breast had been. The rest of the woman's face was so badly cut up it would have been difficult for her own mother to recognize her without those few clues.

The cold calm he had sought now filling his body and mind, Tormand was able to look more closely. Despite the mutilation there was an expression visible upon poor Clara's face, one that hinted she had been alive during at least some of the horrors inflicted upon her. A quick glance at her wrists and ankles revealed that she had once been bound and had fought those bindings, adding weight to Tormand's dark suspicion. Either poor Clara had had some information someone had tried to torture out of her or she had met up with someone who hated her with a cold, murderous fury.

And someone who hated him as well, he suddenly thought, and tensed. Tormand knew he would not have come to Clara's bedchamber for a night of sweaty bed play. Clara had once been his lover, but their affair had ended and he never returned to a woman once he had parted from her. He especially did not return to a woman who was now married and to a man as powerful and jealous as Sir Ranald Sinclair. That meant that someone had brought him here, someone who wanted him to see what had been done to a woman he had once bedded, and, mayhap, take the blame for this butchery.

That thought shook him free of the shock and sorrow he felt. "Poor, foolish Clara," he murmured. "I pray ye didnae suffer this because of me. Ye may have been vain, a wee bit mean of spirit, witless, and lacking morals, but ye still didnae deserve this."

He crossed himself and said a prayer over her. A glance at the windows told him that dawn was fast approaching and he knew he had to leave quickly. "I wish I could tend to ye now, lass, but I believe I am meant to take the blame for your death and I cannae; I willnae. But, I vow, I *will* find out who did this to ye and they will pay dearly for it."

After one last careful check to be certain no sign of his presence remained in the bedchamber, Tormand slipped away. He had to be grateful that whoever had committed this heinous crime had done so in this house for he knew all the secretive ways in and out of it. His affair with Clara might have been short but it had been lively and he had slipped in and out of this house many, many times. Tormand doubted even Sir Ranald, who had claimed the fine house when he had married Clara, knew all of the stealthy approaches to his bride's bedchamber.

Once outside, Tormand swiftly moved into the lingering shadows of early dawn. He leaned against the outside of the rough stonewall surrounding Clara's house and wondered where he should go. A small part of him wanted to just go home and forget about it all, but he knew he would never heed it. Even if he had no real affection for Clara, one reason their lively affair had so quickly died, he could not simply forget that the woman had been brutally murdered. If he was right in suspecting that someone had wanted him to be found next to the body and be accused of Clara's murder, then he definitely could not simply forget the whole thing.

Despite that, Tormand decided the first place he would

go was his house. He could still smell the stench of death on his clothing. It might be just his imagination, but he knew he needed a bath and clean clothes to help him forget that smell. As he began his stealthy way home Tormand thought it was a real shame that a bath could not also wash away the images of poor Clara's butchered body.

"Are ye certain ye ought to say anything to anybody?"

Tormand nibbled on a thick piece of cheese as he studied his aging companion. Walter Burns had been his squire for twelve years and had no inclination to be anything more than a squire. His utter lack of ambition was why he had been handed over to Tormand by the man who had knighted him at the tender age of eighteen. It had been a glorious battle and Walter had proven his worth. The man had simply refused to be knighted. Fed up with his squire's lack of interest in the glory, the honors, and the responsibility that went with knighthood Sir MacBain had sent the man to Tormand. Walter had continued to prove his worth, his courage, and his contentment in remaining a lowly squire. At the moment, however, the man was openly upset and his courage was a little weak-kneed.

"I need to find out who did this," Tormand said and then sipped at his ale, hungry and thirsty but partaking of both food and drink cautiously for his stomach was still unsteady.

"Why?" Walter sat down at Tormand's right and poured himself some ale. "Ye got away from it. 'Tis near the middle of the day and no one has come here crying for vengeance so I be thinking ye got away clean, aye?

Why let anyone e'en ken ye were near the woman? Are ye trying to put a rope about your neck? And, if I recall rightly, ye didnae find much to like about the woman once your lust dimmed so why fret o'er justice for her?"

"'Tis sadly true that I didnae like her, but she didnae deserve to be butchered like that."

Walter grimaced and idly scratched the ragged scar on his pockmarked left cheek. "True, but I still say if ye let anyone ken ye were there ye are just asking for trouble."

"I would like to think that verra few people would e'er believe I could do that to a woman e'en if I was found lying in her blood, dagger in hand."

"Of course ye wouldnae do such as that, and most folk ken it, but that doesnae always save a mon, does it? Ye dinnae ken everyone who has the power to cry ye a murderer and hang ye and they dinnae ken ye. Then there are the ones who are jealous of ye or your kinsmen and would like naught better than to strike out at one of ye. Aye, look at your brother James. Any fool who kenned the mon would have kenned he couldnae have killed his wife, but he still had to suffer years marked as an outlaw and a woman-killer, aye?"

"I kenned I kept ye about for a reason. Aye, 'twas to raise my spirits when they are low and to embolden me with hope and courage just when I need it the most."

"Wheesht, nay need to slap me with the sharp edge of your tongue. I but speak the truth and one ye would be wise to nay ignore."

Tormand nodded carefully, wary of moving his still-aching head too much. "I dinnae intend to ignore it. 'Tis why I have decided to speak only to Simon."

Walter cursed softly and took a deep drink of ale. "Aye, a king's mon nay less."

"Aye, and my friend. *And* a mon who worked hard to help James. He is a mon who has a true skill at solving such puzzles and hunting down the guilty. This isnae simply about justice for Clara. Someone wanted me to be blamed for her murder, Walter. I was put beside her body to be found and accused of the crime. And for such a crime I would be hanged so that means that someone wants me dead."

"Aye, true enough. Nay just dead, either, but your good name weel blackened."

"Exactly. So I have sent word to Simon asking him to come here, stressing an urgent need to speak with him."

Tormand was pleased that he sounded far more confident of his decision than he felt. It had taken him several hours to actually write and send the request for a meeting to Simon. The voice in his head that told him to just turn his back on the whole matter, the same opinion that Walter offered, had grown almost too loud to ignore. Only the certainty that this had far more to do with him than with Clara had given him the strength to silence that cowardly voice.

He had the feeling that part of his stomach's unsteadiness was due to a growing fear that he was about to suffer as James had. It had taken his foster brother three long years to prove his innocence and wash away the stain to his honor. Three long, lonely years of running and hiding. Tormand dreaded the thought that he might be pulled into the same ugly quagmire. If nothing else, he was deeply concerned about how it would affect his mother who had already suffered too much grief and worry over her children. First his sister Sorcha had been beaten and raped, then his sister Gillyanne had been kidnapped—twice— the second time leading to a forced marriage, and then there had been the trouble that had sent James running for the shelter of the hills. His mother did not need to suffer through yet another one of her children mired in danger.

"If ye could find something the killer touched we could solve this puzzle right quick," said Walter.

Pulling free of his dark thoughts about the possibility that his family was cursed, Tormand frowned at his squire. "What are ye talking about?"

"Weel, if ye had something the killer touched we could take it to the Ross witch."

Tormand had heard of the Ross witch. The woman lived in a tiny cottage several miles outside of town. Although the townspeople had driven the woman away ten years ago, many still journeyed to her cottage for help, mostly for the herbal concoctions the woman made. Some claimed the woman had visions that had aided them in solving some problem. Despite having grown up surrounded by people who had special gifts like that, he doubted the woman was the miracle worker some claimed her to be. Most of the time such *witches* were simply aging women skilled with herbs and an ability to convince people that they had some great mysterious power.

"And why do ye think she could help if I brought her something touched by the killer?" he asked.

"Because she gets a vision of the truth when she touches something." Walter absently crossed himself as if he feared he risked his soul by even speaking of the woman. "Old George, the steward for the Gillespie house, told me that Lady Gillespie had some of her jewelry stolen. He said her ladyship took the box the jewels had been taken from to the Ross witch and the moment the woman held the box she had a vision about what had happened."

When Walter said no more, Tormand asked, "What did the vision tell the woman?"

"That Lady Gillespie's eldest son had taken the jewels. Crept into her ladyship's bedchamber whilst she was at court and helped himself to all the best pieces."

"It doesnae take a witch to ken that. Lady Gillespie's eldest son is weel kenned to spend too much coin on fine clothes, women, and the toss of the dice. Near everyone—mon, woman, and bairn—in town kens that." Tormand took a drink of ale to help him resist the urge to grin at the look of annoyance on Walter's homely face. "Now I ken why the fool was banished to his grandfather's keep far from all the temptation here near the court."

"Weel, it wouldnae hurt to try. Seems a lad like ye ought to have more faith in such things."

"Oh, I have ample faith in such things, enough to wish that ye wouldnae call the woman a witch. That is a word that can give some woman blessed with a gift from God a lot of trouble, deadly trouble."

"Ah, aye, aye, true enough. A gift from God, is it?"

"Do ye really think the devil would give a woman the gift to heal or to see the truth or any other gift or skill that can be used to help people?"

"Nay, of course he wouldnae. So why do ye doubt the Ross woman?"

"Because there are too many women who are, at best, a wee bit skilled with herbs yet claim such things as visions or the healing touch in order to empty some fool's purse. They are frauds and oftimes what they do makes life far more difficult for those women who have a true gift."

Walter frowned for a moment, obviously thinking that

over, and then grunted his agreement. "So ye willnae be trying to get any help from Mistress Ross?"

"Nay, I am nay so desperate for such as that."

"Oh, I am nay sure I would refuse any help just now," came a cool, hard voice from the doorway of Tormand's hall.

Tormand looked toward the door and started to smile at Simon. The expression died a swift death. Sir Simon Innes looked every inch the king's man at the moment. His face was pale and cold fury tightened its predatory lines. Tormand got the sinking feeling that Simon already knew why he had sent for him. Worse, he feared his friend had some suspicions about his guilt. That stung, but Tormand decided to smother his sense of insult until he and Simon had at least talked. The man was his friend and a strong believer in justice. He would listen before he acted.

Nevertheless, Tormand tensed with a growing alarm when Simon strode up to him. Every line of the man's tall, lean body was tense with fury. Out of the corner of his eye, Tormand saw Walter tense and place his hand on his sword, revealing that Tormand was not the only one who sensed danger. It was as he looked back at Simon that Tormand realized the man clutched something in his hand.

A heartbeat later, Simon tossed what he held onto the table in front of Tormand. Tormand stared down at a heavy gold ring embellished with blood-red garnets. Unable to believe what he was seeing, he looked at his hands, his unadorned hands, and then looked back at the ring. His first thought was to wonder how he could have left that room of death and not realized that he was no longer wearing his ring. His second thought was that the point of Simon's sword was dangerously sharp as it rested against his jugular.

"Nay! Dinnae kill him! He is innocent!"

Morainn Ross blinked in surprise as she looked around her. She was at home sitting up in her own bed, not in a great hall watching a man press a sword point against the throat of another man. Ignoring the grumbling of her cats that had been disturbed from their comfortable slumber by her outburst, she flopped back down and stared up at the ceiling. It had only been a dream.

"Nay, no dream," she said after a moment of thought. "A vision."

Thinking about that a little longer she then nodded her head. It had definitely been a vision. The man who had sat there with a sword at his throat was no stranger to her. She had been seeing him in dreams and visions for months now. He had smelled of death, was surrounded by it, yet there had never been any blood upon his hands.

"Morainn? Are ye weel?"

Morainn looked toward the door to her small bed-chamber and smiled at the young boy standing there. Walin was only six but he was rapidly becoming very helpful. He also worried about her a lot, but she supposed that was to be expected. Since she had found him upon her threshold when he was the tender age of two she was really the only parent he had ever known, had given him the only home he had ever known. She just wished it were a better one. He was also old enough now to understand that she was often called a witch as well as the danger that appellation brought with it. Unfortunately, with his black hair and blue eyes, he looked enough like her to have many believe he was her bastard child and that caused its own problems for both of them.

"I am fine, Walin," she said and began to ease her way out of bed around all the sleeping cats. "It must be verra late in the day."

"'Tis the middle of the day, but ye needed to sleep. Ye were verra late returning from helping at that birthing."

"Weel, set something out on the table for us to eat then, I will join ye in a few minutes."

Dressed and just finishing the braiding of her hair, Morainn joined Walin at the small table set out in the main room of the cottage. Seeing the bread, cheese, and apples upon the table, she smiled at Walin, acknowledging a job well done. She poured them each a tankard of cider and then sat down on the little bench facing him across the scarred wooden table.

"Did ye have a bad dream?" Walin asked as he handed Morainn an apple to cut up for him.

"At first I thought it was a dream but now I am certain it was a vision, another one about that mon with the mismatched eyes." She carefully set the apple on a wooden plate and sliced it for Walin.

"Ye have a lot about him, dinnae ye."

"It seems so. 'Tis verra odd. I dinnae ken who he is and have ne'er seen such a mon. And, if this vision is true, I dinnae think I e'er will."

"Why?" Walin accepted the plate of sliced apple and immediately began to eat it.

"Because this time I saw a verra angry gray-eyed mon holding a sword to his throat."

"But didnae ye say that your visions are of things to come? Mayhap he isnae dead yet. Mayhap ye are supposed to find him and warn him."

Morainn considered that possibility for a moment and then shook her head. "Nay, I think not. Neither heart nor mind urges me to do that. If that were what I was meant to do, I would feel the urge to go out right now and hunt him down. And, I would have been given some clue as to where he is."

"Oh. So we will soon see the mon whose eyes dinnae match?"

"Aye, I do believe we will."

"Weel that will be interesting."

She smiled and turned her attention to the need to fill her very empty stomach. If the man with the mismatched eyes showed up at her door, it would indeed be interesting. It could also be dangerous. She could not allow herself to forget that death stalked him. Her visions told her he was innocent of those deaths but there was some connection between him and them. It was as if each thing he touched died in bleeding agony. She certainly did not wish to become a part of that swirling mass of blood she always saw around his feet. Unfortunately, she did not believe that fate would give her any chance to avoid meeting the man. All she could do was pray that when he rapped upon her door he did not still have death seated upon his shoulder.